Fields of Grace

Books by

Kim Vogel Sawyer

Waiting for Summer's Return

Where Willows Grow

My Heart Remembers

Where the Heart Leads

A Promise for Spring

Fields of Grace

Fields of Grace

A Novel by

Kim Vogel Sawyer

BETHANY HOUSE PUBLISHERS
Minneapolis, Minnesota

Fields of Grace
Copyright © 2009
Kim Vogel Sawyer

Cover design by Paul Higdon
Cover photograph by Steve Gardner, PixelWorks Studios, Inc.

Scripture quotations are from the King James Version of the Bible.

Published by Bethany House Publishers
11400 Hampshire Avenue South
Bloomington, Minnesota 55438

Bethany House Publishers is a division of
Baker Publishing Group, Grand Rapids, Michigan.

Printed in the United States of America

Library of Congress Cataloging-in-Publication Data

Sawyer, Kim Vogel.
Fields of grace / Kim Vogel Sawyer.
p. cm.
ISBN 978-0-7642-0508-8 (pbk.)
1. Immigrants—Fiction. 2. Mennonites—Fiction. I. Title.
PS3619.A97F54 2009
813'.6—dc22

2009025049

For *my parents,*
who instilled in me a pride in my heritage;

and for *my grandchildren,*
who will carry that heritage into the next generations

". . . MY GRACE IS SUFFICIENT FOR THEE:

FOR MY STRENGTH IS MADE PERFECT IN WEAKNESS. . . ."

2 CORINTHIANS 12:9

1

Mennonite village of Gnadenfeld in Molotschna Colony, Russia

Late May, 1872

Lillian Vogt wept against her husband's chest, using his striped nightshirt to muffle the sounds of her heartache. The boys, sleeping in the loft directly overhead, must not be disturbed. Lillian had held back any sign of regret or worry during Reinhardt's announcement of their plans at the dinner table. Somehow she'd found the strength to smile and assure their sons they were facing a grand adventure. But now, in the quiet of her bedroom, snug with Reinhardt in their familiar feather bed, the fear exploded into tears.

"Shh, Lillian." Reinhardt rubbed his palm up and down her spine. "You and I had already made the decision to go to America. So why this crying?"

With a gulp, Lillian pulled back to peer into Reinhardt's face. The flickering candlelight made him appear harsh and forbidding. She lowered her gaze and toyed with the edge of the white cotton sheet. "But on our own . . . leaving behind our things . . ." Fresh tears welled and spilled over. "I need time to prepare myself for this journey. Can we not wait for the explorers to come back with a report of the land? It frightens me to think of going ahead . . . without knowing what awaits us."

Reinhardt sighed, his breath stirring her loose curls. He tugged her beneath his chin and rested his cheek against her flaxen hair. "You know we cannot wait. It may be another year before the explorers return. Henrik will be eighteen in only three more months."

His ominous tone stilled Lillian's protests. Yet anger rolled through her, filling her chest so thoroughly her lungs resisted drawing a breath. Her family could remain right here in their little village were it not for broken promises. So often her people had suffered the consequences of broken promises. Had they not come to the *steppes* of Russia and tamed the land, building their farms and villages secure in the promise of practicing their Mennonite beliefs free of government involvement? Now leaders had decided not to honor their promises, and once more her people were forced to make agonizing choices.

But, truthfully, there was no choice. The mere idea of dear, scholarly Henrik with a gun in his hands sent shivers down Lillian's spine; the reality would be unconscionable. Of course they must go. But oh! How hard it would be to leave her home and all she cherished. Her own grandfather had helped found the prosperous village of Gnadenfeld. She had been born in this village, as had her three fine sons.

In her mind's eye, she pictured Henrik's first shaky steps, taken in the grassy yard beneath the flowering *kruschkje* tree. She crunched her brow. "Do pear trees grow in America?"

A gentle chuckle vibrated Reinhardt's chest. "I do not know, *mienje Leefste*."

Reinhardt was a good man who loved her, but he rarely called her his dearest. His doing so now warmed her, but it also prompted concern. For him to use such tender words, she knew his emotions must also run deep at the prospect of leaving their home.

"Just as Eli plans to take his wheat seed, we will take seeds with us and grow *kruschkje* if we cannot find them. Will you then feel more at home?"

Lillian feared it would take more than a pear tree in the yard for her to feel at home in America, but she decided not to burden Reinhardt with the thought. She twisted slightly to look into her husband's face. "Eli has agreed to come?"

"He did not even hesitate when I suggested it."

Although Lillian knew of Eli's devotion to Reinhardt after having been taken in by Reinhardt's family when he was orphaned as a small boy, the thought that he would abandon his thriving farm to travel to America puzzled her. "But he has no son to protect from military service."

"*Nä*, but he loves Henrik like a nephew. And he has farming skills that will help us survive until the others come and we can establish a village." A mirthless chuckle once more rumbled. "My skill at cobbling, no matter how masterful, will not put food on our table in the new land. Having Eli come, too, is *en Säajen*."

"A blessing . . . yes . . ." A bigger blessing would be if Eli were married. Then she would have a woman with whom to travel.

Reinhardt planted a kiss on the top of Lillian's head. "Go to sleep now, *mienje Leefste*. You will need rest to face the work of tomorrow. We must leave for Hamburg in only two more days."

Lillian rolled to her side and nestled into her pillow. But the images behind her closed lids of her beloved Gnadenfeld kept her awake far into the night.

Henrik stomped his feet against the hard-packed road with such force he wondered if the hand-sewn seams holding the soles to the kidskin vamp of his boot would burst. Every day for the past three months he had met Susie Friesen behind her father's butcher shop at the end of the school day. Despite his pleasure in studying, meeting Susie was usually the day's highlight. But not today.

Sidestepping a parked wagon, Henrik slipped between two mud-brick houses to proceed free of the watchful eyes of those on the dirt street. Everyone in the village seemed to stare and whisper, surely aware of his family's plans to leave Gnadenfeld ahead of the others. Even though his father had only informed them at their dinner table last night, news spread quickly. Had Susie already heard the whispers? Would she accept the news better than he had?

He reached the back door of the butcher shop with its attached living quarters and waited, as had become his routine, for Susie to appear. When Susie slipped out the planked back door a few minutes later, Henrik knew by the expression on her face that the rumors had found her ears.

In all their times of talking, not once had Henrik touched Susie—not to hold her hand or slide his fingers along the line of her jaw the way he itched to do. As a proper Mennonite girl, she had kept three feet of distance between them, and as a proper Mennonite boy he had not made untoward advances. But today it seemed natural for her to dash across the short expanse of grass and throw herself into his arms.

His pulse pounded like a blacksmith's hammer as he curled his arms around her and held tight. He asked, unnecessarily, *"Weete dü?"*

Her face against his chest, she nodded. He felt her shoulders heave in one silent sob. Yes, she knew. And she was no more pleased than he with the plans.

Henrik tipped his head slightly, grazing her warm hair with his cheek. The sparse whiskers that had only recently begun peppering his cheeks by midafternoon caught in her silky hair, pulling loose a few yellow strands. But Susie made no effort to remove herself from his embrace.

Henrik swallowed. How could Father expect him to leave? All he knew—and loved—could be found in Gnadenfeld. "I do not wish to go." He forced the words past the lump of agony that filled his throat.

Susie pulled back, nearly toppling him with the unexpected movement. Her blue eyes wide, she stared into his face. "But you must go! You cannot remain here and be forced into military service. My heart would break if you were hurt or . . . killed."

The fear on Susie's face mirrored what Henrik had seen in his mother's eyes. Resentment choked him. Did no one have confidence in his ability to fend for himself? Slinking away seemed the coward's response. Henrik squared his shoulders, drawing in a deep breath. "I would not be killed. I can take care of myself."

Susie's fine brows dipped down. "You . . . you would go? To war?"

Henrik turned his head to look across the neatly sown fields surrounding the village. The tenacious spirit that had allowed the Mennonites to carve the harsh *steppes* of Russia into flourishing farms resided within Henrik, too. Truthfully, he had no desire to use that tenacity in marching in military parade or aiming a weapon at a man who pointed one back at him, but pride—a pride his father had repeatedly tried to extinguish—kept him silent.

Susie's soft sigh brought his attention back to her. She twisted a few strands of her long hair around her finger and gazed at him with a mournful expression. "Even if you . . . you chose to fight, I . . . I would still love you, Henrik." Before he could respond, she spun and dashed into the mud-brick building.

Henrik stood for long moments, staring after her. Although

he had suspected Susie carried deep feelings for him, he had not expected her to make a profession of love. They were young, after all—only seventeen. But in these times, with so much upheaval, maybe age didn't matter.

He took a slow backward step, his thoughts racing. If he were married, then he would be considered a man. Capable of making his own decisions. And he could choose to go, or stay. A band wrapped around his chest, constricting his breathing. Father might see his desire to wed as rebellion, and rebellion was instantly squashed. For a moment Henrik considered the certain argument that would ensue. Then he remembered Susie's sweet face, her sorrow-filled eyes, and her whispered proclamation that she loved him.

He would not leave her. He *would not.*

"You *will* go."

Lillian placed her hand over her husband's wrist, a silent request to temper his harsh tone.

Reinhardt shook her hand loose. "And I will listen to no more arguments."

Henrik set his jaw, and Lillian's heart ached as she met her oldest son's stony gaze. She understood his reluctance to leave his home. In her opinion, allowing him to voice his thoughts could do no harm, but she knew Reinhardt would never permit anything that hinted at defiance. So she offered her son a sympathetic look and said softly, "It is difficult, Henrik, I know, but things will work out. You will see."

Six-year-old Jakob sat up like an attentive little gopher. "We get to go on a big ship, Henrik! With sails that puff out like this." He filled his cheeks with air and held the breath.

Reinhardt tapped the top of Jakob's head. "*Jo, jo,* we know you are excited, but eat your supper before it gets cold."

Jakob blew out his breath in a noisy whoosh, flashed Henrik a grin, then spooned a bite of potatoes into his mouth.

Lillian smiled indulgently at Jakob. The child's sunny personality always brought a lift to her heart. Nothing—not even leaving their home and all they knew—could dampen Jakob's exuberance. She glanced at her middle son, Joseph. He sat silently, eating his meal with his head low. Did he see their move as an adventure, like Jakob, or did he resent being uprooted, like Henrik? She supposed she would never know. Joseph rarely shared his thoughts. Of her three sons, she knew Joseph the least, and as always a touch of sadness accompanied the realization.

When all had cleaned their plates, Lillian announced in a cheerful voice, "I have a surprise. I made *pluma moos* for dessert. Who would like some?"

Although the thick prune-based soup was a rare treat, only Jakob waved his hand in the air. "I want some, Mama! Me, please!"

Joseph pushed away from the table, the chair legs screeching against the planked floor. "I need to pack my clothes. Excuse me, please." He ambled to the staircase in the corner, his hands in the pockets of his trousers.

Henrik, too, rose. "I am going to take a walk."

Lillian flicked a worried glance toward Reinhardt. Would he demand that Henrik stay? Always Reinhardt insisted the boys ask permission rather than state their intentions. But this time Reinhardt merely nodded. Henrik strode out the front door.

Relieved that they had avoided a conflict, Lillian looked at Reinhardt. "No *pluma moos* for you? The cream will not keep—it needs to be eaten."

Reinhardt opened his mouth to answer, but a knock at the door interrupted. Lillian crossed to open it. Eli Bornholdt stood on the stoop with his hat in his hands. She offered him a warm smile. "*Wellkom*, Eli. Reinhardt and Jakob were just about to have some *pluma moos*. You have some, too."

There was no other man in the village whom Lillian would invite so casually to her table, but Eli was like family. His broad grin thanked her for the invitation, and he moved quickly to the table and seated himself. Lillian dished up bowls of the cool, fruit-laden soup and handed them around. Then, wiping her hands on her apron, she said, "You enjoy your treat. I am going to . . ." She backed toward the door, waving her hand.

Eli and Reinhardt leaned forward and began talking about the trip, and she slipped out. Although Henrik had indicated he planned to go for a walk, she spotted him sitting on a bench at the edge of their little yard in the dappled shade of their *kruschkje* tree, which was now just beginning to throw off its blossoms and show the promise of fruit. Who would harvest their pears this year?

Turning her attention to her son, she linked her hands behind her and walked toward him with deliberately slow steps. If he desired to be alone, her unhurried approach would give him the chance to rise and flee. But he remained in his elbows-on-knees pose.

When she reached the bench, she pointed to the empty spot beside him with her brows raised high. He gave a slight nod, and she sat, resting her hands in her lap.

She sent him a sidelong look. "It will not be so bad, Henrik." How she wished she could smooth the creases from his youthful brow. But he was no longer a little boy to be placated. "And who knows? When the explorers return, maybe the Friesen family will also choose to make the journey to America, like so many other villagers."

Henrik jerked his head to face her. "How did you know

I was speaking of Susie when I mentioned staying here to get married?"

A smile tugged at Lillian's lips. Ah, children—did they not realize a mother read much in her child's eyes? "I suspected. She is a fine girl, and I understand your fondness for her."

Henrik shifted to stare straight ahead. The evening sun, sliding toward the horizon, cast his face in a rosy glow. "The Friesen family has no sons. They have no reason to leave."

Lillian knew many of the families with sons coming of age planned to leave to escape the military service requirement. But other families were concerned about the Russian government's reforms that took away the control the Mennonites had always held over their own villages. Were the Friesens included in that number? She couldn't remember. "They might still come."

Henrik pinched his lips into a scowl. "Two years from now . . ."

"Two years is not so long."

"But school! I want to finish school. I want to be a teacher, not a farmer. Father says we will all have to farm to survive."

Lillian experienced true remorse at the thought of Henrik working in fields rather than studying books. He had always been a thinker, and it seemed a shame to waste the gift of a good mind.

"And what if our villagers settle somewhere other than where Father takes us? How do we know we will find the same location that the explorers pick for the community?"

No assurances came to Lillian. She would not make promises that might not be kept. With a sigh, she admonished gently, "There is no sense in borrowing trouble, Henrik."

Henrik stood and fixed her with a look of betrayal. "You always take Father's side. I know you want to stay, too, but you will go because Father wants to go."

Lillian jumped to her feet and caught Henrik's hands. "I go because I want you safe."

"Safe." Henrik snorted. "Why does everyone think I am such a *kjint* that I cannot even serve in a military hospital without being harmed?"

She squeezed his hands. "No one thinks you are a child, Henrik. And I know the government officials say our young men can help in medical care rather than bear arms, but just being in the barracks with the Russian soldiers . . . harm could come to you." Lillian's worries went beyond physical harm. What kind of influences might her son's young, impressionable mind encounter when away from home and the bounds of faith?

For long moments Henrik stood with his mouth clamped tight, staring across the shadowed yard. Finally he met her eyes. "But do you wish we could stay?"

"Jo." She swallowed the lump of longing that threatened to strangle her. "I wish we could stay. I love Gnadenfeld and our house, but wishing does not change the facts. If we stay, you—and eventually Joseph and Jakob—will be forced to serve in the army. Our God instructs us not to kill. We cannot support an organization whose purpose is to take lives. As hard as we find it, we must start over in a place where we can live freely, not bound by the rules of a government that has no respect for our beliefs."

"But so far, Ma? Must we go so far?"

The anguished question made Lillian long to wrap him in her arms and rock away his hurt the way she had when he was little. But Henrik was nearly a man. A hug from his mother would not cure the pain he now carried. She gave his hands another squeeze. "Yes, son, we must go very far."

Henrik pulled loose from her grasp. "I will take that walk now."

Lillian watched him stride away through the waning light. The slope of his shoulders and his low-slung head reflected a despondency that matched the somber backdrop of gray shadows and darkening sky. Blinking back tears, Lillian sank onto the bench and lowered her head.

She wished she could pray, but what would prayers avail? Would the czar change his mind about military service? Would Reinhardt change his mind about leaving? No. So she held her prayers and her hurt inside and remained on the bench until the long shadows enveloped her.

2

Eli slipped the paper tickets from his jacket pocket and laid them on the table's hand-rubbed top in a neat row. "There they are—enough for all of your family and for me. We will board the *Holsatia* in Hamburg on the morning of June fifth."

Little Jakob wriggled in his seat. "A ticket for me, too, *Onkel* Eli?"

Reinhardt sent the boy a sharp look. "Eat your *pluma moos* and leave the talking to the grownups."

The child picked up his spoon and slurped a bite. But, unabashed, his bright eyes bounced back and forth between the men as the conversation continued.

"It is a merchant ship, but they have turned hallways into sleeping rooms with bunks that fold down from the wall at night and push back up for space during the day. Most of the passenger list is made up of Germans, so we will be able to communicate with others on the way." Eli chuckled, winking at Jakob. "We can speak the High German and pretend we are always in worship service, *jo*?"

The little boy rewarded him with a gap-toothed smile, and

Eli continued. "Because it is a merchant ship, berths are only for the crew members. I was unable to get a private berth for you and Lillian. We will all be in the sleeping hallways."

"Bunks?" Reinhardt frowned briefly, but then he shook his head. "It does not matter. We will be on the ship for little more than a month. We can tolerate bunks as long as it means we will reach America."

Eli nodded. The idea of sharing a sleeping space with dozens of others did not appeal to him, either. Living alone, he had become accustomed to privacy. Yet he wouldn't complain. Didn't his Bible tell him to be content in all circumstances? Surely this included being satisfied with a bunk on a ship.

"This means we will arrive in early July, giving us time to travel on to Kansas, build a shelter, and prepare the ground to receive seed for October's planting." For a moment, Eli worried his lower lip between his teeth. Would the soil of America receive and nourish their hearty winter wheat as well as Russia's plains had for the past century?

The thought of wheat reminded him of something else. Resting his elbow on the table, he leaned toward Jakob. "Jakob, could you help me tomorrow?"

Jakob paused with his spoon in his fist. "Help you?"

Eli's cheeks twitched with the desire to smile at Jakob's exuberance, but he forced himself to retain a stoic expression. "*Jo.* I have a very important job. Are you big enough, do you think?"

Jakob sat up straight, throwing his skinny shoulders back and lifting his chin. "I am big enough!"

Swallowing a chuckle, Eli nodded. "*Goot.* I was hoping you would be. You come to my house tomorrow morning. You will help me choose the very best wheat kernels to take to America."

The boy's shoulders slumped. "Choose wheat kernels? That is not important."

Eli raised his eyebrows and stared at Jakob. "Not important? Why, it is the most important job there is! Our good, strong wheat kernels that grow even under the snow and hard ground of Russia have never seen American soil. We want America to know what good wheat we grow—the best wheat! So we must take the very, very best kernels to plant in the new land. Only those kernels that are bright red and hard as little stones will be strong enough to make the journey."

While Eli spoke, Jakob's blue eyes grew wider and wider.

Eli waved his hand. "But if you do not think you can choose good kernels, then—"

"I can do it!" The child bounced in his seat. "I can do it, *Onkel* Eli. I can!"

Eli exchanged a quick smile with Reinhardt. "I knew I could depend on you, Jakob. Just wait until America sees what fine wheat we bring. The country will be glad we came."

"And now"—Reinhardt placed his hand on Jakob's shoulder—"go wash your face and climb into your bed. If you are going to do such important work, you need your rest."

Jakob hopped down from his chair and raced to the enclosed stairway at the corner of the dining room. His pounding footsteps shook the rafters.

Eli released a laugh. "That one will never let grass grow beneath his feet."

Reinhardt shook his head. "You will have your hands full tomorrow with him. But thank you for keeping him busy. Lillian will be able to accomplish much work tomorrow without him putting his nose in the way."

"He will be a big help to me," Eli insisted. "I trust him to select the plumpest seed kernels for transport."

Reinhardt snorted but didn't argue. "Are there restrictions on what we can take with us on the ship? I know Lillian would like to bring our goosedown mattress and her mother's china dishes, but that will require a second large trunk."

Eli glanced at the handcrafted hutch holding the white dishes scattered with roses. There would be no pretty dishes in his trunk, and for a moment he experienced a twinge of remorse at what his life lacked. He had no need for fancy dishes, but what must it be like to have a wife who valued such things?

"Each traveler is allowed one trunk." Eli traced four tally marks on the table with his finger and then crossed through the row. "So your family will be able to take five. Will that be sufficient?"

"It will have to be."

The front door opened and Lillian entered, bringing in the scents of evening. Her cheeks were flushed, and Eli wondered briefly if she were upset or if the night air had produced the high color. She crossed directly to the table and scooped up the dishes and spoons. Reinhardt barely glanced at her as she bustled to the large bricked *Spoaheat* in the corner of the kitchen and dipped water from the reservoir into a wash basin.

Eli's ears tuned to the creaky footsteps of the boys in the loft overhead, to the gentle splash of water accompanied by the clink of dishes in the basin, to Lillian's soft hum as she saw to her evening chore. So different it all was from the silence of his little house at the edge of the village. A spiral of longing wove through him. These sounds meant family—something he hadn't truly known since he was a small child. He was thirty-eight already—an old man. Would God ever bless him with a family? Or would he forever live vicariously through his foster brother Reinhardt?

Across the table, Reinhardt released a heavy sigh. "Being allowed one trunk per traveler is good news. I am relieved we are not limited to one trunk per family. That would barely hold our clothing. We must have my cobbler tools and our household necessities for starting over, as well as a few heirlooms to make the new land feel like home, since we must leave our furniture behind."

Lillian peeked over her shoulder. "Did you visit *Oomkje* Hildebrandt today and ask if he had more trunks for sale?"

"He is special-crafting one for us, larger than his usual storage trunks." Reinhardt laughed softly. "He can start a whole new business now, making travel trunks for our people. According to Hildebrandt, at least half of the village plans to leave as soon as the explorers return."

Lillian sent Reinhardt a smile, then turned back toward the basin. The tenderness in her gaze left Eli feeling like an interloper. He stood abruptly. "*Nä-jo*—all right, it is late, and we all have much work to do tomorrow. I will go now. Lillian . . ." He waited until she turned to meet his gaze. "Thank you for the *pluma moos.* It was *en gooda schmack.*"

Her nod and smile acknowledged his compliment.

Striding toward the door, he plopped his hat on his head. "Be sure to send Jakob over early. It will take most of the day to fill a bag with choice seed." He stepped into the night without awaiting a reply.

Eli hid a smile as young Jakob lifted his straw hat and swiped his hand over his forehead, leaving behind a trail of grime. Jakob's little face crunched into a scowl. "*Onkel* Eli, I am tired. Can we stop now?"

The normally bouncy boy looked wilted from his long morning of sorting seeds. Assuming a serious look, Eli pointed at the burlap sack hanging on the edge of the workbench. "Is the bag full?"

Jakob tipped his head and carefully examined the bag. "The bottom part is."

Eli swallowed twice to hold back his laughter. "But until the top part is also full, we cannot quit. We will need a full-to-the-top bag of choice seed to plant in America."

Jakob sighed, but he leaned over the seed bin and scooped up another handful. With his forehead wrinkled in concentration, he plucked seeds from his cupped palm and dropped a few into the bag. "*Onkel* Eli, what does America look like?"

Without looking up, Eli answered, "I have not yet been to America, so I cannot say. But if God made it, as we know He did, I trust it will be a place of beauty."

"So it will be a *goot* place to live?"

Eli raised his gaze from the seed bin to Jakob. The worry in the boy's eyes stirred compassion. "For sure it will be."

"Then why is Henrik so angry?" Tears pooled in Jakob's blue eyes. "He wants to stay here and not go to America at all. He and Papa yelled at each other last night, and when Henrik came to bed his face was all red."

Eli gently chucked Jakob's chin. "Henrik will be all right. He is just used to being here, and he feels *schrakj* about leaving."

The child's eyes flew wide. One tear lost its position on his lashes and spilled down his round cheek. "*Henrik* is scared? But he is almost grown-up!"

A chuckle rolled from Eli's chest at Jakob's shock. "Even grown-ups get scared sometimes, Jakob."

"Even you and Papa?" Jakob's jaw dropped open.

Cupping Jakob's chin, Eli guided the boy's mouth closed. "Even your papa and me. Starting over again in an unknown place is scary. Being scared need not shame you. But letting fear keep us from doing right . . ." Eli pointed one finger at the boy to emphasize his words. "*That* we must not do, because it means we do not trust God to take care of us."

Angling his head, Jakob squinted up at Eli. "So going to America is right?"

Eli nodded. "I believe it is. The Bible teaches us not to kill. Military men kill. They kill in battle, but still, it is killing. Our people cannot disobey God's Word and take part in killing, so even if it makes us scared to leave our home and go someplace new, we must go."

Very slowly, Jakob bobbed his head up and down. "I can do it." With his fingertips, he skimmed away the remaining moisture from his cheeks. "And I will be brave instead of scared."

"Good for you." Eli pointed to the bin. "Now come, let us try to add another inch to our bag before we stop for lunch."

Jakob leaned forward to continue the task. After another hour, they stopped to enjoy a lunch of bread, cheese, and pickled pears. Jakob ate just as much as Eli, and his full belly brought on a bout of yawning that Eli couldn't ignore. He finally tucked the boy in the corner of the barn on a pile of empty burlap bags and allowed him to nap while he filled the remainder of the seed bag himself.

Periodically while he worked, he glanced at the sleeping child, and each time a fond smile curved his cheeks. In sleep, Jakob looked so innocent. The paternal tug at Eli's heart didn't come as a surprise—he'd experienced it frequently over the years with Reinhardt's sons. But it was stronger now that he knew Reinhardt's family and he would be making a trek across the ocean and settling in a new land, dependent on one another.

If Henrik continued in rebellion, Reinhardt's focus would certainly be on him. The younger boys would require attention, and Eli was more than happy to provide it. A sigh lifted his shoulders. As much as he loved Reinhardt's boys, he wondered if he would ever have the opportunity to nurture his own children.

Having grown up an orphan, cared for by the Vogt family yet never really belonging, Eli carried a deep need for family. His own family. So far, God had not granted that gift. And if he left this village for the untamed lands in America, it seemed a fair assumption that it would be years before the desire was fulfilled . . . if at all.

Jakob snuffled in sleep, rubbing his fist beneath his nose before turning onto his side and curling into a ball. Once again, Eli smiled at the boy. For now, having a role in raising his foster brother's sons would be enough. *But, Lord, someday . . . ?*

3

Lillian stood silently beside the wagon. Six well-filled trunks rested in the wagon's bed. Joseph, Henrik, and Jakob sat atop the handcrafted wooden boxes. Jakob's straight-up pose reflected eagerness, but both Henrik and Joseph hunched forward as if bearing a weight on their shoulders.

Reinhardt sat on the wagon's seat with his fingers curled around the reins, his shoulders tense, ready to go. But she remained on the hard-packed road of her dear Gnadenfeld and peered through the early-morning mist at the structure that had been her home for the past twenty years.

Just a simple house, constructed of Mennonite-fired mud bricks and a thatched roof, nearly identical to all the others on the street. Yet it was hers, and looking at it in the soft rosy glow of dawn while white specks winked in the canopy of pale gray sky brought a rush of memories that had to be relived before she could turn her back and drive away.

How many meals had she prepared at the bricked stove? The table on which those meals had been served remained in the house, empty of dishes. At least the dishes would make the journey—they now rested in one of the trunks, sandwiched securely between layers of clothing and bedding.

She closed her eyes for a moment, replaying images of their years in this little house. She could picture each of her sons sitting in the tall wooden chair, their baby mouths opening for a spoonful of mush. In her imagination, she walked up the tiny enclosed staircase to the loft, where first one bed, then two, and finally three stood in a neat row. A smile pulled at her lips as she recalled leaning forward and brushing kisses on warm cheeks before whispering nighttime prayers with the boys.

Henrik had come into manhood in this house; all three sons had been born in the feather bed tucked into the far corner of the main floor. How could she possibly leave this house of memories? Her nose stung, and she crunched her eyes more tightly closed to hold back the tears that pressed behind her lids.

"Lillian?"

Reinhardt's voice popped her eyes open. She turned slowly and looked up at him.

"We must go now. It is a long journey to Hamburg, and if we do not reach it in time, we will miss the ship." He held out his hand. "Come."

Drawing in a deep breath, Lillian cast one final, searching gaze across the house and yard before taking Reinhardt's hand. Settled on the high seat, she sent a quavering smile back toward her sons. "*Nä-jo*, here we go."

Jakob bounced on his bottom and clapped his hands, but Henrik turned away, his face sullen. Joseph met her gaze, but his expression was empty, emotionless. Somehow Joseph's lack of response was harder to bear than Henrik's open resentment.

With a glance at Reinhardt, she whispered, "I am ready."

She clutched her shawl around her shoulders as the wagon lurched forward. Torn between regret and relief that they would not drive through the center of the village where she would look, one last time, upon the neat marketplace and their beloved chapel of worship, she focused on the swishing tails of Eli's team of horses that pulled the wagon. Eli rode alongside the wagon on a third horse, and a fourth one trotted behind the wagon, bobbing its head at the restraining tether.

Eli had expressed hope that he could sell the horses in Hamburg before they embarked, since the ship would not allow livestock. Her heart ached at the thought of so much left behind. Trusted animals, beautiful furniture, lifelong friends . . . But at least, she comforted herself as the wagon rolled into the open country, many of the friends would follow after the explorers returned with their report.

Dear God, go before us. Guide us to Your place of choosing.

She grasped Reinhardt's arm. "Have you decided where we will build our new home?"

Reinhardt pulled the reins to the left, guiding the horses around a deep rut in the road. "The one letter that has come from the explorers spoke of railroad lands for sale at good prices in Kansas. According to the letter, the prairies there resembled the *steppes* of Russia and, judging by the tall grasses, would be suitable for farming. So Eli and I have decided to ask about it when we reach New York. If land is still available, we will make our new home in Kansas."

"Kansas . . ." Lillian rolled the word across her tongue. She tried to envision how a place called Kansas might look, but her mind was too cluttered with the view of her familiar homeland.

Jakob stood behind the driver's seat and curled his hands over his parents' shoulders. "Mama, *Onkel* Eli says America will be good because God made it. If Kansas is in America, then that means Kansas will be good, too, right?"

Lillian patted Jakob's hand. "I am sure you are right, Jakob.

Now sit back down. The road is bumpy, and I would not want to see you bounced from the wagon bed."

Jakob laughed. "I like to bounce!"

"Sit down, Jakob."

At his father's low-toned command, Jakob sank back onto a trunk. But he twisted this way and that, peeking past his parents' heads to examine the road ahead.

Behind him, Henrik and Joseph spoke in hushed tones, and Eli whistled a tuneless melody. Aware of her companions' activities yet feeling oddly separated from them, Lillian scanned the area as they traveled. Knowing this would be her last glimpse, she found importance in every detail of the ground, the sky, and even the span of openness in between.

The Mennonites' wheat fields, harvested of their hearty winter wheat only one month ago, were now speckled with stubble rather than waving with tall stalks of ripe wheat. The stubble allowed a view across the rolling landscape, where she could watch the sun climb higher in the ever-lightening sky. The fireball seemed to shrink as it rose, yet the heat grew more intense as the morning progressed. Before long, she discarded her shawl and tugged the brim of her bonnet forward to shade her eyes.

They passed through small villages and larger towns, over winding roads where other travelers in less burdened wagons pulled around them to disappear over bends. By the time the sun hovered directly overhead, the horses' footsteps were plodding rather than brisk, and the boys' mumbled chatter had long since ceased. A glance in the back of the wagon found all three boys drowsing, little Jakob lying sideways across a trunk and Henrik and Joseph with chins on their chests.

She touched Reinhardt's sleeve. "Can we not stop for a drink and something to eat? We would all benefit from stretching our legs a bit."

Reinhardt transferred both reins to one hand and used his free hand to remove his gold watch from its hidden pocket in his jacket. He scowled at the watch's face, looked skyward, then slipped the watch back into his jacket before pulling back on the reins. "Whoa."

The horses came to a stop with snorts and giant nods of their heads. Eli brought his horse even with the wagon seat and halted.

"Lillian thinks we should have a drink and some food," Reinhardt said.

Eli grinned. "I will not argue against Lillian's idea."

The boys roused, and everyone climbed out of the wagon. Joseph and Jakob chased each other in circles while Lillian pulled cheese sandwiches, dried fruit, and a water jug from a woven basket. Reinhardt spoke a blessing, and then they sat in the grassy area beside the road to eat. They ate their fill in silence while the breeze cooled their sweaty brows and noisy birds scolded from the brush.

When they'd finished, Jakob tapped Reinhardt's shoulder. "Are we in Germany yet, Papa?"

Reinhardt scratched his chin, shaking his head. "*Nä*, son. Not yet. But by the time the stars come out in the sky tomorrow, we will be in Germany."

Jakob heaved a huge sigh. "I am tired of sitting on that trunk. My bottom hurts."

With a light chuckle, Reinhardt warned, "Well, climb back in the wagon anyway or your bottom might hurt for a different reason."

Jakob clambered over the side without another word of complaint. Joseph and Henrik joined him more slowly, and even Lillian delayed climbing back onto the seat. Her hips felt stiff from the long drive; sitting held no appeal. She rose on her tiptoes to whisper in Reinhardt's ear. "Might the boys and I walk behind the wagon for a while?"

His brows came down, and by his frown Lillian felt certain he would refuse her request. But then a gentle smile crinkled his eyes. He leaned forward and spoke in a voice intended only for her ears. "Your bottom is hurting, too?"

She hunched her shoulders and giggled, her gaze skittering sideways to Eli in case he had heard. But he went on rubbing his horse's nose, unaware. *"Jo."*

Reinhardt clapped his hands once. "Boys, your mother wants to walk. Do you want to join her?"

With a joyful cry, Jakob leapt from the wagon and bounded to her side. The older boys also hopped down. Lillian took Jakob by the hand and swung a smile on each of her sons. "While we walk, let us sing. It will make the time pass more quickly."

Reinhardt brought the reins down on the horses' rumps, and the wagon rolled forward. She and the boys fell into step. Lifting her chin, she began to sing. "Oh, for a faith that will not shrink . . ."

Eli stifled a yawn while he waited for Reinhardt to emerge from the inn. He wouldn't mind sleeping in a stable with the horses, but he knew Lillian would prefer a bed for their final night on this side of the ocean. They were dusty and travel-rumpled, and they would all appreciate a bath and change of clothes. Lillian even hoped to wash out the clothes they had worn for their four-day journey before packing them in a trunk.

"Eli?"

Eli turned toward Lillian. Her dark eyes were underlined with purple smudges of weariness.

"Do you suppose Reinhardt will be able to get three rooms? The city is so crowded."

Eli let his eyes roam the busy street before facing her again. "If not at this inn, surely there will be one with three rooms available somewhere. There are several inns along the street."

The boys remained in the back of the wagon, as Reinhardt had instructed, but all three looked up and down the street, their eyes wide. Eli surmised they would enjoy the opportunity to explore. Hamburg, with its bustling streets, tall businesses crowded side by side, and noisy street vendors must incite curiosity after living their entire lives in the tiny village of Gnadenfeld. Obedience held them captive, however, and Eli sent Joseph an approving nod when their gazes met.

Reinhardt strode from the building, his shoulders drooping. He rested his arms on the edge of the wagon and gave Lillian a weak smile. "We have three rooms. And the innkeeper said he would arrange baths for each of us, although it cost extra."

"It is worth paying extra." Lillian wrinkled her nose. "We all smell so bad the ship captain might not let us board."

"If we have tickets, we can board." Reinhardt turned to address Eli. "There is a livery stable on the next street. The innkeeper said the liveryman might be interested in purchasing your horses. Let us unload our trunks and get Lillian and the boys settled in the rooms, then we can go speak with him."

Eli nodded and swung down from his saddle. He tied the horse's reins to a wagon wheel, and then he, Reinhardt, and the two older boys carried the trunks into the inn. The rooms were plain but clean, with plump feather mattresses on the beds. His aching body felt relieved already, knowing it would have the pleasure of a comfortable bed for one last night.

Before leaving the room where the two older boys would sleep, Reinhardt pointed sternly in the boys' direction. "You stay here until Eli and I return. Take your baths and change into clean clothes, and then you may visit your mother's room. But do not leave the inn. Tonight we will all go to supper together, but I do not want you wandering the city."

Joseph and Henrik exchanged a quick look of disappointment, but they nodded.

Eli followed Reinhardt to the wagon and untied the reins from the wheel. As he rode, he repeatedly patted the animal's sleek neck. He had to sell the horses—they couldn't go along, and he needed the money to help with expenses when they reached America. Yet he couldn't deny wishing he didn't have to part with his animals. They had been faithful servants as well as companions on his lonely farm. It pained him to leave them with strangers.

After a thorough examination from teeth to tail, the liveryman made Eli a fair offer. With a weight in his chest, Eli accepted the payment. He stroked each beast's nose one last time before turning his back and leaving the livery.

As they moved down the busy street, Reinhardt gave Eli a clap on the back. "*Nä-jo*, it is time for baths, supper, and a good night's sleep. Tomorrow we go."

Despite the difficulties of the past days and the challenges that waited ahead, Eli felt a small rush of anticipation. Tomorrow they would go. *God, what do You have waiting for us in America?*

4

Lillian tightly held Jakob's hand and watched the porters carry her family's trunks up the wooden plank to the ship. The men had promised to put the trunks beneath their assigned bunks, and she had little choice but to trust them.

People waiting to board the ship jostled her. She pulled Jakob against her side to protect him. Catching Joseph's eye, she admonished, "Stay close. We do not want to lose you, too." The boy took one step closer to her shoulder.

So much activity! Her heart pounded in apprehension as she scanned the teeming wooden pier. Somewhere Reinhardt and Eli searched for Henrik. Of all the boys, Henrik should be the least likely to wander off. Yet just moments ago Joseph had asked the question, "Where is Henrik?" And they'd realized he was no longer with them. A prayer winged from her soul: *God, protect him and bring him back to us!*

Jakob yanked on her skirt. "Mama, people are getting on the ship! Are we getting on the ship?"

Lillian's mouth went dry at the sight of the throng moving one by one up the narrow gangplank. Should she, Joseph, and Jakob get in line? She had their tickets—they could board and wait for Reinhardt and the others on the ship.

Joseph scowled at Jakob. "We cannot board until Father comes. What if they close the gate and we are on the ship without Father and Henrik? Do we want to sail away without them?"

Lillian murmured her thanks for Joseph's sensible reply. Of course they must wait. But Jakob continued to tug at her, eager to cross the gangplank and get on the ship. She gave his shoulder a firm jerk. "Stand still, Jakob! We will not board until our family is all together."

Jakob stuck out his lower lip and folded his arms across his chest, but he stopped fidgeting. Bobbing heads of passersby blocked her view, but Lillian continued to scan the crowd for Reinhardt or Eli. Just when panic had nearly sent her stomach into spasms, she spotted Reinhardt's familiar black hat. She rose on tiptoe, and relief flooded her when she realized he had Henrik by the collar of his jacket, propelling him along. Eli followed on their heels.

She pressed Jakob into his brother's hands. "Joseph, keep Jakob with you and stay right here. Do not move!" She worked her way through the crowd to meet her husband and oldest son in the center of the pier. "Oh, Henrik!" Although he remained caught in Reinhardt's grasp, Lillian embraced him. "What a fright you gave me! How did you get separated from us?"

Reinhardt gave Henrik's jacket a yank that pulled him free of Lillian's arms. "Tell your mother how you came to be separated from us."

Despite his father's demand, Henrik clamped his jaw and looked to the side in silence.

Color rose in Reinhardt's face. "He did it on purpose. He wanted to go back to Gnadenfeld." He released Henrik with a sharp jerk that pulled his jacket askew. *"Onndankboa benjel dü."*

Henrik's cheeks streaked red as he spun to face his father. "You call me an ungrateful boy? I am neither a boy nor ungrateful. I am a man with my own ideas!"

"Bah!" Reinhardt slashed his hand as if erasing his son's words. "A man thinks of others before himself. But you think *only* of yourself." He pointed at Lillian. "How dare you frighten your mother this way!"

For a moment, remorse flashed in Henrik's eyes, but it disappeared when Reinhardt continued.

"You would sneak back to Gnadenfeld after all we have done for you? Everything we left behind, we left because of you!"

"Did I ask you to leave things behind for me? I wanted to stay! I would perform my duty and then come home again, but *you* said we had to leave!" Henrik's voice, normally low-toned, came out as a screech. "It was not my choice!"

"I gave you no choice because you are still a foolish boy and I am your father." Reinhardt banged his thumb against his chest. "I know what is best. You will honor me and do as I say." He leaned forward, his nose inches from Henrik's.

The two, nearly identical in height and build, squared off with matching brown eyes flashing. Each clenched his fists.

Lillian clapped her hands over her mouth. Might Reinhardt strike his son . . . or vice versa? She started to step forward and intervene, but a small body shot past her. Jakob wrapped his arms around Henrik's waist.

"*Brooda*, my brother, do not be angry. Come with me on the ship." The little boy lifted his face to Henrik, his expression pleading. "I want you to come with me."

Henrik caught Jakob's arm as if to push him away, but then his grasp relaxed. He dropped to one knee and slid his hand onto Jakob's shoulder. "All right, Jakob. I will come."

Jakob threw himself against Henrik's chest, and Henrik scooped him into his arms as he rose. Carrying Jakob, he turned toward the gangplank without another word. Lillian shot Reinhardt a relieved look, but Reinhardt's hard expression didn't change. He cupped her elbow with one hand and reached toward Joseph with the other.

"Let us board before the ship leaves without us."

Once on board, Henrik lowered Jakob to the deck but kept a grip on his hand. The little boy's eagerness to explore matched Henrik's desire to escape. Maybe by staying together, they could keep each other out of trouble.

Henrik glanced at his father's stern profile. Guilt pricked, but anger squelched it. He shouldn't feel guilty for resenting this move to America. Wasn't he almost eighteen—a man? He'd been told his whole life he was intelligent; Ma often praised him for his ability to make good decisions. But Father treated him as though he were no older than Jakob. Embarrassment stung anew as he remembered being hauled to the ship's boarding dock like a wayward child.

Jakob stepped on the lowest rung of the railing, and Henrik curled one arm around his little brother's waist to prevent him from toppling. He clamped his free hand over the cool iron bar that formed the top rail and peered at the people standing on the boarding dock. His heart skipped a beat when he spotted a young woman with sunshine yellow braids much like Susie Friesen's. Would he ever see Susie again?

He blinked, turning his attention away from the yellow-haired girl to others who clustered on the pier and lifted their hands in farewell. Jakob waved animatedly, as if he personally knew everyone down below. None of his brother's enthusiasm touched Henrik. Dread sat like a stone in his stomach at the thought of leaving

Susie, leaving Gnadenfeld, leaving all that was familiar. Yet Father insisted he had to go.

Honour thy father and mother. The biblical command had been fed to him from his earliest memories. He'd had few opportunities to rebel, given the numerous watchful eyes and wagging tongues in Gnadenfeld that witnessed and willingly reported any misdeed, real or imagined. Henrik had obeyed partly out of honor and partly out of fear of unpleasant consequences. All the while, he had looked forward to the day he would leave the school in Gnadenfeld to attend a Mennonite-approved university.

But now his long-held plans had been thrust aside in favor of traveling to America. Did they have Mennonite-approved universities in America? Henrik snorted, his arm crushing Jakob tightly against his aching heart. Father and Eli called America *"de Launt üt ne Je'laäjenheit"*—the land of opportunity. Well, once there, Henrik would be eighteen—a man fully grown—and he would seek his own opportunities, separate from Father's plans.

"Come, Jakob." Henrik caught Jakob beneath his armpits and lifted him from the rail. "Let us go below deck and find our bunks."

Jakob huffed his disapproval. "But I want to look around the ship!"

"We can explore the rest of the ship when we are out on the water."

Although Henrik sensed Father's sharp-eyed gaze on his back as he guided Jakob toward the stairway leading to the lower levels of the ship, he didn't turn back to look.

Lillian awakened to the sound of retching. Forcing her heavy eyelids open, she squinted into the deep shadows and tried to determine the source of the sound. Was it Jakob, who slept directly above her on his shelf bed?

The retching came again, longer and more intense. She was able to discern that it came from somewhere ahead and to her left, not from above. Ducking low to avoid bumping her head on the underside of Jakob's bunk, she rolled from her lumpy mattress. She stood for a moment, waiting for her eyes to adjust to the dim light. Lanterns glowed from the far end of the hallway, but little of the light reached the center of the sleeping hall.

In a few moments, she was able to make out a woman's form leaning over the edge of her bunk with her arm clamped over her stomach. After two weeks aboard the ship, Lillian had become accustomed to the gentle up-and-down movements of the great boat on the water, and she had no difficulty advancing the few feet needed to reach the woman.

An unpleasant odor reached her nostrils as she neared the woman, but she swallowed hard and touched the woman's pale cheek. The heat surprised her, and she yanked her hand back.

The woman stared at her with glassy eyes. "Oh, please help me. I am sick. So sick . . ." Apparently the fever that had begun sweeping across the passengers less than a week out to sea had captured a new victim.

"What is it?" A cranky voice came from farther down the line of bunks. "Who is talking?"

In a whispered tone, Lillian replied, "Someone is ill. I am assisting her. Go back to sleep."

"Ill?" The voice became more shrill. "Another one? Get her to the sick bay!"

The shrill-voiced woman's lack of compassion stirred Lillian's indignation, even though she understood the worry behind the demand. She didn't want her Jakob, who slept in the women's bay rather than the men's because he was so young, exposed to this fever. At least two people had succumbed to the illness despite the doctor's prescription of caudle and bed rest.

"Are you going to get the steward to move her or not?" The woman's strident voice roused several others, and a distressed murmur carried through the sleeping hallway. The ill woman would need to be moved to the sick bay quickly before a disturbance broke out.

"*Jo, jo*, I will get the steward." Lillian pressed the feverish woman back into her bunk with a whispered promise. "You stay here. I will get you some help."

Lifting her skirts, she stepped around the evidence of the woman's sick stomach and made her way to the stairway that led to the middle level of the ship. The crew's quarters were at the opposite end of this level. Lillian could never remember the official name for that end—stern? aft?—although Jakob would know. The little boy followed the crew members and asked endless questions. To her maternal delight, the men seemed quite taken with him and never sent him away.

The timbre of the sea filled her ears as she moved down the hallway to the steward's cabin. Below, in the sleeping hallway, the engines' noise covered almost every other sound, but here on the next level, the sea's music reached her. The ocean's vast openness—a sound difficult to define yet impossible to ignore—made her long for the open prairie of home.

The surface of the water, stirred by the wind, gave the appearance of a wind-tossed wheat field. The sound of the sea was the same gentle swoosh as wind coursing over tall, untamed grasses. Of course, here on the ocean, the swoosh was accompanied by the steady slosh of water against the sides of the ship. Yet, in spite of the unfamiliar harmony, Lillian couldn't deny the ache of homesickness the song of the ocean created in her soul.

She reached the steward's cabin, tapped lightly on the door, and waited. Snuffling noises and an irritated grunt let her know the man had awakened. The door swung open to reveal a disheveled man with hair standing on end.

He looked at her, blinked twice, and then groaned. "Another one must be moved to sick bay?"

Lillian nodded, shifting her gaze away. The steward hadn't bothered to button his shirt to the top, and the sight of the pale, smooth wedge of exposed skin made her clutch the high collar of her own frock in embarrassment.

"Very well." He closed the door, and Lillian listened to more shuffles, thuds, and muffled curses before the door opened again. He stepped out, fully clothed and with a hat covering his hair. "Ready."

He followed Lillian to the women's sleeping hall, and she assisted him in drawing the ill woman to her feet. The steward made an awful face when he saw the mess on the floor, and he muttered something about sending down a cabin boy to clean it up. The other women remained in their bunks, covers pulled up to their chins, and watched in silence as Lillian and the steward guided the ill woman out of the sleeping hallway. Three abreast on the stairway to the lowest deck, where the ship's doctor had set up a crude hospital ward, was a tight fit, but Lillian turned sideways and they managed.

The steward opened the door to the ward, and the smell that wafted from the room nearly turned Lillian's stomach inside out. Slop buckets sat in a row, waiting to be carried out and emptied. Lanterns swung from hooks in the ceiling, casting an eerie glow over the rows of cots where patients lay, their faces pale and shiny from fever. Groans and soft sobs competed with the roar of the engines, creating a heartbreaking symphony of suffering.

Lillian helped the woman into an empty cot while the steward roused the doctor, who slept sitting in a chair propped against the wall in the corner. She stepped back as the doctor placed his hand on the woman's forehead and heaved a sigh. Then he caught Lillian's arm and gave it a shake.

"You get out of here now." The doctor's stern voice, coupled with the fierce downthrust of his eyebrows, made Lillian's pulse race. "And stop in the washroom to scrub yourself good before you go back to your bunk."

With her hand over her nose, Lillian turned to go. Her gaze skipped across the cots once more, and the sight of a head of wavy black hair fired her heart into her throat. She dashed forward and dropped to her knees beside the cot. "Reinhardt!"

5

Lillian ran her hand over Reinhardt's hair. Heat emanated from his scalp, and she cringed. "Oh, Reinhardt . . ."

His fever-bright eyes met hers, and a worried scowl puckered his chapped lips. "Lillian, *mienje Leefste*, are you ill?"

"Nä, nä." She quickly explained her reason for being in the sick bay. "But when did you come here? You were fine at dinner." She thought about their evening meal, only hours ago. Reinhardt had been unusually quiet, but she hadn't suspected his silence was anything more than dislike of the bland meal on his plate. Now she realized his picking at the flavorless dish of boiled butter beans had a deeper, more significant root.

"Eli brought me shortly after bedtime. I was worried I would make the others ill." His face contorted, and he rolled to his side. Lillian snatched a pail from the end of the cot and held it beneath his chin. When the bout passed, he slumped back onto the thin mattress.

She used the handkerchief from her pocket to wipe Reinhardt's mouth. "What else can I do for you?"

"You need not do anything. I will be fine."

His tone made Lillian smile despite the shock and worry of finding him here. "Maybe the ship's cook has some chamomile tea. I will ask, and then I will brew you a pot. It will help settle your stomach."

Reinhardt shook his head, perspiration beading on his forehead. "*Nä,* Lillian. You must stay away from here. You might get sick, too."

"But how can I leave you?"

Just then a hand curled around her upper arm and yanked her to her feet. "I told you to get out of here!" The doctor's purple-rimmed eyes narrowed to angry slits.

Lillian wrenched free of his grasp. "This is my husband!"

The doctor's expression momentarily softened, but then he grabbed her again and tugged her toward the door. "I will see to him like I do all the others. But the longer you stay, the more likely you will pick up and spread the illness. So you stay out." He pushed her into the hallway and closed the door behind her. From behind the closed door, she heard him order, "Go wash yourself!"

With tears blinding her, she stumbled up the stairs and made her way to the women's washroom. Leaning over the porcelain basin, she splashed tepid water onto her face and then scrubbed her hands and arms. While she scrubbed, a prayer rang through her heart: *Make him well, dear Lord; make my husband well.*

Clean again, she returned to the sleeping hallway. A dark spot of wet wood marked the place of the woman's sickness. Apparently the steward had sent someone to mop up the mess. Unfortunately, the odor still lingered. Lillian stood beside her bunk and ran her hand over Jakob's thick blond hair and pressed a kiss on his round cheek. The little boy slept, oblivious to his mother's attention.

Assured he was fine, she curled in her bunk. Closing her eyes, she repeated her prayer for the Lord to make Reinhardt well, and then she added a postscript: *And please protect my sons from the illness.* She fell asleep with the prayer hovering on her heart.

In the morning, hand in hand with Jakob, Lillian walked to the dining room. They entered the room where other passengers already crowded around the tightly crammed tables and benches. She scanned the area and spotted Henrik and Joseph standing with Eli alongside the wall, near the beginning of the serving line. Taking Jakob's hand, she wove between others, muttering, "Excuse me . . . excuse me, please . . ." Although the room was small, it took several minutes to reach her sons.

Eli leaned toward her, keeping his voice low. "I must tell you. Reinhardt—"

She nodded. "I saw him in the sick bay last night." The image of Reinhardt's sweaty, pale face flashed in her memory. She hugged Jakob to her side and pushed her quavering lips into a smile she hoped offered assurance to her sons. "But he says he will be fine, and I believe him. God is watching over him. So we must trust."

"Yes, of course we trust." Eli gave a solemn nod. Then he turned to the boys. "*Nä-jo,* shall we get in line to eat?"

Henrik and Joseph fell in line with little enthusiasm. Lillian could hardly blame them. At home, breakfast consisted of eggs, sausage, potatoes, and bread. But on the *Holsatia,* every morning the ship's cook plopped a lump of gray oatmeal into a bowl and didn't even offer cream or sugar to flavor the unappealing fare. The noon and evening meals offered no enticement, either, but at least the food was filling and she didn't have to prepare it in the sleeping bay the way she had heard was required of some travelers on other ships.

After they all had received their bowls of oatmeal, they sat together at the end of one long table. As was their custom, they joined hands for a prayer. In Reinhardt's absence, Eli offered the blessing.

Jakob put a bite of oatmeal in his mouth and promptly spit it back out. "Mama, this is *suä*."

Lillian frowned. "Jakob, do not be ungrateful. Eat."

He smacked his spoon onto the planked table. "But it tastes bad."

Henrik took a careful bite and grimaced. "He's right. The cook must have used *suä* milk."

Eli replied, "With no cow on board to provide fresh, of course the milk has soured by now. But even oatmeal made from sour milk is better than what the doctor is giving to your father."

Jakob stared at Eli, his eyes wide. "What must Papa eat?"

Placing his elbow on the table and bending forward so his face was near Jakob's, Eli twisted his mouth into a horrible scowl. "Caudle. Gruel mixed with ale. It smells much worse than *suä* milk, I can tell you, and tastes terrible."

Lillian hid her smile. Although "gruel" sounded bad, she knew the flour and water paste could be quite tasty if flavored with sugar, molasses, or other spices. Eli might be exaggerating, but she knew his tale was meant to distract Jakob.

"Mama says medicine is supposed to taste bad," Jakob said.

Eli grinned at Lillian. "My *Mutta* always said the same thing. The worse it tastes, the better it is at making you well." He sat up straight and scooped up another spoonful of oatmeal. "So your papa will be well soon just so he does not need to drink any more caudle." He pointed to Jakob's bowl. "And to keep you well, you must have a full stomach. So eat your oatmeal and pretend it is pudding, *jo*? Then it will go down easier."

Jakob sighed but obeyed. To Lillian's relief, Joseph and Henrik ate, also. When they finished, they carried their bowls to the washbin. Jakob caught Lillian's skirt and tugged.

"Mama, may I go? Franz said he would show me how the catharpings are tied."

"Catharpings?" Lillian shook her head in confusion.

Henrik glanced at her and answered, "Ropes, Ma. They are part of the sail rigging."

Although the ship was powered by a steam engine, Lillian had noticed the crew releasing large square sails in the afternoon. Little Jakob had explained that the sails caught the wind and helped propel the ship, thereby saving some of the fuel needed to feed the engine. By the time they reached America, Jakob would certainly know all that was needed to be a skilled sailor.

"So may I go, please? Franz said he would teach me to make the special knots." Jakob danced in place, eagerness lighting his round face.

"Who is Franz?"

"My friend, Mama!"

"One of the sailors?"

"The *best* sailor. He knows *everything*!"

Lillian laughed softly and smoothed her hand over Jakob's hair. "All right, *tigja Benjel*, go ahead. But do not be a nuisance."

Jakob started to dash off, but Henrik caught his hand. "Wait for us, Jakob. Joseph and I would like to learn the knots, too. Who knows . . ." A cunning gleam lit his eyes. "Maybe we will be sailors someday."

Jakob dragged Henrik out of the dining room while Joseph trailed after.

Lillian watched them go, a strange pressure building in her chest. Why had none of the boys expressed concern for their father? Jakob was young and easily distracted by the promise of learning to tie knots. But Joseph and Henrik were old enough to realize the illness could be serious.

Ever since Reinhardt had announced they would be leaving Gnadenfeld, Lillian had sensed her older boys slipping away. Henrik's comment about becoming a sailor had almost felt like a warning. Would this new start in America mark the end of the family life she cherished?

"Do not look so troubled."

Eli's voice jarred her from her musings. She looked at him in silence.

A soft smile curved his lips. "They are only curious. They will not come to harm learning to tie knots from a German sailor."

Lillian forced a light laugh. "Of course not." But she didn't divulge the real reason for her unease. Eli wouldn't understand. He wasn't a mother. Catching her skirts, she moved toward the wide doorway leading to the deck. Outside, the wind tried to chase away the melancholy feelings of moments ago.

She paused beside the railing and peered across the broad expanse of sea meeting sky. Everywhere she looked, regardless of direction, there was nothing but blue. She hadn't realized the world was so big—and she so small—until she'd climbed aboard this ship. In Gnadenfeld, the narrow scope of her village defined her world. Now the perimeters of her world were beyond measurement. Awe at the sheer might displayed before her eyes made her shiver.

When she turned to look at Eli, she saw his face pucker with concern. "Go below deck if you are cold," he told her. "We do not wish for you to take ill, too."

Accustomed to following Reinhardt's directions, Lillian took no offense at Eli's counsel. Yet she didn't want to leave the sight of the sea. She fisted the tails of her shawl and crisscrossed them over her body. "I am not cold."

Here she could inhale the salty, fresh scent of the brisk air and listen to the lovely chorus of whistling wind and sloshing sea. Below deck, the smell of unwashed bodies made her stomach turn, and the engine noise made conversation difficult. Out here, she had room to stretch out her arms if she wanted to; below, even with the beds folded up, the area was cramped with trunks lining the walls and so many people milling in the narrow space. She would certainly be safer from the sickness here in the open air, regardless of the chill.

Eli angled his face toward the distant horizon. "The view from here . . ." He shook his head, his shoulders rising and falling in a mighty heave. "So much water and sky makes my chest feel empty and yet full at the same time."

Lillian cast a sidelong glance at him. Not many men spoke of simple things like scenic views or feeling empty. In times past, had she ever heard him utter phrases that could be woven into poetry? With a start, she realized she and Eli had never conversed without Reinhardt present. The thought made her take a step away from him. Should she be standing on the deck with Eli, even here on a ship in the middle of the Atlantic Ocean?

He turned and looked at her. "Is something wrong?"

She shook her head, embarrassment at her behavior silencing her tongue.

"Are you sure you do not find my odor offensive?" A grin climbed the corners of his lips, making his beard twitch. "I know I have not bathed recently, but the wind should be carrying *en Kjarpa Je'roch* away from your nose instead of toward it."

Despite herself, Lillian burst out laughing. Never would she have thought of discussing something like body odor so casually! But then, she had never before been trapped in a sleeping hallway with so many people. One could either laugh or cry over the unpleasantness. She found the laughter refreshing.

He laughed, too, his eyes crinkling merrily. "It is good to hear you laugh. It tells me you are not worrying overmuch about Reinhardt."

At the mention of Reinhardt, Lillian immediately sobered. How could she be laughing when her husband lay ill? She shifted away from Eli and bit down on her lower lip.

His fingertips grazed her elbow. "Lillian?"

She turned her face to meet his serious gaze.

"Reinhardt is strong. The others who died . . . one was elderly and one had suffered fever before coming on board, so was already weakened. I do not believe we need worry about Reinhardt."

"*Nä, nä,* of course we need not worry. God will take care of Reinhardt." Gusts of wind loosened strands of hair from Lillian's heavy bun. The tendrils slapped against her cheek, and she tucked them beneath her bonnet. She frowned across the sea. "Does the wind feel cooler to you?"

Eli lifted his face, seeming to sniff the air. He turned a slow circle, and then his brows came down sharply. "Look in the east. How dark is the sky! I think maybe a storm is brewing. We should find the boys and go below."

Lillian grasped her shawl more tightly as another gust nearly tore the woven covering from her shoulders. *"Jo."* She shivered, fear striking for the first time since boarding the ship. "I hope we will not be tossed about too much."

Eli released a low chuckle and stepped away from the rail. "A big, sturdy ship like this can take high waves. It will be like riding a galloping horse, but we will be safe." He glanced again at the sky, and concern flashed through his eyes before he formed a cheerful smile. "Come. We do not want to get wet if rain should start to fall. Let us find the boys . . . quickly."

6

Henrik folded his arms across his stomach and fought nausea as the ship groaned its way over the next crashing wave. The rise-and-roll motion had already caused several others to empty their stomachs, but Henrik was determined he would not succumb. His resolve faltered, however, as waves continued to rock the ship. When would this storm pass?

For more than six hours, he and his fellow passengers had remained below deck, crammed shoulder to shoulder since they had been advised to sit on the floor rather than climb into bunks. With all of the portholes closed against the lashing rain, the stench was nearly unbearable, and the walls of the sleeping hallway seemed to press in on him. Sweat beaded across his forehead. Although Jakob's friend Franz had assured them the ship could withstand the storm, Henrik questioned the man's confidence. With each rise and fall, the ship groaned like a wounded animal. That sound alone could drive a man mad even without the pounding rain and roaring wind.

Joseph, on his right, bumped his arm with his shoulder. "Scared?"

Henrik forced a blithe tone. *"Nä."* He planted his feet, pressing his back more firmly against the wall, as the ship began another rolling lift. His stomach protested the motion, and he sucked in air through clenched teeth. "But I am bored. I wish we could get up and walk around."

Joseph nodded slowly. "If we could move around, I would go to the women's hallway."

Henrik grinned.

Red crept up his brother's neck. "To make sure Ma and Jakob are all right, I mean."

Joseph's statement didn't fool Henrik, but he decided not to tease his brother. "If I know Ma, she is leading the women in singing hymns." Did he admire or resent his mother's cheerful nature? At that moment, he wasn't sure.

Joseph leaned his head against the wall and closed his eyes. "I feel sick."

"Try not to think about it," Henrik suggested. He hoped his brother wouldn't add to the foul smell of the hallway. "Think about something else—something pleasant."

Eli, who had sat quietly beside Joseph with his eyes closed, seemingly asleep, leaned forward. He wrapped his arms around his knees and faced the boys. "Henrik gives good advice, Joseph. Even the Bible, in the fourth chapter of Philippians, tells us that we should think upon whatsoever things are lovely. So, Henrik, tell us something pleasant to get our minds off"—Eli pinched his nose shut, which gave him the appearance of an ornery youngster—"the not-so-pleasant. When you think 'lovely,' what comes to mind?"

Immediately an image of Susie Friesen flashed through Henrik's mind. Pain stabbed his middle, and he knew it was unrelated to the tossing of the ship. If remembering Susie was meant to bring pleasure, he'd just experienced the opposite. He shook his head.

Without a change in expression, Eli turned to Joseph. "What about you? What pleasant things do you recall?"

Joseph sighed, a grin lifting the corners of his mouth. "Racing Jakob. Fishing. Sleeping in my soft bed in our loft. Eating Ma's cooking instead of what the cook serves on the ship." He smacked his lips. "I would like some of her *Rasienenstretsel.*"

Henrik's mouth watered at the thought of biting into a thick slice of the raisin-studded pastry.

Eli chuckled. "*Jo*, everything you say brings good thoughts, Joseph. And you know?" He raised his eyebrows, bumping Joseph lightly with his elbow. "All of those things you will do again once we are off of this ship. You will race your brother, throw a line into the water to fish, sleep in your bed in a brand-new loft, and enjoy your mother's fine cooking. This present time of not-so-pleasant will pass, and it will all be just a memory. But those things you cherish will be lived again. That is a good thought, too, hmm?"

Joseph nodded thoughtfully, a pleased smile lighting his face. But Henrik frowned. Perhaps the things Joseph had mentioned could be relived, but how would Henrik ever regain the sweet times he'd shared with Susie? What if her family never left Gnadenfeld? And even if her family did come to America and somehow met up with his family, so much time would have passed. Someone else might turn her head while he was far away.

He leaned against the wall and squeezed his eyes shut. Maybe sleep would make the time pass quickly.

Eli woke with a jerk. Something was different . . . but what? After a moment, he realized his ears no longer buzzed with the roar of wind, the slash of rain, and the groan of the ship's wooden ribs against the push of the sea. Instead, he heard the rumble of the engines. During the two days they had battled the storm, the engines had remained silent. Surely this sound meant the storm had finally passed.

He stumbled to his feet, holding the wall to keep his balance. After the long stretch of sitting—they had only moved from their positions to go to the toilet—his legs felt wobbly and unsure. Around him, men sprawled on the stained floor. Snores competed with the engines' steady roar. With one arm across his nose to shield himself from the pervasive odor, he used his free hand to unlatch the closest porthole and fling it wide.

Outside, a pinkening sky and a sea as smooth and shiny as glass greeted his eyes. *Oh, thank You, my Father, for Your safe delivery.* The prayer formed without a thought, and he repeated it for good measure. Surely God's hand had been upon them all through that long, perilous storm.

Crouching down, Eli shook Henrik's shoulder. The boy roused, blinking in confusion. He rubbed his eyes as he sat up. Eli told him, "The storm is over. I am going up on deck and then to the sick bay to check on your father. You open the portholes and let in the morning air, hmm?"

Henrik yawned and nodded. Scratching his head, he pushed to his feet, nudging Joseph as he did so. Eli crept from the hallway, careful to avoid stepping on the hands or feet of sleeping passengers. On deck, he grasped the damp railing and sucked in great drafts of fresh, crisp air. The foul odor that had plagued his nostrils for the past days washed away.

Turning, he kept hold of the rail with one hand and opened his jacket with the other. The wind flapped his jacket against his sides and flattened his rumpled shirt to his belly. Letting his head flop back, Eli closed his eyes and relished the clean air pulling at his hair, his beard, his clothing. It was almost as good as a bath.

"Was tun Sie heraus hier?"

Eli opened his eyes and spun from the railing. Jakob's friend Franz stood a few feet away, fixing Eli with a puzzled look. Eli supposed the sailor had reason to question what he was doing; he must look like a child standing with his face to the wind and his arms outstretched.

Grinning, Eli answered in German. "Outside I came to breathe the fresh air." He sniffed, his chin high. Then he pushed his lips into a fierce grimace. "The sleeping hallway . . . very smelly."

Franz's blue eyes sparkled as he laughed. The boy was not much older than Henrik, Eli realized. But he spoke with authority. "I will send a cabin boy down with bucket and mop. A clean floor and open portholes will make an improvement."

"Jo." Eli nodded in relief. *"Dank."*

"Sie sind willkommen." Franz started to leave, but then he turned back, his face hopeful. "The little yellow-haired boy . . . Jakob . . . he is eager to be out again?"

Although Eli hadn't seen Jakob during the long storm, he knew the child would be very eager to clamber all over the ship once more. *"Ach, jo."*

Franz's smile flashed. "Good. He reminds me of my own little brother, Friedrich. I only see him when we port in Hamburg, and it is not nearly often enough." For a moment, sadness colored the young man's expression. But then he brightened. "But Friedrich says he will be a cabin boy one day, so who knows? Perhaps we will sail together."

"Perhaps," Eli mused.

"I must return to work." Franz pointed at Eli. "Be careful out here alone. The sea is calm this morning, but the deck is slippery from the rain. We would not want to lose you overboard."

Eli gave a solemn nod and shifted away from the railing. Franz disappeared around the corner. Eli remained on deck, watching the sun dapple the water as it rose from its hiding spot behind the sea. The sky changed from pink to streaky yellow and orange and finally robin's egg blue. And that change seemed to signal to the others on board that it was time to be up.

One by one, people spilled from the lower levels to cluster on the deck and chatter excitedly. Eli, his moments of solitude spent, went to check on Reinhardt. During the days of the storm, several more people had been taken to sick bay, but only one man had been deemed well enough for release. He hoped Reinhardt might rejoin his family soon. Those who remained in the sick bay when the ship docked might not be allowed to enter America.

Halfway down the stairs, he encountered Lillian and Jakob on their way to the deck. "The storm is over, praise the Lord."

Lillian's wan face evidenced the rolling boat's effect, but she offered a smile. "Praise the Lord indeed. And how good it feels to be up and moving around." She glanced at Jakob, who fidgeted beside her. "I am certain I would not have been able to keep him still for even one more hour."

Eli chucked Jakob under the chin. "Your friend Franz asked about you. He thinks, like your mama, that you are ready to run and play on deck."

Jakob giggled, hunching his shoulders. "I like Franz." He turned a pleading gaze on his mother. "May I find Franz, Mama? May I?"

Lillian smiled warmly at her son. "You and your friend Franz—I am thinking you will miss him when we leave the ship."

Jakob nodded so hard his thick blond hair flopped on his forehead. "*Jo*, I will miss him. So may I go see him now?"

"After breakfast." Lillian softened the denial with a stroke of her slim hand over Jakob's hair. The boy stuck out his lower lip, but he didn't argue.

Eli said, "I am going to the sick bay to see how Reinhardt fares this morning. The doctor probably will not let me in—when we took a sick man down yesterday, he made us stay in the hallway and only allowed the sick one in. But I will knock on the door and ask."

Lillian's shoulders slumped for a moment. "Thank you, Eli. The doctor told me to stay away, and I have honored his demand, but I wish he would send word. I suppose he is too busy caring for the sick to think about sending messages."

Eli nodded, but his thoughts turned to what he had glimpsed through the doorway to the sick bay: a sheet-wrapped body, ready for burial. Lillian didn't need such an image in her mind. "Go on up on deck, but be *fäasejchtijch*. All of the rain has made things slick."

Lillian grasped Jakob's hand. "We will be careful. Thank you for the warning." She and Jakob moved past him, and he continued to the lower level. A light tap on the door to the sick bay brought no response, so he pounded a little harder.

The door opened just enough to reveal one red-rimmed eye, which looked him up and down. The doctor's voice barked, "You do not look sick."

Eli linked his hands respectfully over his stomach. "I am not ill, and I am sorry to disturb you. But I came to check on one of your patients—Reinhardt Vogt. He is doing better?"

"Vogt . . . Vogt . . ." The door widened enough for Eli to see the doctor's face. The man blinked twice, his expression blank. Then his lips twisted into a grimace. For a moment it appeared he would close the door, but then he slipped into the hallway. "You are family?"

A chill of foreboding crept up Eli's spine. "He is . . . my brother."

Lowering his gaze, the doctor rubbed the underside of his nose for a moment, as if gathering his thoughts. His head still down, he mumbled, "Reinhardt Vogt died during the night."

The words struck like a shotgun blast to the middle. Eli stumbled backward. Reinhardt . . . dead? Eli's legs began to shake, and he groped for support. With both hands pressed to the solid wall, he fought a wave of sorrow that threatened to knock him to his knees.

"I lost three passengers during the storm." The doctor spoke in a detached, tired voice empty of sympathy. "Now that the sea is calm, we can have burials."

Eli knew the doctor meant that the deceased would be dropped overboard. But such a fate for his lifelong friend and foster brother defied acceptance. "B-but you c-cannot—"

"Well, we cannot keep them on board," the doctor snapped. Then he drew in a deep breath, and when he spoke again, kindness underscored his tone. "It is still a week to dry land. The bodies . . . will not keep. There is no other choice."

Slowly, Eli bobbed his head in agreement even while his heart rebelled. How could they dump Reinhardt's body into the water? How would he tell Lillian? How would she bear the pain? Suddenly he pushed away from the wall. "I . . . I must go tell his wife and . . . and sons." Poor little Jakob—would he understand? And Henrik and Joseph . . . As young men, they needed a father's guidance. *Oh, dear Lord, why? Why?*

Without another word, the doctor stepped back into the sick bay, and Eli moved to the stairway. His feet might have been crafted of lead, so hard it was to lift them to each riser. His heart lay somewhere in the pit of his belly, a stone of dread and sorrow.

He must break the news gently. Even now, more than thirty years after the death of his own parents, a harshly delivered message from a neighbor was embedded in his brain. "They are gone, boy, and tears will not bring them back. So hush." Years later, he understood that the man's callous behavior was a mask for the shock of finding young Eli crying beside the wrecked wagon under which his parents lay. But at the time it had seemed as though no one cared.

He reached the deck, surprised by the bold yellow sun glowing overhead. Shouldn't it be shadowy and dark when he carried such a horrible burden? People stood in small, animated groups with smiling faces, happy to have left the storm behind. But inside Eli, a new storm brewed. The sun, no matter how warm and bright, could not light his soul.

7

Lillian raised the mug to her lips and took a sip of coffee. The brew was strong and black, the way Reinhardt liked it. She drank it because it was all that was available, but she would have preferred to sweeten it with two heaping spoonfuls of sugar and a dose of thick cream.

Eli planned to use some of the money from the sale of his horses to purchase milk cows when they reached their destination. How she wished they'd already arrived in Kansas. How pleasant it would be to live in a house rather than sharing a narrow space with so many others; to stand on solid ground rather than finding one's balance on a constantly rocking deck; to prepare hearty meals that not only filled the stomach but pleased the tongue.

In one more week they would reach the harbor at New York, the cook had said at breakfast. The good news had sent everyone from the dining room with smiles on their faces, including her boys. It had given her heart a lift to see a smile on Henrik's too-often-sullen face.

Now she sat alone at the table, listening to the excited chatter of passengers outside on the deck and the clatter of dishes in a washtub from the cooking area. Closing her eyes briefly, she offered a silent prayer of gratitude for protection during the storm, for the promise of reaching land soon, and for the opportunity to live freely. Like the comfort of her woven shawl, contentedness enveloped her. One more week and their new life could begin.

"Ma?"

At the single-word query, a hush seemed to fall across the deck. Lillian experienced an odd tingle of awareness. Peering over her shoulder, she spotted Henrik and Joseph in the wide doorway. The sun behind them cast their faces in shadow, but she sensed a reluctance to draw near. The boys' reticence coupled with the silence of the watching passengers told her something was amiss. No doubt her boys had been up to mischief.

She laughed softly. "You two look as if you have been caught stealing cookies from the crock." She extended her hand to them. "Come here and tell me what misdeed you have performed."

Instead of approaching, they separated, and a third person in sailor garb stepped between them. He carried a small bundle, and Lillian rose when she recognized Jakob's form draped in the man's arms. Fondness warmed her when she saw her son's closed eyes and relaxed posture.

Sighing, she shook her head. "Less than an hour of play, and already he naps?" She shifted her attention to Henrik. "Why did you not carry him down and put him on his bunk?"

Henrik took two forward steps, moving out of the shadows. "Ma . . ."

Lillian's heart caught at the broken tone and the bright tears swimming in his eyes. Behind him, the doorway suddenly filled with other passengers straining to peek in at her. Trepidation made her pulse race. "Henrik?"

But Henrik remained silent, his chin trembling. Joseph hovered in the doorway, as if holding back the crowd. Lillian faced the sailor. His sorrowful expression flipped her stomach upside down.

"What is it?" Rushing forward, she touched Jakob's hair.

The little boy didn't stir. His arms hung limply. Lillian caught his hand and raised it to her lips. "He is sleeping, *jo*?" Even as she asked the question, her heart knew the answer. "Jakob, *mein kjestlijch en Sän*, wake up now for Mama."

A single tear slipped from the sailor's eye to his chin. It quivered there for a moment before plopping onto Jakob's chest. "After the rain, with everything wet and slick . . ."

Lillian fought the urge to cover her ears with her hands. She did not want to hear this man's words.

"He loved to climb on the ratlines with me. But . . . this time . . . he slipped, and his foot caught. When he fell, his head . . . he . . ."

"No!" Lillian scooped Jakob from the sailor's arms. She hugged him to her aching chest. He lay motionless in her grasp. Only then did she notice the rivulet of blood running from his left ear.

The sailor reached out one hand but stopped inches short of touching Jakob. "The captain said he broke his neck. He . . . he did not suffer."

Lillian stared at the young man. Did he believe his words would bring her comfort? Suddenly realization dawned. "You are Franz."

He nodded.

Jakob's sweet voice echoed in her mind: *"Franz is the best sailor!"* Fury consumed her like a fire devouring dry leaves. Her body trembled with the effort of containing a hatred she hadn't known she was capable of harboring. "Jakob called you his friend. But you betrayed him. You let him climb where it was not safe. You let him fall. You let him *die*!" She flayed the young man with her words, even as tears poured down his face. "You killed my son!"

Had she ever spoken such hateful words to anyone? No, never. But a pain this intense had to be excised, and she knew no other way than to fling it at someone. Franz—this stranger with tears staining his tanned, square face—provided a willing target. He stood silent and defenseless against her anguished rage.

She opened her mouth to release another torrent of words, but Henrik leaped forward. "Ma! *Nä!* Franz did nothing wrong. He tried to stop Jakob. He told him no, not to climb on the ropes today. But Jakob laughed and said he was *ne Op*—a monkey." Henrik's voice broke on a sob. "He . . . he would not listen, Ma."

Lillian slowly shifted her gaze to peer into Jakob's still face. Yes, her *kjestlijch en Sän*—her precious son—would want to be a monkey and climb after the long, stormy days of sitting. She could envision him laughing, scampering away from Franz's reaching grasp, his bright eyes teasing as he called, "Try and catch me, Franz!"

Tears flooded her eyes, distorting her vision. She crushed Jakob close to her heart, burying her face against his neck. "Oh, Jakob . . . Jakob . . ." She sank to her knees, still cradling her son. Henrik knelt beside her with his hands on his thighs, his throat convulsing.

Franz crouched in front of her. "*Frau* Vogt, I am sorry. So very, very sorry." His pain-filled eyes beseeched her to forgive him for not saving her little boy.

But Lillian's throat closed in her own agony of grief. She could offer no absolution to this young man. Or to herself, for she had entrusted Jakob into his hands. She and Franz bore Jakob's blood jointly; they must both suffer the pangs of guilt.

After a few moments, Franz pushed to his feet without a word and walked on stiff legs past Joseph, who hadn't moved from the doorway. At Franz's departure, the onlookers who had gathered outside the door also drifted away. The murmur of their voices floated to Lillian's ears, but she kept her head down.

Sunlight spilled through the open doorway, bathing Jakob in

its yellow beams. She examined her son's face, memorizing every detail. How peaceful he looked—so innocent with his round cheeks and curling lashes. His full lips were parted slightly, as if a deep sleep claimed him, but no milk-scented breath escaped his lips.

A shadow fell across Jakob's body, and she looked up, frowning, ready to tell the intruder not to shield her child from the warmth of the sun. Eli towered above her. Sadness darkened his eyes.

A sob rose from Lillian's throat at his sympathetic expression. "How did you hear? Did Franz tell you?"

Slowly, Eli hunkered down on his haunches. His gaze bounced from Jakob to Lillian's face. He shook his head slightly, as if confused.

Pressing Jakob's cheek to her own, Lillian began to moan. "How will I tell Reinhardt our little boy is gone? Our precious boy . . . our sweet baby . . ." Tears flowed, but she took several calming breaths. She must be strong for Henrik and Joseph. Turning to Henrik, she said, "Go to your brother. Joseph needs you."

With a sober nod, Henrik rose and crossed to Joseph. The two huddled together with Henrik's arm around Joseph's shoulders, their dark heads close. Both Joseph and Henrik were dark of hair and eyes, like their father. Only little Jakob had Lillian's fair hair and blue eyes. Reinhardt had often whispered how glad he was that one of the boys carried their mother's coloring. Jakob's sunshine hair and sky-blue eyes matched his sunny disposition.

Oh, Reinhardt, losing our sweet boy will crush you. How could she bear to look into her husband's eyes when he learned of Jakob's death? An idea struck—a selfish one, yet it would remove a great burden from her. Lillian bit down on her lower lip for a moment. Hesitantly, she lifted her face to meet Eli's gaze.

"Eli, will you . . . will you take this news to Reinhardt for me? I . . . cannot leave Jakob's body untended, and it will do Reinhardt no good to see his child in death while he lies ill." She blinked rapidly, clearing her eyes of tears. "Will you tell him, please?"

Eli slumped forward, his head low. He covered his face with one hand, and his body shuddered. His obvious sorrow heightened her own sense of loss, and it took every bit of self-restraint she possessed not to dissolve into wild weeping. Her chest felt as though it might explode, but she held back her sobs and waited for Eli to gain control of his emotions.

At last he looked at her. The pain in his eyes pierced her. How deeply he loved Jakob, too. "Lillian . . ." She had to tip her head toward him to hear his raspy, whisper-soft voice. "I talked with the doctor this morning and . . ." He paused, a swallow making his Adam's apple bob. Stretching out his hands, he grasped her upper arms. His fingers cut into her flesh. "Last night, Reinhardt slipped away. He, like Jakob, is with his Maker now."

Nä! Had Eli not held her, she would have toppled sideways. *Oh, Lord, it is too much! I cannot bear it! Please, my Father* . . . Did she utter the prayer or did it only groan from her heart? What a cruel blow, to hear of Reinhardt's death while cradling the lifeless body of her youngest child. All her life, she had been told she could place her trust in a loving Father-God, but how could a loving God perpetrate such heartache on one of His own?

She pushed the rebellious thought aside and tried to rise, but hindered by Jakob's weight and her trembling legs, she collapsed in a heap. Eli wrapped his arms around both her and Jakob and lifted them. His breath stirred her hair as he spoke. "I will take you to the sick bay where you can say good-bye to Reinhardt. The doctor says we must have a burial today."

Lillian stared into his face. The others who had died had been wrapped in cloth and lowered into the sea. At home for a burial, shovels of dirt covered the casket bit by bit, giving one an opportunity to offer a slow good-bye. But at sea, there was a soft splash and the body was swallowed all at once. How could she say good-bye so abruptly to Reinhardt and Jakob?

The very thought of her beloved husband and son lying in the bottom of the ocean sent a spasm of revulsion through her frame. She shook her head wildly. "*Nä. Nä.* They must have a place of rest on land. Please, Eli, tell the captain—"

Eli gave her arm a squeeze. "Lillian, there is no other choice. Their bodies . . . by the time we reach land . . ." He glanced over his shoulder at Henrik and Joseph, who stood together, staring at them with wide, distressed eyes. Facing Lillian again, he ended on a whisper. "We must do what is best for everyone."

"Oh, but, Eli . . . not in the sea . . ." A sob choked off her words.

Eli cupped Jakob's head with his big hand. "We give only their shells to the ocean. Their souls are already with God, Lillian. Their souls are running free."

His tender voice did little to soothe her. Hugging Jakob more firmly to her breast, Lillian pressed her cheek to his hair. "I cannot. I cannot, Eli. Please . . ."

He opened his mouth, no doubt to express another argument, but a sudden gasp and soft thud from behind him captured their attention. Eli spun, and Lillian looked past him. Joseph lay sprawled on the floor. Henrik knelt beside him.

"Joseph!" Lillian stumbled forward, her heart pounding. Had the boy fainted from grief?

Eli dashed to Joseph's side. "Joseph?" Gently, he patted Joseph's cheek. Eli's head jerked upward, and he pinned Lillian with a worried scowl. "We must take him to the sick bay at once. He is burning up!"

8

"You will not take Joseph to that useless hospital room!" Henrik leaped to his feet and balled his fists. Already his father had died under the care of the doctor. Henrik could not let Eli entrust Joseph to the man's ineffective ministrations.

Eli slipped his arms beneath Joseph's shoulders and knees and lifted him. "We have no choice, boy." Although he frowned at Henrik, he spoke gently. "Joseph is ill—the other passengers will not allow him to stay in the sleeping hallway."

"Then we will find a spot . . . somewhere. And Ma will care for him." Henrik looked from Eli to his mother. Her pale, stricken face brought him up short. She didn't look capable of caring for herself, let alone a sick boy.

He squared his shoulders. He was the man of the family now, and he would decide what was best. "Or I will see to him myself. But you will not hand him over to the doctor who let my father die." The reality of all that the family had lost in such a short time tried to double Henrik with grief, but somehow he remained upright, fixing Eli with a glare. "Give my brother to me." He held out his arms.

An apology flashed in Eli's eyes, but he shook his head and pushed past Henrik. "I am taking Joseph to the sick bay and then I will help prepare Reinhardt's body for burial. Stay with your mother and give her comfort." He strode around the corner.

Henrik stared after him, shock holding him in place. After a few stunned seconds, he spun on his mother. "Will you let him take Joseph? You might as well sign his death certificate yourself!" Ma looked at him with worry and grief in her red, swollen eyes, but he refused to back down. "Go after Eli and tell him to give Joseph to me."

Slowly, Ma shook her head. Tears poured down her cheeks. "Eli is right, Henrik. You cannot care for Joseph—the others on the ship will not allow it. And what if you became ill, too? Then what . . . what would I do?" A sob heaved her shoulders, and she adjusted her hold on Jakob's still form.

Clutching his hair, Henrik groaned. "But how can we let Joseph go into that room with the illness? He might not come out again!"

"Henrik . . ." Ma begged him with her eyes. "We must tr—"

"Trust?" The word burst from Henrik's chest on a tide of fury. "We must *trust*, is that what you were going to say? Trust whom? Trust the doctor? Trust God?" Henrik laughed, a hollow sound completely devoid of humor. "What good has it done us to trust? Father is dead; Jakob is dead; Joseph is sick . . ." He leaned forward, staring in disbelief at his mother's white face. "How can we *trust*?"

Ma's face crumpled. "But, Henrik, what else can we do? We *must* trust. If we have no faith, then . . ."

Henrik waited for her to continue, but the thought remained incomplete. Unable to look into Ma's grief-contorted face any longer, he lowered his gaze. His eyes fell upon Jakob's lifeless body.

A pain more scorching than anything he'd experienced before sliced through his chest. If only they had remained in Gnadenfeld, Jakob would still be running, laughing, teasing. If they hadn't boarded this ship, they wouldn't have encountered the illness that claimed his father's life and that might—right now—be draining the life from his remaining brother.

Spinning from the sight of little Jakob in his mother's cradling arms, Henrik pressed his fists to his eye sockets. Colors burst behind his closed lids, an explosion of pain and grief. They had left Gnadenfeld because of him. To save him from harm. But at what cost? Thrusting his arms downward, he stormed out of the dining room. He heard his mother's frantic voice call his name, but he barreled around the corner and across the deck and thundered down the stairs two at a time.

He nearly knocked over two men coming up, but he didn't pause to apologize. He must find a place to hide from the wrench of guilt. Like a frantic animal, he paced the lower levels of the ship, seeking a cubby or closet that would provide refuge. But after several minutes of frenzied searching, the futility of the hunt brought him to an exhausted halt.

He dropped onto his bunk and buried his face in the bend of his elbow. There was no place of escape. He would carry this burden of guilt to his own grave.

"Ashes to ashes, dust to dust . . ."

Lillian almost scoffed. How absurd the captain's solemn utterance. Dust . . . in the ocean waves? A hysterical bubble of laughter threatened to escape her throat. But she held it in. Earlier that day, she had listened to the mournful wails of another woman whose husband had died of the fever. She would not resort to such undignified mourning.

Sad-faced passengers surrounded Lillian and Eli. Henrik remained below, huddled on his bunk. Although Lillian worried he would later regret not saying good-bye to his father and brother, she didn't have the strength to argue with him. So she allowed him to mourn on his own, alone.

Her chest tightened, constricting her breathing, as she watched two sailors lift and suspend Reinhardt's cloth-wrapped body over the side of the ship. At the captain's nod, the men let go. A splash signaled the ocean receiving its gift and Lillian gasped, covering her mouth with one hand.

Then the men lifted the smaller bundle. Unthinkingly, Lillian stumbled forward, reaching for her son. But strong hands cupped her upper arms, drawing her against a firm chest. A voice, low and tender—Eli's—whispered in her ear. "Let him go now, Lillian. You must let him go."

The captain had allowed her the day to mourn. To bathe her son's sturdy body, to comb his thick, sunshiny hair, to rock him and sing him his favorite lullabies one final time. But now, as the sun set, painting the sky with jeweled tones of blazing pink, purple, and yellow, she was forced to release her *kjestlijch en Sän* to the ocean's care. The captain looked at her, his gaze asking a silent question: *Are you ready?*

Again Lillian almost released a scornful laugh. Was a mother ever ready to bid a permanent good-bye to her child? But somehow, inexplicably, she found the strength to raise and lower her chin in a nod. After a moment's pause, another splash—much softer than the first one—reached her ears.

Lillian pulled in a breath that seared her from the inside out. How cruel that her heart continued to beat, her lungs continued to take in air, while her husband and her dear child had no life in them! The captain, sailors, and several passengers filed by, offering condolences, squeezing her hand, promising to pray for her. She murmured her thanks for their inadequate words, understanding they gave the best they knew to offer. But even as she responded in a calm, even tone, she felt strangely distanced from herself.

Surely she was caught in a dream. Tomorrow she would awaken and laugh with Reinhardt about her ridiculous imagination. Together they would watch Jakob clamber over the ratlines while Joseph challenged him to climb higher. In her mind's eye, she could see Jakob's impish grin, hear Reinhardt's laugh and feel his arm around her waist. She crunched her eyes closed, absorbing herself in the scene inside her head.

"Lillian."

She scowled, resisting the intruding voice.

"Lillian, we must talk."

The images faded as Lillian opened her eyes. The other passengers were gone. She and Eli stood alone on the deck. Anger swelled. Why had Eli disturbed her?

"Can we go into the dining room and sit at a table?"

Wind, cool and damp, slapped her face. Gooseflesh broke out over her body. She drew her shawl closer around her shoulders. She wanted to go below, curl up on her warm bunk, and let sleep claim her. If she were sleeping, she could dream. If the Lord granted her heart's desire, Reinhardt and Jakob would appear in those dreams. She turned, intending to go to the stairs, but Eli put his hand on her back and steered her into the dining room as if she had uttered agreement.

He pressed her onto a bench, then sat across from her, folding his hands on the scarred tabletop. "Lillian, I think we must talk about Kansas."

Kansas? The plans she and Reinhardt had made seemed to be

from a lifetime ago. How could she possibly think of Kansas now that her husband was gone?

"I am not going to Kansas." The strength of her voice surprised her. Perhaps the anger roiling through her insides had given her courage. "Kansas was Reinhardt's plan for all of us. Since all of us cannot go, I will not go."

Eli shot her a startled look. "Then what will you do?"

Lillian gave a little jolt. "Return to our home in Gnadenfeld, of course." In Gnadenfeld, the villagers would reach out, as they always did, to a widow and her orphaned children. But no . . . she couldn't return to Russia. Henrik would be pressed into military duty. She must go on, as Reinhardt had planned. Yet how would she and the boys survive without his guidance and care? Fear rolled over her like a wind-tossed wave, threatening to bury her in its icy depths. She pressed her fingertips to her trembling lips and stared at Eli.

He leaned forward, stretching one hand across the table to gently grasp her wrist. "Lillian, all day I have been thinking of what is best. We cannot go back without Henrik facing grave consequences. Reinhardt wanted him safe from military duty. Reinhardt would want us to go on. And . . . I believe . . ." He paused, swallowing hard. "I believe Reinhardt would wish for me to see to the needs of his wife and sons."

Lillian pulled her wrist free, clasping her hand over the flesh still warm from his touch. "You want us to travel on . . . together?" If Eli were Reinhardt's birth brother, the situation might be acceptable. A brother-in-law could assume the role of helper. But Eli wasn't Reinhardt's brother. As close as a brother, perhaps, but not bound by blood. Continuing this trek with Eli would be unseemly at best, debauched at worst.

Above the thick, dark hair of his beard, Eli's cheeks glowed red. "I know it seems . . . improper . . . but it does not need to be.

If . . ." Red blotched his neck. "If we were husband and wife, no one would think ill of our traveling together."

Lillian bolted from her seat. "H-husband and wife?" She stared at him in horrified disbelief. Not even an entire day had passed since she'd learned of Reinhardt's death, and already Eli wanted to claim her as his wife? In all of her years of acquaintanceship with this man, she had never found a reason to dislike him. But at that moment, looking into his blushing face, she loathed the sight of him.

He stood, gesturing to the bench she had vacated. "Please, Lillian, sit down. Hear everything I have to say. Then, if you refuse me, I will not ask you again."

He waited, his expression pleading, while she battled the urge to run from the room. But at last weariness drew her back to the bench. She sat, and he sank down, too.

He cleared his throat. "I know it is sudden. You have much on your heart, and you think me unkind for suggesting this scheme."

She refrained from nodding in agreement.

He pinched his chin, his fingers disappearing in his thick beard. "Please forgive me for adding another burden to you, but time is short. A week and we will reach America. We must decide what to do."

As much as Lillian didn't want to admit it, he spoke the truth. They must make decisions. As a child, she had followed her father's guidance; after marrying Reinhardt, she had submitted to her husband's decisions. How simple it would be to acquiesce to Eli and allow him to guide her.

"You suggest . . . marriage?" She forced the words past the lump in her throat.

"Jo." He nodded, the movement jerky, but he spoke with assurance. "We can travel on without anyone's disapproval if we

are husband and wife. You, Henrik, and Joseph will have a man to provide for you and to protect you. The boys will have a man to help them grow up in the Mennonite faith. That is important."

Lillian carefully considered his arguments. While she saw the sense of his suggestion, one question remained. But how could she ask it? She had loved Reinhardt. Slipping into his bed had never been distasteful. But although she knew, liked, and respected Eli, she could not profess to feelings stronger than simple friendship. Would he expect her to be his wife in every sense?

The silence lengthened, and Eli heaved a huge sigh. "I know you have much about which to think. I will not press you for an answer tonight. You take your time. Pray about it."

Lillian licked her lips. Yes, she must seek the Father's will.

Eli went on quietly. "If you decide yes, the captain will marry us before the ship docks." He pulled in a deep breath that expanded his chest. "If you decide yes, we will start out in the new land as a new family."

He didn't say what they would do if she chose to decline his offer.

9

Eli crept to the deck, mounting the stairs on tiptoe to be as quiet as possible. His fellow passengers slept; he didn't want to disturb them. But he must follow Henrik. Only moments ago, he had wakened and spotted the boy slipping around the corner toward the stairs.

In the three days since they'd lowered Reinhardt and Jakob into the sea and moved Joseph to sick bay, Henrik had been uncommunicative, holding himself aloof from everyone. Eli had witnessed Lillian's despondence at her eldest son's withdrawal, and her heartache ate at him. Henrik must be made to see how his coldness affected his mother. A quiet chat at night, with no listening ears of other passengers or with Lillian at hand to interfere, might be what was needed to bring a change in Henrik's behavior. At least, Eli prayed it would be so.

The moon hung high and bright in a cloudless sky, bathing the deck in soft light. Henrik sat with his back against the wall, his arms wrapped around his knees and his gaze heavenward. Wind ruffled his brown hair and lifted the open flaps of his jacket. For a moment, Eli resisted approaching him. The boy looked deep in thought.

Should he intrude? But then an image of Lillian's worried face, her eyes glistening with unshed tears, drove him forward. As he approached, Henrik turned his head. A scowl creased his face.

"I came up here to be alone."

Eli sat and pulled up his knees, imitating Henrik's pose. It provided a bit of warmth against the night air. He looked at the bone white moon suspended in a velvet black sky and spoke in a mild tone. "You have been alone for days. Is it not time to set aside your pout?"

Henrik huffed and pressed his palms to the wooden deck, poised to jump up and flee.

Quick as a striking snake, Eli threw out one arm and caught Henrik's wrist, preventing him from rising. "We must talk."

The boy's expression soured. He jerked his wrist free. "I have nothing to say."

"Then listen." Eli shifted his head to look directly into Henrik's narrowed eyes. "You want to be a man. I understand that. Every boy is eager to assume manhood, and in only weeks you will reach the age of manhood. But there is more to manhood than age, Henrik. There is maturity, which includes setting aside one's own wants to see to the needs of others.

"Your mother has suffered great loss. She has need of your presence now, of your support and understanding." Again, Lillian's pain-filled face appeared in Eli's memory, spurring him to assume a sterner tone than he had ever used with Henrik. "By holding yourself distant, you are piling more hurt on her already broken heart. Is that what you intend?"

Henrik's scowl didn't ease, but he shook his head. "I am not trying to hurt Ma."

"Then what is it?"

The boy stared into Eli's face, his lips puckered. Eli waited, silent, giving Henrik the opportunity to collect his thoughts. But several minutes ticked by without Henrik speaking. Finally, Eli opened his mouth to question him again.

"I have been trying to figure out how I will take care of Ma and Joseph." The words blurted out, as if Henrik shared them against his will.

"I see." Eli offered a slow nod. He glanced at the speckled pathway cast by the moon on the water and then looked again at Henrik. "Have you reached a decision?"

Henrik's sigh formed a brief cloud in the cool night air. "I will have to work, at least until Joseph is old enough to earn money to provide for Ma. When he is old enough, I will go to a university, just as I had planned in Russia, and become a teacher. When I have my certificate, then I will take care of Ma and give Joseph his freedom to pursue his own dreams."

Eli's heart swelled. Henrik had been using his time of isolation to make good plans. He only wished the boy had shared his ideas with his mother; her worry would have been eased considerably had she realized she was at the center of his thoughts.

"I can see you want what is best for your mother and your brother."

Henrik nodded and looked away. The pinched look around his eyes led Eli to believe other thoughts rolled through the boy's mind, but he wouldn't press him to reveal them. Sometimes a man needed to hold thoughts inside.

"When do you plan to tell your mother this idea?"

Henrik's shoulders rose and fell in one shrug.

"We reach New York in only a few more days." Eli waited for acknowledgment. When none came, he added, "I, too, have an idea for caring for your mother."

Henrik turned his face in Eli's direction, and suddenly Eli felt shy. Yet Henrik wasn't a little boy to be kept out of decisions. He should be told. So Eli drew in a big breath and admitted, "I have offered to marry Lillian and be a provider for her and for you boys."

Henrik spun, fully facing Eli. "Marry her!"

"*Jo*, that is right."

The boy shook his head. "B-but Father only just died. Mother loves him still. How can she marry you?"

Eli felt heat rise in his cheeks. He didn't need Henrik's reminder that Lillian held no love for him. Setting aside his deep desire for a wife who was devoted to him was difficult, yet he believed taking care of Lillian was the honorable thing to do.

"People marry for many reasons." Eli spoke to himself as much as to Henrik. "Love is one reason. You are right in that . . . that love beyond Christian caring does not exist between your mother and me. But sometimes a union is made because it is the sensible choice."

Eli swallowed the disappointment that accompanied his words and went on firmly. "For your mother and me, getting married is sensible. We respect and admire each other, and we share a faith in God. We both love you boys. It is a more solid foundation than many have, and I believe, for the two of us, it will be enough."

He tugged his jacket flaps together to block the slight spray of water that spritzed over the edge of the deck. "I respect your desire to become a teacher, and I know your mother wishes to see you complete your education. If she and I marry, then you need not provide for her. You could go to school, just as you had hoped, and not be burdened with caring for a mother and brother."

"Has Ma agreed to marry you?"

Eli crunched his eyebrows. "She has not given me an answer yet." Lillian would need to decide soon. The days were slipping by quickly.

Henrik pushed to his feet. "I will talk to her in the morning. She needs to hear my plans."

Eli rose and put a hand on Henrik's shoulder. "Yes. Talk to your mother. She hungers for time with you. And it will do her much good to know you are concerned for her."

"I am more than concerned. I am—" The boy stopped, turning his face toward the water and pressing his lips together.

"You are . . . ?" Eli prompted, giving Henrik's shoulder a slight squeeze.

But Henrik stepped away from his touch. "Nothing. I will speak to Ma in the morning." He strode away.

Eli watched Henrik until he disappeared around the corner. He should follow, return to his bunk, and sleep, but he remained on deck, shivering in the night breeze.

If Lillian agreed to Henrik's plan, then Eli would not be needed as a provider. He would have lost not only his dear foster brother Reinhardt, but all of Reinhardt's family, too. He would be—just as he had been at the age of six—alone.

Lifting his face again to the moon, where it seemed a placid face peered back at him, he asked himself a question: Was it selfishness or selflessness that had prompted him to ask Lillian Vogt to become his wife?

"Oh, Henrik." Lillian embraced her son, pulling his head into the curve of her shoulder just as she had when he was a little boy. He didn't fit as well, but still it felt good to hold him, if only for a moment. She released him and cupped his cheeks, offering a quavering smile. "I am so proud of you for wanting to take care of your brother and me."

Henrik nodded, his face solemn. He shifted slightly on her bunk, making the straw-filled mattress crackle. His gaze flitted briefly to the bunk Jakob had occupied, which was now folded against the wall behind their heads. Did the sight of that unused bunk pierce him with pain as it did her?

Her son cleared his throat and swiped his hand over his face. "I looked in on Joseph this morning. The doctor said he is much improved. He should be well enough to leave the ship when we dock."

Lillian nearly sagged with relief. Two constant prayers had hovered on her heart: *Lord, bring healing to Joseph* and *Lord, return my Henrik to me.* Now it seemed both prayers had been answered. A dark thought intruded: If God had answered her prayers to restore Reinhardt's health and to protect her children, perhaps her family would still be intact.

She refused to give that thought root. Instead, she chose to praise God for Henrik's change in attitude. Warmth flowed through her chest as she recalled his fervently worded plan of caring for her and Joseph. He was such a good boy.

Tipping forward, she kissed his cheek. Whiskers pricked against her lips, and she reared back in surprise. Her boy was fast becoming a man. "I thank you, Henrik, for your concern."

"So you will let me provide for you?"

Lillian opened her mouth to give a positive response, but something held her tongue. Was it fair to expect Henrik to assume such responsibility at his young age? He had hopes and dreams that deserved fulfillment. God had gifted him with intelligence. Henrik was a scholar—Lillian had always recognized that. If she accepted his offer, he would be forced to push his dreams aside for her. That didn't seem right.

Licking her lips, Lillian formed a cautious response. "*En Sän,* I love you, and I want what is best for you. Will you give me time to pray and seek God's will? I must have complete peace before I give you an answer."

A scowl briefly puckered Henrik's forehead, but he nodded. "Very well, Ma. I understand. I will give you time to pray."

She caught his hand. "And you pray, too, Henrik. We must follow God's will."

The scowl returned, more fierce than before. He gave another brusque nod and rose from the bunk. But then he stood, staring down at her with an unreadable expression. "Ma?"

"Yes, son?"

He shook his head. "Nothing. You . . . you pray, and we will talk again tomorrow." He departed, leaving Lillian alone. Since the storm, when they had all been forced to remain in the hallway all day and all night, most passengers avoided the sleeping hallways when they could. Lillian appreciated the privacy, for it gave her an opportunity to think and pray without distraction.

She sat with her eyes closed, her mind bouncing back and forth between Henrik's offer and Eli's. Which would benefit her sons most? Which held God's will for her? She spent the entire morning wrestling with herself, but when noon arrived, she still had no answer. With a sigh, she rose from the bunk and stretched, easing the taut muscles in her back and neck.

Slowly, she walked up the stairs to the upper level. Passengers filled the sunny deck, waiting for the cook to ring the dinner bell. Some stood in groups, visiting quietly; others sat with their backs against the wall, snoozing; still others paced slowly back and forth. A couple ambled from her left, their hands clasped and their gazes pinned to each other's faces.

Envy struck, harsh and unyielding. She missed Reinhardt. She missed having a husband to hold her hand and peer into her face with a smile that spoke of devotion. Although he had never been overtly affectionate, Lillian always felt secure in Reinhardt's love for her. A lump of sorrow filled her throat, and she swallowed hard to hold back the tears that longed to follow.

She turned away from the couple, and her gaze fell upon Henrik and Eli. They stood side by side at the edge of the deck, leaning their arms on the railing. As she watched, Henrik pointed at something out on the water. Eli nodded, then he put his arm across Henrik's shoulders and gave a quick squeeze before leaning again on the rail.

Something pleasant coiled through Lillian's middle at the sight. Was this glimpse of Eli and Henrik meant to provide her answer? In every way, they appeared to be father and son. Realization swept over her. Eli might not love her, but he loved her boys. He had promised to care for them as well as for her. She knew he would encourage both Henrik and Joseph to love and follow God. Marrying Eli, although perhaps awkward for her, would be best for her sons.

She needn't wait to make a decision. The answer stared her in the face from twelve paces away. Catching her skirt between her fingertips, she squared her shoulders and moved toward Eli and Henrik to give her answer.

10

Lillian stood in the center of excited female attention. All through the long voyage, the women had mostly kept to themselves, but today every woman on board, from the youngest to the oldest, took an interest in Lillian.

For today was her wedding day.

Lillian allowed the women to fuss, one smoothing the wrinkles in her dark blue dress, another tucking stray wisps of hair into her bun. Someone had unpacked a delicate lace scarf of purest white and pinned it to Lillian's hair. She had no flowers to carry, but a blushing young woman had offered a cluster of bright ribbons tied in the middle with a loose knot. The rumpled ends trailed over Lillian's clasped hands and lay like a sleepy rainbow against her full skirt.

While gazing down at the flurry of bright colors, the image suddenly blurred. Despite her best efforts to leave the past in the past, she couldn't help but think of the day she'd pledged her love and life to Reinhardt. That day, her heart had been so full, she feared it would burst from her chest. Joyous anticipation had made her giddy. *Oh, Lord, how I wish I could feel . . . something . . . for Eli.*

A woman should not enter into a union so beautiful and holy as marriage with only emptiness in her soul. She blinked rapidly to clear away the tears in her eyes.

The women, their fussing complete, stepped back and nodded their heads in approval. They knew nothing of her inner turmoil. The woman Lillian had helped to the sick bay stepped forward and cupped her cheek. "You look lovely, *Frau* Vogt."

Lillian fought an urge to snatch the scarf from her head, toss the bright bouquet of ribbons on the floor, and confess that she did not want to marry a man she did not love. But what choice did she have? She must proceed with her plans; she must do this for her sons. Eli was a good man—a kind man who was willing to set everything aside to meet the needs of his foster brother's family. Eli would see that Henrik went to school and that Joseph grew into a godly man. Squaring her shoulders, she staunchly lifted her chin. So she didn't love Eli. There were worse things than a loveless marriage.

She sent a tremulous smile around the circle of eager faces. "I thank you all for your help. You have been very kind."

Like a wave, the women moved in unison and propelled her toward the stairway. She stepped onto the deck and turned the corner to find Eli, the captain, and Henrik waiting.

The captain's serious, chin-held-high pose brought an air of formality to the simple setting. Just as she had chosen her best dress, Eli and Henrik had donned their finest suits. Although the jackets and pants bore wrinkles from their time in the tightly packed trunks, Lillian still appreciated the touch of elegance the fine clothes provided.

A hand applied lightly to her back sent her forward, away from the supportive circle of women, and she stepped to Eli's side. His Adam's apple bobbed up and down, and then he angled his elbow for her to take hold. Her fingers trembled as they made contact. His muscles quivered beneath her fingertips, and she jerked her gaze to his face. Was he also nervous? She watched his hazel eyes drift from her head to her toes and up again. When he met her gaze, a slight smile curved the corners of his lips, forming a look of tender approval—one a groom fully in love with his bride might give.

Her cheeks grew hot, and she quickly faced the captain.

The man cleared his throat, opened a little book, and began to read. "On this day we join together this man and this woman in holy matrimony . . ."

With his hands clasped tightly behind his back, Henrik listened to the captain read the wedding ceremony. The man's emotionless tone contrasted starkly with the myriad of feelings coursing through Henrik's middle.

He glanced at his mother's flushed face, and anger rose above all the other emotions. What did she think she was doing marrying *Onkel* Eli? Why hadn't she trusted her own son to take care of her? His chest constricted painfully. He knew why. She blamed him for being on this ship—for the loss of her husband and youngest child. She didn't want to be beholden to the one who had inflicted so much pain.

He could no longer look at Ma's solemn profile. Jerking his head to the side, he focused on a gull that circled far in the distance, a tiny speck floating above the water. *She is only doing this out of desperation. She and* Onkel *Eli do not love each other!*

As if from a distance, he heard the captain say, "Elias Bornholdt, do you take this woman to be your legally wedded wife?"

Without a moment's hesitation, Eli said, "I do." Did a note of eagerness underscore his response?

"Lillian Vogt, do you take this man to be your legally wedded husband?"

Time seemed to halt as Henrik held his breath, waiting for her reply. *Say no, Ma! Say no, and I will take care of you. Somehow I will make it up to you for causing Father and Jakob to die. You do not have to marry him!*

But Ma's airy voice proclaimed, "I do."

A war took place in Henrik's soul when his mother and *Onkel* Eli—no, his *stepfather* Eli—turned from the captain to face the cluster of passengers who served as witnesses. People rushed forward to shake Eli's hand, kiss Ma's cheek, and bestow well wishes on the newly married couple.

Henrik knew he should offer congratulations—and his blessing. But he could not. Tugging off his coat and string tie, he strode away from the merry celebration. Ma had made her decision without considering his feelings. Why should he worry about her now?

Eli dropped onto his bunk and rested his head on his linked hands. The great boat rocked gently while the boards vibrated with the pounding of the engines. Over the past weeks, his ears had become used to the engines' roar. The sound was now a disharmonious lullaby. He closed his eyes, replaying moments from the evening's events while he waited for sleep to claim him.

The passengers, eager for a reason to celebrate, had turned his marriage to Lillian into a party. The cook had prepared a smoked ham, slicing it very thin so everyone got a taste. One passenger brought out a violin, and several couples danced to the merry tunes. Eli had been unable to resist tapping his toes, but he knew better than to ask Lillian to dance. Mennonites did not dance.

Besides, he had seen in her sky-blue eyes the heaviness of her heart. She might have accepted his proposal, but she still belonged to Reinhardt. For years Eli had dreamed of having his own family. Of shedding the feelings of isolation and loneliness. Now he had a family—a lovely wife and two fine sons—but he still felt alone.

He sighed, opening his eyes and peering up at the underside of the bunk above his. How strange to be married yet still lying in this bunk alone. How disheartening to be married to a woman who still wore her dead husband's ring. When they had spoken with the captain, the man had asked if they would exchange rings. Lillian had looked at the gold band on her finger as if surprised to see it there. Then she shot Eli a flustered look. He assured her it was fine to keep her familiar ring—he had none to offer. The gratitude in her eyes at his declaration had created a longing he couldn't describe.

Yes, she bore Eli's name, but she was his in name only.

He brought down his arms and rolled to his side. Across the aisle, Henrik lay on his bunk with his face toward the wall, presumably asleep. Eli decided not to poke him and find out if he was pretending. Frustration at Henrik's abrupt departure after the wedding ceremony welled, but he forced the feeling down.

In watching Reinhardt father his sons, there had been times Eli believed his foster brother was unnecessarily hard on them. Especially on Henrik. Eli reminded himself that Henrik had lost much. His home, his father, his little brother, his security . . . and now, maybe in his eyes, he had also lost his mother. It would take time for Henrik to adjust to all of the changes. Surely if Eli were patient, and if he assured Henrik of his place in the family, the boy would eventually accept Eli's new position as stepfather.

Eli's heavy eyelids drooped, weariness finally taking hold. But suddenly Henrik rolled over, and his gaze collided with Eli's. Immediately the boy's eyes narrowed. Eli deliberately relaxed his face. He wouldn't give Henrik fuel to feed the fury sparking in his eyes. For long seconds they lay, listening to the snuffles and snores of the men around them. Just when Eli thought Henrik would roll back again, the boy shot a resentful whisper across the aisle.

"The party . . . it is over?"

"*Jo.* It was a fine time. You missed eating smoked ham." He didn't add that Henrik had missed giving his mother a kiss of congratulations.

"I was not hungry." Henrik worked his lower jaw forward and back for a moment. "I spent the evening with Joseph."

The words came out like an accusation—as if Eli had no right to enjoy himself at a party while Joseph remained in the sick bay. But Eli exercised patience. "Did you have a nice visit?"

A grimace creased Henrik's youthful face. "It is *stinkje* in that room. I wanted to bring Joseph out."

"What did the doctor say?"

"Tomorrow."

Eli nodded. Good. Then Joseph would enjoy one day on deck, resting and soaking in the sunshine, before they reached New York and began their journey to Kansas by train. He yawned. Once more, sleep tugged at his eyelids.

"I told him you and Ma married."

Eli's eyes flew wide. "What did Joseph say?"

"He is not happy. He thinks it is too soon for Ma to be marrying."

The words didn't take Eli by surprise. The boys were old enough to be familiar with societal dictates. In Gnadenfeld, a second marriage less than two weeks following the death of a spouse would have been too soon. But they were no longer in Gnadenfeld—they were starting a new life. He fixed Henrik with a steady gaze. "Your mother did what was best."

"Best?" Henrik hissed the word. "It is best to marry someone we know she does not love? What kind of life is that?"

Eli drew in a deep breath. "We could not travel on together as an unmarried man and woman—we had to become man and wife or return to Russia. And we could not return to Russia."

Even in the dim light, Eli saw Henrik's cheeks flame red. The boy's face contorted, but was it anger or anguish that created the deep furrows in his brow? Eli went on quietly, "As I already told you, your mother and I are suited to one another. We will all be fine together. Just wait and see."

With a snort, Henrik rolled over, presenting his back.

Although exhausted, worry robbed Eli of sleep. *Dear Lord, have I made a mistake?*

11

Oh, look!" Joseph pointed, his eyes wide.

Eli smiled down at the boy. "*Jo*, it is something, for sure."

Moments earlier, the cry had risen: "New York! New York!" The passengers, in a rush of anticipation, had scrambled up onto the deck. Eli stood at the rail with his arm tucked protectively around Joseph. The sun, creeping upward, lit the view by inches, making it seem as though the mighty city rose from shadows. Buildings stretched side by side as far inland as the eye could see. The ever-rising sun bathed the cityscape in gold while decorating the cloudy sky above in streaks of purple, orange, and pink.

"Nature makes a special welcome for us."

Awe filled Joseph's voice, bringing a lump to Eli's throat.

The ship sailed slowly up the bay, and Joseph excitedly pointed to the multitudes of factories, churches, stores, and public buildings. Eli laughed softly, enjoying Joseph's enthusiasm. After his long days of sickness, Joseph was still pale and weak, and Eli wondered if he should make the boy move away from the rail and sit down to rest. But he decided a little excitement would do him good.

The ship docked, and a cheer rose. Dozens of people pointed at the oval-shaped structure built of rosy brown stones. Some released cheers of excitement, but Eli also witnessed a few tears. Tears pricked behind his eyes, too. This was Castle Garden—the place where they would be given permission to enter the wonderful land of freedoms called America. But it also meant a release of the old. A bittersweet thought.

A flag, anchored to a pole mounted high on the building's roof, snapped in the morning breeze. Eli stared at the flag's red and white stripes. They took on the appearance of fingers beckoning him to come, to live in peace, to feel at home. Unconsciously he leaned toward the flag, sadness melting away as he became filled with an eagerness to put his boots on the ground of his new homeland.

But then a crewman bellowed for everyone to return to the sleeping hallways. "Workers will load your belongings onto tugboats. Then they will organize the trunks in the emigration center. Once all the baggage has been removed from the ship, you will be allowed to disembark!"

With groans and muttered complaints, the passengers filed back to their bunks to wait. Eli nearly wore out his watch's cover flipping it open every few minutes to check the time. Surely the hands had stopped moving, so slowly time crept by. But finally all of the trunks, boxes, and bags had been removed, and they were given permission to leave the ship.

"Stay with me," Eli warned Joseph and Henrik when the boys bolted for the stairs. Standing on one foot and then the other in impatience, they waited for Lillian to join them. Together, they mounted the stairs and fell in line with the other passengers anxiously pushing their way down the plank and onto dry ground.

Eli put his arm around Joseph as they moved down the wide plank. The boy's slight frame seemed to possess no strength, and Eli sent up a silent prayer. *Lord, let him be accepted into America. Do not let the officers deny him entrance.* After all the family had gone through to make it to America, they couldn't be sent back now.

"Careful," Eli said as he and Joseph left the plank and stepped onto the rocky ground. Throngs of people—passengers from the *Holsatia* and also two other ships that had docked in the harbor—filed toward the corridor leading to Castle Garden. Three large groups melded into one. Shoulder to shoulder they moved, voices chattering in a hodge-podge of languages. So many smells converged that Eli's nose twitched in opposition to the assault. He was forced to stop abruptly when a man pushed in front of him, and someone bumped him hard from behind. He glanced over his shoulder and discovered Henrik on his heels. Lillian clung to Henrik's elbow.

The boy's sullen expression made Eli want to grab Henrik by the collar and shake him the way Reinhardt often had. But knowing how much it would upset Lillian, he refrained. Instead, he pasted on a bright smile. "Look! A flag waves hello to us. It welcomes us to our new home."

Lillian looked up, smiling slightly. Then her eyes flitted briefly to Joseph, and worry pinched her brow. "I trust it will welcome all of us."

Eli leaned down to whisper in Joseph's ear. "I know you are tired, boy, but when we meet the inspectors, you must stand straight and look them in the eye. Can you do that?"

"*Jo, Onkel* Eli." The boy grimaced. "I mean . . . Father."

Henrik's soft snort reached Eli's ears. Eli gave Joseph's shoulder a light squeeze and spoke loudly enough for Henrik to hear, too. "You need not call me Father, Joseph. That is a special name reserved, rightly, for your father. *Onkel* Eli is fine."

The relieved expression that crossed Joseph's face reminded Eli of Lillian's response to being allowed to wear Reinhardt's ring. *I know it is too early, Lord, for them to accept me. But please let acceptance come. Let us be a real family.*

They came to a bricked sidewalk wide enough for them to walk four abreast. Eli stretched his hand to Lillian, but Henrik bolted forward, filling the space between his mother and Eli. Eli bit down on the end of his tongue, reminding himself to give Henrik time to adjust to the changes in his family. As a group, they entered Castle Garden through a double door. A glass dome overhead cast the entire scene in light. A dozen uniformed men herded the new arrivals like cattle, calling out what Eli presumed must be instructions, but he didn't understand the language.

Lillian slipped past Henrik and leaned close to Eli. "What are we to do now?"

With one arm around Joseph and the other clasping Lillian's elbow, Eli watched the officers' hand gestures. "I think we are to get into this line leading to that table over there."

Lillian nodded, releasing a soft breath. They joined the long line of bedraggled newcomers. Henrik kept his face angled downward, a stubborn set to his jaw, but Joseph looked around, wide-eyed. He pointed to the high, domed ceiling.

"*Onkel* Eli, what is this place? It reminds me of a cathedral in Berlin."

Eli looked upward and whistled through his teeth. "A fancy building, for sure." He grinned and poked Joseph's shoulder. "What a nice welcome for us to America, *jo*? Here we are, poor people from a foreign land, entering a building worthy of hosting kings and queens."

The man in front of them turned around. "The captain of the ship told me this building used to be a theater. A woman singer named . . ." He scrunched his face, tapping his whiskered chin with his finger. Then his expression cleared, and he pointed at them. "Lind . . . Jenny Lind . . . from Sweden gave concerts here. But not anymore."

Eli thanked the man for his explanation, and the line moved forward a few inches. A constant buzz of voices filled the air, making Eli's head ache. The air was thick and hot, and Lillian fanned herself with the tails of her shawl. Henrik swayed slightly, as if emulating the movement of the ship's deck. A glance down the line showed several others also swaying in place.

Eli hid his smile. After weeks at sea, it did seem odd to stand on a firm surface. But it felt good—secure. He had no desire for more rocking. Of course, next they would travel by train, and surely the cars would rock on the track. He fingered his pocket, where his leather wallet sat fat and warm against his ribs. Maybe he should splurge and buy tickets for a private berth. After sleeping in a hallway, surely each of them would appreciate some privacy.

He turned to ask Lillian's opinion, but she and Henrik were talking quietly, their heads close together. Weariness was etched into her face. Eli's fingers itched to smooth the tired lines around her eyes. She shifted and caught him looking at her. Color splashed across her cheeks, and his ears went hot.

He licked his lips. "Lillian, I wonder if—"

"It is our turn," Henrik interrupted.

Eli looked forward and realized the man at the table was ready for his approach. The fire in his ears traveled down his neck to his chest. "I apologize." He gestured for Lillian to step up to the table, and she crossed in front of him with Henrik at her side. Eli guided Joseph forward with a hand on his back. As a unit, they faced the balding officer.

A second man stood behind the table. He asked, *"Sprechen Sie Deutsch?"* Eli gave an eager nod. The seated officer asked questions in English, the man behind the table repeated the question in German, and Eli replied in German. Then the man behind the table translated his answers into English. Eli listened closely, trying to pick up a few words. The information he shared must match the ship's records, Eli realized, and his heart clutched when he viewed Reinhardt's and Jakob's names with the word *gestorben* inked in beside them. *Gestorben*—the German word for deceased. He hoped Lillian wouldn't see the list.

All of their names, birthdates, former place of residence, and future plans were recorded and matched with the captain's records. When they were finished, Eli's close attention garnered him one new English word to savor: *wife*. He hadn't wished Reinhardt dead—he still mourned the loss of his foster brother and dear friend—but now Lillian was his wife, and he must honor his vows and do whatever he could to bring her contentment.

The officer waved them on, and they were shuffled through another line that led to a curtained area. Murmuring from others let Eli know a doctor would examine each of them behind the faded green curtain. A shiver of nervousness went down his spine, and he prayed for the Lord to calm his fearful thoughts.

Suddenly a wail rose from behind the curtain. Moments later, the curtain parted and an older couple in clothes worn by the Polish emerged. The woman cried loudly, and the man's wrinkled face twisted into a horrible expression of worry and confusion. A uniformed man bustled forward and escorted the couple out a side door.

Eli's heart pounded. The people had been rejected. Even though he had never seen the man and woman before, his heart turned over in sympathy. He looked at Joseph, who stared after the couple with fright-filled eyes, and he prayed again that the boy would pass inspection.

The doctor crooked his finger at Eli. Shoulders square, he followed the black-suited man behind the curtain. He didn't much like being poked, tapped, and having his teeth checked as if he were a horse, but he bore it without complaint. The doctor put an X on a paper, handed it to Eli, and sent him back out. An officer waiting outside the curtain checked his paper, nodded, and gestured for him to step aside. Eli interpreted these actions as meaning he had received approval to enter the United States, and he couldn't stop a smile from growing on his face.

But then the doctor gestured for Joseph. Eli held his breath, sweat breaking out over his body. The ship's doctor had released Joseph, but would this doctor look at the boy's pale face and sunken cheeks and deem him unfit to walk on American soil? Eli counted the seconds, his heart thudding, while he stared at the curtain and waited. After several minutes, Joseph emerged, holding up a paper that also bore an X.

Oh, thank You, our dear loving Lord. Eli nearly collapsed with relief. He slung his arm around Joseph's shoulders and squeezed him tight. Joseph beamed up at him and blew out a little breath followed by a soft giggle.

Henrik received his release, and then Lillian stepped behind the curtain. He and the boys waited, release papers in hand, watching the curtain. After a few minutes, the doctor pulled the curtain aside and looked at Eli. He said something in English. Eli only understood the word *wife*, but since the man's voice went up at the end, Eli knew he was being asked a question. He took a forward step and guessed at the right answer.

"*Jo*, Lillian Bornholdt . . . *mein Frü—mein* vife . . . wuh-ife."

The doctor fired a quick series of statements that left Eli shaking his head. The doctor looked around, his face pinched into a scowl of impatience, and then he raised his hand and waved at someone. The ship's captain jogged over. The doctor repeated his earlier words.

The captain spoke in German. "Your new wife is nervous

about the doctor checking her. He asks for you to come behind the curtain and offer support."

Eli's chest went tight. As her husband, his presence during the simple exam would not be improper. But how would Lillian react? And how would the doctor interpret her reaction? He sent a helpless look at the boys, but neither Joseph nor Henrik offered any assistance. Truthfully, by Henrik's crooked grin, it seemed he took pleasure in Eli's discomfort. Henrik's behavior stirred Eli's resolve. If Lillian needed support, he would provide it.

Drawing in a breath, Eli nodded and pushed the curtain aside. He crossed to Lillian. "What is wrong?"

Lillian's fear-filled eyes appeared almost black in her colorless face. "He put his hands on me."

Eli glanced at the doctor. "In a forceful manner?"

A flush filled her cheeks. "*Nä*. But it seemed too . . . familiar."

Eli understood. Lillian's modesty protested the doctor's examination, yet it must be accomplished or they would not be allowed to move on. He whispered, "It will be all right. Let him check you. I will stay so you do not come to harm."

Lillian swallowed, and tears glittered in her eyes, but she nodded. While the solemn-faced doctor performed the examination, Eli averted his gaze to prevent further embarrassment for Lillian. When the doctor marked an X on the paper and handed it to Eli, he nodded his thanks, slipped his hand beneath Lillian's elbow, and escorted her from the curtained-off area.

Outside the curtain, he shot her a bright smile. "See? All went well, and now we have consent to continue."

She heaved a huge sigh that spoke more eloquently than words could. His smile grew. He had just performed his first duty as her husband, and she approved of it. Warmth flooded him. Henrik scurried to his mother's side, but Eli deliberately stepped into the boy's pathway. "Henrik, stay close to Joseph and help him, if need be."

Henrik opened his mouth, but Lillian gave a barely discernible shake of her head. With a fierce scowl, Henrik moved to Joseph's side.

Had Lillian just chosen Eli's presence over her son's? Eli's heart set up a mighty pounding, and his hand trembled as he cupped her elbow. "We will need to retrieve our trunks and make arrangement for transport to a hotel. This way."

They dodged groups of other newcomers and made their way to the far side of the crowded room. The passengers' belongings were stacked in rows on a raised platform that apparently once had been a stage. After a few moments of searching, they located their things. To Eli's relief, all six trunks were there. The lids were loose, however, and Lillian ran her hand over the one marked with Reinhardt's name.

"Someone has been in this trunk."

Eli touched her shoulder. "Officials search the trunks to be certain we brought nothing of danger. I was assured this is customary." Franz had explained the procedure to Eli. He had also given Eli a slip of paper with the symbols for both Russian rubles and American dollars.

"There are sharpers who will prey on your ignorance of American ways, *Herr* Bornholdt," Franz had said, "so think before you hand over any money. You will trade your money at the Bureau of Exchange in Castle Garden. Even after you have exchanged your money, carry this with you. It will help you understand the similar values of rubles to dollars so you are not cheated."

Eli had already determined how much American money he should receive in place of his rubles, but he would do as Franz advised and keep the paper until he memorized the value of the dollars and coins. He didn't care to be seen as a fool. His first practice would be paying someone to transport their trunks to the train station.

"You stay here with the trunks," he said to Henrik and Joseph. "See over there?" He pointed to a window with a large sign above it. The sign bore a line of print and several symbols, including an intertwined "P" and "Y" for the Russian ruble. "Your mother and I must exchange our rubles, and then we will make our way to the train station to determine schedules."

"We will leave for Kansas right away?" Joseph was again sagging with tiredness.

Eli gestured to the nearest trunk and waited until Joseph sat before replying. "*Jo,* we should go as quickly as possible rather than spending money on hotels in the city. The sooner we go, the sooner we can purchase our land and begin building our new home." Besides, the less time spent lingering in the city, the less likely Henrik would find an opportunity to slip away.

From the folds of her apron, Lillian tugged loose a money pouch and handed it to Eli. Reinhardt's rubles, he realized. Lillian sat beside Joseph and slipped her arm around his shoulders. "I will wait here with the boys while you exchange our money."

The look of trust she turned on Eli nearly melted him. *Our money,* she had said. Not his and hers, but theirs. Eli battled an urge to lean forward and place a kiss on her cheek. Instead, he spun on his heel and charged toward the money exchange station.

12

Why did you give him Father's money?"

Henrik's accusatory words and sharp glare pierced Lillian's heart. She took his hand. He didn't curl his fingers around hers, but neither did he pull away. "My son, you seem to have forgotten your lifelong relationship with your *Onkel* Eli. You know your father trusted him. They planned this journey to America together. Just because your father is now gone—" An ache rose within her, making her throat grow tight. She swallowed and continued. "Just because your father is gone does not change who Eli was, and is, to us. He will take good care of us."

Henrik frowned toward the Exchange Bureau and muttered something unintelligible.

She leaned forward, tipping her head. "What did you say?"

"Nothing. It does not matter." Turning, he plunked onto a trunk and sat with his arms folded and his head down. Joseph leaned against Lillian's shoulder, and she absently patted his knee. She scanned the area, seeking Jakob's active body. When she realized what she was doing, she couldn't hold back a soft moan.

Although many days had passed, she still instinctively looked for her little Jakob.

She tilted her head and delivered a kiss on Joseph's warm, dark hair. The boy stirred, offering a shy smile. It pained her that it had taken the loss of Jakob, and Joseph's illness, to awaken a closer bond with her middle son. Yet gratitude brimmed that they could sit together, mother and son, with his head nestled on her shoulder. If only the cost had not been so high. . . .

Tears stung her nose, so she sought Eli to distract herself from sad thoughts. She found him at a window, engaged in conversation with a man dressed in a blue, official-looking suit. They talked for a long time, with Eli repeatedly raising and lowering his broad shoulders as if confused by some of the things the man said. Finally, Eli approached, weaving between other arrivals. To Lillian's relief, a wide smile lit his face.

He crossed directly to Lillian. "All of our money is now in American dollars, and I have good news. Next to the Exchange Bureau, a man gave me information about train schedules. Already I have purchased our tickets."

He consulted a wrinkled piece of paper. "The Pennsylvania Railroad leaves in the morning from the New York Station and will carry us to Chicago, Illinois. Then we take the Chicago line to St. Louis, Missouri. From there the Union Pacific Railroad will take us to Topeka, Kansas."

At the word *Kansas*, Lillian's heart leapt. Oh, if only Reinhardt and Jakob could be here! Pushing aside the dismal thought, she focused instead on the confident, knowledgeable tone Eli used. His sureness gave her a sense of security. "Topeka, Kansas," she repeated. "Is that where we will live, then?"

Eli raised one brow and scratched his head. "*Nä*, but the ticket-master told me there will be railroad men—land speculators, he called them—in Topeka who will tell us about land for sale. We will decide, after we reach Topeka, where we will build our new home."

Lillian rose and clapped her palms together. "*Nä-jo*, then let us find a hotel for the night and be well rested for travel by morning."

"That is the other good news." Eli rocked on his heels, looking pleased with himself. "We need not spend money on a hotel. We can stay right here in Castle Garden tonight."

Lillian glanced around the cavernous room teeming with jabbering people. Where would they lay their heads to rest? The sight of Joseph's pale face brought a rush of protectiveness. Her son needed quiet and a comfortable bed if his health was to be fully restored. "We will stay *here*?"

"It will save us much money, and the ticketmaster says we will be safe." Eli stepped forward and put his hand on her shoulder. "One more night amongst many others, and then we will have our privacy. I have made arrangements for us to occupy two private berths on the train."

Eli's hand seemed to grow heavier on her shoulder as worries filled Lillian's head. She bore his name. Did he now expect her to share a berth with him as if she belonged to him in every sense? She stared into Eli's hopeful face, concern making her heart pound. The feelings of security that had wrapped her in peace only moments ago now fled, leaving her nervous and uncertain.

He tipped his head, puzzlement creasing his brow. "Lillian? Is something wrong?"

How could she voice her fears with Henrik and Joseph listening to every word? She shook her head, forcing a smile for the sake of her sons. "*Nä, nä*, all is fine. A . . . a private berth will be welcome after sleeping in the ship's hallway." Stepping away from his touch, she caught Joseph's sleeve and tugged him to his feet. Then she stretched her free hand to Henrik. "Come, boys. Let us find a washroom and give ourselves a thorough scrubbing before I take out some dried meat and crackers from my trunk for our lunch."

Flanked by Henrik and Joseph, she scuttled away with Eli's confused face etched in her memory.

Henrik dropped onto the padded seat of the railroad car next to Joseph and peered out the window at the bustling New York train station. So many tracks, running in every possible direction. Where did all those tracks lead? Surely not all of them went to Kansas.

According to Father, Kansas was a favorable place because the explorers had indicated it resembled the *steppes* of Russia. A flat, open plain. Fields of tall, wild grass. Just like the area that surrounded Gnadenfeld.

Were there universities in Kansas? Probably not. The state was too new. Frustration stirred in Henrik's belly, firing his temper. He wanted to live in a city, not on the plains!

He wished he'd been allowed to explore the huge city of New York. Just a walk down one of those cobblestone streets to look into the windows of some of the buildings would have satisfied his craving for something new and exciting. But Eli had hustled them to the train station first thing in the morning, even though their train wasn't scheduled to leave until shortly after noon. Henrik had asked, very politely, for permission to look around a bit, but Eli had firmly refused even before Ma shook her head. Henrik might have ignored his uncle's words—the man had no right to tell him what to do—but he wouldn't distress his mother.

A piercing whistle blew, followed by a shuddering *chug-chug*, signaling their departure. Henrik pressed his fingertips and nose to the window, examining every detail of the busy station one last time. The train began to move in short jolts that forced Henrik to curl his fingers around the edge of the seat. As the locomotive gained speed, the ride became smoother, although the rocking motion encouraged Henrik to keep a grip on the seat lest he vibrate off the cushion and fall on the floor.

Outside the window, the station disappeared by sections. The view changed to buildings, and finally to countryside. Not until they left the city completely behind did he turn away from the window and let out a sigh. On to Kansas, just as his father and Eli had intended.

He shot a quick look at Eli, who slumped on the bench across the small berth. His uncle's eyes were closed, his bearded chin against his chest. No wonder his uncle was tired. Every time strange noises had awakened Henrik during the night, he had found Eli alert and watchful. Henrik had tried to stay awake, too, to guard his mother and brother, but weariness had pulled him back to sleep.

Joseph tapped Henrik's arm. "Do you think *Onkel* Eli will stay with us in our berth the whole way?" His voice was whisper-soft, making it difficult for Henrik to hear him over the clatter of the train's wheels against the track.

Henrik nodded.

Joseph made a face. "If he stayed with Ma, we could each have our own seat."

Without replying, Henrik turned back to the window. He should be pleased that Eli hadn't forced his way into Ma's berth. As her legal husband, he had the right. But he had settled Ma in her berth across the narrow hallway and then told the boys, "*Nä-jo*, let us go to our berth now." Henrik had seen Ma's tense shoulders relax at his proclamation, and he should have been grateful. Yet, somehow, his uncle's consideration rankled. Why must Eli always be so perfect? And why was he being so thoughtful? What did he want in return? Was it the packet of money that he had kept after exchanging their rubles for dollars? Or was it something else—something Henrik felt uncomfortable even contemplating.

In the past, Henrik had viewed Eli's involvement in their lives as a way of repaying Father's family for giving him a home. But now Father was gone; Eli could go his own way. Yet he remained, claiming he desired only to see to Ma's needs. But his interference kept Henrik from assuming leadership for his remaining family. If Henrik had been in charge, he would have insisted they remain in New York, where he could have found a job in one of the many factories. He could have learned to speak English and then attended a university. He could have visited the docks each day, watching for the arrival of more of Gnadenfeld's residents. In time, he might have reunited with Susie.

Resentment made Henrik's stomach churn.

Joseph tapped him again. His brother's thin face took on a thoughtful expression. "Do you think, when we get to Kansas, Ma and *Onkel* Eli will have children together?"

"What?" Henrik barked the word. The mere thought of Ma having babies with *Onkel* Eli made him break out in a sweat.

"Children," Joseph said again. "I thought maybe—"

"Do not speak of such things," Henrik hissed. "It is indecent!"

Joseph's cheeks splotched red, and he tucked his chin low.

Henrik knew he should apologize for his harsh reaction. Joseph missed his little brother. So did Henrik. Cheerful little Jakob had lit up each room he'd entered. Life seemed dull and joyless without the little boy's giggle and ornery grin. But while a baby might help fill the void Jakob's passing created, another child could never replace Jakob. There was no point in wishing for something that couldn't be.

He forced a kinder tone. "Having children is a private matter, Joseph, between grownups. It is not for us to discuss." Besides, a man and a woman should not create a child together unless love bound them to each other.

"But . . ." Joseph licked his lips, glancing at Eli as if to ascertain the man was really sleeping. "They are married. Married people have children . . ."

"Ma and Eli only married so they could travel on together. They do not love each other the way Ma and Father did." The thought of love shared between a man and woman immediately brought Susie Friesen to mind, and Henrik added in a sour tone, "I do not wish to speak of it anymore."

Joseph's head bobbed in silent agreement. Then he yawned and shifted on the seat. "I think I will take a nap like *Onkel* Eli."

"Good." If Joseph slept, too, Henrik would be left in peace. Peace . . . Truthfully, his soul had not known peace since the day Father had announced his intention to leave Gnadenfeld. Glaring out the window at the unfamiliar sunlit landscape, Henrik wondered if peace even existed in America.

Lillian lifted her feet onto the bench and leaned into the corner. Thick draperies, held back with gold-tasseled cords, framed the window. She had lowered the top pane, and hot air coursed into the enclosed berth, stirring the curtains as well as her hair. The scene outside beckoned her to admire the lush landscape and towering trees thick with dark green leaves, but her focus was turned inward.

She had misjudged him. When Eli had mentioned two private berths, she hadn't expected he would allow her an entire berth to herself. No, she'd assumed he would join her. She glanced around the space—small, certainly, but more than adequate for one person. The benches, well cushioned with tufted emerald green velvet pillows softening the seats and backs, allowed one to travel comfortably for the four-day journey.

Guilt niggled as she considered Eli, Henrik, and Joseph sharing a similar space. She should invite Joseph to join her. Then Eli and Henrik would have more room to stretch out. But she would wait until tomorrow. For now, she appreciated the privacy.

How long had it been since she'd been able to enjoy a moment of complete solitude? Not since she was a little girl escaping to the fields after school instead of going home as her parents instructed. Her one small rebellion. She remembered her mother waiting in the doorway, switch in hand, to mete out punishment for her disobedience. Yet those hours of uninterrupted pleasure, running through the fields with her arms outstretched or lying flat on her back, gazing at the clouds and drinking in the sight and sound of the open prairie, had always been worth the momentary sting of the switch against her legs.

Her mother had been the disciplinarian in her childhood home, but Lillian had always deferred to Reinhardt in disciplining their sons. With Reinhardt gone, would Eli now take over that position? Would Henrik submit to Eli's authority? Reinhardt had kept an especially close watch on Henrik. At times she had thought him overly attentive—Henrik was, underneath, a good boy, even if prone to flights of fancy.

She could understand Henrik's desire to learn—to sample fresh and exciting experiences—because she'd harbored exactly the same desires as a child. Yet she also knew her parents' close rein had prevented her from stepping into dangerous situations. She sensed Henrik's continued restlessness. Could she, without Reinhardt's firm hand, keep him reined in and safe from worldly influences?

Sorrow pressed like a weight on her heart. Oh, if only Reinhardt were still here! If only little Jakob could grow to manhood! But wishing changed nothing. Reinhardt and Jakob were gone.

She, Henrik, and Joseph remained. Somehow she would find the strength to provide the guidance her boys needed to be God-honoring men.

Heavenly Father, help me guide my boys in Your ways. Without effort, a song formed in her heart. She opened her mouth and burst forth with *"Auf, Auf, Mein Herz, mir Freuden,"* one of her favorite hymns from the *Glaubensstimme*, the songbook used in the little church in Gnadenfeld for as long as she could remember.

Although "Awake, My Heart, With Gladness" was traditionally an Easter hymn, the idea of starting anew in a fresh land seemed to pair well with the heart-stirring phrases. The words offered an encouragement to meet the challenges that lay ahead with joy and anticipation rather than fear and concern. Yet, for reasons she didn't want to examine, this time the music failed to melt away her worries.

13

Ma! Ma!" Joseph's excited shout roused Lillian from sleep. She sat upright and blinked into surprisingly bright light. The boy held the curtains wide, allowing sunlight to pour through the window. "Topeka, Ma! We're here!"

Lillian looked out onto a city scene similar to many others they'd witnessed over the past days of travel. Wood- and rock-constructed buildings lined a wide street. The train chugged slowly, its whistle warning the townspeople of its approach. By craning her neck, she could glimpse the station ahead. A long, scrolled board mounted above a covered walkway held one word: TOPEKA. The same word from their tickets. As Joseph had gleefully exclaimed, they'd reached their destination.

Lifting her hands to her hair, she chided, "Drop the curtain, Joseph, so we might ready ourselves without observation."

Joseph let the curtain fall, but he peeked through the narrow slit between the two heavy panels while Lillian brushed her hair, braided it, and fashioned the waist-length plait into a thick knot at the back of her neck. A change of clothes wasn't possible with their trunks stored in a boxcar at the back of the train, but she smoothed her full skirt as best she could and tugged at Joseph's shirt in an attempt to remove the worst of the wrinkles.

The train's whistle let out one long blast that accompanied the brakes' ear-piercing squeal. Both she and Joseph braced themselves against their seats as the train screeched to a shuddering halt. The moment it stopped, Lillian snatched her apron from the end of her bench and whipped it around her waist.

A light tap sounded on the paneled door of their berth. Joseph bounced up and opened the door before Lillian had finished tying her apron. Her hands scrambled to complete the task, but Eli caught her mid-tie. Although adequately covered, the idea of his seeing her perform part of her dressing duties sent fire through her cheeks.

Apparently he found the situation disconcerting, as well, because he averted his gaze, angling his face down the hallway instead of into the berth. "This is Topeka," he said unnecessarily. "I spoke with the conductor, and he gave me instructions for finding the men who can sell us land. I wonder . . ."

He turned his head slowly, by inches, as if fearful she would still be doing something he shouldn't see. She clasped her hands at her waist and met his gaze directly, although she wanted to hide her flaming cheeks behind her palms. His shoulders heaved in a deep breath, and a grin teased his lips.

"I wonder if, rather than going to a meeting with land sellers, you would like to take the boys to an eating place and have a good meal?"

Lillian's stomach growled at the thought of a decent meal. *"Ach, jo."* The train's fare had not been much better than the meals served by the ship's unimaginative cook.

Eli's eyes crinkled with his smile. "The conductor tells me a restaurant can be found over the bridge and down a street called Kansas Avenue. This will give you and the boys a chance to learn to recognize the name of our new state. He assures me the food is very tasty and plentiful." He removed his wallet from his jacket pocket and withdrew two crisp bills. "Take this. I have been teaching Henrik the dollar amounts, so he understands the costs. You and the boys enjoy a meal. I will go see the land sellers and meet you at the restaurant when I have made arrangements for a purchase."

"Then you will eat, too?" Lillian fingered the bills. It wasn't fair that she and the boys should have the pleasure of a hot, flavorful meal while Eli went hungry.

"*Jo*, then I will eat, too. Thank you for your concern." The warmth in his eyes made her face flood with heat again. He gestured for her and Joseph to step into the aisle. "Now you go. I will see to our trunks, but I cannot take them until I have found a wagon. The conductor said the land sellers will be able to direct me to a wainwright." He spun on the worn heel of his boot and walked away.

She held Henrik's elbow, allowing him to escort her off the train. Joseph scuffed behind them as they crossed over a wooden bridge and then turned onto a street marked with the word *Kansas*. The boys gawked into store windows, their eyes round and curious, but Lillian looked at the sky. It was bright blue and dotted with fluffy white clouds—a beautiful sight. Seeing that blue sky, reminiscent of the canopy from her childhood wanderings in the fields outside of Gnadenfeld, made her feel at home, even though the town was new and strange.

The smell of fresh bread and cooking meat reached her nostrils even before they stepped onto the boardwalk of a wood-sided building with a tall, square front. White paint glistened in the sun, and dark blue shutters stood guard on either side of the windows and the centered door. Henrik guided her to the door, but Lillian hesitated.

She glanced at her travel-rumpled skirt and then at the crisp, checked curtain hanging behind the glass. Surely a building as clean and neat as this on the outside would be even neater on the inside. Although her stomach begged her to proceed, she remained stiff and unmoving on the sidewalk. She had never eaten in a restaurant before, but she felt certain their wrinkled, sweat-stained clothes would be unwelcome here. And what would she do if they spoke to her in English?

Henrik gave her arm a little yank. "Come on, Ma."

She took a step away from the door. "I . . . I do not think we should go in."

"But *Onkel* Eli said for us to eat," Joseph said. "He will meet us here later. I'm hungry."

Lillian worried her lower lip between her teeth. She didn't know where to find Eli to tell him they couldn't enter the restaurant. A long bench sat beneath one of the windows. She supposed they could sit and wait for Eli to come to them. While she considered this possibility, the door swung open and a young woman wearing a snow-white apron over a dress the same color as the shutters offered her hand in welcome.

The young woman spoke, but Lillian was unfamiliar with the words. She shook her head, wrinkling her brow and flipping her hands outward to indicate her lack of understanding.

Tipping her shining blond head, the woman said, *"Hollandisch? Russisch? Deutsch?"*

Lillian's heart skipped a beat at the recognizable word. *"Jo, Deutsch."*

Soft laughter spilled from the girl's lips. She said in perfect German, "Ah, welcome to Aunt Toadie's Kitchen. Please come in."

Joseph bolted through the door, and Henrik guided Lillian after him. Inside, Joseph peered around with his mouth open. Even Henrik's gaze flitted from the glossy wooden floors to a huge tin fixture holding dozens of candles above their heads.

"Follow me, please, and I will seat you."

Round tables draped with blue-checked cloths filled the space, which was larger than Lillian had expected. Potted plants—some leafy and green, some covered with blooms—created a gardenlike appearance. Fat candles glowing on each tabletop and in scrolled-tin wall sconces lit every square inch of the white-painted room. Lillian tried to make herself as small as possible as they followed their hostess to a table in the corner, near a large rock fireplace now empty of a blaze.

The girl gestured to the spindle-backed chairs that surrounded the table. Her full rosy lips curved into a smile. "Please be seated. I will see to your needs."

"Dank," Lillian said. Clearly this girl's beauty went below the surface to her soul. She glanced at Henrik and caught him staring at the girl.

"*Sie sind willkommen*. My name is Nora, and it is my pleasure to serve you. Aunt Toadie baked pork chops today. May I bring some to you?"

The good smells filling the dining room convinced Lillian that any food served here would please their tongues. *"Jo, bitscheen."*

With another nod, Nora glided away toward a set of wooden double doors.

Henrik watched her until she disappeared behind the doors. Then he turned and caught Lillian smiling at him. He fussed with the edge of the white napkin lying on the table, carefully clearing all expression from his face. Lillian bit the insides of her cheeks to keep from giggling. Perhaps Henrik was finally beginning to forget Susie Friesen.

True to her promise, Nora served them an enticing meal of seasoned pork chops, mashed sweet potatoes swimming in butter, whole green beans, and fluffy rolls on homey, blue-speckled plates. While they ate, she hovered beside their table, visiting with them as if they were elite guests rather than common immigrants. Joseph peppered her with questions, all of which she answered without hesitation. They learned she had been raised in the eastern United States and even had attended a university in New York City. Upon graduating, she had traveled to Kansas in response to her great-aunt's plea for help in her restaurant.

"Since I am able to speak fluently in four different languages, I can converse with many of the immigrants who arrive on the trains."

Henrik's brows formed a sharp V. "If you have such education, why do you work as a server?"

Nora laughed lightly, proving she took no offense at Henrik's bold query. "I have few skills other than speaking in many languages. But I see that ability as a gift. I believe this is where the Lord guided me, allowing me to use my ability to help newcomers like yourselves feel welcome."

"You have made us feel very welcome," Lillian assured her. Her fondness for this young woman grew with each passing moment.

"Then I am satisfied." Nora flashed another smile around the table. Then she looked up. "Oh! Another guest. Excuse me." She scurried toward the front door. Lillian looked over her shoulder. Eli had arrived. Half rising, Lillian waved at him.

Eli tipped his hat to Nora, then strode directly to their table. He sat across from Lillian and removed his hat. Looking at their empty plates, he licked his lips. "*Nä-jo*, it appears you had a *goot* meal for sure."

Moments later, Nora brought him a plate of thick chops. Lillian sipped hot, sweet coffee and listened to Henrik and Joseph visit with Nora while Eli cut into his pork chops. When he had finished, he wiped his mouth with a napkin, placed it beside his plate, then patted his stomach.

"*Ach*, that was very good. The best since we left Gnadenfeld."

Nora poured coffee from a tall enamel pot into Lillian's cup and then picked up Eli's empty plate. "*Danke schoen.* I will tell Aunt Toadie you approved of the meal. May I bring you a piece of pie?"

After a moment of thought, Eli shook his head. "My stomach is full. But *dank*."

Nora bid the family farewell and hurried toward the doors that led to the kitchen.

Eli leaned his elbows on the table. "I tell you what I have gotten done since you left the train."

Lillian marveled at all Eli had accomplished in the past hour. After visiting with a railroad representative and making arrangement for the purchase of 240 acres of land near a town called Newton, he had bought a wagon—"Called a prairie schooner," he said with a wink at Joseph—and two pairs of oxen to pull it.

"Not horses?" Henrik's tone carried scorn. Eli's choice surprised Lillian, too. In Gnadenfeld, he had been known as a fine horseman. Surely he would prefer horses.

"Oxen are sturdy beasts," Eli said without a hint of remorse, "better suited to this hard landscape. One had a calf not long ago, so she will give us milk for our journey. They will take us to our land, and then they will take turns pulling the plow I bought." His expression turned dreamy. "This land, Lillian, is meant to receive seed. We will be successful here. I feel it in my bones."

Henrik's soft snort didn't even make Eli flinch.

"We must go back to the railroad station now and load our trunks onto the wagon. Then we will purchase supplies at the general store, and off we go to our new land!"

Joseph propped his elbows on the table's edge, imitating Eli's pose. "How will we know where to go? Are there roads?"

"*Jo*, boy, there are some roads. But look here." Eli slipped a round disc from his pocket and held it on the palm of his hand.

Joseph leaned in eagerly, and even Henrik angled his head to see. "The wainwright gave this to me. It is a compass." He pointed to a tiny hand quivering on the dial. "See here these letters? They mean north, south, east, and west. This will help us stay on course."

Joseph nodded and his hair flopped over his forehead. "The ship's captain used a tool like this to keep us on course on the ocean."

"I am certain the captain's tool was much more complex than this," Eli responded, "but it will suit our purpose." He grinned at Lillian. "Newton is southwest of Topeka, so . . ." Turning again to Joseph, he said, "The compass is very smart and this little pin shows us where north can be found. So if the compass points north, what line on the compass will point to our new home?"

Joseph jammed his finger against the glass cover on the disc halfway between S and W. "Here!"

"*Jo,* good job. You will make a fine navigator for us."

The boy beamed. Eli slipped the disc back into his pocket and looked at Lillian. "We will be required to stop in Newton and ask for someone to accompany us to the piece of property I purchased. The land sellers sent a telegram to let them know to expect us."

Everything was falling neatly into place, just as Reinhardt had planned. Lillian vacillated between gladness that their dreams were coming true and grief that not all members of her family were here to see the dream unveiled.

Eli pushed his palms against the table, rising. "Now we must buy our supplies. Come. We want to leave Topeka before evening. From now on, we camp until we reach our land, and I do not know how many cities with stores we will find in between. So we must make good and thorough selections while we are here and supplies are plentiful."

Then he faced Joseph again, his eyes twinkling. "Speaking of selections, Joseph, I have a special job for you."

Joseph pressed his palm to his chest. "For me?"

"*Jo.* I met a man who will sell us some chickens. Our wagon has a place to hang a chicken cage, so I am thinking it would be good for us to have fresh eggs as we travel and for when we reach our land. Oxen and horses I know, but I did not raise birds on my farm. You fed the neighbor's chickens in Gnadenfeld. Do you think you could choose for us some good laying hens?"

Joseph nearly danced with excitement. "*Jo, Onkel* Eli! I will choose the very best ones!"

Eli slung his arm around Joseph's shoulders, and they headed for the outside door. Lillian followed, words of praise for Eli filling her mind. Eli placed such confidence in Joseph. The boy would surely flourish beneath Eli's attention and care.

Then she glanced at Henrik, and her heart fell. His sullen expression had returned. It would take more than letting him choose chickens to reach Henrik.

14

Can you build an outdoor fire?" Eli asked Lillian as the boys headed off to look for dead limbs.

She lifted her chin. "I built many fires in *ne Oweback* at home. An outdoor flame cannot be any harder to strike than one in an oven."

Eli noted that weariness lined her face, making her appear older than her thirty-eight years, yet she expressed no complaint, only a willingness to do what was needed. She walked to the jockey box hanging on the wagon's sideboard and flipped it open. Slipping the packet of wooden matches into her skirt pocket, she drew in a breath and pointed to the roadway they had just covered.

"I am going to look along the road for rocks to circle my cook fire." She glanced across the area where Eli had indicated they would camp. "I would not wish this grass to catch the flame."

"That is sound thinking." Eli wanted to tell her how much he appreciated her positive, hardworking attitude, but a lump blocked his throat, holding the words of praise inside. He released the two lead oxen from their yoke and called a warning: "Watch the grass for snakes."

Lillian jolted, momentarily ceasing her progress. Then she bent over and snatched up a sturdy twig. She continued, slashing the grass with her stick.

Quite a woman, his *frü*. His *wife*. He savored the American word as he guided the oxen to the back of the wagon and tied their leads to a rear wheel. Although marrying Lillian had been a decision born of necessity, he already recognized his long-held brotherly fondness for her deepening to something more. His gaze followed her, watching her stoop to lift a rock and drop it in the pouch made with her apron, then walk a few steps farther, her head turning this way and that in search of sizable stones. The bouncing wagon ride, with wind-carried dust constantly pelting them, had worn him down. Lillian could be no less weary, yet she didn't sit in the shade and complain. Instead, she gathered stones so she could safely build a fire to prepare their supper.

Eli scratched an ox's head while considering the cheerful spirit Lillian possessed. With all she'd lost, she should be mired in grief. But not once since the day she'd held Jakob's lifeless body in her arms had she spoken of either Reinhardt or Jakob. She didn't look back, but forward—to the future. Their future . . .

His thoughts skipped ahead to nightfall. Until this time there had been separate areas for sleeping. But tonight there were no hotel rooms or berths or sleeping hallways to keep them apart. How could he offer Lillian at least the semblance of privacy? He and the boys could throw pallets anywhere and lie in a row, but Lillian? She needed her own spot.

He ran his hand along the smooth line of the bonnet covering the sturdy bed of the wagon as he moved to release the second pair of oxen. In his mind's eye, he reviewed the crowded space inside the wagon. Trunks and supplies filled the bed, but maybe they could lay a feather mattress across the trunks for Lillian. Then he and the boys could sleep on pallets beneath the wagon, where they would have some protection.

The boys' banter carried to his ears, and he looked up to see them heading toward the wagon with their arms full of twigs. Lillian came from the opposite direction holding the corners of her apron, which hung low and tight with its load. His heart seemed to double in size, filling his chest. His family . . .

Swallowing, he raised his hand and waved. "Hurry now! Night will soon fall, and we want to have a nice meal together before we sleep."

Lillian proved an adept fire builder, and soon she had a pan of *Bobbat*, a hearty bread laden with meat and dried fruit, baking over a snapping fire. A tall coffeepot balanced on the rocks guarding the fire, the liquid boiling while the *Bobbat* baked. Good smells lifted on the breeze, nearly turning Eli's stomach inside out with anticipation. He and Henrik kept busy smoothing out the ground beneath the wagon and then laying out their bedding. Joseph freed the three speckled hens from their cage and watched them scratch in the dirt near the wagon.

Dusk fell, soft and rosy, with the wind gentling as the sun slinked toward the horizon. Lillian removed plates from the back of the wagon and called, "*Nä-jo*, Joseph, put the clucks in their box so we can eat."

They sat in a circle around the fire, and Eli prayed for their simple meal, adding, "Thank You, our Father, for providing us with a new home. Take us safely to it and may it provide our needs according to Your riches in glory. Amen."

"Amen," Lillian whispered, the simple expression carrying a deep note of appreciation.

For a moment their gazes met across the flickering fire, and Eli wondered if the high color in her cheeks came from the fire's heat or from a heat within. Before he could explore the answer, Joseph held out his plate.

"Cut me a big piece, Ma. I am starving."

Laughing, Lillian divided the *Bobbat* into four wedges and served each of them. Eli forked up a big bite, his mouth watering. Usually well-flavored with fresh sausage and plump raisins and baked in a mud-brick oven, the open-fire *Bobbat* contained chunks of dried beef and chopped dried apricots. Despite the differences, it was every bit as good as the original version. He ate with relish, as did his companions. No one talked; they were too tired, Eli supposed, to think of words to say. When they finished, Lillian pushed to her feet and reached for the plates.

But Eli shook his head. "*Nä*, you cooked; we men will clean up."

Henrik made a face, but he stood and headed for the water barrel.

"No water, boy." Eli's words stilled Henrik in his tracks. "We only have the two water barrels, and I do not know when we will have the chance to fill them again, so we must use the water sparingly. We will only use water for drinking and cooking."

Joseph sat straight up. "No bathing?" Elation filled his voice.

Eli swallowed a chuckle and opened his mouth to confirm Joseph's assessment, but the dismay on Lillian's face made him offer a compromise. "Your mother will dip a cloth, and we can use that to wash our faces and hands. If we come upon a creek, we will bathe and give our dishes a thorough scrubbing. But for tonight we will scrape these plates and pan good with a fork and make do." Turning to Lillian, he said, "You have had a long day, Lillian. Go . . . ready yourself for sleep while the boys and I clean the dishes. I—we—Henrik and me—made a bed for you in the wagon."

In the waning light, he watched color again climb her cheeks.

"The boys and I"—he pointed to the pallets—"will sleep there."

She nodded, the loose strands of hair from her bun swirling around her face. "*Dank*. But I . . . I need . . ." Her gaze skittered around the camp, her lower lip caught between her teeth and her brow furrowed.

What caused her such anxiety? Finally, understanding dawned. Although the topic was not one he would usually address with a woman, it was necessary. And she was his wife, after all. Leaning forward, he whispered, "The trees will provide a barrier. Take the lantern from the end of the wagon to light your way."

Another quick nod served as a reply. She spun and dashed away.

The sound of distant thunder awakened Lillian. She sat up and blinked into the gray gloom, confusion making her pulse race until she remembered where she was. Tipping her head to the side, she peered beneath the edge of the bonnet at the dark sky. What odd thunder Kansas possessed! Usually thunder rolled and then stopped, but this thunder continued—a persistent rumble. She shifted to her knees, and the wagon springs squeaked.

A shadowy figure appeared at the end of the wagon. "Lillian . . . you are awake?"

She tugged her blanket to her chin and nodded. "*Jo*. The thunder wakened me."

"It is not thunder. Come."

In the minimal light, she saw that he offered his hand. After a moment's pause, she took it and allowed him to help her from the wagon. She held the blanket around her shoulders like a shawl, shivering although the breeze wasn't cool. "What is it?" Why she felt the need to whisper, she couldn't explain. But to speak aloud would be to desecrate this predawn hour.

"Look." Eli hunched his shoulders, bringing his face next to hers and pointing straight ahead.

Stars still dotted the sky, only a soft blush of pink on the eastern horizon promising that the sun would soon appear. Deep shadows covered the land, but by squinting, Lillian was able to make out a large, moving mass of . . . something. Horses? No, these creatures were too short to be horses. But something large, with hooves. The thunderous sound came from the pounding of their feet against the hard earth. Dust rose like a cloud above the herd, and the ground quivered beneath her feet.

Her breath coming in little spurts, she repeated her earlier question. "What is it?"

Eli's hand rested on her shoulder. "I am not sure, but I think they might be what the land speculator called buffalo. He said they look like humpbacked, hairy cows."

Lillian shrugged further into her blanket, straining to get a better glimpse of the hairy cowlike animals. But the herd of buffalo—if indeed that is what they were—headed away from them, the thunder sound becoming more distant. After a few moments, they seemed to disappear into the morning gloaming, only a puff of dust staining the sky to provide evidence that they had been there at all.

Lillian looked up into Eli's face. He stared after the herd, amazement tingeing his features. His hand still rested on her shoulder, so she stood very still, waiting for him to remove it rather than disturbing his concentration.

Finally, he heaved a sigh and shifted, looking into her face. "I think we are very fortunate, Lillian, to have seen the buffalo. The land speculator told me nearly all of the herds have been wiped out by hunters. But there they were on our first morning, waking us with the sound of hooves against the sturdy ground that will receive our wheat seed." He sighed deeply, serenely. "This is a *goot* land, Lillian."

Suddenly he seemed to realize his arm was around her because he jerked his hand away so abruptly her blanket slipped. He jammed the hand into his pocket, as if afraid it might do something else of which he didn't approve.

As casually as possible given the uneven beat of her pulse, she shifted the blanket back into place and then fussed with her braid, which fell over her shoulder. Her pretended indifference had the desired effect—he released a breath and pulled his hand loose to run it through his hair. "It is early, I know, but maybe you could start our breakfast? The earlier we start, the more progress we make today toward our land."

She nodded and headed around the wagon. "You wake the boys, and I will—" Her words died when she realized a fire already crackled. She looked at Eli. "You have been up for a long time already if you got a fire started."

He shrugged, his grin sheepish. "I kept it going all night."

She gawked at him. All night? Had he slept at all?

"I thought it best to keep wild animals at bay, and then, too, you would not be troubled with the work of building a fire first thing."

Lillian examined the gentle blaze and the neatly jumbled pile of sticks waiting beside the rock circle to feed the fire. Throughout her marriage, Reinhardt and she had performed their own duties. He worked as a cobbler to earn their living, and she kept the home. She would never have attempted to cobble a shoe, and never had Reinhardt assisted with her chores. Yet Eli had readied this fire for her. The simple act touched her deeply.

"Dank." She heard the tremulous note in her own voice, and she swallowed, adding in a firmer tone, "It is very kind, but you must not stay up every night tending a fire. You will need your rest if you are to have energy to drive the wagon."

"Ach." He waved his hand. "It is no trouble, and I can doze on the seat, since I have Joseph to keep us on course."

They laughed together softly over Joseph's fascination with the compass. A sliver of gold appeared on the horizon, and Eli shifted his face to the rising sun. A deep breath expanded his chest, and a contented smile stretched across his face.

"Ah, here is the sun. Another day. A day of freedom." He slapped his stomach with both open palms. "We will have breakfast; then I will read to us from the Bible for a good start on our day, *jo*?"

Lillian nodded. "I would like that." Then she blurted, "You are so *schaftijch* this morning."

His lips twitched, his eyes sparkling. "Is there a reason I should not be cheerful?"

She wished she could snatch back the words. Reinhardt had been surly and uncommunicative most mornings. Not until after his coffee did he speak without grumbling. Having a man greet the day with smiles rather than snorts was alien but pleasant. But making the comparison was most surely disloyal to Reinhardt's memory.

She tossed her blanket into the back of the wagon and lifted out a skillet. She carried it to the fire and set it on the rocks to heat. "Please wake the boys and have Joseph check the hens' box for eggs. I will prepare a hearty breakfast, but first . . ." She waved her hand toward the scrub trees off the road. "I must visit the trees."

15

Henrik shielded his eyes with his hand and peered down the road, then drew in a breath of anticipation. "I see a town ahead!"

Beside him on the wagon seat, Eli nodded slowly. "*Jo*, boy. I see it, too."

After four days of traveling by wagon, with Eli skirting cities, Henrik was ready to see people and buildings—anything besides scrub trees, prairie grass, and little jumping critters that barked like dogs but scurried like overgrown mice. Didn't this new country hold anything of interest?

When he'd asked Eli why they couldn't visit the towns along the way, Eli had chuckled in his frustrating way and said, "For what purpose would we visit? We cannot speak their language. There would be nothing to say. Besides . . ." He had raked his fingers through his beard, lowering his voice. "I do not wish to be taken advantage of. If we stay away from people, we are safer."

Recalling the conversation, Henrik snorted in disgust. Safer . . . and bored. He shifted on the seat to face Eli. "Will we stop at this town?"

Ma leaned between them from her spot inside the wagon bed. "It might be wise, Eli. The water barrels are low—we could replenish them in town."

Henrik held his breath while Eli worked his jaw back and forth, considering Ma's comment. When the man nodded his agreement, Henrik nearly shouted with glee. But when they pulled into the town, Henrik's elation dampened. The town was small, only a few wood-sided buildings lining a dirt street and a spattering of houses beyond. The wood siding on all buildings was bone white and unpainted rather than gray and weathered, which told Henrik they had been recently constructed. Railroad tracks dissected the town east to west, dividing it into two halves.

Eli drew the oxen to a halt beside the tiny train depot, the only building in town wearing paint. A man stepped from the little structure and pushed his hat to the back of his head, examining their wagon.

With a smile, Eli said, "*Goodendach*—hello."

The man lifted his chin. "Hello."

Shifting on the seat, Eli pointed to the water barrels that hung from the wagon's sideboard. *"Wota?"*

After a moment's pause, the man lifted his hand and gestured to Eli. Eli hopped down, and Henrik started to follow. But Eli shook his head. "*Nä*, you stay here with your mother and brother. I will see to filling the barrels."

Henrik huffed in frustration. The town wasn't much—that was obvious—but at least it would be a change from the prairie. Why couldn't he explore? He plunked back onto the seat hard enough to make the springs squawk in protest and watched Eli and the man walk around behind the building. In moments, Eli returned, a smile on his face.

"We can fill our barrels from the water tank, no charge. He

called this place Cottonwood Station. And I think he said we are halfway to Newton."

Halfway? That meant at least another four days of sitting in this wagon, staring at the rumps of oxen, and tasting dust. Henrik leapt to the ground. "While you fill the barrels, I am taking a walk through town."

Eli's eyebrows formed a sharp V. "We will not be here long."

"I need to stretch my legs." Henrik made a show of arching his back, grimacing with the movement. "What will it hurt for Joseph and me to get some exercise? We are tired of sitting."

Ma leaned out of the wagon. "Let them go, Eli." Her hair hung in her face, her eyes tired. "It will do them good."

Without waiting for Eli's reply, Joseph hopped down from the wagon and scampered to Henrik's side.

"Come, Joseph." Henrik grabbed the sleeve of Joseph's shirt. His brother waved at Ma and then fell into step beside Henrik.

A half dozen horse-drawn wagons stood along the edge of the street, the horses lazily nodding under the sun. The boys encountered a few townspeople, who looked them up and down with idle interest, but no one spoke to them. That suited Henrik fine. As Eli had said, they didn't speak the same language. Listening to—and not understanding—English made him feel foolish. And he hated feeling foolish.

The only person with whom he had enjoyed visiting since they reached America was Nora, back at the little restaurant in Topeka. In their conversation, she had mentioned a university being built right there in the city. His heart twisted with desire to return to Topeka, spend time with Nora, pick up as much English as he could, and then enroll in that university. But he couldn't leave Ma and Joseph right now.

He and Joseph reached the end of the business district, and

Joseph kicked a stone in the road. "Should we turn around and go back?"

"*Nä*, not yet." Henrik turned a slow half circle as he answered. Tall grass grew in scraggly patches alongside the foundation of the building at the edge of town. Henrik shook his head, disgusted. Someone should take a sickle to that grass—it created a good hiding spot for snakes or spiders. Suddenly, from the depth of one thick clump, the glint of sun on something shiny caught his eye. A coin, perhaps?

"Stay here and watch for the wagon," he told Joseph; then he strode to the clump and hunkered down. Cautiously, in case he startled a snake, he pushed the blades of grass aside, revealing the source of the glint. Three skinny-necked green-glass bottles stood in a crooked row against the building's stone foundation.

Henrik sent a quick glance over his shoulder. Joseph stood with his back to him, looking toward the railroad station with his hand cupped above his eyes. Convinced he was unobserved, Henrik lifted the center bottle from its hiding spot. Liquid sloshed in the bottom half.

After another furtive glance left and right, he popped the cork and put his nose over the narrow opening. He recoiled at the smell, but as he did so, a memory surfaced. When he was thirteen or fourteen, he and Father had traveled to Volgograd. He'd encountered two Russian youths passing a thick jug back and forth. With wide grins, they'd offered him a sip. The smell coming from the jug had sent Henrik scurrying to his wagon. The youths' scornful laughter still rang in his mind.

He'd been too afraid to try the liquid then, but he was no longer a boy. He was a man. He lifted the mouth of the bottle to his lips.

"Henrik!"

Henrik jerked, nearly spilling the bottle's contents. He quickly replaced the cork and rose, holding the bottle by its neck behind his leg. "What?"

Joseph pointed. "*Onkel* Eli is coming."

Henrik angled his body away from his brother and slipped the bottle into the waistband of his pants. A tug of his jacket hid the bottle from view. Then he joined Joseph in waiting for the wagon. He assumed a casual pose, but beneath his shirt, his heart pounded like Father's hammer on the cobbling bench.

Eli called, "Whoa," and the oxen obediently halted. "*Nä-jo*, boys, climb in."

Joseph started to climb in the back, but Henrik stopped him. "Sit up front with Eli for a while." He stretched his mouth into a yawn. "I want to lie in the back and rest."

Joseph trotted around the wagon and hoisted himself onto the high seat. Henrik clambered over the back and slumped into the narrow space between the trunks and the wooden hatch. The top of the bottle's neck poked into his ribcage, and he shifted slightly to remove the pressure.

The wagon lurched forward, and Ma sent a hopeful smile in his direction. "Did you enjoy your walk, son?"

He nodded. "*Jo*. But I am tired, Ma." Without waiting for her response, he leaned his head into the corner and closed his eyes. The wagon bounced along, the growl of the wooden wheels against the rough road a familiar sound. Henrik crossed his arms over his middle. The glass bottle felt warm and smooth against his skin. As soon as night fell, he'd sneak away from camp and sample the contents of the bottle. Those Russian boys had seemed to enjoy drinking from their jug. Henrik looked forward to a few moments of pleasure.

"Eli? Eli, wake up."

The panic underscoring the whispered command filtered through Eli's sleep-foggy brain and brought his eyes open with a snap. He blinked several times, trying to focus. At last his eyes adjusted enough to recognize Lillian on her knees beside the wagon, peering at him.

She scuttled backward as he rolled from his sleeping pallet and emerged from beneath the wagon. They both stood at the same time, only inches apart. Her golden hair, unfettered, tumbled across her shoulders, gently lifting in the night breeze. A white voluminous gown encased her body, with a dark blue shawl draped around her shoulders. She might have been an angel, so lovely the vision.

He swallowed hard. "W-what is it?"

"I am sorry to wake you, but . . . Henrik is gone."

Eli scowled. He leaned forward, peeking beneath the wagon. Joseph lay snoring on his pallet, but only a crumpled blanket lay across Henrik's pallet on the far side of the wagon. "Maybe he is visiting the trees," Eli offered.

Lillian shook her head. "That is what I thought when I saw him leave the camp. But he has been gone a long time—much longer than what would be needed. And . . ." She bit down on her lower lip, her brow furrowing.

"What is it?"

She crunched her lips into a pained grimace. "When he left, he kept peering back, as if afraid someone was watching. He acted strangely, Eli."

Eli's concern for the boy rose. "Which way did he go?"

Lillian pointed, and Eli held back his relief that she pointed to the grassy fields across the road rather than the road itself. If Henrik had headed down the road, Eli would suspect he'd intentionally run away. But a trek across the tall grass in the minimal light of the moon meant he could be wandering. Maybe his looking back was merely out of worry that he would disturb their rest.

Eli put his hand on her shoulder, trapping a wavy lock of hair beneath his palm. The feel of the silky tresses sent a jolt of reaction through his belly. He resisted snatching his hand away and offered a comforting squeeze instead. "Go back to bed and do not worry. He might have found it difficult to find the wagon in the dark." But as he spoke the words, a log in the campfire snapped, sending up a tiny flutter of sparks. Wouldn't the fire's glow guide Henrik back again? He chose not to share his thought with Lillian. "I will light a lantern and find him."

"*Dank*, Eli."

He waited until she climbed back into the wagon before plucking a lantern from a hook on the side of the wagon and lighting its wick. Then he set off in the direction Lillian had indicated. He made no effort to move quietly—he wanted any four-legged creatures to hear his approach and scatter. Holding the lantern well in front of him, he let his gaze rove through the circle of yellow, seeking any clue to Henrik's whereabouts.

Crushed grass showed the path their feet had taken earlier in the evening to visit the trees. Eli stood in the center of the mashed area, turning a slow circle and peering into the night. He tilted his head, listening intently. Only the gentle whisper of wind across the grass, the hoot of an owl, and the distant call of a coyote greeted his ears. But then, so softly he almost thought he imagined it, he heard a chuckle.

Scowling in confusion, he tipped his head and squinted his eyes shut in an effort to focus on listening. The laughter came again, less subdued, and somewhere to his left. Turning, he moved slowly in the direction of the sound. He stumbled when he went over a small embankment, but when he righted himself, the lantern light swung across Henrik's frame stretched flat in the grass with his arms propped behind his head. Eli charged forward and held the lantern close to Henrik's face.

The boy scrunched his face into a horrible scowl and covered his eyes with his hands. "*Onkel* Eli, blow that out." His speech slurred, each word extended to unnatural lengths.

"What is wrong with you, boy, leaving the camp and worrying your mother? Get up." Eli grabbed Henrik's sleeve and yanked him to his feet.

Henrik staggered, squinting at Eli. "Careful. You almos' knocked me down." He glared with one eye, crunching the other one shut.

Eli shook his head. "What is the matter with you? Did you fall and hit your head?" He reached to run his hand over Henrik's scalp.

Laughing, Henrik ducked away. His movements were clumsy, uncontrolled. He stretched his arms outward and waved them to keep his balance. Then, his footing established, he laughed again. "*Nä, nä*, I am fine. I am better fine than I have ever been before."

Eli got a whiff of Henrik's breath, and understanding dawned. "Have you been drinking?"

Henrik threw his shoulders back and assumed an innocent expression with wide eyes. "Drink . . . ing?" He hiccupped in the middle of the word.

The answer confirmed Eli's suspicions. "Where did you get liquor?"

Henrik covered his lips with one finger.

"Where did you get liquor?" Eli made his voice stern, leaning close.

But Henrik remained silent, smirking behind the finger on his lips. Fury filled Eli. So this was why Reinhardt had kept such a close watch on the boy—he was prone to dangerous foolishness.

Grabbing Henrik by the collar of his shirt, he began hauling him toward camp. Henrik squawked in protest, flapping his arms in wild circles, yet he had no choice but to go along.

When the flicker of firelight shone ahead, Eli came to an abrupt halt and released Henrik. The boy stumbled sideways and nearly fell, but somehow he managed to catch his balance. He stood wavering before Eli with a shamed expression on his face.

"I . . . am sorry, *Onkel* Eli. I only wanted to feel hap . . . py." Hiccups continued to interrupt the words. "Are you go . . . ing to beat me?"

Truthfully, the thought had crossed Eli's mind. A few licks might pound some sense into the boy. But Eli couldn't do it. *I must father this boy, dear Lord, but how would You have me do it?* In that moment, Eli missed Reinhardt with a fierce ache. He drew in a deep breath and released it slowly, bringing his temper under control. "Is the liquor all gone?"

"All gone," Henrik repeated. "Ev . . . ery drop."

"Goot." Eli curled his hand around Henrik's neck. "You have had your 'fun.' But there will be no more such fun, do you hear me, boy? This time I will let it go because everyone is entitled to make one mistake. But to make the same mistake twice is to act with deliberate foolhardiness. Next time, you will get that beating. Do you understand?"

Henrik blinked twice. "Will you tell Ma?"

Eli clamped his jaw so hard his teeth hurt. Should he keep this from Lillian? Surely the truth would hurt her. She didn't need any more worries. But he decided it was best to leave Henrik wondering. "Not tonight." He gave the boy a little shove toward camp. "Lie down on your pallet and go to sleep. No more mischief."

Henrik stumbled toward camp, his shoulders slumped and his head sagging. Eli followed close on his heels, holding the lantern to illuminate the way. As soon as they entered the camp, Lillian popped her head out of the wagon. She curled her hands over the wagon's hatch. "Henrik, you are all right?"

"He is fine." Eli bustled forward. He watched Henrik roll onto his pallet, then gave Lillian's hand a reassuring pat. "He is tired from wandering. Let him sleep. Talk in the morning."

"Thank you for finding him, Eli."

Eli blew out the lantern and returned it to its hook. "*Bitscheen.* Go back to sleep now, Lillian. All is well." But as he crawled back onto his pallet, his words mocked him. All was certainly not well.

16

Lillian wiped her sweaty brow with a wilted handkerchief. Although the wagon's bonnet extended over the seat, the angle of the sun prevented the canvas from offering even a thumbnail of shade. The sun beat down relentlessly, creating a burning sensation on her skin. She stared at the glistening hides of the oxen. How the poor beasts managed to keep plodding forward when just sitting beneath the shimmering rays made her want to collapse, she would never understand.

Her temples pounded. She twisted her head one way and then the other, trying to relieve the tension in her neck muscles. The movement didn't help a great deal, and she knew why. The tension went more than skin deep. It pressed from the very center of her soul.

The wagon's front right wheel hit a rut, and she grabbed the seat to keep herself from tipping against Eli's arm. Since the night Eli had gone searching for Henrik, he had insisted the boys ride in the back and allow their mother to sit on the wagon seat. She wondered at the reason for the change. Eli had seemed to enjoy pointing out unique land features or sharing his knowledge of plants with Joseph and Henrik, and she hadn't minded riding in the back. Truthfully, the wagon's bed provided more protection from the endless wind and blistering sun. But Eli had directed her to sit on the seat, so she did.

Angling a quick glance sideways, she took in Eli's stiff posture and firmly set jaw. The easy smile she had come to expect was nowhere in sight. The days on the trail had stolen his lightheartedness. Might it return when they reached their destination? His change in demeanor extended to the boys. He seemed emotionally distanced from them. Especially from Henrik, although she noticed he kept her oldest son under his watchful gaze at all times.

Something had happened that night Lillian had sent Eli after Henrik, but neither of them volunteered any information. And Lillian was half afraid to ask. So she pondered in silence while tension ate at the muscles in her neck and gave her a headache no powders could cure.

She peered over her shoulder at her sons. Despite her headache, a smile tugged at her cheeks. They lay across trunks in the back of the wagon, heads on bent elbows, eyes closed, napping. Her heart swelled at the innocent picture they painted. Her boys . . . Mother-love, fierce and aching, rose in her breast. *Lord, let this new land treat my sons kindly. Let them blossom and grow into the men You desire them to be. Give us grace, Lord.*

Suddenly, Eli cleared his throat, and she spun to face forward. At the quick movement, little dots danced in front of her eyes, and she grabbed hold of the edge of the seat as a wave of nausea attacked.

Eli sent her a worried look. "You are all right?"

She was hot, her head hurt, and her heart ached. But complaining wouldn't change any of it. "I am all right."

His head bobbed in a slow nod. "By tonight, if I am thinking correctly, we should reach Newton. Then one more day of travel and we will be at our land."

Lillian's heart lurched in her chest. "Oh, Eli, that will be wonderful."

A hint of a smile appeared on his lips. "*Jo, wundascheen* for sure." He grimaced and rolled slightly on the seat, lifting one hip and then the other. "I will be very happy to climb down off this wagon seat for good. All of this sitting has made me ache in places that usually do not have cause to ache."

A giggle formed in Lillian's throat, but a remembrance chased it away. The day they had left Gnadenfeld, Reinhardt had given her permission to walk for a while after teasing her about her sore bottom. *Oh, Reinhardt, I miss you so, my husband!* Tears sprang into her eyes, and she blinked rapidly to prevent Eli from seeing them.

But he looked at her with a scowl. "Lillian? What is it?"

"I . . . I . . ." She swallowed the explanation before it formed on her tongue. What good would be served by speaking of Reinhardt? He was gone, he wasn't coming back, and Eli was her husband now. Sniffing hard, she brought the tears under control. "I have a headache."

Eli's lips pursed in sympathy. "Maybe a doctor in Newton can prescribe something for you."

"*Nä, nä*, it is only from the sun."

He didn't look convinced.

She rushed on. "I have headache powder in the trunk. When we stop, I will take some. But . . ." She turned a hopeful look on him. "If we are going to reach Newton by evening, maybe we can stay one night in a hotel?" A soft bed would be pure pleasure.

"Nä." His answer came so quickly, she knew he didn't give her suggestion one second of consideration.

Puzzled, she asked, "Why not?"

Eli's jaw thrust out stubbornly. "Because I say no."

He had never been so dictatorial. The stern refusal, coming from Eli, who had always been considerate in the past, stung like a slap. Lillian jerked her gaze forward and clasped her hands tightly in her lap. She stared ahead at the little puffs of dust rising from the oxen's hooves, at the thick grass growing alongside the road, at a hawk circling overhead. But she carefully refrained from glancing at Eli.

After a few minutes of tense silence, he spoke again, his tone kind but firm. "We will camp within walking distance of Newton. Then, in the morning, you and the boys will stay at the camp while I walk to town and fetch the agent who will show us to our land." He flicked a glance over his shoulder into the back of the wagon, his brows low. "It will be best that way."

Although he didn't explain why it would be best, the grim line of his mouth discouraged her from questioning his reasons. But the way he'd glanced at the back of the wagon made her wonder if it had something to do with Henrik.

As the wagon rolled to a halt, Henrik poked Joseph. His brother sat up, blinking sleepily from his perch on an oversized trunk.

"Climb on out of there and collect fuel so your mother can build a fire," Eli called to them. "Our last night of camping on the trail. Tomorrow we will reach our land."

Joseph clambered over the side of the wagon. "Really, *Onkel* Eli? Tomorrow we will be on our farm?"

A light chuckle rolled from the big man—the first Henrik had heard from Eli since the night Henrik drank the liquor. "*Jo*, boy," Eli answered, "but it will take us some time to build the farm. We will still sleep under stars for a while, but we will sleep under stars that cover our own land. And that will make it better."

Joseph whooped and socked the air. "Our own land! No more riding in the wagon!"

Henrik leapt from the wagon. The jar of his feet connecting with the hard ground sent a tingle through his soles. He wriggled his toes within the confines of his boots and looked across the prairie. Although the sky had dimmed as evening fell, there was enough light to make out gray shapes rising from the grassy plain not far away—no more than two miles. This was the town called Newton. But Henrik wouldn't get to see it; Eli had made that clear.

He'd overheard the conversation between his ma and uncle, and he had come close to sitting up and telling Ma why Eli wouldn't take them into town. But he'd held his tongue, unwilling to risk his mother's disappointment. Facing his guilt over Father's and Jakob's deaths, as well as Eli's censure, was enough of a burden.

Grabbing Joseph's shirtsleeve, he said, "I see a fallen tree down by that creek. Help me drag one of the dead limbs over for Ma's fire."

Eli called after them, "Do not dally. We stopped later than usual so Newton would be in sight. Night will fall, and I do not want you caught away from the camp with no fire's glow to guide you back."

"*Jo, Onkel* Eli." Joseph began whistling a merry tune. Henrik couldn't decide if he resented or envied his brother's cheerful attitude.

During supper, Henrik stared toward town. Lights came on one by one, turning the city into a living creature with many winking eyes. He caught Eli's hooded gaze watching him, and he focused on his plate instead of the lights. As had become their custom, he and Joseph washed the dishes. They made use of the creek water, rather than only scraping the plates clean. With the dishes tucked back in their trunk, Henrik headed for his pallet, but Eli beckoned him to the edge of the camp.

"Tomorrow early, before the sun rises, I will set out for Newton. I want to be on the land developer's doorstep as soon as he opens for business so we can be on our way by midafternoon for sure." Eli's heavy hand descended on Henrik's shoulder. "You, your mother, and brother will be here alone. I do not expect trouble, but I want you to be alert."

Henrik resisted heaving a sigh. Eli might be able to suck Joseph in by bestowing responsibilities, but Henrik was more world-wise. He recognized the ploy, and he wouldn't be duped by it. Eli only wished to trick Henrik into staying well away from town.

Eli leaned in, lowering his voice to a gruff whisper. "In your father's trunk, wrapped in sheeting, is a loaded rifle."

Henrik gawked at his uncle. He knew of no men in Gnadenfeld, except Susie's father, the butcher, who owned a gun. He couldn't imagine his father purchasing one.

"He bought it in Hamburg for protection while traveling and for hunting when we reach our land." Eli's hand tightened. "If trouble should strike—strangers causing problems or a need for help to come quickly—I want you to take out the rifle and fire it straight in the air. It is loaded with two shots. Only fire in the air once. Save the second shot in case you need to point it at . . . an enemy."

Henrik licked his lips, his heart thudding hard against his ribs. "Do you think I will have need?"

Eli shook his head. "I do not expect trouble, but it is always best to be prepared. Can you do this, Henrik?"

All suspicions of Eli tricking him with manufactured responsibilities fled in light of his uncle's serious tone. "I can do it."

"Goot." Eli gave Henrik's shoulder a thump and then dropped his hand. "To sleep now. I will keep watch during the night. I will wake you when I leave."

Henrik rolled onto his pallet and curled on his side with Joseph pressed against his back. Eli sat facing the flames, his back to the wagon. He hunched forward and propped his elbows on his knees with his head dropped back. Did he examine the stars? Or was he praying? Henrik drifted off to sleep without knowing.

Someone shaking his shoulder roused him. He opened his eyes to find Eli leaning over him. Henrik tossed aside the blanket and stumbled to his feet. He rubbed his eyes and peered around. Stars glittered in a dusky gray sky, but no sign of the sun yet touched the eastern horizon. Sunrise was still at least an hour away.

"I am leaving now." Eli kept his voice to a mere whisper. "Keep the fire going—I broke up another dead limb last night, so you have plenty of fuel. And remember what I said. Take good care of your mother and brother."

As Eli disappeared into the shadows, Henrik assumed Eli's place by the fire and fed twigs to the flames. He yawned frequently, fighting the urge to lie down again. Eli would never know. But if he lay down, the fire would die. He knew they must preserve the matches, so instead of sleeping, he kept the fire going.

Ma rose with the sun, and she wakened Joseph to care for the chickens. While Joseph gave the chickens their feed, Henrik hobbled the oxen's legs and led them to the grassy area near the creek to eat. By the time the animals had eaten their fill, Ma had breakfast ready. Henrik eagerly took his plate of fried eggs and salt pork.

Ma looked at him, one fine eyebrow higher than the other. "Would you bless our food, Henrik?"

Father—and then Eli—had always prayed for their meals. Self-consciousness attacked Henrik, and his face grew hot. He spluttered something nonsensical.

Ma quirked her lips into a half grin. "It is all right, son. I will pray." She lowered her head and offered a simple blessing.

For Henrik, the food didn't go down easily, despite Ma's fine cooking and the musical accompaniment of birds in the brambles near the small creek. Why hadn't he been able to offer a blessing for the meal? It wasn't as if he never prayed . . . although he realized with a shock he couldn't remember praying since they'd left Gnadenfeld. Had he left God behind on the *steppes* of Russia?

When they finished eating, Ma sent Henrik and Joseph to the creek for a bath. Henrik resisted leaving Ma alone in the camp, but she shooed him off, telling him she would be fine with the clucks and the oxen. Henrik bathed as quickly as possible and returned to camp with his clothes sticking to his damp body. Ma was waiting, scissors in hand.

"Let us make ourselves presentable for our new land." She gave first Henrik and then Joseph a haircut. Henrik knew they needed it—Joseph's hair curled well over his ears, and Henrik's was so long it tickled his neck. Even though little hairs worked their way beneath his shirt to prick him, it felt good to have close-cropped hair once more.

After his haircut, Joseph crawled into the wagon to read, and Ma took out some mending. She sat on the ground, leaned against the wagon wheel, and ran the needle in and out, slowly closing the hole in one of Joseph's socks. Henrik paced the ground around the wagon, watching the road leading to and away from their camp. If anyone approached, he would fetch the rifle and be ready.

By midmorning three wagons had passed by, but none had stopped, and Henrik's short night was catching up with him. He yawned repeatedly, shaking his head to battle sleepiness. How did Eli manage on so little rest?

Ma, watching him, let out a soft laugh. She put her stitching aside and crossed to him, placing her hand on his crossed forearms. "Come and sit, Henrik. You'll wear out the soles of your boots with your marching to and fro."

"Eli told me to keep guard, so . . . I am."

Ma clicked her tongue against her teeth. Her thin, lined cheeks didn't match the girlish sparkle in her eyes. "Even guards occasionally sit. Come. Have a cup of coffee and relax." She glanced at the sun. "Surely Eli will be back soon with the developer and we will be on our way."

Although Henrik kept his eyes on the road, he followed Ma to the fire and sat, accepting a cup of rich coffee. He sipped the hot brew, sweat breaking out across his back. It tasted good, and he took another sip.

"Are you . . . happy we will soon reach our land, Henrik?"

Henrik set the tin cup on his knee and toyed with the curved handle. No, happiness did not lift his heart when he thought of establishing a home on the prairie. Over their days of travel, the endless view of rolling plains covered in tall grass had brought no rush of eagerness to claim a portion. This dream of owning land in America was Father's and Eli's, not his.

A verse from Philippians—one his father had taught him when he was young—floated through his mind: *Not that I speak in respect of want: for I have learned, in whatsoever state I am, therewith to be content.* Had the author of the Scripture been forced to set aside his deepest dreams to fulfill someone else's calling?

"I will be glad to be in one place" was Henrik's careful answer.

Mother's sad eyes met his. "My son, you will become a teacher one day. Eli has promised me that he will see to it."

Henrik nodded, but he wondered if Eli would keep that promise. Especially now, when he was still so angry about Henrik's misbehavior. Henrik stared into the yellow flames. The licking tongue consuming the dry wood became an image of the sun overhead consuming him—melting away his hopes and dreams. His stomach churned with a swirl of mixed emotions.

"Son?"

He looked up.

"What happened between you and Eli?"

Henrik sucked in a breath. Of course Ma would know something had happened. Eli had been edgy ever since that night, not even speaking cheerfully with Joseph or Ma. Henrik's mind raced for an explanation that would be truthful yet spare the ugliest details. He couldn't confess his recklessness to Ma and lose even more of her confidence.

"Henrik?"

He opened his mouth to reply, but a puff of dust down the road captured his attention. Someone was coming. Tossing the coffee into the dry grass, he rose and peered toward town. A one-horse buggy, with two men on its leather seat, approached camp.

Henrik straightened his shoulders. "Here is Eli."

17

Eli stood on quivering legs and surveyed the area by inches. His pulse tripped hard and fast. His land . . . "Do you see, Lillian? Is it not fine?"

Lillian stood, tipping forward to peer from beneath the bonnet of the wagon. Both boys leaned over the seat, looking, too.

Eli aimed a wide grin at the boys. "This is where we will build our farm."

For as far as the eye could see, grass waved like a rolling sea. Tall grass, thick, telling Eli the ground would be well suited to growing wheat. A band of wind-twisted trees marked one edge of the claim, and a trickling creek—a branch of the Arkansas River, the developer said—served as a barrier on the opposite side of their property. Water, trees, good fertile soil . . . and a wife and sons with whom to share it. For what more could a man ask?

Seated in the buggy in front of them, the developer, *Herr* Wiens, turned to face backward. He snatched his hat from his balding head and smiled at them over the top of his folded-down leather bonnet. "What think you of the land, *Herr* Bornholdt?"

Eli replied in the same cultured German the man used. "Pleased

I am with our purchase, *Herr* Wiens. The land is all you promised it to be."

The man nodded. His scalp, shiny with sweat, glowed in the late-afternoon sun. "Since it meets with your approval, I will return to Newton. I wish you folks well." Facing forward once more, he tugged his brown bowler low on his forehead and picked up the reins. "Hee-yaw!" His horse heaved against the rigging, and the buggy turned a neat circle. *Herr* Wiens offered a parting wave.

Lillian and Joseph answered with waves of their own, but Henrik kept his hands curled over the back of the seat. He met Eli's gaze. "How far from a town are we out here?"

Eli shrugged, although he knew the answer. *Herr* Wiens had graciously drawn a rough map of the area, showing Newton to the south, King City to the west, Creswell to the east, and McPherson Town to the northwest. The larger communities of Newton and McPherson Town were farthest away, but both had railroad stations he could use to transport his wheat after harvest next spring.

"Where will we get supplies when they are needed?"

At Henrik's question, Lillian's face pursed with worry.

Eli rushed to assure her. "We are within a half day's distance of two towns where supplies can be purchased. No cause for worry—our needs will be met." Eli turned his head right to left, taking in the landscape once more. "On this *wundascheen* land, our needs will surely be met."

He clapped his hands once. "*Nä-jo*, let us get out of this wagon and plant our feet on the ground. Then we will have a prayer of thankfulness to God for bringing us safely to our home." Although he spoke in a cheerful tone, pain pierced his heart. Reinhardt and Jakob had not been delivered safely to this land. He would forever carry a hole where his foster brother and nephew had been, yet it would be wrong not to show appreciation to God.

Lillian must have had a similar thought, because her chin

crumpled briefly, her brow creasing into a series of furrows. But as quickly as the pain-filled expression formed, it cleared, and a soft smile curved her lips. "That is a fine idea, Eli. Come, boys."

Eli helped Lillian down and Joseph scrambled out the back, but Henrik remained as if nailed to the wagon bed. Joseph stepped next to his mother and looked up at Henrik. "Henrik, are you coming?"

With a sigh, Henrik hopped over the seat and joined them. They stood in a circle. Grass swallowed them to their hips. Their shadows stretched across the thick grass as if laying claim to the land. Eli clasped his hands beneath his chin and closed his eyes. Words poured from the depth of his soul—words of gratitude and praise for the gift of land, the gift of freedom, the gift of family. Eli laid every heartfelt statement at the feet of his Father's throne and then closed the prayer with a humble plea. "And, our dear Lord, may we live together in such a way that we bring glory to You in our home and on this land. In Your Son's most precious name I pray, Amen."

He opened his eyes to find Lillian wiping a tear from her cheek. She offered a tremulous smile that sent a shaft of warmth straight through the center of his chest. He answered with a broad smile and threw his arms wide.

"*Nä-jo*, family, there is much to be done before the sun sets! Let us get to work."

Henrik made good use of a sickle to clear an area to serve as a campsite while Joseph and Eli removed the bonnet and bows from the wagon. They used the wood and canvas to put up a tent that Lillian and the boys could share. Eli intended to sleep outside, where he could stare at the sky and count the stars that hovered over his land. Had he ever done such a whimsical thing in Gnadenfeld? He didn't think so. He paused in his work, pondering why this piece of Kansas land meant so much. And the answer came quickly: Because this land he shared with a wife and sons.

In Gnadenfeld he had been alone, longing for family. Now his desire had been granted. Not in the way he would have wanted, but yet, the longing had been fulfilled. His feet would not be the only ones to tromp the ground, his hands the only ones to dig in the dirt. No longer would he lie listening to his own heartbeat in his ears. From this day forward he would hear the sounds of voices and laughter and, perhaps, at times, weeping. But never again would he be alone.

Eli drew in a big breath of Kansas air, his chest expanding until he could hold no more. Then he let it out in an audible *whoosh*.

Joseph grinned at him, the expression impish. "It smells different here. Good, *jo*?"

"Jo. Sea goot."

Joseph laughed, and Eli joined him, finding pleasure in their joined laughter. Then he put his hands back to work.

By dusk the area was well organized with the wagon bed empty and their supplies stacked neatly at one end of the tent. There was little room left for pallets beneath the tent roof, but Lillian claimed she would merely place her mattress on top of the trunks, just as she had inside the wagon.

She served a supper of beans, pork, and poor man's fare: a thick mush made of cornmeal. *Herr* Wiens had given them a fifty-pound bag of cornmeal, claiming that here on the plains it was a common provision. Eli ate it after dousing it with a serving of beans, but he wasn't convinced he wanted to grow accustomed to American food if cornmeal was a mainstay. He'd rather eat *Bobbat* made with flour from his own hearty wheat.

After supper, Henrik reached for the plates, but Lillian pulled them back. "*Nä*, son, we are no longer on the trail. We are home.

And at home, dishwashing is my chore." She peeked at Eli, as if seeking his approval.

He found himself unable to offer so much as a nod. Her words, "we are home," resonated in his heart. *Oh, Lord, thank You that Lillian's heart and mine are joined in claiming this land as home.*

Lillian watched Eli lift the chunk of sod over his head. Muscles bulged beneath his sweat-soaked shirt. She released a breath of relief when he heaved the block into place. Wiping his brow with his sleeve, he turned and caught her looking. A grin immediately formed behind his beard.

"So, Lillian, you thought I would drop it on my head? That would be entertaining for you, I am sure."

Over the past week, Eli's gently teasing nature had reappeared. The stern man of the last few days on the trail had departed, and Lillian discovered she enjoyed the presence of the smiling, light-hearted Eli. She only wished Henrik would follow Eli's example and set aside his surly manner.

"I would find very little amusement in all that dirt on your head and clothes. I do the washing, you know."

His chuckle brought a lift to her heart.

"But," she continued, tapping her chin with one finger, "that wall seems high enough now. We won't bump our heads, anyway. And the sooner you put a roof over the walls, the sooner we can move in."

Eli had chosen to structure their first home of sod. They had seen many such homes while traveling from Topeka to Newton. The thick grasses held the soil together, making it possible to cut sizable blocks. The blocks stacked neatly, and a splash of water served as mortar. With Henrik's help, Eli had put up walls to form two side-by-side sod houses: one twelve feet square and the other eight feet square, both with doorways facing the east. The larger one he claimed was for her and the boys, the smaller for himself.

Hard-packed dirt would serve as the floor, and there would be no windows, but the dwellings were intended to be temporary. Lillian was pleased she wouldn't need to reside for long in the house built of dirt blocks. Even the larger one would be cramped with three people living within its meager space, but somehow she and the boys could manage until after the first crop was harvested and Eli would have the means to build a real house of wood.

Eli stood with his hands on his hips, examining the rough structure. "The roof will be trickiest." He paused for a moment to nibble his dry lower lip. "I have Henrik and Joseph scouting for branches long enough to stretch all the way across from one wall to the other. The branches must be light enough not to crumble the top of the wall, yet sturdy enough to hold a layer of sod."

"You will put sod on top, too?"

Eli's hair bounced on his forehead as he nodded. He needed a haircut, but Lillian felt shy about suggesting it. "*Jo*, or when rains come, the wet will come through the roof. Branches alone will not hold the rains at bay."

Lillian lifted her apron to clear perspiration from her face. "I wish trees were not so scarce. I miss having shade trees." Seeds from the *kruschkje* tree in Gnadenfeld waited in a little pouch in the bottom of her trunk to be planted next spring. But it would take years for one of those seeds to grow a tree large enough to provide shade . . . or pears.

Eli's eyes held sympathy. "I know. These trees are so wind-bent, they remind me of little old men. We must use the wood from the trees wisely. But at least we are not without a means of fuel. Between the buffalo chips and the grasses, we will be able to fuel your oven and, later, the fireplace I build into your sod house."

Eli's resourcefulness amazed Lillian. Before starting the houses, he had constructed an outdoor *Spoaheat* so she could bake. Instead of mud bricks, which Reinhardt had used in Gnadenfeld, Eli took clay from the creek bank to form the oven. She assumed he would use clay for the fireplace, too. She didn't know where he had learned such practices, but she was grateful. Reinhardt had been wise in asking Eli to accompany them to America.

As always, thoughts of Reinhardt made her chest twist in agony. But she deliberately pushed the pain aside. Focusing on the past would benefit no one. She must look ahead. And ahead was a roof so she could sleep surrounded by walls rather than between the flapping folds of a canvas tent.

"*Nä-jo*, I will fetch you a drink of water and then let you return to work."

His laughter followed her as she lifted the empty bucket and headed for the creek. "*Jo*, Lillian, you need not hint. I will finish this wall so I can get busy on the roof."

When Lillian turned from the creek to return to their building site, she stopped for a moment to admire all Eli and the boys had accomplished in six short days. In addition to the clay oven and the two sod houses awaiting roofs, a makeshift fence constructed of stacked sod posts and stripped branches provided an enclosure for the oxen. Using two of the bows from the wagon and a roll of chicken wire purchased in Newton, Eli had built a sturdy chicken coop four times the size of the crate the chickens had called home on their journey from Topeka. The crate rested on its side within the enclosure, providing a simple shelter for the clucks.

The sickle's blade had required sharpening twice already, but the area around the sod houses, including a large patch for a garden, was neatly cleared, with the grass stacked into sheaves to dry. Eli planned to show the boys how to twist the long, thick blades into fat "logs" that she could use in her oven in place of buffalo chips.

As soon as the houses were completed, Eli intended to start clearing the fields to receive his red wheat kernels, but first he must travel to McPherson Town or Newton to purchase a plow. The journey would take most of a day and he would go to town alone, he had already warned her. His cheery whistle reached her ears, and she realized she would miss having him near on the day he chose to complete that errand.

The bucket's weight on her arm reminded her she had been standing in one spot for too long. With a little jerk, she started her feet in motion. She moved cautiously, careful to avoid sloshing water over the rim—she mustn't be wasteful. Carrying water from the creek that ran a quarter mile from the sod houses was her least favorite chore. Eli had promised to dig a well before the ground froze, and she would welcome that convenience. When she passed the tent, she retrieved a dipper, dropped it into the bucket, and then carried it to the sod house, where Eli thumped the final sod square into place.

"Ah . . ." He licked his lips as he reached for the dipper. His Adam's apple bobbed with his noisy swallows. He downed two full dippers before backhanding his mouth and calling, "Boys! Come and have a drink!"

After a few moments, Joseph and Henrik trotted from the direction of the creek. Each dragged a branch behind him, and they dropped the limbs before reaching eagerly for the dipper. Their tanned faces and sun-streaked hair made them seem like strangers to Lillian, but their eyes—dark brown like Reinhardt's—remained familiar. Joseph's eyes sparkled with a vitality he had lacked in Gnadenfeld, while Henrik carried a resigned air that brought sadness to Lillian each time she glimpsed it.

She watched them gulp the water, taking turns with the dipper, and she tipped her head as unbidden thoughts attacked her mind. One son embraced the new land with both arms; the other held it at bay. Joseph seemed to have been given something through their travel adventures; Henrik had left important parts of himself behind. Two sons—two extremes. How might she bring Henrik to Joseph's joyous acceptance?

The boys, their thirst satisfied, turned back toward the creek, but Eli held out his hand.

"Wait. I wish to speak to you about something important."

The teasing tone he'd used only moments ago had disappeared. Lillian held her breath, wondering what serious topic he might introduce.

"Tomorrow is Sunday—the Lord's day. " His gaze bounced from Lillian to each of the boys as he spoke. "We have labored hard this past week, and I am *sea stolt* of your uncomplaining attitudes and good efforts."

Lillian's heart swelled as Joseph stood taller, his shoulders squaring with Eli's words of praise. She, too, was proud of how her sons met the challenges without complaint.

Eli continued. "I think, in honor of the Lord's day, we should take time for a service."

"A service?" Joseph held his hands outward, peering around. "But we have no *Kjoakj*!"

Eli ruffled Joseph's hair. "*Ach*, boy, we do not need a church building to have a service."

Joseph hunched his shoulders and grinned.

Henrik folded his arms across his chest. "What kind of service will we have?"

Eli took in a breath. "A simple worship service. I was thinking we could read a passage of Scripture, pray together, and"—he grinned openly at Lillian—"your mother could lead us in some hymns."

The service, although different from any held in a church, appealed to Lillian. "I like the idea, Eli." She turned to the boys.

"Is it not a good idea? Since it may be months before we have an opportunity to attend a real church service, we should start our own practice of worship together."

"For sure." Joseph nodded hard.

Henrik dropped his crossed arms and slipped his hands into his pockets. "It would be fine." His voice held no enthusiasm.

"Goot." Eli rubbed his palms together. His enthusiasm was enough for all of them. "And after our service, we will rest—no working, just like in Gnadenfeld. But today is not Sunday, and still there is work to do." He flicked both hands at the boys, as if shooing them. "Gather more limbs. Your mother wants a roof on her sod house!"

18

The month of August melted away beneath a sweltering sun. Every day, from sunrise to late afternoon, Henrik trailed behind Eli and forked into piles the grass Eli whacked off with the sickle. Joseph then wrestled the piles into sheaves. Even though they stopped for frequent water breaks, Henrik's throat always felt parched. There were times he wanted to lift the bucket's rim to his mouth and drain it dry. Yet he believed no amount of water could replace the sweat that had poured from his body to be absorbed by the rich black dirt.

But after today's work, the land would be completely cleared. Eli could then use a plow and turn the soil to receive seed. All across the claim, drying grass stood in bundled sheaves, reminding Henrik of a pen rendering of Indians' tepees from a penny dreadful Joseph had discovered along the road. Wouldn't Joseph whoop with excitement if a real Indian brave stepped from behind one of those sheaves?

After long weeks of seeing no one except his family members, Henrik might even welcome a visit from a red-skinned man. The longer they worked this land, the more he yearned for Gnadenfeld, Susie, his friends, his school . . . and the life he'd known before.

He stopped for a moment, leaning on the pitchfork's handle while Eli kept moving, his swing of the sickle so rhythmic the man more closely resembled a steam-powered machine than a human. Henrik examined his hands—his blistered, calloused hands—and he wanted to moan. Not because of pain. He could bear the physical discomfort. But his hands had become the hands of a farmer. Not of a teacher.

Joseph panted to Henrik's side. His face, tanned brown by the sun, shone with perspiration. "Do you think it is almost time for Ma to bring the water bucket?"

Henrik squinted at the sun. Perhaps an hour had passed since Ma's last visit to the field. "Maybe."

Without breaking stride, Eli called over his shoulder, "Your mother will bring the bucket soon, boy, do not worry. She will not forget us."

Joseph quirked his lips into a grin. Lowering his voice to a whisper, he said, "That is *Onkel* Eli's way of saying 'return to work.' "

Henrik held back a disparaging grunt. Eli had a way of telling one what to do without giving direct orders. Ma said he was being diplomatic; Henrik saw it as manipulation. Either way, he didn't like following Eli's commands. He would turn eighteen in two more days, which marked the beginning of manhood. He was old enough to make decisions for himself. He would leave this homestead and find a college!

Joseph plodded to the closest pile of freshly raked grass, his face aimed toward the sky. Henrik followed his brother's gaze and spotted a hawk circling far overhead. Henrik envied the bird's ability to spread his wings and soar above the earth, unburdened by cares and work and worry.

Snatching up the rake again, he jammed the prongs into the grass and viciously swiped the fallen blades into a pile. Life—his life—was weighted down. How could he soar with the burdens he carried? His home in Gnadenfeld . . . gone. His father and dear little brother . . . gone. Susie . . . gone. His opportunity to attend university . . . gone. In the back of his mind, his mother's words whispered, *Eli promises you will become a teacher.* But here he was, raking hay instead of studying books.

"Here comes Ma!"

Joseph's cheerful shout shattered Henrik's musings. He dropped the rake and sauntered to meet Ma. Joseph dashed ahead of him and received the first drink. In his haste, he sloshed water down his front. "Be careful, Joseph!"

Ma clicked her tongue, lowering her brows in displeasure. But she aimed the silencing look at Henrik, not Joseph.

Henrik clamped his jaw to hold back further words of complaint. Joseph handed him the full dipper, and Henrik cupped it with both hands to be certain every drop of water found its way to his mouth. After three dipperfuls, he passed the dipper to Eli, who drank noisily but without spilling.

Eli swiped the droplets clinging to his mustache and beard with the back of his hand and grinned at all of them. "Nothing like cold water on a hot day to revive a man." He glanced at Joseph's blotchy shirt front. One brow arched higher than the other. "Were you unable to hit your mouth, boy?"

Joseph ducked his head, his expression sheepish.

Eli laughed and ruffled the boy's hair. "It felt good, did it not, to get a little splash of water on your skin?"

Joseph shrugged.

"*Nä-jo*, then I think you should enjoy it again." Quick as a gopher darting into its hole, Eli plunged the dipper into the bottom of the bucket and slung its contents over Joseph's head.

Joseph took a backward step, his arms held away from his body and his mouth open in surprise. Eli stood with his hands on his hips. A wide grin split his sunburnt face in two. Henrik stared at the man, unable to believe what he'd just witnessed. Eli was no child to play games. Yet by his teasing grin, it seemed he had just challenged Joseph.

Joseph burst out laughing. He ran his hands down his face, flipped the water from his palms, and laughed again. Shaking a finger at Eli, he said, "*Onkel* Eli, I will get even with you."

"Oh-ho, you think you can pull one over on Eli?" Eli shook his head from side to side, his twinkling eyes never wavering from Joseph's face. "We will see, boy; we will see . . ." He turned and strode to the sickle, lifted it, and returned to work. Joseph, still giggling, trotted back to the field, too.

Henrik glanced at Ma, and at the look on her face, a chill went down his spine. Admiration, appreciation, and—he swallowed—affection. Ma's blue eyes shone with affection for Eli. He'd seen her look at Father in that way. But at Eli? He spun and stomped to his rake.

He raked with a vengeance, fury giving him energy that defied the heat and the long hours of labor. Eli had effectively drawn Joseph and Ma to his side. But Henrik wouldn't be drawn in. Eli had stolen his only opportunity to absolve his guilty conscience for Father's and Jakob's deaths. Couldn't the man understand the only reason they boarded that ship for America was because of Henrik?

He paused, pressing his forehead against the end of the fork's handle. If he were solely responsible for taking care of Ma, he could make it up to her. But Eli saw to Ma's needs. And Ma seemed perfectly content to allow him to provide for her. Raising his face to the clear sky, Henrik sent up a silent question: *How, then, will I ever be able to release this unbearable burden of guilt?*

Lillian lifted the tray of *Perieschkje* from the clay oven, careful not to place her thumb on the flaky pastries near the edge of the black baking pan. Back in Gnadenfeld, she had stuffed her *Perieschkje* with finely chopped pork and cabbage. She had no cabbage or pork with which to fill her folded-over tarts, but chopped and boiled dried beef, mixed with wild onions and mushrooms, served as a substitute. She held the tray of well-filled miniature pies under her nose and inhaled. If they tasted as good as they smelled, her family should voice no complaints.

Her family . . . She had seen Henrik's reaction to Eli's playful moments earlier that afternoon. How she wished Henrik would begin to see them as a family. Certainly, it wasn't the same as when they lived in Gnadenfeld. No ornery Jakob filled her days with laughter and fun. No strong husband cradled her in his arms at night. Now unending work made the days slip by, and exhaustion helped her sleep, despite aching for Reinhardt's presence. But Eli was a good man—a man who worked hard to create this farm for them, a man who could be a father to Henrik, if only Henrik would accept him.

She set the tray of pastries on the trunk that served as their table and dropped a length of toweling over the top to keep the flying bugs from sampling their dinner. The wind tried to carry the towel away, so she weighted the corners with rocks. That task complete, she entered her sod house and brought out plates and cups. Setting the table, she once again marveled at Eli's cleverness. He had fashioned four stools by tearing apart his own travel trunk.

It had pained her to see the well-built trunk turned into scrap lumber, but what other choice did they have? There was no Mennonite furniture maker's shop nearby where they could purchase a table and chairs. They ate all of their meals outside unless it rained, which she had discovered was a rare occurrence. The sod house's close walls left little room for moving around. When winter came, they would be cooped up all the time. While the weather permitted, she intended to be outside as much as possible.

Just as she finished setting the table, she spotted Eli and the boys coming from the field. Eli and Joseph walked side by side with Eli's arm hooked around Joseph's neck. Although she couldn't hear him, she knew Joseph was jabbering. She shook her head, smiling indulgently. That boy talked to Eli more than he had ever talked to anyone. Eli's praise had released a confident side of Joseph that was beautiful to see.

Then she noticed Henrik trailing behind the pair, his head down and feet scuffing through the dirt. Her heart sank.

She must do something to bring joy to Henrik. Lifting her hand, she waved for them to hurry. "I have made *Perieschkje*! And the wash bowl is ready. Wash and eat!"

The three made good use of the wash bowl and towel; then they sat around the table and folded their hands while Eli gave the blessing. Lillian served the pastries, watching for their reaction to the unusual contents.

Joseph's eyebrows rose as he chewed rapidly. "Mmm, Ma. These are good. Different."

Henrik examined his pastry, tipping it one way and then the other. "What did you put in there?"

Lillian laughed softly. "Whatever I could find." She shared the contents of the filling, smiling when Henrik took another big bite.

Across the table, Eli shook his head. "Lillian, you are an amazing woman. You take what meager things we have and make something good."

His praise warmed her. She ducked her head to hide her flaming cheeks. "I am not the only one who makes good of whatever is available." She patted the stool.

"*Ach*, we could not eat the trunks." Eli reached for another pastry. "But when I go to town, I will visit a mill and bring back some lumber. The animals, they will need a shelter. And this winter, when we are unable to be outside working, I want to use the tools I brought and make some furnishings for the house I will build after harvesting our wheat."

Henrik shot Eli an interested look. "You are going to town?"

"Of course. How else will I get a plow? I had to leave mine in Gnadenfeld—it would not fit in the trunk." His chuckle didn't hide the remorse in his voice over leaving his prized possession behind.

Henrik rested his elbows on either side of his plate. "Which town?"

Eli shrugged with one shoulder. "I think McPherson Town. It is not any farther than Newton, but according to *Herr* Wiens, it is a good-sized community. And I will not need to ford any streams to get there. That will make for easier travel for the oxen."

"Will we all go?"

Lillian hadn't seen Henrik show such eagerness in weeks. Would Eli agree to take Henrik along?

Eli twisted his lips into a grimace and shook his head. "I am sorry, Henrik, but no. For two reasons." Eli held up one finger. "I need the wagon bed to carry back a load of lumber. It will take much lumber to build a shelter for the animals. There will not be room in the bed for people, too, what with the lumber and the plow." He flicked another finger upward. "And all of us gone means no work gets done. It will be an all-day excursion, and there is too much to do here for us all to take a day from working."

Henrik pushed his plate aside.

Eli put his hand on Henrik's shoulder. "We will all go one time before the snow flies. When we buy supplies for the winter months. Does that sound fine?" He waited, but Henrik didn't answer.

Finally, Eli sighed and dropped his hand. He looked at Lillian. "*Nä-jo*, Lillian, that was a very good meal. Will you go to the creek now for water to wash the dishes?"

Lillian sent him a puzzled look. "Do I not always go to the creek for my dish water?"

Eli lifted his chin in a nod. "*Jo*, I suppose you do. You best hurry, then. Because"—he stood, his gaze flitting briefly to Joseph—"I am going to jump in the water and muddy it up."

Joseph sat straight up, dropping the last bit of his pastry. "Swimming, *Onkel* Eli?"

Eli tweaked Joseph's ear. "Swimming, for sure, after a long, hot day like this one." He quirked one brow. "But you would not have any interest in swimming, am I right?"

Joseph nearly sent his stool flying, he jumped up so fast. "I do! I like to swim!" He turned to Henrik. "You are coming, too, Henrik?"

But Henrik rose slowly, his jaw set in a stubborn line. "*Nä*. You go ahead. I am going to light a lantern and read instead."

Lillian waited for Eli to encourage Henrik, but he threw his arm around Joseph's shoulders and the pair headed for the creek without a backward glance. Lillian watched them go, nibbling her lower lip. If Eli stopped trying to reach Henrik, all would be lost. Despite Henrik's lack of response to overtures, she must encourage Eli not to give up on her son.

Henrik moved toward the sod house, his hands in his pockets and his head slung low. If Eli wouldn't encourage Henrik, she would. Calling his name, she hurried after him. He stopped but kept his face angled away from her.

Lillian tangled her hands in her apron. "You have worked hard this week. Why not swim, Henrik? Spend some time with Joseph and . . . and your stepfather." She held her breath as she uttered the title. Somehow Henrik must begin to accept Eli's position in his life.

Henrik spun around. The fury in his face sent Lillian stumbling backward a step. He withdrew his clenched fists from his pockets and stood, bristling. Tension fairly crackled between them, and Lillian felt as though her booming heart might explode. She had never feared her son, but in those tense, anger-filled moments, she wondered if he might actually strike her.

Finally Henrik drew in a deep breath and relaxed his fists. His firmly clamped jaw released, and he lowered his head, shaking it slightly as if arguing silently with himself. Then he met her gaze. The anger she'd witnessed had dimmed to a mere spark in his dark eyes.

"Unlike Joseph, I still remember my father. I have no desire to replace him." His low, even tone sent a chill through her frame. "But I wonder, Ma, if you already have."

Lillian opened her mouth to protest, but Henrik strode around the sod house. She didn't follow. Because she realized she had no words of defense to offer.

19

Eli crested the gentle ridge that led to their land claim. It took much self-control not to smack the reins down on the backs of the horses and urge them to race the remaining few miles. Wouldn't his family be surprised to see horses pulling the wagon? When he had left early that morning, one pair of their faithful oxen stood within the wagon's yoke, but a good trade with a farmer in McPherson resulted in acquiring two wagon-broke bays. They were not young horses, but they had many good working years left.

Eli admired the horses' gleaming hides, both the color of stained mahogany. The female bore a white stripe down the center of her nose that matched the stocking on her right foreleg, but the male was solid reddish brown. A more handsome pair of animals Eli had rarely seen, and now they were his. But he hadn't asked the man for the horses' names. He would allow Joseph the pleasure of naming the pair.

He chuckled, thinking of how Joseph had named their chickens. The silly clucks even came when he called. The boy had a way with animals, for sure. Maybe he would be a rancher when he grew up, or a farrier. Both would take skill with animals. Joseph was still young, but not too young to be thinking of the future. He would have a talk with the boy soon.

As he guided the horses off the rough road and onto the untamed prairie, the wagon jolted sideways. The bed's contents clunked as they shifted. "Who-o-oa," Eli soothed, giving the reins a gentle tug to slow the great beasts. "It would not be wise to bounce out any of that cut lumber or my new plow." Nor did he want to lose the surprise he'd secured for Henrik.

The thought of Henrik didn't bring a fond chuckle. Instead, Eli's stomach clenched with dread. It seemed no matter what he did, Henrik disapproved. He glanced into the wagon bed at the burlap-wrapped package tucked behind the seat. Surely that gift would please the boy.

His thoughts skipped to tomorrow—Henrik's eighteenth birthday. In Gnadenfeld, his family would have hosted a celebration and invited their neighbors to wish Henrik well in adulthood. Food would have been abundant, with fellowship that lasted well past bedtime.

Here they had no neighbors to invite. It would only be Lillian, Joseph, and he wishing Henrik well. Eli knew it would be very little compared to what he would have received in their Mennonite village, but perhaps the small taste of Gnadenfeld rolling around in that burlap bag would diminish the sting of disappointment.

Eli looked ahead at the cleared patch of ground waiting the plow. So dark and rich-looking, that Kansas soil. Surrounded by thick prairie grass, it offered the illusion of a large package wrapped in brown paper. The image seemed appropriate, because Eli viewed the land and the opportunities it afforded as a gift.

His chest swelling with gratitude, he offered a familiar prayer: "*Dank Jie, dia Gott*, for this land. May its bounty bring You glory." Tomorrow was Sunday—a day of worship, rest, and celebrating

Henrik's birthday—and then on Monday he would put his new steel plow and the remaining pair of oxen to work turning the ground.

The wagon rattled around the cleared field, and Eli spotted Joseph and Henrik walking toward the sod houses from the creek. Homemade fishing poles bounced on Joseph's shoulder, and Henrik held a string of fish. Eli licked his lips in anticipation of that fish dipped in cornmeal and fried to a crisp. Even poor man's fare appealed to him when it served as batter for fresh fish from the creek on their property.

He knew the moment the boys spotted him, because Henrik came to a halt and Joseph threw his hand in the air in an excited wave. Then the younger boy dashed to the sod house and disappeared inside. When he emerged he was empty-handed, and Lillian followed, wiping her hands on the apron she always wore over her dress. Her smile was evident even from this distance.

Eli's heart turned over at the sight of his family awaiting his return. Had he ever felt as needed, as happy, as fulfilled as in those moments? His hands curled around the reins as the urge to hurry the horses once more attacked. But he held the team to a slow, steady *clop-clop* until he reached the sod houses. The moment he drew the team to a stop, Joseph rushed to stroke the nose of the big male. The horse nickered softly and nudged Joseph's shoulder. Eli, watching, smiled. Yes, the boy had a way with animals.

"*Onkel* Eli, where did you get horses? Where are Buff and Brody?" Although excitement underscored the tone, Joseph kept his voice low so as not to startle the horses.

With a chuckle, Eli leapt over the side. He grinned in Lillian's direction before turning to Joseph. "I made a trade—two oxen for two horses. A good trade, I think. Are they not a fine pair?"

"A very fine pair!" Joseph peeked over his shoulder. "Look at them, Ma. Are they not pretty?" Before Lillian could answer, the boy dashed around the wagon to peer into the back. His eyes grew huge. "Look at all the wood!" Turning, he gestured Henrik forward. "Look, Henrik! There is enough wood to build two barns, I think!"

Henrik peeked over the wagon's side. His lips pulled into a lopsided sneer. "You are *domm*, Joseph."

"I am not dumb!"

"Boys . . ." Lillian voiced a soft reprimand.

Eli sauntered over and ruffled Joseph's hair, diffusing the situation. "This wood will not be enough for a big barn, but it will provide a shelter for the horses and oxen. A small shelter will have to do until we harvest our wheat. Then, with that money, we can build a bigger barn."

"And a house?" Joseph asked.

"And a house," Eli agreed.

Joseph ran his hand down the shiny blade of the plow. "You bought wood and a plow . . . What else?"

Eli lifted a bushel basket from the back of the wagon and held it toward Lillian. She skipped forward and tugged aside the burlap covering. She clapped her hands together in obvious delight. "Cabbage! Oh, Eli, I can make sauerkraut!"

"*Jo*, we must have kraut for the winter." Eli set down the basket and dug beneath the leafy balls. "I bought a dozen heads, and the man gave me"—he lifted out four sweet potatoes, two in each hand—"a little something extra."

"What a treat!" She took the potatoes and showed them to Henrik. "We will have something special for your birthday supper tomorrow, Henrik!"

Still beside the wagon, Joseph reached for the remaining burlap bag. "And what is this?"

Eli snatched up the bag before Joseph could touch it. "That is a surprise, boy."

Joseph's dark eyes lit with excitement. "A surprise? For me?"

Eli shook his head, grinning. "You are not the one with a birthday tomorrow." He glanced at Henrik, hoping for a positive response. But Henrik swung the string of fish, his face impassive.

Joseph's lower lip poked out in a pout. "I wish you had brought something for me, too."

"You get to name the horses," Eli said, and Joseph's pout disappeared. Cradling the burlap bag in both arms, he turned to Lillian. "It seems I am just in time for supper. Fish, *jo*?"

Lillian bustled forward to take the string of fish from Henrik. "With beans and wild potatoes."

Eli's stomach growled at the mention of potatoes. The half bushel of potatoes they'd purchased in Newton hadn't lasted long, but when digging up the sod to build the little houses, he and Henrik had discovered a starchy root that resembled sweet potatoes but tasted similar to white potatoes. Lillian had wasted no time in learning to cook the root.

Eli said, "Whatever you fix is fine." Henrik stood silently beside his mother. "Boy, will you help me unload the wagon while your mother cooks the fish? These horses are ready to be released from their rigging."

Henrik nodded.

"*Dank*. I will put your surprise away." He dipped his chin toward the bag in his arms, still hoping for some response from Henrik, but none came. With a sigh, he headed for his little sod house with wide strides. He set the bag in the corner and gave it a pat. To himself, he whispered, "Do not let Henrik's attitude take away the joy of homecoming. The welcome from Lillian and Joseph is enough."

Yet as he stepped back into the waning sunlight, he couldn't deny that some of the shine of those golden moments had been rubbed away.

After supper, Henrik wiped his mouth with the tail of his shirt and stood. "Ma, I am going to take a walk." In Gnadenfeld, he had enjoyed walking through his village as the sun sank toward the horizon. The sights and smells of the place of his birth had always brought him an element of peace, no matter what challenges the day had offered.

Now, on the threshold of manhood, he felt the need to recapture that peace. Even though there was no village square, no thatched mud-brick houses, and no friends to meet, maybe a walk would allow him to remember those days of walking, thinking, dreaming.

Eli swallowed his last bite of fish and held up one hand. "Wait, Henrik. I will walk with you."

Ma's face lit with pleasure at Eli's announcement, and Henrik looked away before she read irritation in his eyes. If he'd wanted company, he would have invited Joseph. "I prefer to walk alone."

Eli paused mid-rise. He looked at Ma as if seeking her guidance. But before Ma spoke or moved, Eli straightened fully and turned to face Henrik. "I think I will come anyway. I have some things to discuss with you."

Henrik released an aggravated huff, but Eli didn't hear—or at least, he didn't react. They fell into step and walked between the sod houses, following the path their feet had carved to the creek. On either side of the wide path, thick grass stood almost waist-high.

Eli frowned at the grass lining the pathway. "I should cut down some of this growth. Wild creatures could hide and surprise your mother on her way to the creek."

Henrik added nothing. Maybe if he remained silent, Eli would return to the sod house and allow him the seclusion he desired.

Eli kicked at the grass for a moment or two, then pointed to the smooth creek bank. "Let us sit, *jo*?"

Blowing out another breath he hoped communicated his impatience, Henrik trailed Eli to the creek bank. He waited until Eli plopped down, and then he sat a few feet away, tucking his legs up and wrapping his arms around his knees. He stared across the creek toward the sun, which seemed to increase in size as it made its descent toward the horizon.

Now that they were seated, Eli fell silent. So Henrik sat, listening to the sounds of the prairie. Some, such as the wind stirring the grass and the slap of a fish leaping in the creek, were similar to home. But others—the discordant croak of frogs and the howl of an animal that resembled a scrawny dog—were new. Henrik tipped his head, trying to determine how far away the howling dog might be. But with everything so flat and open, it was difficult to discern. He closed his eyes, listening more intently, and Eli cleared his throat. At the disruption, the frog temporarily ceased its chorus. Eli filled the sudden silence.

"I did much thinking on my trip into McPherson Town."

Henrik looked at Eli.

The man raked his fingers through his beard, his brows beetling. "I drove past a school, and it made me remember how much you wish to be a teacher."

A cord of longing wound itself through Henrik's chest. He tightened his hands on his knees and held back words of agreement.

"I had trouble in town, Henrik." Eli grimaced, shaking his head. "The language . . . not knowing the English words makes a problem."

Henrik sighed, shifting to peer across the creek again. He didn't need Eli's reminder of how difficult it would be to see his dreams to reality in this new country.

"I wondered how I could help you learn the English so you can go to a university and study." Once more he paused, but Henrik remained silent and waiting. If Eli had a plan, he would listen, but he wouldn't offer any help. Eli licked his lips and continued. "And I reminded myself of how a baby learns to talk—by listening to others speak. One by one, the words are learned, until he can converse like everyone else."

Henrik snorted. "Everything is learned in that manner. Step by step, piece by piece, until the task is mastered." His chest ached with longing to be the one to teach those steps, to see the light of recognition dawn, to build success in his students.

"Jo." Eli nodded enthusiastically, as if he and Henrik had hit upon some great secret. "And so I know the way for you to learn the English is to be with English-speaking people. You must work beside them, live near them, listen to them, and speak with them." Eli's words tumbled out faster and faster. "When you have mastered the language, then you can attend the university and study to become a teacher right here in America."

"Universities take money." Confrontation laced his tone, but Henrik did nothing to temper it. He wouldn't allow Eli to ignite his dream only to dash it with an inability to see it through to completion.

"I know this, boy," Eli countered evenly. "I have been thinking of how to pay for your schooling. Your father and I talked about it even before we left Gnadenfeld. He wanted to set money aside from our first harvest to help you. But he said you should work to earn some of the money, too." The sun dropped lower, throwing long shadows over both men and giving Eli's narrow face a serious appearance. "He believed—and I agree—that one appreciates better something that has been earned."

Henrik nodded slowly. "I am not opposed to earning money for school." If only he could be freed from the work on the homestead, he would earn every penny. But he didn't mention that to Eli.

"Goot." A smile curved Eli's cheeks, but quickly it disappeared. "It is good to make a plan, Henrik. A plan gives you something to hope for, something to work for. But plans . . . well . . ." He crunched his face into a scowl. "Sometimes they happen slowly."

Henrik thrust his jaw forward, his shoulder muscles tightening into a knot. "How . . . slowly . . . will my plan unfold?"

The grimace that crossed Eli's face tempted Henrik to jump up and flee. But his uncle's next words held him in place. "The length of one harvest."

Henrik's mind spun. Eli would plant the seeds in October, allowing them to soak up the winter snow and grow plump beneath the ground, then emerge tall and strong in the early spring. The wheat would be harvested by mid-May. Eight months.

He murmured, "Two-thirds of a year . . ."

"Jo." Eli's voice, soft as the wind that whispered over the seeded tops of the grass, sounded melancholy. "I know it seems a long time for one your age. A year can feel like a lifetime. But it will pass quickly. In no time, I will sell the wheat, have money in my pocket, and give you half of Reinhardt's portion to help pay for school."

Henrik stared at Eli. "Half of Father's portion? But there are three of us with Ma, Joseph, and me."

Somberly, Eli nodded. "But I will honor your father's decision. He and I planned to work side by side and share equally of the harvest's reward. He intended to give half of his earnings to you for school. It will surely not fund everything you need to become a teacher, but it will give you a good start. Does this seem fair to you, Henrik?"

Henrik considered the information, his heart thudding so hard he thought he could hear the beat in his ears. Eli would give him the proceeds of one-half of Father's share of the harvest! But should he take it? Mother and Joseph would need money, too. Was it fair for one person to take half when two must survive on the remaining half?

"It . . . it is more than fair to me." The words came out strangled. He felt as though his tonsils were in a knot.

"Then we have an agreement." Eli held out his hand, and Henrik took it. They exchanged a firm handshake, and then Eli leaned back, propping himself on his elbows. "It is good to have a plan. . . ."

Henrik nodded. Now he could look forward to the future instead of dreading it. His time here was limited. He would go to school, become a teacher, just as he'd always wanted! A part of him wanted to thank Eli for helping him, but then he realized he could have seen his goal through without Eli's help. It might have taken longer, but he would have accomplished it. Why thank Eli for something he would have done all on his own eventually?

"Boy, I would like it if you would do something. . . ." Eli sat up, fixing Henrik with a steady gaze.

"What?"

Eli clamped his hand over Henrik's shoulder. "I know you are not happy that your mother married me. I know you are not happy to be in America. I understand, and I do not fault you for your feelings. But your continued glumness causes your mother great pain."

Guilt pressed as Henrik considered the source of his mother's pain: leaving their home, losing Father and Jakob. His breath came in little spurts as he battled the rising culpability.

"Now that you know you will be able to go to university and become a teacher, just as you have wanted, will you throw aside your sad face? For your mother's sake? I would like her last months with you to be pleasant ones, not hurtful."

Henrik hung his head. Even knowing he could count down the days until freedom to pursue his dreams, remorse still clung to him like the smell of sweat after a long day's work in the sun. But he could pretend. For Mother's sake, he would try.

His head still low, he muttered, "I will do my best."

"That is all I could ask of anyone." Eli squeezed Henrik's shoulder and then rose, brushing off the seat of his pants. "*Nä-jo*, boy, I will leave you to yourself now. Thank you for talking with me." He ambled up the path, leaving Henrik alone to ponder this new turn of events.

20

"For this thing I besought the Lord thrice, that it might depart from me. And he said unto me, my grace is sufficient for thee: for my strength is made perfect in weakness.' "

As they had each Sunday since their arrival, they sat together on one of Lillian's quilts in the shade of the sod house for their worship service. Eli's voice rumbled above the whine of the wind, sending shivers of pleasure up and down Lillian's spine. How she loved to hear God's Word uttered in his masculine voice—like the voice of God Himself.

" 'Therefore I take pleasure in infirmities, in reproaches, in necessities, in persecutions, in distresses for Christ's sake: for when I am weak, then am I strong.' " Eli closed the Bible. For a moment his thick palm caressed the worn black leather cover. Then he glanced around the little circle they formed. "Let us pray." He lowered his head and closed his eyes. Lillian and the boys did likewise.

Lillian felt a smile grow on her face as Eli praised their heavenly Father. She and Reinhardt had prayed together, but she remembered more petitions than praises. The idea of praising God even when troubles knocked at the back of one's heart brought a feeling of contentment and fulfillment beyond anything she'd known before. As Eli prayed, she offered her own silent request for God to bestow the same measure of contentment on her sons—especially Henrik.

Then, remembering Eli's praises, she sent up a heartfelt thank-you that on this Sunday morning Henrik seemed less withdrawn. He had even given her a kiss on her cheek when she wished him a happy eighteenth year. The simple gesture had filled her heart with joy.

"Amen." Eli lifted his head, took in a deep breath, and then offered a bright smile. "*Nä-jo*, let us have our lunch, and then we will have a special time of celebrating Henrik's birthday."

Ordinarily, Sunday lunch would be a simple affair to avoid tasking oneself on the Lord's day of rest. But given the special occasion of a birthday, Lillian believed God would forgive her for taking extra effort.

She waved her hands at Henrik and Eli. "You stay here. Joseph and I will prepare the table." Joseph jumped up, and soon their trunk-table was spread with Lillian's finest linen tablecloth embroidered at each corner with pink roses, delicately painted bone china dishes, and silverware Lillian had polished to a high shine. She invited the others to pull up their stools, and then she retrieved Henrik's birthday dinner: the sweet potatoes Eli had brought from McPherson Town and cabbage rolls in a thick sour cream sauce.

"Mother, you made *Holubtsi*?"

Lillian laughed aloud at Henrik's surprise. "You did not guess? The wind has carried the smell from the *Spoaheat* to our noses ever since we sat down to worship together."

A gust lifted the edge of the tablecloth, and Joseph whacked his hand down to hold it in place. He giggled, hunching his shoulders impishly. "The wind must have pushed the smell past Henrik's nose."

They all laughed, and Lillian set the tray in the middle of the table. She perched on her stool, and they joined hands. But instead of offering grace, Eli looked at Henrik.

"On this day when you become an adult, would you like to offer the blessing?" The hesitance in Eli's voice made Lillian's heart flutter with apprehension. Would the request bring a return to sullenness? After their lighthearted morning, she wished for Henrik to maintain a cheerful countenance. To her joyful relief, Henrik offered a meek nod.

Tears stung behind Lillian's nose as she listened to her son recite a simple blessing for their food. When he added, "Bless the hands that prepared this food," he gave her hand a gentle squeeze, and the tears spurted. When she raised her face, two warm tears rolled down her cheeks.

Henrik looked at her in alarm. "Mother?"

She swished the tears away, releasing a trembling laugh. "*Ach*, ignore me, Henrik. It is just that you are no longer my little boy, and a mother has to mourn such changes." She reached for the tray of *Holubtsi*. "Here now. You take the fattest ones."

No one seemed to mind that shredded wild potatoes and dried beef replaced the traditional rice and ground sausage that would have filled the cabbage leaves in Gnadenfeld. Instead, they ate with great appreciation, showering Lillian with compliments. Conversation flowed smoothly, with Henrik contributing nearly as much as Joseph, and Lillian thought she had never been happier. Perhaps coming into the age of manhood had reaped this change in Henrik. Or perhaps God had finally answered her prayers. Whatever the reason, she celebrated the time of fellowship with her sons and Eli.

When the last cabbage roll had been consumed, Eli stood. He rocked back on his heels, a mischievous grin tipping up the corners of his lips. "And now it is time for my surprise."

Lillian winked at the boys as Eli strode across the ground, his arms swinging with eagerness. He stepped inside his little sod house, and when he emerged he held the burlap bag he had taken from the back of the wagon.

"What is it? What is it? Open it, *Onkel* Eli." Joseph bounced on his stool.

Eli shook his head. "*Nä*, boy, this is for Henrik to uncover." He held the bundle to Henrik, who took it gingerly. The bag slipped from his hands, landing in his lap, and he smacked his hands over it to keep it from rolling off of his knees.

"Whatever it is, it is heavy." Henrik untied the string holding the bag closed and reached inside. His eyes grew huge as he looked up at Eli. From the wide grin stretching across Eli's face, it appeared the man gained more pleasure from the gift than the receiver did. The sack fell away, and Henrik held aloft a round, striped *Or'büs*.

Joseph clapped and cheered. "Watermelon! Henrik, *Onkel* Eli brought you a watermelon!" Then his elation faded, and he bit down on his lower lip while worry crinkled his face. "Oh . . . but it is your birthday gift. So will you eat it . . . all by yourself?"

Henrik cradled the melon in his lap, stroking his chin with his thumb and forefinger. Lillian, recognizing the teasing light in his eyes, fought clamping her hand over her mouth to hold back laughter while Henrik left Joseph in breath-holding suspense.

Finally, Henrik rolled the melon onto the trunk's top with a shrug. "I suppose I can share my birthday gift." Then, winking at Lillian, he pinched his finger and thumb together, indicating a scant amount. "But make Joseph's wedge no bigger than this."

"Henrik!" Joseph protested, but when everyone else began to laugh, he joined in.

"Did you make *Rollküake* to go with the *Or'büs*, Ma?" Henrik asked.

Lillian pursed her lips in disappointment. Oh, how wonderful it would be to eat the little fried cakes with their watermelon—a true taste of home. "*Nä*, the melon is a surprise to me, too, so I did not know to make *Rollküake*."

Eli said, "I maybe should have told you, but I wanted to keep it a surprise."

Henrik shrugged. "Watermelon is enough of a surprise." He waved his hand toward the watermelon. "You slice it, *Onkel* Eli."

Eli rubbed his palms together. "Do you have a knife, Lillian?"

Lillian, joy filling her at the relaxed conversation Eli and Henrik shared, retrieved her largest knife and handed it to Eli. He turned the melon into wedges with several deft whacks that sent juice splattering across the tablecloth.

Eli passed the wedges around. "Spit the seeds into your plates. We will save them and, next spring, plant our own *Baschtan*—watermelon field. Then, when the others arrive, the waiting field of melons will help them feel at home in this new land."

Joseph paused in eating. He tipped his head and peered at Eli, juice running down his chin. "Do you think the others will find us here, *Onkel* Eli?"

Eli shifted his head to look across the prairie. "I pray so, Joseph."

For a few moments, the wistful words cast a shadow of melancholy over the gathering. Lillian sought words that would return them to their time of cheerful chatter, but before she could speak, Henrik reached across the table and tapped Joseph on the top of his head.

"We found this place, did we not? And we had never been here before. The same land sellers who brought us here will be watching for more immigrants. So the others will come, for sure. And just to make sure," Henrik went on, his expression thoughtful, "when we all go to McPherson Town, we can send a letter to Gnadenfeld, telling the others where we bought land. That will help them find their way here."

With a satisfied grin, Joseph returned to his piece of watermelon. Eli caught Lillian's eye and sent her a look that said very clearly, *"See? Your Henrik will be all right."* She smiled in return, shifting to watch Henrik bite into the flesh of his watermelon wedge. With juice stains on his cheeks and wind-tousled hair curling across his forehead, he held the appearance of a young boy. Yet today she had been given glimpses of the man he would become. Her heart lifted with hope. Yes, her Henrik would be all right.

Fall crept ever nearer, bringing changes to their prairie landscape. Lillian paused in her bread making to bask in the assortment of bold colors—flowers in blues, pinks, and yellows. When one type died away, another variety sprang to life. Eli had taken to gathering a handful of whatever he could find at the close of the day, and the flowers brought a splash of color and cheer to their table, as well as a patter to Lillian's heart.

Reinhardt had not been a sentimental man. A good man, a good provider and a fine husband and father, but rarely sentimental. She couldn't imagine Reinhardt bringing her wild flowers. Yet it seemed perfectly natural for Eli to do so, and it endeared him to her in a way that sometimes frightened her more than thrilled her. If she opened her heart to Eli, would memories of Reinhardt slip away forever? That worry kept her from voicing the gratitude that sprang up within her when Eli handed her his nightly bouquet.

A distant rifle blast startled her into kneading the dough again. Soon Henrik would trek across the grass, pride on his face and some sort of game in his hand. Eli had taught Henrik to fire the rifle, and between Henrik's skill at hunting and Joseph's fishing prowess, there was always food on the table. At first Lillian struggled with preparing wild game—she was accustomed to pork, chickens, and the occasional beef from a butcher shop. No internal parts, feathers, or fur in sight. But the desire to feed her family pushed her past the revulsion at gutting and preparing the rabbits, squirrels, and geese that Henrik brought home.

The young man claimed he would bag a buffalo and dry its meat for the winter, but not since that early morning on the trail had they seen any of the great lumbering beasts. They found evidence of their presence: Hundreds of dried mounds peppered the prairie, providing needed fuel for their fire. But the animals seemed to have disappeared.

Lillian used her arm to push her hair from her face. The endless wind tore strands loose from her bun, and sweat pasted the tendrils to her cheeks. She wondered when the temperature would drop for good. The mornings were cooler, crisp and scented with dew, but the afternoons were just as hot in late September as they had been during their arrival in mid-July. Eli assured her summer would not last forever, but sometimes she wondered if he might be wrong just this one time.

If she squinted, she could make out Eli's form at the far side of the wheat field. He never seemed to tire, urging the oxen onward, onward, while placing one foot in front of the other with no discernible break in stride from morning to dusk. The field that would receive the wheat seed changed week by week as Eli turned the soil once, twice, and then again, bringing from the depths the rich minerals that would nourish the hearty kernels of wheat.

Sometimes at night, she heard Eli creep across the grounds. She followed him once, curious, and found him standing at the edge of the moon-bathed empty field, hands in his pockets. He had jumped at her approach, but then at her query had explained he liked to imagine the wheat growing tall. It was easier to dream of his first American harvest in the starlight, he had sheepishly told her.

Remembering it now, Lillian smiled. Yes, a very different man from Reinhardt was Eli. But a better man? She wouldn't allow herself to think such a thing, let alone voice it. Reinhardt was her first love, the father of her children. He would always hold the greater part of her heart. But did that mean nothing was left for Eli?

With a little huff, she turned her attention to her dough. She didn't have time for fanciful thoughts. There was work to do. Automatically her hands divided the lump of dough into six equal portions. She knew the routine by heart: Pat, pat, pat to form loaves; rub goose fat into the bottom of the pans; plop the smooth, speckled loaves into the black, well-used bread pans; then set the pans on top of the clay oven to rise one last time before baking.

The task complete, she cleaned her hands in the wash bucket. Only a few inches of water remained in the bottom. She glanced at the sun. Although it still burned hot, it sank toward the horizon earlier these days. She should fetch water before the sun set. Eli didn't approve of her going to the creek at dusk since he said she was more likely to encounter wild creatures at that hour.

Lifting the buckets from their spot beside the sod house, she headed for the creek. Halfway down, she met Joseph coming up. He proudly showed her his string of five whiskered catfish. She smiled her appreciation. "They will taste good for tomorrow's breakfast. Clean them and put the fillets in a pan of salted water to keep."

The boy rolled his eyes. "I know what to do, Ma."

Instead of scolding, Lillian hid a smile and continued her trek to the creek. Over the past two weeks, she had witnessed adolescence sneaking up on Joseph. His voice cracked from high to low without warning, his moods swinging nearly as quickly. Reinhardt had held little patience with Henrik's changeable behavior during those awkward years, but she sensed Eli would meet Joseph's changes with understanding rather than strictness.

She gave herself a little shake. What was wrong with her today, constantly comparing Reinhardt to Eli? She crouched at the edge of the creek and pushed the lip of the bucket into the gently flowing water, forcing the buoyant bucket well beneath the surface. At the same time, she pushed aside all thoughts of Eli and searched her mind for images of Reinhardt. Despite her efforts, no pictures sprang to mind.

Her hands stilled. A chill wiggled across her body, an unpleasant taste flooding her mouth. She stared into the creek, her own distorted reflection showing wide, dismayed eyes. Cold water splashed over her hands, filling the bucket, but she remained in her bent-forward pose, the chore of retrieving water forgotten.

"Reinhardt, Reinhardt . . ." She moaned aloud, tears blurring her vision. "How could I forget your dear face?"

Henrik's disdainful comment from weeks ago filtered through her memory: *I wonder, Ma . . . if you have replaced him.*

At that moment, a youthful, exuberant shout carried across the prairie. "Pa! Pa! I caught catfish for tomorrow's breakfast!"

21

Eli stopped in his tracks, but the oxen kept going, forcing him to stumble forward two or three steps before calling, "Whoa." The beasts obediently halted, and Eli removed the trace from around his shoulders and turned toward the sod houses. Had he heard correctly?

Joseph stood at the edge of the field, holding aloft a dangling string of plump fish. "Pa! Catfish!"

Joseph had called him Pa! Eli's heart flipped upside down. He waved one unexpectedly shaky hand and said, "*Jo*, boy, they look fine." His voice broke much the way Joseph's had been cracking lately. He cleared his throat and added, "Very fine." But his words didn't refer as much to the fish as the heady feeling of being called Pa.

With another wave, Joseph scampered toward the sod houses, the fish bouncing on the string. Eli watched until the boy disappeared inside the larger house. But even then he remained rooted in place, replaying the wonder of the past moments. Joseph had called him Pa as if it were the most natural thing in the world to do. As if Eli had been his pa for years.

A shadow snaked across the grass beside the sod houses, then

Lillian stepped into full sunlight, her hands curled around the rope handles of their buckets. Her shoulders slumped with the weight, but even after she set the buckets on the ground, her posture didn't change. Eli's heart turned another flip, but this one was of apprehension. Had Lillian heard Joseph's words, too? Would she disapprove of her son calling someone other than Reinhardt Pa?

Spinning, he looped the trace around his shoulders once more and chirped to the oxen. As he trailed the beasts, guiding the plow to complete its final turn of the soil, he reflected on the past months. Although the role of husband and father had been thrust upon him by circumstance, he believed he had risen to the challenge.

Over the years he had observed the men of his community. He had deliberately chosen characteristics to emulate or reject, planning for the day when he would have a family of his own. He believed, with a rare touch of self-pride, that he had chosen wisely. With the boys he was firm but fair, with Lillian honest and tender. He assumed the biblical role of leader for the family, but he explained the reasons for his choices to stave off resentment and to open the door for understanding.

His treatment had reaped positive results. Lillian exhibited contentment despite the hard work and carrying the pain of much loss. Henrik had set aside his brooding attitude. And now Joseph called him Pa. What better sign of acceptance could there be?

He pulled one trace while calling, "Gee." His hands gripped the plow handles, expertly guiding the blade. On the straight stretch again, he allowed the word *Pa* to echo through his head. The only better word, he concluded, would be *husband*. But it might be too much to ask for Lillian to truly accept him as such. For too long he had been her foster brother-in-law, Reinhardt's best friend, her children's surrogate uncle. She viewed him as a friend, but a friend wasn't what Eli wanted to be.

Alongside the field, bright yellow flowers waved on scraggly stems, reminding Eli of the bouquets he carried to the supper table each night. Lillian received them with a smile of pleasure, but he longed for more. In his imagining, she took the flowers, smiled, and raised up on tiptoe to bestow an appreciative kiss on his cheek . . . or his lips.

His face went hot, and he twisted his hands on the handles, tipping the blade sideways. Quickly, he righted the plow and shook his head to clear the image. It would not benefit him to dwell on youthful flights of fantasy. Clicking his tongue on his teeth to encourage the oxen to complete their last cross of the field, he admonished himself for his greedy thoughts. Lillian had taken his name to obtain a chaperone and to give her boys security. Nothing more. Besides, both he and Lillian were nearing forty. The days of starry-eyed gazes and hand-holding were long past. At his age, he must be practical. Instead of wanting more, he should be thanking God for blessing him with a taste of family life.

His gaze jerked toward the sod houses. Neither Joseph nor Lillian had emerged. Worry gripped his heart. Might Lillian be berating Joseph for granting the title to someone other than his father? Eli couldn't imagine her being harsh, but Reinhardt's death—even though they never spoke of it—was not long past. She might think it too soon.

Whatever she decided, he would support her. As much as he longed to be a true husband and pa, he would not trample Lillian's feelings to satisfy his own longings. But he would forever savor the wonder of that moment when Joseph had met a deep desire of Eli's heart by calling out, "Pa!"

Lillian tucked the quilt beneath Joseph's chin and placed a kiss on his forehead. She touched Henrik's shoulder in lieu of a kiss. "Sleep now, boys. We have much work to do tomorrow." One thing they needed to do was dress the deer Henrik had shot. Lillian cringed. If gutting a rabbit was distasteful, how would she ever manage to prepare a deer?

Henrik shifted on his makeshift bed, the dried grass crackling beneath him. "Do you think we hung the deer high enough that no animals will reach it?"

An image of the deer hanging head-down from the tallest tree on their property, its throat slit and glazed eyes staring, flashed through Lillian's mind. She shuddered. It might be a blessing to her if some animal did cart it away during the night. But how disappointed Henrik would be. He'd exhibited such pride when he'd dragged the deer home this evening. Plus they would need the meat to carry them through the winter. The dried beef they'd brought from Gnadenfeld was nearly gone.

"Eli says it is high enough, and Eli is usually right," Lillian assured her son. "Now sleep."

She lifted the canvas flap, cut from the wagon canopy, and peeked out. Eli was nowhere in sight. Heaving a sigh of relief, she stepped into the trailing end of twilight. The tall coffeepot still sat beside the coals of her cook fire. She retrieved a tin cup from the wash pan and crossed to the fire. As she poured the dark, aromatic brew, she heard footfalls behind her. She straightened so quickly she splashed hot coffee across her hand.

Hissing, she plunked the pot down. In seconds, Eli was at her side. He took the cup and guided her to the wash bucket. Without a word, he submerged her hand in the cool water. She tried to tug loose, but he held tight, counting slowly in a calm, low tone. When he reached twenty, he lifted her hand from the bucket and gently wiped it dry with her apron.

"Does it burn yet?" His fingers encircled her wrist.

In the dim light cast by the half-moon, Lillian read concern in his eyes. Her pulse had increased when he startled her, and it continued to race. She shook her head. "*Nä, nä,* it is fine. You . . . can let me go."

He looked down and gave a little jolt, as if surprised to still be holding her hand. He released her quickly and took several scuttling steps away from her. His hands slipped into his pockets, and he rocked back on his heels. "I set your cup beside the bucket, if you still wish to drink it."

Lillian reclaimed the cup and sipped. The remaining coffee no longer held any appeal, but it helped bring her racing pulse under control. "I . . . I thought you had gone to bed." She couldn't allow him to think she had come out to have time alone with him.

Eli sighed, his head dropping back. His thick beard lifted slightly with a swallow. "I went, but I could not sleep. I . . . am troubled, Lillian."

The somber tone lured Lillian into taking two steps toward him. "Troubled?" As she voiced the simple question, remorse smote her. At supper, she had offered little to the conversation. Joseph's sudden change from "*Onkel* Eli" to "Pa" on top of her inability to conjure an image of Reinhardt had sent her far inside herself. It wasn't Eli's fault—she shouldn't hold him accountable for Joseph's choice or her own negligent memory—yet she had purposely distanced herself from him. She had sensed his discomfort at the table, but she'd done nothing to ease it.

He shifted his head to meet her gaze. For long seconds he stood, his head angled, hands deep in his pockets and his lower lip caught between his teeth. Then he released a sigh that carried clearly to her ears. Slipping his hands free, he crouched beside the fire and propped his elbows on his knees. Staring into the coals, he finally responded.

"I am troubled because you are troubled." He lifted a hand and shook his head as if anticipating an argument. "Do not deny it. We both know it is true." Another hard swallow communicated the depth of his concern. His head low, he offered, "I will speak to the boy—will tell him I am his uncle and not his father."

Lillian opened her mouth to protest, but even though Eli made no gesture to hush her this time, words did not spill out. After a few seconds of tense silence, she clamped her lips shut and cradled the cooling coffee cup between her palms.

Eli kept his head low. "This will make things well between us again?"

She couldn't deny the hurt in his voice. Hanging her head in shame, she sighed. "I am sorry, Eli."

He chuckled softly. "For what are you sorry? You cannot help how you feel."

No, she had no control over her feelings. Yet she should be able to control her actions. Punishing Eli for something outside of his control wasn't right. She blurted, "But you will hurt Joseph's feelings if you tell him he cannot call you Pa." Truthfully, she had considered chiding Joseph herself, but she couldn't find the courage to do so.

Eli gave one slow nod. "*Jo*, that might be true." He lifted his head, his unblinking eyes met hers. "But right now I am more concerned about you and your feelings."

Lillian drew closer to the fire, clutching the cup so tightly the handle bit into her palm. "Please do not think of me first."

His brow crunched. "But why not? You are my—" Eli abruptly turned his head toward the softly glowing coals. The unspoken word hung on the night air as loudly as if it had been shouted.

Oh, Lord, how do we make this work? The prayer winged from her heart, bringing a sting of tears. She had committed herself to Eli. They worked side by side each day, but each night they went their separate ways. This marriage, although it solved many problems, was unnatural. Confusing. Dissatisfying.

With hesitant steps, Lillian closed the distance between them and poured the contents of her cup into the flickering flames. The coals popped and hissed, sending up a cloud of steam. The remaining glow disappeared, shrouding her and Eli in dark gray shadows. Setting the cup aside, she sat across from him and linked her fingers in her lap.

"Eli, I think it is all right for Joseph to call you Pa. It makes him feel secure, and he needs security with all of the changes that have come into his life."

Eli shot her a questioning look, and she thought he would argue. When he didn't, she continued quietly. "My withdrawal from you tonight had more to do with me and something that happened earlier in the day. I should not have allowed it to make me act differently toward you. I am sorry."

Concern crinkled his brow. "Do you want to tell me about it?"

She had hurt him, yet he treated her kindly. No recrimination or retaliation, just a desire to help set things to right. To her acute embarrassment, her eyes filled with tears.

Eli leaned forward, planting one knee against the ground. "Lillian, what is it?"

Rarely had Reinhardt expressed patience with her tears. He had never been harsh with her when tears threatened, but he usually slipped away to avoid facing them. She had always tried hard to control her emotions so Reinhardt wouldn't be uncomfortable.

But at the sight of tears, Eli didn't get up and leave. His tenderly voiced question, combined with the deep shadows in which she could hide, gave Lillian courage. She whispered, "I was at the creek, looking at my own reflection, and I realized . . . I cannot remember Reinhardt's face."

Eli seemed to freeze, and then he settled back to sit on his heel. "I . . . see."

Once the confession had found its way from her mouth, she felt as though a dam had burst. Words tumbled out. "Do you realize we never talk about Reinhardt, Eli? It's as if—as if he and Jakob never existed. I think of them every day. I look for Jakob, I listen for Reinhardt. The surprise of not finding them has dimmed, yet a part of me still looks and listens, waiting and hoping.

"They haunt my dreams at night, but even then their faces are fuzzy. Reinhardt and I lived together for twenty years, Eli, but now . . . his image is lost to me." She gulped, swallowing salty tears.

Eli rose, his knees cracking with the sudden movement. He stood looking toward her but not meeting her gaze. "I am sorry, Lillian, at the depth of your pain. But . . ." He drew in a deep breath and released it slowly. When he shifted to face her, his smile was sad. "It is late. We should rest. There is much work to do tomorrow between planting my wheat seeds and preserving the meat from Henrik's deer."

Confused by the abrupt closure to their conversation, Lillian nodded mutely. He held his hand toward her, and she allowed him to assist her to her feet. The moment she stood, he released her hand and backed away.

"Good night, Lillian. I—" His shoulders squared sharply. "I will pray you see Reinhardt clearly in your dreams."

Eli slapped aside the canvas door flap and stormed into his little sod house. He wanted to pace, to unwind his tangled thoughts and expend the hurt that weighted his chest, but there wasn't room to take more than a couple steps.

With a groan of frustration, he flopped onto the quilt covering the mound of dried grass that served as his bed and covered his eyes with the crook of his elbow. Behind his closed lids, he envisioned Lillian from moments ago, moonlight barely tingeing her features. But even in the scant light, he had read the truth in her eyes.

She would never stop loving Reinhardt. What a fool he had been to imagine that he could build a family with Reinhardt's wife and sons. In their busyness to establish themselves on this land, their talk had been on the present and future, not on the past. But the past still lived in Lillian's heart. Lillian belonged to Reinhardt and always would.

He kicked off his boots. The solid *thunk* of the heels against the hard-packed floor echoed against the sod walls and pounded home the realization that he was married, but slept alone. Married, but unloved.

"Why, God?" The words rasped from his tight throat. "You took my first family—my *Mutta* and *Foda*. I had a substitute family all those years of growing up. Then I spent my adult life alone. Is it too much to ask for my own family now?"

Eli listened, but the Voice of God didn't reply from heaven. Only wind—whistling Kansas wind—filled his ears. He released a heavy sigh, the big expulsion of breath carrying away a bit of the hurt Lillian's words had inflicted.

He had vowed before God and witnesses to honor Lillian, and he would keep the vow. He would provide for her and her sons, build her a home that would shelter her, continue to be her friend. But when the others came, and they established a village on this prairie, she would no longer require his presence. As had been the tradition in Gnadenfeld, the men of the community would see to the needs of a widow and her children. When the others came, Eli would move her off this farm and into town.

He nodded, a plan forming in his head. There would be no dishonor in dissolving their marriage. A marriage that was not consummated could be disjoined by the church. A dissolution would free Lillian to live with Reinhardt's memory, unbothered by the presence of her husband's foster brother. And it would free Eli to seek a wife who would love him. At his age, he probably would never have children, but perhaps God would bless him with stepchildren who—

A picture of Joseph waving the string of catfish intruded into his thoughts, bringing with it a pain so sharp it doubled him in his bed. He crunched his eyes closed, willing the image to fade, and forced his thoughts onward.

If God blessed him with stepchildren, he would love and nurture them, just as he had tried to do with Joseph and Henrik.

Rolling to his side, he offered one more whispered plea: "*Mein Gott*, let me honor my vows, but put a shield around my heart. Only let me feel love that will result in good . . . for me and for Reinhardt's family."

22

Lillian covered her mouth with her apron and coughed. She and Henrik had built a fire pit well away from the sod houses and her clay oven, but the wind snatched the smoke and carried it to her while she went about her chores. Henrik stood guard beside the fire, steadily feeding green twigs on top of the dried buffalo droppings. With each addition, a new cloud of gray smoke billowed. How could he tolerate standing so near when from a distance the smoke choked off her breath?

A rack constructed of slender boughs from scraggly berry trees that grew along the creek, now denuded of their fruit, arched low over the fire. Strips of deer meat, cut only that morning from the carcass, which survived its night in the tree, draped over the boughs. More strips lay in uneven rows on a bed of dry grass, waiting their turn to be placed over the smoking pit. Before heading to the field with Joseph, Eli had given instructions on drying the meat.

An uncomfortable feeling wiggled down her spine as she remembered Eli's unsmiling face at the breakfast table. His tone when instructing Henrik hadn't been unkind, but neither had he sounded like Eli—not the Eli they had come to know over the past months. Although Joseph had come in for the noon meal, Eli hadn't, claiming he had too much work to do to take time to eat. But Lillian suspected he intended to avoid her. His distant treatment pained her more deeply than she could understand. Especially on this day when Henrik prepared his first large kill and the red wheat kernels carried from their home in Russia would be placed in the waiting soil—both events worthy of a family celebration.

She scooped up the pile of clothes for washing and called to Henrik, "I am going to the creek. Will you be all right?"

He lifted a hand in reply, waving her on, before tying a bandana over his nose like a bandit. She hugged the pile of dirty clothes to her chest and made her way to the creek. Setting aside the clothes, she removed her shoes and stockings and placed them on the bank. On bare feet, she crept into the water. The shock of cold sent shudders through her frame, but she quickly adjusted.

Piece by piece, she scrubbed the clothes against a large rock half submerged in the water. Her skirts soaked to the knee, clinging to her legs and making movement awkward, but she worked the clothes up and down against the surface of the rock until every item was as clean as she could make it.

She bemoaned the lack of soap for scrubbing the soiled articles of clothing. With no store nearby where she could purchase soap, she needed to make lye soap for the family's use. She would check how much lard remained in the crock. She sighed as she spread the week's laundry over bushes and along the sandy creek bank to dry. The work here was never-ending. But at least the washing was finished for the week.

She picked up her shoes and gingerly followed the path back to the sod houses. Henrik remained beside the fire, and Lillian joined him. They pinched several strips, removed those they believed were dry enough to keep from spoiling, and added more to the timber frame. By then her skirts were dry, so she replaced her socks and shoes. A glance at the sky confirmed the dinner hour was approaching, so she returned to the creek with buckets in hands to retrieve water for cooking and washing.

Over the cook fire near the sod house, she fried thick deer steaks with wild onions and mushrooms. The good smell wafting from the pan caused saliva to pool under her tongue. Cleaning the deer had been distasteful, but eating the meat would surely bring pleasure. When the sun hung heavy above the horizon, Eli and Joseph returned from the field.

She looked at Eli's dirty face and laughter bubbled upward. "You have dirt caught in every crease on your forehead. It looks like the map *Herr* Weins drew."

Eli's lips twitched into a weak grin, but he didn't make a teasing response, and Lillian's laughter quickly died. While Eli and Joseph washed, Lillian set the table. She smiled in satisfaction at the meal. The steaks sent an enticing aroma into the air. She had also fried thinly sliced wild potatoes and tossed them with fresh-churned butter. Eli's palate would be well satisfied—the meal was fit for royalty.

Cupping her hands beside her mouth, she called, "Come and eat!"

To her surprise, rather than approaching the table, Eli stalked to the fire pit and spoke with Henrik. After a moment, Henrik ambled away from the pit, and Eli took Henrik's place.

Lillian caught Henrik's sleeve. "Is Eli not eating?"

Henrik glanced toward the pit and gave a one-armed shrug. "Someone must watch the meat. He said I should eat, and he will eat later. Leave a steak for him."

Lillian sank onto her stool, defeated. Not even when Joseph volunteered to bless the food did her heart cheer. She ate, listening to Henrik and Joseph compete over who did the hardest work that day, but she contributed nothing. She might as well have been eating shoe leather for all the enjoyment she took in the succulent steak. Eli's absence—both literal and figurative—created an aura of despondence she found difficult to shake.

When she and the boys had finished, Henrik returned to the pit and Eli sat alone at the table, methodically eating his now-cold steak and potatoes. When he finished, he carried his empty plate and fork to the wash pan and handed them to Lillian.

"That was a *goot* meal, Lillian. Thank you."

The compliment, uttered in a polite yet emotionless voice and without the warm spark in his eyes to which she had become accustomed, made her want to cry. She managed to push her lips into a quavering smile. "You are most welcome, Eli. Tomorrow I will prepare a hearty stew with wild potatoes and onions and cabbage. Does . . . does that sound good?"

"Whatever you cook will be fine." He took a slow backward step, lifting his arm toward Henrik. "I believe I will help Henrik with the meat. Excuse me, Lillian."

Excuse me, Lillian. The words echoed through Lillian's head as Eli turned and strode across the ground to the pit. *Excuse me, Lillian*—as courteous as could be. But he might have been addressing a stranger rather than his wife.

Spinning toward the wash pan, Lillian berated herself. What was she doing, trying to entice Eli to smile at her? Why, she behaved like a ninny! She scrubbed the plates and clanked them into a stack beside the wash pan. Just yesterday she bemoaned an inability to remember Reinhardt's face, and today she missed Eli's smile. Perhaps she was becoming senile. Her conduct made no sense—not even to herself.

The dishes done, she returned to the creek to gather the laundry. The wind had lifted a few items and tumbled them aside. A pair of Joseph's pants had rolled down the bank; one pant leg trailed in the water. Huffing in annoyance, she yanked the pants up and shook them. Droplets of water spattered her, glistening in the waning sunlight. The tiny droplets resembled tears, and before she knew it, real tears flooded her eyes.

Collapsing on the creek bank, she hugged Joseph's damp pants and blinked to chase away the tears. How she wished she had someone to talk to! In Gnadenfeld there had always been people nearby—Reinhardt, her cousins, her church friends. But here there was no one. Except Eli.

With a start, she realized the source of her frustration: how much she had come to rely on Eli's companionship over their months together. In Gnadenfeld he had been Reinhardt's friend; here, on the prairie, he had become hers. But now the friendship had drifted away like the smoke from Henrik's fire. Left behind was the lingering scent of what used to be, leaving Lillian with stinging eyes and a bruised heart.

Not until that moment did she realize just how much Eli meant to her. Not as a provider or someone to guide her sons or even as Reinhardt's beloved foster brother, but as a friend. *Her* friend. She wasn't sure how she had lost his friendship. She knew it had happened last night, when they talked together over the dying fire, but she couldn't understand why he had changed.

With a sigh, she rose. To her surprise, while she sat musing beside the creek, twilight had fallen, the sun a thin red line beneath a pale yellow glow on the horizon. Stars dotted the dusky gray-blue sky, and shadows lay long across the ground. Eli had cautioned her frequently about the danger of being at the creek after dusk. Wild animals came out at night to drink and hunt. She didn't care to become prey.

Quickly, she piled all of the clothes into her arms and turned toward the path that led to the clearing. She moved as fast as her skirts would allow, her gaze darting back and forth through the tall grass. Her heart pounded harder and harder, fear creating an unpleasant tang at the back of her mouth, while she waited for an animal to leap out and attack.

Halfway up the gentle rise, a loud rustle sent her heart pounding in her throat. Suddenly, a large shadow loomed in front of her. She let out a cry of fright and tossed the clothes in every direction.

"Lillian!"

At Eli's startled voice, she froze in place. She stared at him, her hands over her thudding heart. "E-Eli?"

"For sure it is Eli. What else did you expect?"

"I . . . I thought . . ." She bent over and hastily began gathering the scattered clothing.

Eli assisted her. When they had picked up all of the items, he took her elbow. "I have asked you not to go to the creek after the sun is down."

"I know. I am sorry. The time sneaked away from me."

"You must pay attention, Lillian. This time it was me who found you, but it could very well have been a wild creature. Will you bide my warning in the future?"

Scuttling along beside him with pant legs and shirtsleeves dangling over her arms, Lillian experienced a jolt of elation. He had come for her because he was concerned. He wouldn't be concerned if he didn't harbor affection for her. Perhaps the friendship hadn't disappeared for good. It merely needed to be rekindled.

"I will bide your warning," she said breathlessly.

"Goot." They reached the sod houses, and he dumped the clothes he carried into her arms. "One more day of planting, and then I will dig your well. After that, you will not need to make so many trips to the creek. But even so . . ." His voice held a note of admonition.

She nodded quickly. "Do not worry. I will watch the sun."

"*Dank*, Lillian." His face showed relief.

"Eli . . ." Lillian drew in a deep breath that brought her rapid pulse to a normal rhythm. She met his gaze squarely and uttered in a near whisper, "Thank you for caring enough to come looking for me."

The dirt-encrusted creases in his forehead pressed together into a snarl and then released. His mouth opened, closed, opened, and closed again with snap. He gave a gruff nod, spun on his heel, and stalked away.

The final two weeks of September passed in a flurry of activity, hardly giving Lillian time to draw a breath between chores. Now that the wheat kernels were in the ground, Eli turned his attention to improving things around their sod houses. As he had promised, he dug a well. After lamenting having to choose the location without the assistance of a water diviner, he prayed for guidance and pushed the shovel into the soil.

Lillian fretted during the three days of digging, watching Eli disappear into the hole, wondering if water would spill in and cover him before he could climb the rope to the top again. Eli fretted that no water would be found and all his digging would be for naught. But late on the third day, his exultant shout let them know his worry was unfounded. As was Lillian's—he was out of the hole long before the trickle became a rush. And by the morning of the fourth day, Lillian was able to plunge a bucket into the hole and bring up cold water.

While Eli dug the well, Joseph and Henrik dug a trench for an outhouse. Lillian made no effort to hide her relief that they would no longer have to make use of the bushes on the far side of the property. With two digging, the boys finished their trench the same day Eli struck water. Deciding that covering the outhouse took precedence over the well's cover, Eli and the boys set to work carving out squares of sod from the land across the creek to enclose the trench.

Using two long boards purchased in McPherson Town, he constructed a seat. A strip of canvas left over from the wagon bonnet served as a door. When the outhouse was completed, he looked at Lillian. "No more visiting the trees, *jo*, Lillian?" A hint of orneriness twinkled in his eyes. "Do you want to be the first to try it out?"

Though fanned by a cool, early-autumn breeze, Lillian's face flamed. As if she would go in and make use of the outhouse while her family waited in a row outside the canvas door! She stammered out a *nä* and scurried back to the sod house. But later—away from Eli and the boys—she allowed herself a hearty laugh. That little bit of teasing gave her hope that Eli's lighthearted nature might have returned . . . and would stay.

Despite her efforts to coax a smile or engage him in conversation, Eli maintained a cautious distance. It extended to the boys, as well, and Lillian's heart ached for Joseph. The boy also withdrew, losing some of his bounce with Eli's change in demeanor. When Henrik asked what was wrong with Eli, Lillian explained he was tired from working so hard. Joseph seemed to accept her answer, but Henrik raised one brow in skepticism. Although he didn't press his mother for more information, he seemed to watch Eli closely, as if trying to make sense of him.

One morning near the end of the first week in October, Lillian was preparing for the weekly laundry when a loud whoop made her look up. Joseph, who had been caring for the chickens, scampered to Lillian's side.

"Ma, what was that?"

Henrik stepped from the animals' enclosure with the milk bucket. He, too, looked puzzled. "Did someone shout?"

The cry came again, and this time Lillian recognized the shouter. "Eli?" Dropping her armload of clothes, she captured Joseph's hand. "Come. He is at the field."

Henrik put the bucket inside the sod house and trotted alongside them. They discovered Eli at the edge of the field, pacing back and forth while punching his fists in the air. Lillian came to a panting halt. "Eli, what is wrong?"

"Wrong?" He spun to face them. A huge, bright smile, so long absent from his face, sent her heart into pattering double-time. Without warning, he caught Joseph's hands and led him in a wild, stomping jig. Joseph giggled, and Lillian covered her mouth with her hands to hold back her own merriment. How boyish and carefree Eli looked, dancing in a circle with Joseph.

The pair ended their jig, and Eli tugged Joseph tight against his side while releasing another raucous whoop. "Look out there! Do you see? The seeds have sprouted!"

Lillian put her hands on her knees and peered across the field. Slender green shoots peppered the cleared ground, pointing toward the sky like tiny arrows. Her heart leapt in excitement. She gasped, clasping her hands beneath her chin. "Oh, Eli!"

"My first American crop!" He gestured Henrik closer. "Look there, Joseph and Henrik. Wheat! Our Turkey Red wheat poking its head above the ground to peek at the Kansas sun! Just as it sprouted across the ocean, now it sprouts here." He closed his eyes, his grin wide. "*Ach*, I can see it at the end of winter, shooting higher and higher after its sleep under the blanket of snow, losing its green and turning as yellow as the sun, the stalks heavy with our hearty wheat kernels."

When he opened his eyes, twin tears glistened in the corners. "Can you see it, too, Lillian?"

Lillian stared at him. Farmers viewed their bounty much differently than merchants, she realized. Although Reinhardt had taken pride in his craft as a shoemaker, she had never witnessed such elation in the end result. But looking into Eli's excited face, she thought she understood how God must feel when a baby was born—the joy of creation.

She nodded. "I can see it, Eli."

He sucked a mighty breath through his nose and blew it out. Then, smacking his hands together, he said, "Come. We must pray." He dropped to his knees and closed his eyes. Lillian motioned to her sons, and the three of them quickly knelt as Eli began to pray. "*Mein Gott*, I thank You for this good rich land. I thank You for the sprouts that poke their little heads from the soil. I thank You for the crop that will grow and will provide for our needs. I thank You for a return on our labor. Bless this wheat, *dia Gott*, and may it be the start of much blessing in America. Amen."

"Amen." Lillian opened her eyes to find Eli reaching for her. She took his hands, and they rose together. Then, instead of releasing her hands, he drew her beneath his chin and wrapped his arms loosely around her. His heart beat in her ear, his chest warm against her cheek and his arms strong on her back. He sighed, his breath stirring her hair. "*Ach*, Lillian, I feel so . . . full."

Lillian swallowed. She, too, felt full. Before she could completely examine the pleasurable feeling, Henrik gave a little cough, and Eli abruptly dropped his arms and stepped away from her.

Color flooded Eli's tanned cheeks. "*Nä-jo*, now that we have all seen the wheat, we should return to work." He hurried off. The boys ambled toward the sod houses. But Lillian crouched down, running her fingertips over the tender tips of the closest shoots of new wheat.

Looking up at the cloud-dotted sky, she smiled. "Dear God, thank You . . ." The wheat wasn't the only thing blooming on this prairie. Something inside of her had just sprung to life.

23

What was I thinking?" Eli kicked at a tuft of grass and plunged his trembling hands into his pockets. He slid a quick, accusing glance skyward. "Did I not ask You to guard my heart? And did You see what I did back there? I held her." He stopped abruptly, as if colliding with a wall. "I held her."

In his lifetime, Eli had received few hugs. He remembered his mother hugging him when he was a little boy, but after her death he could count on one hand the number of times someone had embraced him. Each time had been special, cherished, because of the rarity of the gesture. But this time—taking Lillian into his arms—had been different from all other times before.

He aimed another vicious kick at the grass and forged onward. After days of keeping himself at a safe distance, of being considerate without investing his emotions, he had completely undone himself in one moment of excitement. "*Ach,* what was I thinking?" The words exploded, more forcefully than before, scaring two quail from the thick grasses.

Once again he stopped. Stooping, he plucked a long piece

of grass and twisted it between his fingers. The blade spun as erratically as his thoughts, bouncing this way and that. By the time he tossed the blade away, he had come to a conclusion: His thrill over the sprouted seed had spilled over, compelling him to share it. So he had danced with Joseph and hugged Lillian. The hug was only an expression of delight; it didn't need to mean anything more.

But as Eli retrieved the sickle and began trimming the grass behind the sod houses, a persistent thought niggled in the back of his mind: That hug was no accident. He had deliberately chosen to share his excitement with Lillian because, deep down, he wanted to share every part of his life with her.

"Joseph, pay attention." Henrik pointed to the arithmetic book. His finger sent a long shadow across the page as he tried to make his brother understand. "See here? You have to bring the next number down and continue dividing until what is left of the dividend is too small to receive the divisor. Then, if there is any part of the dividend left over, you record it here as a remainder."

Joseph stuck out his lower lip. "There are too many steps, Henrik. I don't care about long division."

Shaking his head, Henrik shot his mother an impatient look. "Joseph prefers to be *duslijch*."

Ma pursed her lips. Her hands paused in stitching a patch onto Henrik's work trousers. "Your brother does not wish to be stupid, Henrik. He is merely tired of sitting still. You have been studying all morning. Maybe you could take a short break?"

"And do what?" Henrik threw his arms wide. Rain fell steadily outside, trapping them in the sod house for the third day in a row.

Ma sighed, poking the needle through the fabric. "Read a book?"

Henrik slapped the arithmetic book closed and paced the short expanse of open floor. "I only brought three with me besides the study books, and I have read them so many times I have them memorized."

"Then recite something to me."

"Oh, Ma . . ."

Joseph bounced up from the trunk. "We could arm-wrestle."

Henrik blew out a derisive breath. "No contest."

"Come on, Henrik." Joseph rolled up his shirtsleeve. "I have worked hard and built my muscles. See?" He flexed his arm. To Henrik's surprise, a small bulge rose on his brother's skinny arm. "Arm-wrestle me."

"Boys . . ." The warning note in Ma's voice carried clearly over the gentle roll of thunder and patter of raindrops.

"Just arm wrestling, Ma," Joseph pleaded, "not real wrestling."

Henrik slung his arm around Joseph's neck and tugged him close. Surprisingly, Joseph's temple met Henrik's chin. His brother had grown over the past months. "Ma says no, Joseph. Think of something else."

Joseph folded his arms over his chest and twisted his lips into a scowl. "There is nothing else . . ."

"Knock, knock!"

Joseph lost his sulk when Eli's voice called at the door. He scampered the few feet needed to pull the canvas flap aside. "Pa! Why are you in the rain?"

Eli ducked to enter the sod house, but he stopped just inside the door. Water dripped from his hat, clothes, and beard, but he grinned. "I am in the rain because I cannot avoid it. Such a rain! Steady, but not too hard—a perfect rain to nourish the wheat." He removed his hat and shook his head. Drops flew, spattering Ma, but she smiled rather than ducking away from the moisture.

Eli's gaze seemed to avoid Ma, bouncing instead between Joseph and Henrik. "I have seen to the needs of the animals. The chickens, they cluck in complaint, but the horses and oxen are content to sit and watch the rain fall."

Ma, still busily stitching, commented, "These two boys are far from content. They are getting restless from being trapped in here."

Eli shook his head, clicking his tongue against his teeth. "*Ach,* after all our days of work, you cannot enjoy a few days of rest?" His grin took the sting out of the rebuke. He ran his fingers through his beard. "I thought maybe I would go to the creek and see how well Kansas fish bite in the rain."

Joseph darted for his jacket. "May I go, too?"

Eli chuckled. "*Jo,* that is why I came here first. I thought you boys might be ready to get out." He jerked his thumb in Ma's direction. "Your mother, though—she is probably too *Je'scheit* to sit on a wet creek bank and hold a pole while rain falls on her head."

Henrik half expected his mother to toss aside her stitching and meet Eli's challenge. Lately, it had seemed she went out of her way to please the man.

But she only nodded. "Far too prim for such an activity." Looking up, she arched one brow. "How will you cook the fish if you catch any? The rain prevents me from building a fire."

Eli scratched his head. "Hmm . . . Your mother makes a good point. Maybe we should not go fishing after all."

"Aww!" Joseph smacked his jacket against his legs. "Please, Pa? Even if we just catch them and throw them back, can we not go?"

Henrik wasn't particularly fond of fishing, but when faced with staying inside all day as opposed to getting out for a while, he would willingly fish. "Maybe we could put the fish on a string and leave them in the creek. The rain must stop sometime, and we can cook them after the rain goes away."

"See there?" Eli gestured toward Henrik with his hat, nodding at Ma. "This is why your boy will be a good teacher—he solves problems." He stepped toward the canvas door. "*Nä-jo*, put that jacket on, Joseph, and fetch a hat. You, too, Henrik."

As they walked to the creek, poles bouncing on their shoulders, Eli said, "As soon as this rain quits, we must dig clay and build a *Feaheat* in your sod house. The nights are cool enough now to sometimes need warmth from a fireplace, and your mother will want a way to cook when it is too cold to be outside."

While Henrik appreciated Eli's attention to Ma's needs, he wondered why the man discussed it with him rather than with Ma. But as long as Eli planned to make improvements, there was something else the sod house needed. "We should also build a solid door. The canvas is getting tattered from the wind flapping it all around. And it will not hold out snow when winter comes."

"Sound thinking again." Eli crouched, plucked up a worm that wriggled up from the ground, and wove it on his hook. "I think as soon as the rain passes, we will make a trip to McPherson Town. We can get lumber for doors and purchase supplies one last time before winter strikes."

The thought of going to town—seeing something besides their own plot of rolling prairie—lifted Henrik's damp spirits. He plopped down next to Eli on the creek bank. Wetness seeped through the seat of his pants, making him shiver, but he ignored the discomfort and baited his hook. "So we all will go to town?"

"Did I not promise the family a trip to town?" Eli tossed his baited hook into the creek.

Henrik had learned over the past months that Eli kept his promises. Having the promise of money to attend school had kept

Henrik working faithfully and without complaint until the wheat could be harvested. He threw out his line. Raindrops disturbed the surface of the water, the sound reminding him of eggs frying in grease. Surely the fish were far below, hiding in the calm depths. He might be sitting here getting soaked for nothing. "Are you sure fish will bite during rain?"

Joseph, on Eli's other side, released a snort. "Now who is *duslijch*? Everyone knows fish bite better in the rain."

Eli nudged Joseph with his elbow. "Do not call your brother stupid."

Joseph hunched into his jacket.

Eli continued, "But Joseph is right, Henrik. I learned this from your grandfather. When your father and I were boys, your *Grootfod* took us fishing in the early morning while rain fell. It seems we always brought home many more fish on a rainy day than on a day when the sun shone bright."

As if to prove his point, his line jumped. Eli flipped a brown, scaly fish with a broad mouth onto the creek bank, where it flopped wildly. Although past experience had taught them this particular fish was not as tasty as the grayish, whiskered fish they called *cat-fish*, Eli still grabbed it up. Deftly, he ran a string through its gills, looped the other end of the string around his boot, and tossed the fish back into the water.

Joseph watched Eli ply his hook with another worm. "You and . . . and Father fished together when you were boys?"

Eli chuckled lightly and returned his line to the water. "For sure we did. Your father and I, we did most everything together when we were growing up. We got into our share of trouble, too!" With another laugh, he launched into a story about a fishing expedition that turned comical.

Listening, Henrik wondered why Eli suddenly chose to talk about Father. After Father's death, it seemed everyone had forgotten about him. But now, months later, Eli spoke of him as if he had been the topic of conversation every day. An uncomfortable feeling teased Henrik's stomach as he thought about Father. Thoughts of Father led to thoughts of Jakob. The guilt, which Henrik had tried so hard to escape through hard work, returned in a rush.

Father and Jakob might be sitting on a riverbank in Russia, holding a pole in their hands, were it not for Henrik. Sorrow as fresh as if the deaths had occurred only that morning struck him hard, and tears began to roll down Henrik's cheeks. Raindrops mingled with the tears, hiding the fact that he cried—until he sniffed.

Eli's head shifted sharply, his brows low. "Are you cold, boy? We do not want you to get a chill. Go back to the sod house if you think you might be getting sick."

Although Henrik knew he suffered no physical illness, he willingly put his pole aside. "I think I will go back."

On his way to the sod house, something else occurred to him. Joseph called Eli Pa. He, like Henrik, had always called their father the formal title of Father. Never Pa. The name Pa had seemed too casual, too familiar. Henrik's steps slowed to a stop as another bout of sorrow struck—this time for an entirely different reason. He had loved his father, but he hadn't really known the man. Father had never taken him fishing, or worked side by side with him building a sod house, or talked to him as if his opinion mattered. In a few short months, he and Eli had shared more intimate moments than in all of his years with Father.

Looking back toward the creek where Eli and Joseph perched together under a veil of rain, Henrik acknowledged a deep need to receive more than discipline and instruction from a father. He had been taught to respect his father, but he also desired to be respected in return. From Eli he had received admonishment, but also approval, respect, and warmth. For the first time, Henrik allowed himself to consider Eli as more than Ma's husband of convenience.

Pa . . . The title fit.

Lillian turned and gestured to the boys, who hunkered in the back of the empty wagon. "I can see McPherson Town. Sit up and look."

The wind, chilly and redolent from the days of rain, tugged at her bonnet strings. She held them beneath her chin and smiled at Joseph, who leaned across the back of the seat and broke into a wide-eyed look of wonder. She understood his astonishment. Although they had seen many towns while traveling to their land claim, they had been alone on the prairie for weeks, and the sight of other people was most welcome.

"Do you see, too?" She included Henrik with her question, even though he remained seated rather than kneeling to peek like his brother. "There *are* other people residing in Kansas. I had begun to wonder."

Eli laughed, shaking his head. "You think just because you do not see something, it does not exist? I told you McPherson Town was there, and I brought back evidence of lumber and an *Or'büs*. Yet you doubted."

Lillian smiled in return. His teasing tone let her know he wasn't scolding, and she liked hearing the light note in his voice. Although she and Eli hadn't quite recaptured the same degree of companionship they had briefly enjoyed, he no longer treated her so distantly. She responded quickly. "I did not doubt, but it is good to see for myself." Facing forward again, she drew in a breath. "We have been so busy, there has been little time to think of being lonely. But now that I see a town and people, I realize how much I miss being part of a community."

Eli flicked the reins to hurry the horses the last few yards. "You will be glad when the others come."

She looked at him, nibbling her lower lip. "Will you not?"

His gaze met hers, and his brow puckered pensively for a moment. But then he nodded. "*Jo.* It will be good to have others near again."

Their wagon rolled into town, and Henrik joined Joseph in kneeling behind the seat. Both boys curled their hands over the wooden back and peered around Lillian's head, commenting on various businesses and speculating on what might be found inside. Joseph hoped for candy, while Henrik admitted a new book to read during the winter months would please him.

Eli drew the team to a stop in front of a store where the wide windows offered a glimpse of stacked flour sacks. "This is the general store I visited the last time. They have most everything we will need." The boys started to climb out of the back, but Eli caught Henrik's arm, forcing them to stop. "I am sorry, boys, but we can only buy needed goods—no peppermint sticks for Joseph and no book for Henrik." His face reflected his unwillingness to disappoint the boys. "Until we harvest the wheat, we must be prudent with the funds we brought from Gnadenfeld. Do you understand?"

Lillian watched dismay creep across her sons' faces, but to her great pride, Henrik squared his shoulders and gave a firm nod.

"It is fine." Then he released a humorous snort. "The only books here will be printed in English, and I cannot yet read the English, so what good would it do me to buy one?"

"English candy must taste as good as Russian candy," Joseph said, then hung his head. "But I do not need any."

Eli smiled his approval. "All right, then. Let us go in and

make our purchases. When we are done here, we will go to the lumberyard."

Lillian took Eli's elbow and followed the boys into the general store. The combination of smells unique to a dry goods store—yeast and leather and apples—transported her to the little general store in Gnadenfeld. She drew a deep breath, taking great pleasure in the remembrance.

A woman bustled from behind the counter and addressed them. Being unfamiliar with the language, Lillian drew back. But to her surprise, Eli stuttered out a mixed phrase of Low German and English. He apparently communicated their needs, because the woman smiled and gestured them to the side of the store. Lillian stayed close beside Eli, listening as he made transactions. How quickly he had picked up a few English words! Her pride in him grew as he efficiently exchanged paper money and coins for the goods they would need to carry them through the winter months.

While a store worker organized Eli's purchases into sturdy wooden crates, Lillian perused the bolts of fabric lining one wall of the neat shop. Her dresses had become tattered from constant wear and being scrubbed against a rock instead of a washboard. Delicate floral patterns caught her eye, and she brushed her fingertips over a pale yellow cotton sprinkled with tiny lavender rosebuds.

A hand touched her shoulder, and she spun to discover Eli behind her. He tipped his head toward the fabric. "You have need of this?"

Glancing at the frayed hemline of her skirt, she battled temptation to request yardage for a new dress. But remembering Eli's caution and the boys' willingness to set aside their desires, she shook her head firmly. "*Nä.* I will wait until the others arrive and we have formal church services again. Then I will come back and purchase fabric for a new dress."

Eli nodded, his eyes bright. "I think that is a good plan."

Suddenly, she realized neither Henrik nor Joseph were in the store. Her heart skipped a beat—might Henrik have wandered off again? "Where are the boys?"

Eli took her arm and aimed her toward the wide window. "They are sitting on the boardwalk sharing a penny's worth of gumdrops."

Lillian's lips twitched as she fought a grin. "I thought you said no candy."

He scratched his chin, shrugging. "The boys have worked hard. They deserve a treat. And a penny . . . We can spare a penny."

She shook her head, chuckling indulgently.

The woman approached and spoke to Eli. He nodded, then turned to Lillian. "Our things are ready."

Henrik and Joseph helped Eli load the boxes, bags, and barrels into the back of the wagon. Lillian watched Henrik closely, searching for signs that he might slip away, but he showed no desire to wander. Instead, he bantered with Joseph, followed Eli's directions without a scowl, and tipped his hat to ladies who passed by on the sidewalk.

Standing back, observing the way Eli and her sons worked together, her heart swelled. Even Henrik had apparently accepted Eli's position as head of their household. From all appearances, they had become a family. A true family.

The loading completed, Eli clapped his hands together. "*Nä-jo*, boys. Climb in so we can visit the lumberyard and buy wood to build doors for the sod houses."

Doors . . .

As Eli assisted her onto the seat, Lillian's lovely imaginings dissolved. A true family would have need of only one door because they resided under one roof. As long as she and Eli lived in separate sod houses, they would never be a family in the truest sense.

24

"Oh, Eli, stop!"

Eli, alarmed, drew back on the reins. The horses halted, whickering in disapproval. With home so near, they were no doubt as eager to be back in their shelter as Eli was ready for his bed.

The day's journey to McPherson Town and back, although mostly spent sitting on the wagon seat, had worn him out. Apparently it had done the same for the boys, because both slept soundly, curled between items in the back. The day was not over, however; they still needed to unload the wagon. But the urgency in Lillian's tone pushed aside everything but seeing to her need.

"What is it?"

She pointed ahead, her face alight with pleasure. "The colors! Oh, look at the sky!"

Eli looked. Over the past months, he had observed that Kansas had particularly beautiful sunsets. This one was no exception. He smiled in agreement.

The horses pawed the ground impatiently, but Eli held tight to the reins and watched Lillian take in the glorious sunset. The sweet curve of her lips and the awe in her eyes made him long to reach out, hold her hand, and tip his temple against hers while they admired the sight together.

"So many colors . . ." Lillian's gaze darted here and there, seemingly trying to memorize every inch of the broad sky. She gestured animatedly as she spoke. "Bright pink clouds above, orange and yellow ones nearer the ground, and a purple sky behind. Why, the scrub trees and tufts of grass appear to be penned in ink, so black they are against that color-filled sky!" She laughed aloud, and Eli's grin grew. She glanced at him, and suddenly her delight faded. "You think me foolish."

"Ach, nä." Eli shook his head, curling his fingers around the reins to avoid reaching for her. "I think you are wise to take time to acknowledge God's handiwork. There is a verse in Psalms . . ." He searched his memory for the reference and exact words. "The beginning of chapter nineteen, I believe, that says, 'The heavens declare the glory of God; and the firmament sheweth his handiwork.' In a sight such as this one I see God's glory exuberantly proclaimed."

Lillian stared at him, her lips parted slightly as if amazed. "The sky does seem to be singing praise." She faced forward again, and Eli allowed her a time of uninterrupted thought. Slowly the sun disappeared, the brilliant colors fading as if the scene had been drawn with pastels and the artist had returned to rub the top layers away. When the clouds were deep purple against a dusky sky, Lillian released a contented sigh. Then she gave a little jolt.

"Oh! How dark it is. And there is still work to be done. I am sorry, Eli."

He chirruped to the horses, and they lurched forward. "Do not apologize for taking time to show appreciation for God's creation, Lillian. I believe our hearts are enriched when we pause to give Him praise, to recognize all He gives."

Clouds parted, revealing the first stars. The boys continued to sleep, one of them snoring softly. Night sounds—insects chirping, the wind's endless whisper, and the distant hoot of an owl—provided a sweet melody. Under the cover of shadow, he opened up a bit of himself to this woman with whom he wished to share all. "Sometimes I marvel at the extras God provides. He meets our needs, yes, but so much more. He did not have to make the world a bright, colorful place of beauty. He could have simply provided the things our bodies require to survive. But He also chose to feed our souls. He designed flowers, singing birds, and even little furry barking creatures that pop out of holes and make us laugh. And He created a sky that begins and ends each day with a show of color."

As the wagon rolled to a stop in front of the sod houses, he gathered his final thoughts. Turning to her, he finished quietly. "I think, Lillian, that when we do not pause to admire God's wonderful handiwork in putting this world together, we disappoint Him. Surely He must delight in our wonder when we delight in His creation."

Lillian's eyes glittered, tears trembling on her full lower lashes. She swallowed, blinked, and shook her head slowly. "Eli, you should have been a preacher. That was the most lovely sermon I have ever heard."

Self-conscious, Eli chuckled and rubbed his finger beneath his nose. "*Ach*, such a thought—me, a preacher. I am a farmer, Lillian, nothing more."

"Oh no. You are more. Much more."

The admiration in her tone and the sincerity shining in her eyes filled Eli in a way he had never experienced before. His breath caught as warmth spread from his middle outward, heating every inch of his body. With a trembling hand, he reached to cup her cheek, but just before his fingers connected with her face, a squeak in the back of the wagon intruded.

"Ma?" Joseph's sleepy voice drifted over the gentle night sounds. "Are we home?"

Lillian turned her face slightly toward her son, but her eyes lingered on Eli. "*Jo*, Joseph, we are home." She licked her lips, finally breaking his gaze to look behind them into the wagon bed. "You and Henrik help Eli unload our things, and I will put together a supper for us."

While Eli carried boxes into the sod house, sidestepping around Henrik and Joseph, who stumbled sleepily as they helped, his mind continually replayed Lillian's simple statement. *You are more. Much more.* The words thrilled him but also bewildered him. Much more than what? And the look in her eyes as she had spoken—what had he glimpsed in her eyes of clearest blue? He had seen the soft look before, when she had spoken of Reinhardt. But having that tenderness turned on him while she uttered words of praise had taken his breath away.

He plunked the last flour sack on top of the stack of boxes and peered around the sod house. The storehouse of items shrunk the room, leaving very little space to move around. He stepped outside and crossed to Lillian, where she held a skillet over the fire. The flame's glow lit her face, bringing out the golden shimmer in her hair. He thought of his comment that God hadn't needed to make the world beautiful, but beauty was His gift to mankind. This woman's beauty felt like a gift to him.

Hunkering beside her, he cleared his throat. "I am afraid you will be more crowded than ever with all our winter goods stored with you. I am sorry the sod house is so small. But I promise you, after the harvest, when I build your house, I will make it large—larger, even, than the house you occupied in Gnadenfeld—and it will have many rooms." The dream unfolded without effort.

"There will be a parlor, and a room for eating separate from the kitchen the way the wealthy enjoy, and many bedrooms. One for Joseph and Henrik and—"

He nearly bit his tongue, he stopped so abruptly. What was he saying? He planned to move Lillian to town when the others arrived. He would have no need of a large house.

To cover his blunder, he said, "But house building is months away yet. Maybe I should have Henrik come live with me. It would give you and Joseph more room."

Lillian stared at the skillet, where something bubbled and sent up aromatic steam. "I suppose that could be one solution. . . ."

Eli tensed, his senses suddenly alert. "You . . . you have another idea?"

For a moment, she dipped her head, her face glowing red. From the fire's heat? She rubbed her lips together, flicked a quick glance at him, then focused once more on the skillet. When she spoke, he had to turn his ear toward her to hear. "Maybe you could use the small sod house as a . . . a storehouse. And . . . and we could all . . ."

He held his breath, waiting for her to complete the sentence. But she fell silent. His chest exploded with each booming heartbeat. He finished the sentence in his mind: *We could all live together.* Is that what she intended to say? But wasn't theirs merely a marriage of convenience? She still loved Reinhardt.

You are more. His mouth was so dry his tongue stuck to the roof of his mouth. He wanted to ask questions, to hear her answers, but he couldn't make his lips cooperate.

"Ma?" Joseph stomped to the fire, his face puckered into a cranky scowl. "When will we eat?"

"Only a few more minutes, son. Be patient."

Joseph stalked away, muttering. But even though he departed, Lillian didn't attempt to resume the previous conversation. Eli couldn't find the courage to mention it, either. When the egg and meat mixture in the skillet was ready, they ate in silence, their gazes meeting and then darting apart. By the time they'd finished the simple meal, full dark shrouded the area, and Eli suggested Lillian wait until morning to wash the dishes.

She followed Henrik and Joseph into the sod house and released the canvas flap, sealing them inside without so much as a backward glance. But what did he expect? For her to turn around and finish the sentence that plagued his mind? By now she no doubt regretted her hasty words.

Eli tossed the remaining coffee from the pot into the fire. He waited until the flickering flames completely died, then pushed to his feet and plodded across the ground to his own little sod house.

Pausing outside the door, he looked at the bigger house only a few feet away. Both houses were constructed of sod, both loomed like black shadows beneath the night sky, but what a difference inside the walls. One sheltered people; one confined a person. He didn't want to go into his little house. He didn't want to be alone.

With a heavy sigh, he pushed aside the canvas and forced his feet to cross the dirt threshold. Inside, he stared across the tiny room. Never had the little dwelling felt as dismal as this night.

Lillian dropped heavily onto her feather tick and stared at the dark ceiling. Joseph's soft snore and Henrik's distinct, deep breathing let her know she wasn't alone, yet loneliness sat heavily in her breast. Slowly, as if forcing it through cold molasses, she stretched her arm to the side, to that narrow slice of bed where her husband used to lie. Longing rolled through her as she remembered coiling against Reinhardt's sturdy frame, being warmed by his body, feeling his breath stir her hair.

She traced time backward, to her final night in Gnadenfeld. Less than half a year ago . . . but so much had transpired in those brief months, she felt as though her time in their little village—her time as Reinhardt's wife—was a lifetime ago. Was this lonely ache the reason she had nearly invited Eli to share the sod house with her? She searched her own heart. Did she truly wish to share her bed with Eli, or was it merely loneliness for Reinhardt that had brought about the impulsive invitation?

When they had watched the sunset together, she had felt bound to Eli in a unique way. Eli hadn't scoffed at her fascination at the colors in the sky. Not only had he understood, he had supported her desire to drink in that wondrous beauty. How easily he could have dismissed her desire to admire the sunset given the late hour and the long day, but he had stopped, listened, shared.

Those moments in the wagon when he spoke of acknowledging all God had given that was beyond need flooded back. She had been taught from early childhood that God would meet her needs, and the idea had offered security. But Eli had suggested something more. Did God grant desires as well as needs? Did God give gifts beyond what His children requested? She had never pondered the giving nature of God in such detail before. But the idea that God would bestow over and above what was necessary to survive filled her heart with gratitude. She wished she could burst into a song of praise!

Eli spoke so easily of God, as one would speak of a close friend or family member. A part of her envied his comfortable status with God the creator. But deeper than her envy came a recognition of how his words applied not only to God's gifts but to Eli's gifts.

She and Eli were married in name only. He was only required to meet the physical needs of her family. Yet his giving extended well beyond what was required. In Eli's willingness to offer up all of himself, she witnessed tangible evidence of God extending His loving hand to mankind.

A question filled her mind: When people looked at her, what did they see? She loved God—she had been raised to revere and love God the Father. She believed in Jesus the Son and had received Him as her Savior when she was still a young girl. Yet, examining her own life, she couldn't be certain her belief showed.

Eli glowed with God's love. She heard it in his words, saw it in his attitude and his actions. He lived wholeheartedly what he believed. His expression as he quoted the Scripture from Psalms earlier that evening had been so sure, so serene. How had he developed such a godly demeanor?

The Bible . . . of course. Eli read from it each day. He started his day with the Word—in fact, he shared a snippet of Scripture with her and the boys every morning at breakfast. Hadn't she seen him hunched over his Bible in deep concentration, his finger underlining words? No matter how much work awaited, he started his day in a time of fellowship with God. That must be what helped him carry the essence of God throughout the day.

She, too, must assume his habit. Eagerness made her itch to leap from the bed, light the lantern, and find the Bible Reinhardt had packed in his trunk so she could begin reading immediately. But no . . . lighting a lamp would disturb her sons. She must wait until morning.

Determined to sleep, she rolled to her side and curled into a ball. But her thoughts continued to churn. One troubling idea worked its way to the forefront of her mind. Did she want to read the Bible to grow more like God, or did she hope to evoke a kinship with Eli?

25

Lillian released a sigh of contentment as she closed Reinhardt's Bible. Daily time with God had increased her desire to know Him more intimately, and she savored the blessed minutes of personal fellowship with the Father.

She laid the Bible next to the lantern that sat on the corner of an overturned crate in Eli's sod house. Her woven shawl slipped from her shoulders, and she tugged it back into place, wondering what she could do to pass the time, since she had no other belongings with her. After an early breakfast, Eli had instructed her to spend the morning in his sod house, since he would be breaking a hole in the wall of the larger house in preparation for building a chimney.

She would welcome a fireplace for warmth, and she wondered if Eli would build one for his sod house, too. Even inside the thick walls of the little dwelling, with the new wooden door snugly closed in its frame, today's chill reached her. Yet she wouldn't complain. Up until the past two days, the weather had remained mild. But as the opening days of November drew near—just as she had come to expect in Gnadenfeld—the temperature dropped, bringing the crust of frost on the grass and the fog of one's breath in the morning air.

Eli watched the sky daily for signs of snow. He expressed concern that Kansas snow would either be too light to blanket his budding wheat and send it to sleep for the winter or so heavy it smothered the wheat and killed the tender shoots. When Lillian reminded him God would meet their needs—including the needs of the wheat—he smiled and grazed her chin with his fingertips. The whisper touch, his gesture of gratitude, had sent a tingle of pleasure through her body.

Laughter burst from outside—Henrik's or Joseph's, she couldn't be sure. Since Joseph's twelfth birthday a week ago, it seemed his voice had lowered in pitch each day, completely losing the little-boy tremolo. That change made her miss Jakob even more. *Ah, Jakob, mein kjestlijch en Sän* . . . Would she ever fully release the longing to see her precious little boy run toward her, arms outstretched for a hug, a smile as bright as sunshine on his face? How could she ever cease craving the presence of a child to whom she had given life? Yet over the months, the bitter sting had lessened. God had been good to ease the pain, and thankfulness rose in her breast for His mercy.

Rising from the crate that served as both bench and table, she crossed to the door and cracked it open. Cold air rushed in, stinging her nose. Although she had planned to go out and peek at the progress being made on her fireplace, she closed the door and returned to the crate.

She sat, her skirts brushing the Bible. Shifting slightly, she traced the gilt letters forming the words *Heilige Bibel*. The touch brought a flood of disjointed memories: her father standing in front of the church, a Bible flopped open on his broad hand as he expounded on the meaning of a selected passage; Reinhardt sitting ramrod straight on the bench on the men's side of the church in Gnadenfeld with his Bible held two-handed in his lap; Eli cross-legged in the grass, his Bible sandwiched between his broad hand and his knee, reading passages in an earnest voice.

Each picture included a man from whom she had received instruction, care, and guidance; each provided a glimpse of the man's reverence for God's Word. She scrunched her forehead, picturing their faces. Two stern, one relaxed; all fervent. She was most drawn to the image of Eli, perhaps because he presented a loving, personal view of religion different from what she remembered of the do's and don'ts of her father's and Reinhardt's staunch beliefs.

She flipped open the Bible again, locating the Scripture she had read that morning. The verses were the same ones Eli had shared the first time they had held their private worship service in Kansas. She scanned the text, seeking the word *Anmut*—grace. When she located it, she whispered the phrase aloud: " 'My grace is sufficient for thee: for my strength is made perfect in weakness . . . ' "

A smile grew on her face as she absorbed the meaning of the words. When she lacked strength, God would provide . . . even beyond her needs. And as He provided, she would grow in her knowledge, trust, and desire for Him.

More laughter enticed her from the seat. She eased the shawl over her hair and tied the ends in a knot, then slipped outside. The brisk air lifted her shawl, making her shiver as she rounded Eli's sod house. Abruptly, she halted, gawking in amazement. The north wall of her sod house bore a gaping hole.

Joseph trotted to her side. Grabbing her arm, he tugged her across the grass. "Look, Ma! See how big the fireplace will be?" He bent over, holding his stomach as laughter claimed him. Eli and Henrik exchanged grins, nudging each other with their elbows.

Lillian, looking on, felt like an intruder. She put her fists on her hips. "I have been hearing laughter all morning. What are you doing? You are supposed to be at work, not play."

Joseph staggered to Henrik's side, still laughing. Henrik shook his head at his brother, puckering his face into a stern look, but sporadic peals of laughter escaped his lips.

Eli waved both hands toward the ragged hole. "Play? You think chopping a hole of this size while not collapsing the entire wall is play?"

"Well, something has you all caught up in merriment." She frowned at each of them in turn. "What is it?"

Henrik put his hands behind his back and whistled tunelessly, rocking on his heels much the way Eli often did. Eli held his axe by the head, bouncing the handle against his leg, his expression innocent. Joseph pinched his lips together, his face bright red. None of them offered an explanation.

Shaking her head, she mused, "I thought three *men* were building this fireplace, but it seems there are three *little boys* instead."

If she thought her comment would restore solemnity, she was mistaken. Her words stirred a new, more raucous burst of laughter. With a huff that left a cloud of condensation in the air, she spun and stormed around the corner.

A hand captured her upper arm, bringing her to a stop. She peered into Eli's face. Genuine concern creased his features. "Are you angry? The laughter is not directed at you."

Lillian bit the insides of her cheeks to hold back her smile. Although his heavy beard lent evidence of manhood, he looked boyish with hanks of dark hair poking out beneath his cap and his face puckered in worry. Assuming a hurt air, she sniffed. "You all share *en Sposkje*, but you leave me out."

He blinked twice, his thumb moving up and down on the inside of her arm and sending delicious tremors from her shoulder to her fingertips. "But the joke, it is not on you."

"Even so . . ." The wind caught her shawl again, blowing it askew. Before she could reach to straighten it, Eli took hold of the edges and shifted it to frame her face. In so doing, his knuckles brushed her cheeks. His rough skin, cool to the touch, was unfamiliar yet oddly welcome. She sucked in a little gasp of awareness.

He took a giant step backward. "I will tell you what happened that is so funny," he blurted. His cheeks glowed red above his beard.

Lillian, inching her way toward the sod house door, waved one hand at him and held tight to the knot of her shawl with the other. "*Nä, nä*, that is fine. You men need a joke amongst yourselves now and then. I was only teasing you. In truth . . ." She licked her dry lips, gathering the courage to share her thoughts. "It is good to hear laughter. It brings a lift to my heart and tells me happiness exists here."

"Much happiness exists here." Eli pressed his palm to his heart. "I feel it . . . and it grows day by day. I . . . I have never been as happy as I am here on this land."

The words "Me too" hovered on the tip of Lillian's tongue, but she held them back. How could she be happier without Reinhardt and Jakob? Expressing the thought would be blasphemous. So she said, "I am glad," instead.

The statement seemed to satisfy Eli. A smile spread across his face. Another gust of wind smacked hard from behind, wrapping her skirts around her knees. Eli pulled his hat more firmly over his hair. "It is cold today. You go inside—it would not do for you to get a chill. I must return to work if we want to have that hole sealed by a sturdy fireplace before the day ends."

Lillian took a step toward the sod house. "Will the fireplace be built today, then?"

"Built, but not yet usable," he said. "The clay must harden before you can put a fire in it. Two—three days of waiting. Can you manage that long?"

"I can manage."

His eyes flashed approval. "*Goot.* Now inside with you."

Sitting all alone, she discovered, made for a dreary day. During the years in Gnadenfeld with three boys underfoot, there had been moments when she longed for a few moments of privacy. Now she questioned that desire. How could she have been so foolish?

By suppertime she'd had enough of sitting idly. Chill wind or not, she would feed her men a hot supper to reward their day of hard work. After starting a fire in the *Spoaheat*, she prepared a batch of *Bobbat*, adding to the thick batter finely chopped deer meat and several handfuls of raisins from the supply purchased in McPherson Town.

To fill time while the *Bobbat* baked, she rolled and cut noodles for tomorrow's meal. Fried noodles, mixed with eggs, was one of Joseph's favorite dishes. She sang while she worked, the words of the hymn *"Wach auf mein Herz und Singe"* spilling effortlessly from her lips.

Eli opened the door of his sod house to find her stringing noodles over every available clean surface. He chuckled, bringing an end to her hymn. Then he lifted his hand in invitation. "*Nä, nä*, I like that morning hymn. Keep singing." Raising his chin, he belted out the opening words. "Awake, my heart, and render . . ."

Lillian joined in, her soprano blending perfectly with his baritone. They sang all four verses in flawless harmony, facing one another across a small sea of noodles. When they finished, Eli drew in a deep breath and released it with an "Ahhh." He grinned. "Although that is a morning hymn, it is a good way to end a day, too."

He glanced around the room. "You have turned my sod house into a *Nüdel* factory, I see."

"They will be dry enough by bedtime for me to put them in a crock," she assured him.

"Ach." His face sagged. "I thought you planned to cook them for our supper."

"Tomorrow," she said. "Tonight we have *Bobbat*. It will be ready soon."

Immediately, he brightened. "A *goot* choice! But while we wait, come." He held out his hand, and she took it. They walked together across the brief expanse of grass separating the sod houses. He pushed open her door and gestured her inside.

The once-gaping hole now housed a deep box, mottled gray with drying clay. Lillian bent down and peered up the chimney, then straightened and clapped her hands. "Eli, you are so clever! It will be so nice to cook inside during the winter."

He rocked on his heels, a pleased smile on his face. "*Jo*. It is not so nice as a brick *Oweback*, but it will do until I can build you an oven, and the fire will keep you warm, too." He jerked his thumb toward the outside. "If this cold continues all winter, you will be very glad for that fireplace."

"For sure." She looked around, noticing all the boxes and barrels piled on the opposite side of the room in a disorganized heap. With one eyebrow raised, she said, "What is this?"

Eli looked at the stacks and scratched his head. "We had to push them out of our way so we could work."

Lillian plunked her hands on her hips and gave him a mock scowl. "*Oomkje* Bornholdt, you made a terrible mess of my house! This must be righted before bed."

He smirked. "You are very bossy, *Frü* Bornholdt."

The title—*Frü* Bornholdt—hung in the room, bringing a tense halt to their lighthearted banter. With the boys calling her "Ma" and Eli calling her "Lillian," she hadn't stopped to think of herself as anything other than *Frü* Vogt. But she was *Frü* Bornholdt, Eli's wife. The name took her by surprise, but the greatest shock was realizing she didn't find the sound unpleasant.

Scrambling to restore normalcy, she said, "W-will you now build a *Feaheat* in your sod house, too?"

Eli swallowed, then cleared his throat. "*Nä*. The walls, they do not have enough length to support a fireplace. We had some trouble cutting this hole and keeping the sod wall from collapsing. We wedged a board across the top of the opening to support the wall and coated it double-thick with clay so it will not catch the flames." A smile teased the corners of his lips. "All the laughing you heard came because chunks of sod kept falling on Henrik's head. Joseph said he hoped it would knock sense into him."

Lillian chuckled softly, envisioning the scene. Then she sobered, thinking of her chilly day in his sod house. "But you'll be so cold. Surely the winter, when snow arrives, will be even colder than today. You must have a source of heat, too."

He waved her concern away. "*Ach*, I will be all right. I will cover myself with several quilts and maybe that deerskin from Henrik's kill. It keeps the deer plenty warm enough."

Despite his lack of apprehension, Lillian remained dubious. "I think quilts and deerskin might not be enough." What would she and the boys do if Eli froze to death? Anything might happen in this unfamiliar new land.

Eli continued in a convincing tone. "I will be fine, Lillian. It can be no colder than my attic room in Reinhardt's house when I was a boy."

Although Lillian had known Reinhardt and Eli her whole life—she'd known everyone in the village of Gnadenfeld—she hadn't realized they'd slept in the attic. The attic of her own home had been unbearably hot in the summer and frigidly cold in the winter. She shivered just thinking of trying to sleep in such an uncomfortable room.

"You and Reinhardt slept in the attic? But the Vogts' house was so large. Why did you not use a downstairs bedroom?"

"You misunderstand me, Lillian." Eli rubbed his finger beneath his nose. "Reinhardt had a room in the main part of the house. I slept in the attic."

Lillian stared at him in astonishment. In all her years of acquaintanceship with the Vogt family, she had assumed Eli was treated like part of their family. He and Reinhardt were together constantly, like any other brothers, alternately romping and tussling. To discover this inequity in treatment both troubled and angered her.

Apparently Eli read the dismay on her face because he shrugged. "I had plenty of quilts, and it was quiet—peaceful."

"Even so." Lillian's voice trembled with indignation. "They took you in. They told the entire village they considered you their son. And all the while—"

He stepped forward and curled his hands over her shoulders. "Lillian." She gazed into his serene face. "It does not matter. Do not let this sully your memories of the family. They were good to me. They fed me and clothed me and cared for me, never asking anything in return except respect and obedience, just as would be expected of any child. I was never mistreated or neglected."

A gloomy picture filled Lillian's mind—a picture of a small boy shivering beneath a pile of quilts, all alone and shut away from everyone. "But an attic room! Is that not neglectful?"

"Lillian, had it not been for them, I would have been on my own." He turned stern, silencing her protests. "I thank God for their kindness to an orphaned boy every day. We will not speak of this again unless it is with appreciation for the sacrifice they made in raising a child who was not their own."

His hands slid away from her shoulders, and he stepped back. Sniffing the air, he said, "I believe the *Bobbat* is nearly done. I will get the boys; we will wash up and enjoy a good meal together before restoring order in this room." He strode from the sod house, leaving Lillian alone in front of the newly constructed fireplace.

Her heart ached over all the brief conversation had revealed. Despite his claims to the contrary, she knew hurt lingered in his heart. How often he must have felt discarded and unwanted, trundled away in an unpleasant space while the rest of Reinhardt's family enjoyed comfortable rooms.

And now she also understood Eli's open acceptance of her sons. He didn't want them to experience the same rejection he'd felt as a boy being raised by a man other than his father. So easily Eli could have become bitter, but instead he had chosen to seek his peace in a relationship with God. She felt a swell of admiration for him, but another emotion rose above it.

Lillian believed she was falling in love with her husband.

26

The wind whistled, rising in pitch and volume until Lillian wanted to cover her ears. Then, as quickly as it escalated, it sank to a gentle whisper, teasing her with the idea that it might have blown itself away. Over and over the process repeated, keeping her from drifting into sleep.

Thankfully, the wind wasn't disturbing her sons. Henrik and Joseph slept soundly on their mats across the room, worn out from their day of sod cutting, chimney building, and jollity. They had nearly fallen asleep in their supper plates, tottering off to bed the moment they finished eating. But she lay, wide-eyed and alert, attuned to the wild song of the wind. And thinking of Eli.

Did he sleep? All alone in his little sod house . . . just as he had been all alone in his attic room in Gnadenfeld? The ache in her breast increased with the howl of the wind as she envisioned him as a little boy with covers tugged up to his chin, lying beneath the slanting rafters. Tears pricked at the image, and she blinked rapidly, shattering the unpleasant picture. But the tears still flowed.

"So much unfairness in this life, God," she whispered. She had overheard Eli addressing the Lord on many occasions when he was unaware of her presence. When he prayed with the family, his demeanor reminded her of a minister, but when speaking with God on his own, he revealed the intimacy of his relationship with his Maker.

Over her weeks of Bible reading and everyday communication with God, she had begun quiet conversations with God—conversations that were prayers, yet not bound by formality. She had found purpose in both means of speaking to Him. So it felt perfectly natural to talk to Him open-eyed, snuggled in her feather mattress, rather than with bowed head and closed eyes, on her knees.

"Why must hard things happen, Lord? Especially to children. Eli orphaned and then not truly loved and accepted . . . my own little Jakob falling while playing a game . . ." Her voice caught, images of Eli and Jakob bouncing back and forth in her mind so rapidly she found it difficult to distinguish one from the other. "You must have a reason, but I do not understand. If You can do anything, why do You not remove suffering from our lives and let us be always joyful?"

The wind howled angrily, and she shivered beneath her quilts. "I am sorry if I offend You with my questions. But please, Lord, help me understand . . . and help me find a way to atone for the lack of full acceptance Eli received as a child."

"Lord, help me understand and not resent Lillian for her reaction."

Eli knelt beside his bed, his beard brushing his laced hands as he prayed. Lillian's face haunted him—the look of pity when she uncovered that one small truth of his childhood. So many times while growing up he had seen pity in people's eyes. He'd heard the whispered comments: "Poor Eli . . . Without parents or a home, what will become of him?"

Poor Eli . . . How he'd hated the sound of it! As if his parentless state somehow demeaned him. He'd worked hard to overcome the disgrace of being orphaned. In school, he studied to stay at the top of his class; for Reinhardt's father, he performed twice as many chores as his foster brother; in the village, he helped build houses and barns and repaired wagons for anyone who needed assistance. When grown, he became a prosperous farmer and a respected horseman. Yet, despite all of his accomplishments, the murmur plagued him. *Poor Eli* . . .

He'd thought the pitying murmurs had been left behind in Gnadenfeld. But no, they found him even here on the plains of Kansas. Earlier that evening, when Lillian had looked at him with the sorrowful expression he had come to loathe, the shame came rushing back. Pushing up from his knees, he blew out a mighty breath of frustration.

"I do not wish to be Poor Eli to Lillian. Maybe Capable Eli, Dependable Eli, Needed Eli, or . . . best of all . . . Beloved Eli." His shoulders slumping, he rasped to the empty room, "Will she look at me now and see the man I have become, or will she always see the lonely child?"

The thought of forever being Poor Eli to this woman who had stolen his heart was unbearable. The cold, fiercely blowing wind crept in along the edges of the door and battered the sod house until little bits of grit drifted from his sod ceiling. He stood in the center of the room, listening to the wind howl like many tormented voices, feeling as though his soul joined in the chorus. But standing there shivering on the dirt floor, even if he did it all night, would solve nothing. It couldn't erase the past. Not the past of years ago, and not the past of hours ago.

He blew out his lantern and rolled into the quilt-covered straw mound that served as a mattress. "Lord, take away the memories," he begged. But lying there, cold and alone, he felt like Poor Eli.

Birdsong, joyful and shrill, teased Eli from a sound sleep. He rubbed his eyes, then sat up groggily, looking around in confusion. With no windows in the sod house, it was difficult to determine the hour, but tiny slivers of sunlight sneaked through the cracks around the door. The brightness told him sunrise had arrived some time ago.

He leapt from his bed, scrambling for the clothes that lay across his trunk. How could he have slept so long? The answer came easily—he had lain awake far into the night, bothered by the windstorm and the troubling thoughts concerning Lillian. Suddenly, he realized the wind no longer roared—a welcome change. But would Lillian's pity have drifted away, too?

Sunlight washed over him as he stepped outside. The morning was cool but calm, reminding Eli of the late days of September. He shook his head. This land was as changeable as a rich woman's wardrobe. Would these fluctuating temperatures have a negative effect on his fledgling wheat crop? He supposed only time would provide the answer.

Lillian and the boys sat around a trunk, which Henrik must have pulled out into the sunny yard. Joseph looked up from his plate and grinned. He pointed at Eli with his fork.

"Pa is awake."

Lillian turned on her stool, wiping her mouth with a square of cloth. Her smile offered as much warmth as the sun. "We saved you some fried potatoes and onions. Come, sit. I will fry you the last two eggs." She bustled toward the cook fire, where a skillet waited.

Eli didn't need a second invitation. His stomach growled as the scent of the potatoes reached his nose. He sat on the remaining stool and bowed his head in silent prayer before scooping the remainder of the potatoes onto his plate. They were cold, but he didn't mind. They tasted good. He'd eaten half of the serving when Lillian approached, a pair of perfectly fried eggs centered on her wooden spatula.

"There you are." She rested her hand on his shoulder as she slid the eggs onto his plate. His scalp came alive with her touch, and he involuntarily jerked upright. Her hand fell away quickly, and she shot him a puzzled look. Without a word, she returned to the fire and placed the spatula on the edge of the skillet.

His hand trembling slightly, Eli cut into his eggs and lifted a bite to his mouth. But although they were fried just the way he liked them—with the white fully cooked and the yolk warm and runny—he found little enjoyment in the food. Why had Lillian touched him? His mind skittered back to the many times someone had patted his shoulder, offering condolence with sad eyes.

The boys excused themselves and ambled away from the table, heading for their morning chores. Lillian remained beside the fire, scraping the crusty remains of eggs and potatoes from the inside of the skillet into the flames, while Eli finished his meal. As soon as he was done, she returned to the table and picked up his empty plate.

"Did you get enough to eat? I can fry some more potatoes if you are still hungry."

Her friendly, helpful tone showed no hint of misplaced pity, but his shoulder still tingled from the feel of her hand. He eyed her with suspicion, watching for compassion to creep into her expression.

"*Nä*, I am plenty full, *dank*. And I am behind on my work with my late sleeping. Someone should have roused me." An unintentional note of accusation colored his tone.

Lillian smiled sweetly in response. "You worked hard yesterday.

You earned some extra sleep. The boys are capable of seeing to the morning chores. If you would like to rest, then—"

"Nä." Eli rose, swiping his mouth with his napkin. He tossed the rumpled cloth onto the trunk and turned to leave.

But for the second time that morning, Lillian reached out. Her fingers landed lightly on his forearm, sealing him in place as effectively as a stake driven through the toe of his boot.

"What tasks have you set for yourself today?" Her casual tone stood in sharp contrast to the fierce beating of his heart.

"W-why do you ask?"

She gave a delicate shrug, but her hand didn't move. "I have an idea for an improvement, but I do not wish to take you away from something important."

He lowered his arm, separating himself from her touch. He immediately felt the absence and wished he had remained still. He swallowed. "I planned to twist the dried grass into logs to burn in the *Feaheat* this winter."

"More logs?" She laughed softly, a strand of honey-colored hair slipping free of its bun to frame her cheek. "You already have a pile as tall as me in the corner of the sod house."

"*Jo,* well, it will take much fuel for both warmth and cooking." His voice took on a defensive tone.

For a moment, Lillian's brow creased, but then a smile replaced the slight scowl. "Are the boys able to form the logs?"

"For sure they are." Eli had taught the boys to twist a hank of dried blades so tightly they doubled into themselves, creating bundles the size of a man's forearm. The bundles didn't burn as long as wood or buffalo droppings, but they created good heat. The boys were now adept at forming the grass logs. "But Joseph needs to study. If we were in a village, he would be in school. He has an available teacher in Henrik, so I thought the boys would use a portion of the day to study."

"I see." Lillian nibbled her lower lip, toying with the hem of her apron's skirt. Her disappointed reaction stirred his curiosity. "What did you wish for me to do today?"

Her head shot up, hopefulness lighting her eyes. "I was thinking last night while the wind blew so hard, bringing in the cold, that you will have a difficult time staying warm without the help of a stove or a fireplace." She turned toward the sod houses. "The houses are close together—only three wide paces apart . . ."

When she started walking, Eli automatically followed. She entered the narrow gap between the houses, then spun and faced him, flinging her arms wide. Her eyes shone with excitement, making her seem much younger.

"What if you cut doors into the walls that face one another and built a hall to connect the two sod houses? Would some of the heat from the fireplace reach the smaller house?"

Eli shook his head slowly. Her suggestion wasn't a foolish one. Heat would certainly find its way to the second house, taking some of the chill from the room. If he built the walls even with the smaller sod house, they could stack many of the supply boxes on either side of the walkway in the hall, freeing up the living space of the large sod house. He could see the sense of the idea, but she'd neglected one important detail.

"Lillian, if I were to do what you suggest, we . . . *all* . . . would be residing under one roof."

His subtly emphasized word hit its mark. She stood in shadow, but he saw pink creep into her cheeks. She lowered her gaze and brushed the toe of her shoe over the short cropped grass. "And would that be . . . unpleasant?"

Eli, uncertain he'd heard correctly, took a step closer to her. "What are you saying?"

Her head still down, she lifted her shoulders in a slow shrug.

"We are . . . husband and wife. The boys . . . they are getting along well with you. Perhaps . . ."

Poor Eli . . . living alone in the little sod house . . . The disparaging words trailed through his mind, taunting him. He clamped his jaw for several seconds, gaining control of his emotions before speaking.

"Lillian, we are husband and wife. It was necessary for us to form a union or we could not travel together. But we are not husband and wife as—as you and Reinhardt were husband and wife." The statement pained him, but speaking it aloud also brought a measure of relief. It was time they stop playing the cat-and-mouse game they had developed and accept the truth. "Our marriage has served its purpose. Henrik is here in America, safe from military involvement, and he will have the means to attend university when the crop is harvested. You and the boys are provided for. But . . . when the others come . . ."

His mouth went dry. He looked into her wide, bewildered eyes and forced himself to continue. "When the others come and our village is established, your needs will be met by the villagers. The church has always cared for widows. My presence in your lives will no longer be needed the way it is now."

"W-what are you saying, Eli?" Her voice sounded raspy, as if she battled to bring forth words. "Do you . . . do you intend to leave us here alone?"

Eli sighed, closing his eyes for a moment. Why did her words make him feel like a traitor? Despite his own fickle heart, which had tricked him into falling in love in the middle of a marriage of convenience, he knew their relationship could never be genuine.

He cleared his throat and continued. "You will not be alone when the others come. At that time, we can have this marriage dissolved and be free to pursue our own lives, just as we would have done if Reinhardt had not perished on the ship." She cringed, but

Eli steeled himself against the reaction and completed his thought. "If we share a roof, the minister will not allow a dissolution."

She seemed to shrink as he spoke, slowly wrapping her arms around her middle and turning her face away from him. "W-what of the boys?" Her whispered voice barely reached his ears. "You will walk away from Joseph, who calls you Pa?"

Now Eli flinched, pain piercing his heart as he recalled his joyful response to Joseph's acceptance of him. "We will be in the same village. I will spend time with him, so he will not feel abandoned."

"It will not be the same, Eli."

How well he knew living separately was not the same as melding into one family. But he would not let pity be the glue that bound them. His tone turned brusque. "Be that as it may, I see no other solution. Henrik told me it was wrong to marry you when you did not love me. I argued and told him shared commitment was enough, but I was wrong. God designed man and woman to be as one. That cannot occur without love. So when the others arrive, and this union has served its purpose, we will undo the wrong."

"But, Eli—"

"Do not worry." He held up both palms, both staving off her argument and making a pledge. "I will keep myself warm this winter, and I will honor my commitment to see to your needs. And now . . ." He began moving toward the sheaves of grass that stood in haphazard rows along the wheat field. "I must get busy before the morning is gone."

27

Too hurt to move, Lillian stared at Eli's departing back. How could he have misled her so? Why hadn't he shared these plans before they exchanged wedding vows? Eli had promised to cherish and honor her until death parted them. If he had no intention of keeping his vows, he never should have spoken the words!

Sandwiched between the sod houses in a thick patch of shade, Lillian allowed the hurt to swell until it grew into fury. Then, when the anger became too much to contain, she balled her hands into fists and charged after him. "Eli! Eli Bornholdt, you will stop and talk to me!"

He was nearly to the wheat field, but her high-pitched shriek must have reached him, because he halted and turned, facing her with a disbelieving expression.

She stomped to within three feet of him and stopped, plunking her fists on her hips and fixing him a fierce glare. "Are you a man of your word or *en Läajna*?"

His heavy brows formed a sharp V and his beard bristled. "Lillian, you know I am no liar. I am a man of my word."

"A man of his word would not make promises and then take them back. You said you would see to my needs and the needs of my sons." Her voice trembled with the force of her anger. "Yet now you say you will walk away from Joseph and Henrik after they have come to trust you, to rely on you, to see you as their pa!"

"Lillian . . ." He growled the word, his gaze bouncing behind her shoulder.

She turned her head and found Henrik and Joseph, their arms full of dried grass, staring at her. Waving her hands at them, she ordered, "You boys go to the sod house and study." They didn't move. "Go now!"

At once they dropped the grass and jogged toward the larger sod house. She waited until the door closed behind them before whirling on Eli again.

"*We* made the decision to be married, Eli. You and I discussed it together, and together we deemed it the best solution to our problems. Not once did you mention it would be a temporary solution. It is cruel now to state otherwise without even giving us a chance to be a part of the decision."

Eli's lower jaw jutted, and he folded his arms across his chest. "You say 'us' as if we were a family. But there is no family, only a mother and her sons sharing a piece of property with a man who works the field and cares for the animals." His tone turned hard. "I might as well be a hired hand."

His words cut her as deeply as if he wielded a razor. "How can you say such a thing? Do you not know you are much more than a worker to the boys and me? Joseph calls you Pa, Henrik respects you and follows your instruction, and I—"

"You what, Lillian?" He leaned forward, his eyes sparking with hostility. "You feel sorry for me?"

She reared back, her mouth dropping open. "S-sorry?"

"Jo."

Shaking her head slightly, Lillian tried to make sense of his strange accusation. Before she could process her thoughts, he continued in a harsh voice.

"I have had enough pity to fill my belly a hundred times over. The villagers, always looking at me with sympathetic eyes because I was orphaned, always wondering what would become of Poor Eli, the child who lost his parents. Our agreement did not include your pity, Lillian. I will not receive it."

She flung her arms outward, angling her body toward him. "I am not offering it!"

"Then why do you come to me now—after learning of how I slept in an attic, not a true part of the Vogt family—and ask me to share your roof?"

"Because I want you to understand you are a true part of *this* family—with Henrik and Joseph and me." A sob choked her, and she pressed her fist to her mouth, stifling the urge to cry. Tears would only create pity from his end, and that emotion had no place in this conversation. She took a deep breath, regaining control, and continued. "Here on this land—working together, praying together, laughing together . . . Eli, we have become a family."

She implored him with her eyes and her tone, her heart begging him to understand that he couldn't—he couldn't!—just walk away from what they had built together. "Can you not see?"

"Jo." Eli bobbed his head, his eyes never wavering from her. "I see that we have worked together to meet all of one another's needs . . . save one."

Lillian's breath came in little gasps. Even though he didn't speak the words, she knew what need he referenced: the need to be loved. She felt it, too. She wanted it as much as he did. And she wanted it from him. She waited for him to express the need, to give her the opportunity to open her heart to him. But he remained silent, his stoic face offering no semblance of tenderness.

So she licked her dry lips and bravely whispered, "Do you mean . . . you desire to be more than needed as a worker? You desire to be loved as a father . . . and a husband?"

He jerked as if impaled by a pitchfork. Although he didn't respond with words, she read in his eyes his answer. His hazel eyes pled to have that need fulfilled.

Lifting her foot, she took one forward step. Keeping her voice whisper-soft, no louder than the gentle breeze that teased her skirts and caused one lock of Eli's hair to dance on his forehead, she said, "All you have to do is ask, Eli, and the desire will be met."

His gaze searched her face. His hands shot out to cup her upper arms, his fingers biting into her flesh as if he required her support to remain upright. "What are you saying to me, Lillian?"

Her heart fluttered with such intensity she feared it would take wing and leave her chest. "I am saying that I have grown to love you, Eli. I want to be more than the one who cooks for you and washes your clothes. I want to be your wife."

"Out of pity?" he barked.

She shook her head wildly, twin strands of hair loosening from her bun to smack against her cheeks. "Not out of pity—out of appreciation."

"But . . . but you have only just become a widow . . . so little time has passed . . ."

Must he argue with her heart? Why couldn't he merely accept her words rather than fight against them? Didn't he realize the courage it took to admit how she felt? Wriggling loose of his grasp, she caught his hands and wove her fingers through his, linking herself with him palm to palm.

"I know when counted in days it seems a short time. But think of all we have weathered together. We have lived a lifetime on this land, Eli. We have shared more than many couples share in decades."

Tears flooded her eyes, distorting his image, but she continued in a tremulous voice. "I have examined my heart, and I know that love for you exists deep within me. I cannot bear the thought of remaining here without you. And I know my sons' hearts would break, as well, were you to leave us. Please, Eli. Please be my husband, as you vowed to be."

He pulled his hands free, and for a moment she feared he would turn and stalk away. But then his arms opened to capture her, and she found herself wrapped in his embrace. With a little cry of joy, she burrowed against him, slipping her arms beneath his jacket to circle his torso. She lifted her face, and his lips found hers—warm and moist and flavored of onions. Onions had never tasted so good.

His hand cupped the back of her head, pulling her more firmly into the kiss, and for seconds she forgot to breathe. When she gasped for air, he drew back, concern on his face.

"You are all right?"

Laughter bubbled upward, spilling out in a delightful torrent in conjunction with her happy tears. "I am fine. I am just breathless from your kissing." She rose up on tiptoe to place a quick smack on his lips, then said coyly, "You are a very good kisser, *Oomkje* Bornholdt. What other secrets do you keep from me?"

He held her loosely in his arms, rocking her back and forth while a smile split his face. "My only secret—which I now regret keeping from you—is that I love you. I have loved you for weeks . . . for what feels like forever. I should have told you sooner."

Safe within his embrace, she sighed. "I was not ready to hear it until now."

Suddenly, he frowned. "You are not telling me you love me out of fear that I will leave you without protection and care?"

The uncertainty in his tone created a rush of sorrow. What scars he carried from being alone for so long. "I depend on you,

Eli, but my love for you is not based on what you give me, but on who you are."

His face lit. "Then, to you, I am beloved?"

"*Jo*, Eli. You are beloved."

"Ahhh." His sigh spoke of a satisfaction that went to the core of his soul. "To be beloved is more than I hoped for."

Lillian grazed his beard with her fingers, enjoying the feel of the soft, curling whiskers. "But do you not remember? God gives us more than we expect."

His smile sent her heart into blissful pattering. He drew her close again, resting his cheek on the top of her head. "We are blessed over and above . . ."

As evening approached, nervous anticipation caused a tremble in Lillian's hands, making dinner preparations difficult. Lunch had been a simple affair—dried meat, bread, and fried noodles. So she planned a special supper, a meal befitting the morning's admissions.

Henrik had shot a fat goose at daybreak when a flock honked its way across the sky over the sod houses. The bird now baked in the outside *Spoaheat,* stuffed with bread crumbs, rice, raisins, and walnuts harvested from a tree on the other side of the creek. Lillian set the table with her linen cloth and fine tableware instead of their everyday tin plates. Freshly churned butter sat pale and moist in a bowl next to a loaf of fresh-baked bread.

The boys would take one look at that table and wonder why their mother had gone to so much trouble for a mere Thursday, but Eli would understand. Her pulse quickened as she remembered being swept into his arms and thoroughly kissed. She touched her lips, a smile growing behind her fingers as she relived those moments when Eli literally kissed her breath away.

Guilt nibbled the edges of her conscience. She had relished

Reinhardt's kisses, but he always exercised a restraint, as if afraid to give vent to passion. Eli, however, had held nothing back, and in so doing had opened up a part of Lillian's heart she hadn't known existed.

How she wished for a second kiss. But it would have to wait. She had work to do. Potatoes, sliced thin and layered with wild onions, awaited frying. She carried the skillet to the *Spoaheat*. Soon she would cook in the indoor fireplace, but not until Eli said the clay was dry enough. She fried the potatoes to a crisp in hot, aromatic lard, then set the skillet at the edge of the fire to keep the potatoes warm until the goose finished cooking.

As she removed the pan with the browned bird from the oven, Eli and the boys came from the field. Eli took one look at the goose and raised his eyebrows in approval. Then he looked at the formally set table and gave Lillian a tender smile.

Warmth flooded Lillian's face. She bustled toward the table, holding the goose in front of her like a shield. "Wash up, everyone. Our supper will grow cold if you tarry."

Eli paused on his way to the washbasin to whisper in her ear. "You have gone to much trouble. I must think of a special way to thank you."

The mild heat in her cheeks turned to a blazing furnace.

They sat around the table and held hands while Eli blessed the meal. Was his voice huskier this evening, or was it only her imagination? She couldn't be sure, but she knew she had a heightened awareness of him. When she passed him the butter and their fingers brushed, lightning shot through her midsection. Surely the boys saw the sparks, so intense was her reaction to his simple touch.

But a glance at her sons showed only their enjoyment of the meal. She forced herself to relax and enjoy partaking of the sumptuous feast.

Midway through dinner, Henrik said, "We will need more

feed for the animals this winter. Do you intend to purchase fodder, Eli?"

"Not when there are fields of grass, ready for cutting." Eli carried a forkful of potatoes to his mouth. He swallowed before adding, "Tomorrow and Saturday we will build a connecting hallway between the two sod houses, turning them into one—"

Joseph's head jerked up to stare at Eli. Henrik imitated his brother's response, but he stared at Lillian. She focused on plucking free a bit of meat from the goose's thigh bone while Eli continued.

"—and giving us additional storage space. When that is complete, we will spend next week cutting the grass across the creek and stacking it to feed to our oxen and horses this winter."

Henrik slowly lifted a bite to his mouth, his gaze still fixed on his mother's face. Lillian refused to look directly at him for fear of recrimination in his eyes. She asked, "You will cut the grass on the other side of the creek? But we do not own that piece of land."

"I know," Eli agreed, "and if someone lived on that property, I would not touch the grass. But it is as yet unclaimed. By next spring, when others arrive, the grass will have grown and replenished itself, so we will not hurt anything by harvesting it."

Joseph, his fisted hands holding his fork and knife upright on either side of his plate, leaned toward Eli. "You said we would join the two sod houses into one . . ."

Henrik cleared his throat—a hint, Lillian was certain, to silence his curious brother. But Joseph, unabashed, continued. "Will you build another sod house, then, for you, since you are making your sod house a part of ours?"

Eli's eyes collided with Lillian's across the table. She sensed him asking permission to share the change in their relationship with her sons. With a minute nod of her head, she gave her approval.

"*Nä*, son, I will not build another sod house. Instead, when your sod house and mine become one, then we"—he gestured to indicate all of them seated around the table—"will also become one family, all living together." Suddenly apprehension attacked his features. "That . . . that will be all right with you boys?"

Joseph's forehead wrinkled. "So we will have a two-room sod house." He sat straight up, much like the little barking dogs that popped from holes in the prairie. "Then can Henrik and I move into the smaller room and have our own space?"

Eli looked at Henrik. "Henrik, would you mind . . . sharing . . . a room with Joseph?"

Lillian held her breath, waiting for Henrik's response. Henrik was old enough to understand the true meaning of Eli's question. Would he explode with anger, or would he offer his blessing? He had been so distant and cold the day she married Eli. How she needed her son's approval.

Henrik glanced from Eli to Lillian and back to Eli. His shoulders rose and fell, and he rubbed his lips together as he stared at the half-empty plate in front of him. Then he lifted his head and gave his mother a sad half grin. "I suppose that would be . . . all right."

Lillian battled the urge to burst into song. Although absent of overt enthusiasm, Henrik's simple statement spoke eloquently of his altered attitude. So many prayers had been answered. She clasped his hand and whispered, "Thank you, *mein kjestlijch Sän.*"

He nodded, then returned to eating. Lillian faced forward to find Eli caressing her with a soft, adoring gaze. Once more, the breath seemed to be sucked from her lungs. How could she have overlooked the love this man held for her? *Thank You, Lord, for opening us to one another. Thank You for the gift of this giving, loving, godly man.*

With a little laugh, she picked up the baked goose thigh and carried it to her lips. They finished their meal with light chatter, teasing, and much laughter. While she listened to Eli and the boys discuss where they would store the winter's fodder for the animals, Lillian's thoughts bounced forward to Sunday, when only one sod house would sit on their property. Surely happiness would now be her constant companion.

28

Henrik threw the quilt over the freshly raked pile of sweet-smelling dried grass and stepped back, letting his gaze sweep the small room. Joseph had made his bed in the opposite corner, with a trunk containing their clothes forming a barrier between the two simple beds. A second trunk, which held his collection of books and Jakob's items—things Ma cherished—huddled next to the wood-framed opening to the newly constructed hallway. The two sod houses were now joined into one.

Joined into one . . . The houses were one, and—apparently—Ma and Eli were one. Over the past two days, Henrik had tried to avert his gaze whenever Ma and Eli were in close proximity. The dreamy looks they shared seemed out of place for people their age and gave Henrik an odd feeling in the pit of his stomach.

Joseph clomped into the room, sat on his bed, and leaned against the sod wall. "Henrik, bring the lantern over here." He patted the top of the trunk separating their beds. "I want to work on my whistle, and I cannot see well enough."

Henrik carried the lantern over and set it on the trunk. "Are you whittling again?" Eli had given Joseph a penknife for his birthday. Joseph worked diligently, attempting to turn twigs into usable objects, but in Henrik's opinion, it was a waste of time.

"I like whittling." Joseph hummed tunelessly as he flicked curls of wood onto the floor.

Henrik pointed. "You will clean up after yourself. I do not wish to get a sliver in my foot."

Joseph scowled at him. "Then put on your boots. You sound like Ma when she scolds about leaving socks on the floor. Let me be."

With a grunt, Henrik stomped to the smaller trunk and removed the history textbook. He flumped onto his bed and opened the well-worn book, but he couldn't focus. What were Ma and Eli doing over on their side of the sod house? On previous Sunday afternoons, he, Joseph, and Ma had rested in their sod house while Eli stayed alone in his. But yesterday evening they had put the roof on the connecting hallway, and Eli had given permission for them to use a portion of the Lord's day to move their belongings. Father would have insisted they wait until Monday rather than do any semblance of work on the Sabbath, but in many ways, Eli differed from Father. Sometimes Henrik appreciated the differences, but this time he wasn't so sure. Eli's hurry to get the boys' things moved seemed to indicate an eagerness to be alone with Ma.

He ruffled the pages of his book, frowning toward the doorway. Maybe he should go check on Ma—make sure she was all right. She had grown accustomed to his and Joseph's presence; she might be feeling uneasy, too. He set the book down and started to rise, but just then Eli's voice called from the hallway.

"Boys, may I come into your room?"

Joseph lowered his penknife. "Come in, Pa!"

Eli filled the doorway. A folded piece of canvas lay over his arm. He looked around the room, then smiled in turn at Henrik and Joseph. "I see you have everything put away."

"Jo." Joseph flicked another bit of wood from the smooth stick. "I like having our own room." He wrinkled his nose. "Except Henrik acts like Ma, telling me to clean up after myself."

Eli chuckled, but then he pointed his finger at Joseph. "You listen to your brother. He must share this space, and he has a say in how the room is kept."

Joseph made another face, but he shrugged and returned to whittling.

Eli held up the canvas. "Would you like me to hang this over the doorway to give you privacy?"

Henrik's senses went on alert. The canvas would form a partition to keep Joseph and Henrik separated from Ma and Eli. In their house in Gnadenfeld, Henrik and his brothers had shared the loft. No door closed on the opening at the top of the stairs. Knowing Ma and Father slept directly beneath the loft, with no door creating a barrier, had given him a sense of security as a child.

"Will that prevent the heat from entering our room?" There was a note of suspicion in his tone.

Eli rubbed the underside of his nose with one finger as he seemed to consider this. "*Ach*, we will fold it aside at night when the fireplace burns. I only thought you would like having the choice to close yourselves away once in a while."

Henrik examined Eli's face for signs of hidden motives. He saw none, yet he shook his head anyway. "Joseph and I are used to open doors. The canvas is not necessary."

Eli shrugged. *"Nä-jo."* He gave a quick nod. "Enjoy your restful afternoon. Take a nap before supper. Tomorrow we have much work to do." He turned and left.

Henrik waited a moment, then rose and crossed to the opening. At the opposite end of the hallway, a strip of canvas hung, sealing off the main room where Ma and Eli were now alone.

The uncomfortable feeling returned.

"Are the boys resting?"

Eli sat next to Lillian on the trunk, drawing her snug against his side. How wonderful, the freedom to touch her whenever he wished. Each time she stepped willingly—even eagerly—into his arms, joy rolled through him. Once more he winged a silent prayer of thanks to the Lord for the gift of love from this woman.

"Joseph is whittling, and Henrik has a book open."

She nestled her head on his shoulder and sighed. "So they are fine?"

"They are fine."

"Good."

Sitting with Lillian on the trunk, Eli wished for a sawdust-stuffed sofa or cushioned settee. The trunk was not a comfortable seat, but the only other place to sit together was on Lillian's feather bed. That would not do should one of the boys venture into the room. So regardless of comfort, he would sit here on the trunk. The pleasant company made sitting on the hard surface worthwhile.

He drew lazy curlicues on her arm with his thumb and rested his cheek against her hair. "When we harvest the wheat, I will buy furniture." His breath stirred an errant curl, and he shifted to tuck the strand behind her ear before pulling her close again.

"But you must buy lumber for our house." She tipped her head slightly to peer into his face. "Will there be enough money for both?"

Eli smiled. "This land, Lillian . . . so rich and dark the soil. If our wheat grows as tall and thick as the grasses, I will have a better crop than even the ones we raised in Molotschna." He sat up, angling his body to face her. "The man who owns the grain elevator in McPherson Town wrote down the price of wheat for me, and I memorized it."

Excitement rose within him as he considered the wealth waiting to be claimed. "Last year's crop brought one dollar and five cents per bushel."

Her eyebrows shot upward. Although she hadn't yet learned the American denominations, she understood how many supplies had been purchased in the store for that amount.

"How many bushels will you raise per acre?"

Her genuine interest increased his enthusiasm. All the years he farmed alone, no one cared enough to ask what he grew or what his crop yielded. He took great pleasure in answering Lillian's question. "I purchased two hundred forty acres from the land developers, and I planted about one hundred eighty acres."

"Why not plant it all?"

"It is best to leave some land to go to hay for animal feed."

She nodded, her smile affirming his decision.

"In Gnadenfeld I yielded twenty-five bushels per acre. I expect a better yield here. But even if it turns out to be twenty-five bushels per acre, we could earn close to four thousand dollars for our crop."

Lillian's eyes flew wide. "Four thousand!"

He laughed. "*Jo*, I know! It is a goodly amount." Quirking his lips to the side, he admitted, "It will cost some to ship it to market—maybe six or eight cents per bushel . . . but even then, we stand to gain a great deal. It will meet our needs . . . and beyond."

Remembering that he'd promised Henrik a quarter of the harvest's gain, he quickly inserted, "I promised Henrik he would have money for schooling, so that will come out first." Another thought followed that one. "We have no church."

"*Jo*, this I know. . . ."

"*Nä, nä*, I am thinking tithe. How can we tithe without a church?" Eli tapped his lips with one finger. "We must give back a portion of what we receive. But how?"

The softness in her expression robbed him of breath. She took his hands, giving them a gentle squeeze. "Eli, what a good man you are."

Ah, to hear those words of praise while her fingers were laced between his was beyond pleasure. He chuckled self-consciously. "It is not goodness that leads me to tithe, but gratitude."

Lillian nibbled her lower lip, a pensive frown creasing her forehead. Then she brightened. "You can set the money aside. Then, when the others come and we are ready to build a church for our village, you can give the money to the minister."

"A fine idea!" Eli leaned forward and planted a kiss on her lips. "You have a good head on your shoulders, *Frü* Bornholdt."

She snuggled herself beneath his arm. With her head nestled against his shoulder, she said, "And my good head, along with the rest of me, wishes to take a nap."

"Then nap." He kissed the top of her head, wrapping his arms more securely around her waist. "I will not let you fall." Although the seat was uncomfortable, and although he longed to nap, too, he sat very still and alert, holding tight so his Lillian could rest.

As November drifted away beneath cloudless skies painted a dull blue-gray, making Lillian happy became Eli's new pastime. He sought little ways to win a smile—bringing her unexpected gifts like a brown stone with a glittery gold stripe, smooth from years in the creek, or a bright bird feather in lieu of the flowers that no longer bloomed with fall slipping into winter. The sod house, with its dirt walls and simple furnishings, lacked color, and his token offerings always brought a smile, a kiss, and a whispered thank-you.

They discovered other pleasures, too, after supper when Henrik and Joseph slept in their half of the sod house. Although Eli had often wondered what it would be like to lie with a woman, to offer himself to the one he loved, his imagining had fallen far short of the reality. Never had he felt so accepted, so desired, so beloved. Daily his heart expanded, Lillian's love satisfying every longing he had ever possessed.

The days grew shorter, the sun sinking into the horizon before the day's work could be completed. The wind carried a bite, and Lillian expressed gratitude that she need not cook in the fire pit outside anymore. Eli preferred to have Joseph spend part of his day studying, yet more often than not the boy ended up working side by side with Eli and Henrik, chopping branches from trees to build a bigger fence to enclose the animals or cutting grass for fuel and winter feed. The labor was backbreaking, yet Eli felt rewarded as he watched the mound of hay behind the three-sided barn grow. His animals would not go hungry, and his family would not freeze.

Each morning after milking the female ox, whose belly rounded with the promise of a calf, Henrik set out with the rifle in hand. Some days he returned with a fat rabbit, other days a pair of squirrels or a speckled prairie chicken. His skill provided them with fresh meat so they needn't exhaust the supply of dried deer meat that would sustain them through the months when game was scarce.

Joseph grew taller by the day, and on a day in late November Eli realized with shock that the boy's britches no longer stayed tucked into his boot tops. Although he hadn't intended to venture into McPherson Town until spring, he wondered if he should plan one more trip to buy Joseph new britches. His old ones would not last him through the winter. He approached Lillian with the matter.

She paused in sorting clean clothes into piles. "You would buy new ones?"

He tapped the end of her nose. "They do not sell old ones. So *jo*, I would buy new." Her worried expression raised his concern. "Lillian, what is wrong?"

Without replying, she moved into the hallway. Eli followed,

watching as she stopped and placed her hands flat on the lid of Reinhardt's trunk. She angled her chin to meet his gaze, and twin tears glistened in her eyes.

"We need not buy new. There are several pairs of good britches in here. With a little tailoring, I can make them fit Henrik, and Henrik can pass his britches to Joseph. They should fit him fine."

Her tone sounded even, unruffled, yet Eli sensed she'd kept the statement deliberately unemotional to hide her true feelings. Only twice since they'd arrived in Kansas had Lillian opened Reinhardt's trunk—first to retrieve the rifle and then to remove Reinhardt's Bible. Other than that, the trunk's contents had remained undisturbed.

He rubbed her upper arms with his palms. "I can buy a pair of britches for Joseph. You do not have to use Reinhardt's." How odd it felt to speak the name of his foster brother. Had his days with Reinhardt existed in reality? Surely his life began the day his heart became joined with Lillian's.

She shrugged free and curled her fingers beneath the lid. "*Nä.* It is silly to have these things and not use them. Even Reinhardt would scold if he knew his clothing languished in this trunk. I . . . I will fetch his trousers and . . ." Her words faded away, her chin trembling. Suddenly, she released the lid. It fell with a thud as she covered her face with her hands. Silent sobs shook her frame.

Eli took her by the shoulders and turned her into his embrace. He held her against his chest, his heart thudding with both sympathy and apprehension. Lillian rarely cried. For her to do so now told him she needed release. But uncertainty at the cause of the tears brought apprehension. As soon as she pulled away to wipe her eyes on her apron skirt, he took her face in his hands. "My Lillian, why do you cry? Are you sure you do not wish to leave Reinhardt's things undisturbed?"

She shook her head, stepping away from his touch and reaching once more for the lid. She hefted it open, then stood staring at the neatly stacked contents. Her hands shot forward, and she lifted out two pairs of tan trousers. With a quick flip of her wrist, she lowered the lid, then turned and perched on its edge, cradling the pants in her lap. A sad smile curved her lips when she looked up at him.

"Do not look so worried, Eli. Sometimes . . . women cry. And these tears were necessary. They helped me say good-bye to Reinhardt."

Had she not already made her good-byes on the ship when Reinhardt was lowered into the sea? She must have sensed his confusion, because she patted the spot beside her. Eli sat, and she placed her hand over his knee.

"These past weeks, as we have grown . . . closer . . ." Pink stained her cheeks, and her gaze danced away briefly before returning to his face. "There have been times when Reinhardt intruded in my thoughts."

Eli's gut clutched. Her thoughts had been on another man while lying with him?

"I loved Reinhardt, Eli, and I know he loved me. We married when we were very young, we were together for many years, and our union created three healthy sons. We shared much."

With effort, Eli maintained a calm demeanor, although his pulse galloped like a runaway horse.

"For a while, I wrestled guilt. Was loving you a betrayal of Reinhardt's memory? Especially when . . . with you . . . the loving was so sweet, so sincere . . ." Her gaze skittered away again, the pink blush deepening to a fiery red. Her voice lowered to a whisper. "Although Reinhardt and I shared much, somehow—with you—all of me reaches out. Even the deep, hidden parts of me. Nothing is withheld."

Eli swallowed, unable to respond.

She turned her head slowly until her clear blue eyes met his.

"What we have is beautiful, Eli—and full. I have often prayed for God to ease my conscience, to allow me to move without reservation into a future with you." A leftover tear that had quivered on her lower lashes broke free and ran past her smile. "And I know now I am ready. If I can reach into this trunk and make use of these things that Reinhardt will never use again on this earth, then I know I have said my final good-bye."

She drew in a shuddering breath, her sweet face expressing an acceptance and confidence that put a lump in Eli's throat. "Nothing—no bitter memory, no misplaced guilt, no whispers of used-to-be—stands in the way. I am fully yours."

Overwhelmed with emotion, Eli could not speak. Tenderly, he gathered Lillian close, pressing his cheek to her warm hair. If memories of Reinhardt could not tug her heart from him, surely nothing ever would.

29

Lillian crossed her finger over the calendar box that represented the last day of December 1872 and released a sigh. So quickly the year had flown . . . and so much *life* had been packed into twelve scant months.

This same calendar had hung on the wall of her house in Gnadenfeld. It had traveled across the ocean to be placed on a wire hook and used to count the days lived in a new country. For a moment she considered leaving it—no other pictures or ornaments decorated the sod walls—but practicality won. The year was complete. The calendar should come down.

She plucked the calendar from the wire and held it in both hands. As she stared down at the blocks that signified days spent, tears pricked behind her nose. Although she had considered carrying it to the outhouse where it could serve a useful purpose, she decided to put the calendar in one of the trunks. 1872 had been a year of many challenges and changes. This calendar would help her remember all they had faced . . . and weathered.

Joseph looked up as she crossed the floor and opened her trunk. "You are keeping the old calendar?"

"Jo." Lillian tucked it into the bottom of the trunk, beneath her clothes. Although she knew Joseph wondered why she would choose to save something that had always been discarded in the past, she offered no explanation.

After a moment, Joseph returned his focus to the arithmetic book opened on the trunk top, and Lillian moved to the fireplace to check the pot hanging over the fire. The lard bubbled, sending up a rich aroma. Her stomach growled as she anticipated biting into a fresh *Portselkje.* The fried fritters, laden with raisins, had always comprised their New Year's Eve supper in Russia. Lillian was determined the tradition would be carried over in their new country.

The door opened, and Eli entered with Henrik close on his heels. A blast of cold air accompanied them. Lillian crisscrossed her arms over her chest. "*Ach*, it feels like *schnee*! Close the door *flucks*!"

Eli latched the door quickly, as commanded, and removed his hat and scarf. He shook his head. "It is high time for snow. Not more than a spatter of snowflakes have we seen—and my wheat needs a blanket."

Lillian scurried across the short expanse of floor and tucked herself along his side. Cold seeped from his jacket, causing her to shiver, but she made no effort to retreat. Eli's arms had become her favorite refuge.

Henrik sent Eli a worried look. "Will the wheat die if snow doesn't come?"

Eli tugged Lillian closer. "It has been cold enough to put the seeds to sleep. We have time yet for snow. Besides . . ." He raised one eyebrow and smiled down at Lillian. "The sky is heavy with clouds and very gray. We might get our first snow at the beginning of a new year. Would that not be perfect?"

Henrik stepped toward the trunk where Joseph sat. "Have you not finished those problems yet?"

Joseph rolled his eyes. "I am finished. Do you want to see?"

"Later." Henrik gestured to his blotchy trousers. "I got my pants wet when I watered the animals. I am going to change." He disappeared down the hallway.

Eli nuzzled Lillian's neck with his cold nose. "Mmm, you smell good."

She wriggled until his soft whiskers met her neck. "I smell like hot lard. I am preparing to cook *Portselkje*."

Eli jolted back, clamping his hands over her shoulders and straightening his arms. "For sure?"

"For sure, just like the ones in Molotschna—no substitutes." She removed herself from his grasp and returned to the fireplace. The bowl of dough sat on a rough shelf pressed into the wall. She stuck her finger in the mixture, then popped the dough into her mouth. "We had to celebrate Christmas with fried rabbit instead of our traditional pork roast, and our *Plümekjielke* contained dried venison instead of ham. But we will have *Portselkje* for New Year's Eve, just like always."

"The rabbit went down all right with lots of sauerkraut," Eli said. Lillian appreciated that he never complained about the food she put on the table, even though many of their familiar recipes had taken on new flavors and textures with her modified ingredients. He shrugged out of his jacket and dropped it on Joseph's head as he passed the boy. With a giggle, Joseph flopped the jacket over the trunk and followed his stepfather to the bowl of dough. Both Eli and Joseph pinched out a bit and tasted it.

"Mmm! *Goot*, Ma!" Joseph proclaimed.

"As good as the *Plümekjielke* at Christmas," Eli added.

Lillian sighed. It heartened her to know the hearty prune,

noodle, and meat dish she prepared for their Christmas breakfast had been appreciated, yet she longed for pork instead of the dried deer meat and wild game that filled their bellies. Her mouth watered at the thought of smoked ham, sausage, and spare ribs. Then she chided herself. She shouldn't complain—God was good to meet their needs for food. Yet a part of her hungered for the foods of her homeland.

Tipping her head, she looked up at Eli. "Will you raise a piglet or two in the spring so we can butcher them and have ham in our *Plümekjielke* next year?"

Joseph's bright eyes bounced back and forth between his mother and stepfather. "And we can build a *Meagrope* to render our own lard—then we will have cracklings!"

Lillian nearly groaned with pleasure at the thought of the crisp bits of meat found in the bottom of the rendering tub when the lard was removed.

Eli laughed and flicked Lillian's chin with his index finger. "I will see what I can do. Maybe when I go to sell the calf, I will buy a couple of fat piglets."

She would have preferred a sure response, but Lillian had learned Eli wouldn't make a promise unless he could keep it. She must be satisfied for now. If he said he would try, he would do so. Glancing at the trunk that served as their dining table, she said, "Joseph, please hang your pa's coat on the hook and put away your books. Now that we are all here, we will eat soon."

"*Jo*, Ma."

Lillian spooned out a dollop of dough and eased it into the grease. A sizzle rose, and the fritter bounced in the boiling fat.

Eli crowded close, sticking his nose over the pot. "Why was Joseph studying today? New Year's Eve should be a holiday."

Lillian gently pushed Eli aside and flipped the fritter with a wooden spoon. "Henrik insisted. He said Joseph spent too many study days fishing, so now that the creek is frozen, he must spend his days studying."

Eli clicked his tongue against his teeth. "A hard task-master Henrik will be when he has a classroom of students to supervise."

Lillian lifted the browned fritter from the grease with the slotted wooden spoon. Eli's gaze followed it, and she caught him licking his lips. She laughed, shaking her head. "You are no better than a little boy! You may have the first New Year's cookie."

His grin gave her all the thanks she needed. She rolled the hot fritter in a pan of granulated sugar. The moment she turned from the pan, Eli lifted the oblong fritter between his thumb and finger. He hissed, *"Sea heet!"* He tossed the fritter from hand to hand, sending a tiny shower of sugar across the floor.

"Eli! You make a mess!" Lillian ground the sugar granules into the dirt floor.

After blowing on the fritter, Eli took a big bite. He waggled his brows at her, signifying his enjoyment. With a laugh, Lillian set to work frying the remaining dough. The aroma made her mouth water, but she diligently waited between batches for the lard to boil. She wanted her *Portselkje* to be perfect.

Soon her serving bowl mounded with golden brown, sugar-coated fritters. She set the bowl on the trunk and smiled at Eli, who eyed the traditional treats from his stool at the table. "Call the boys and we will eat."

The fritters disappeared quickly amidst reflections on the past year and plans for 1873. Tears twinkled in everyone's eyes when they spoke of Reinhardt and Jakob, but Lillian appreciated the freedom to mention the names without experiencing stabbing pain or deep remorse.

Joseph snagged the last fritter from the bowl and then paused, sighing contentedly. "These are good, Ma, but it seems strange eating them all ourselves instead of sharing them with neighbors."

Lillian nodded, remembering the knocks at the door, the boisterous cries of *"Froo Niejoa!"* ringing on the night air, and the laughter of friends and family who crowded into the house to eat a fritter before setting off to the next house.

"But think," Eli said, "by next New Year, we will be part of a village. The others will come next spring, build their houses just as we have, and we will knock on their doors and wish them a Happy New Year."

Joseph grinned. "I know on which door Henrik wants to knock—the Friesens' door."

"Joseph," Henrik warned, but Joseph laughed and popped the last of the fritter into his mouth.

Lillian, determined to avoid an argument on the final day of the year, said, "Do you really think they will come by next spring?"

"For sure they will." Eli's confident tone dispelled Lillian's worry. "The explorers will have returned to Gnadenfeld by now. I believe our neighbors are making their plans to come to America, just as we made our plans at the beginning of this year. Now see where we are, and all we have accomplished?" He rested his elbows on the edge of the trunk. "Our God has been good to us, and He will bring the others to us."

A hint of the old rebellion surfaced in Henrik's eyes. "How can you be sure they will come here?"

Recently, despite Lillian's happiness with Eli, she had glimpsed moments of defiance in her oldest son's behavior. She suspected he struggled with allowing Eli to usurp Reinhardt's place in her life and heart, yet she refused to apologize for unreservedly loving Eli. He was a good man, devoted to her and her children, and Henrik would eventually grow up enough to realize Eli was a special gift to them.

A complacent smile crinkled Eli's eyes. "Did you not send a letter to Susie Friesen and her family and tell them where we are and how rich the land?"

Henrik offered a slow nod.

"Well, then, think of that." Eli's voice held no animosity. "Besides, I pray daily for our friends and neighbors to find safe transport to this wonderful land. God has good plans for our people here, and He will see those plans through." Eli lightly bounced his fist off of Henrik's forearm. "Trust Him, Henrik. You will see—our God does not fail."

Lillian washed the dishes with Joseph's help, and then she and her family spent the evening singing hymns, reading from the Bible, and playing *Hinkspiel,* a hopping game. By the end of the hour-long game, they were giggling so hard they could barely stand, let alone hop on one foot. Eli frequently flipped his pocket watch open to monitor the time, and at midnight, they joined hands and bowed their heads for prayer.

Eli cleared his throat. "Our loving Father God, as we say farewell to one year and enter another, we thank You for Your steadfast presence in our lives. We praise You for bringing us to this land. It is a good land, God—" His voice cracked, and Lillian squeezed his hand. She heard him swallow, and then he continued. "May You find us worthy of Your blessings. Protect and guide us. May we bring joy to You as we follow Your ways. Amen."

"Amen," Lillian echoed. She embraced her boys by turn, whispering, *"Froo Niejoa"* to both of them. After returning the greeting, Joseph and Henrik headed to bed. Lillian then turned into Eli's arms. "*Froo Niejoa*, Eli."

"Ah, Lillian . . ." He sighed against her hair, his whiskers tickling her temple. "This will be the happiest year ever, I think. With you and the boys . . . such blessings . . . My life is complete."

He tilted his head and delivered a soft, sweet, full-of-promise kiss on her eager lips.

Lillian sat up, startled from sleep by a single thump on the wooden door. Was someone knocking? She blinked into the room. The flickering firelight cast dancing shadows on the walls and ceiling. Her senses alert, she listened, waiting for a second knock. But the only sounds that met her ears were the crackling fire and Eli's steady breathing.

With a sigh, she lay back down, snuggling her head on Eli's shoulder. His arm came around her, and she smiled. Even in sleep, he held her. She closed her eyes and—*thud! thud!*—the sound came again. This time Eli sat up, dislodging her. She propped herself on one elbow.

"Waut weascht 'et?" Eli looked around in confusion.

Before Lillian could reply that perhaps someone pounded at the door, a volley of thuds erupted outside. This could be no fists on wood, Lillian realized. Both she and Eli jumped from their bed. Eli's nightshirt flapped as he raced for the door. Henrik and Joseph staggered from the hallway, their eyes wide. Joseph crossed directly to Lillian.

"Ma, what is it?" His question mimicked Eli's, but she had no answer for him, either. She put her arm around his shoulder and looked at Eli, waiting for his leadership.

The thuds grew louder, reminding Lillian of the distant sound of hammers on nail heads when the villagers joined together to build a barn. Yet no village existed, and no barns were being built. Her sleep-foggy brain couldn't comprehend what else would make such a raucous noise.

Eli and Henrik stood in front of the door. Eli alternately reached for the crossbar and pulled back. Lillian had never seen him behave so indecisively, which increased her alarm. Adding to the frightful thuds came the cries of the animals. The oxen's low-pitched moos contrasted with the high screams of the horses; the chickens' persistent squawks filled the middle, creating a discordant trio of confusion and fear.

"Pa, do something!" Joseph, nearly as tall as Lillian, clung to her.

Henrik clenched his fists. "We must go out, see to the animals. Open the door."

And finally Eli opened it. The sound of fierce pounding multiplied with the loss of the protective barrier. Outside, white balls fell from the black sky, bounced against the hard ground, and scattered.

"Hoagelsteens . . ." Eli gasped the word.

Hailstones! Lillian rushed to the door. "The chickens! We must—"

Eli grabbed her and pulled her back. "No, Lillian! See how large the stones are? Bigger than goose eggs . . ." He shook his head, his fingers convulsing on her back. "A stone of that size could injure a man. We must stay inside."

"But—" A chunk of sod fell from the ceiling, cutting Lillian's argument short. The clump shattered, and a round, white hailstone rolled free. Joseph picked it up and held it out to his mother.

She looked at the damaged ceiling, her heart pounding. Would the ceiling collapse? She clasped her hands beneath her chin and silently begged for God's protection.

Standing in the doorway with cold wind tossing the tail of his nightshirt around his bare legs, Eli called out, "Dear God, please make it stop!"

For a few frightful seconds the onslaught continued, but then, mercifully, the hail began to abate. Gradually the storm calmed, until only a few stones thunked against the hail-scattered ground.

Even after the deluge stilled, Lillian's ears continued to ring. Eli remained in the open doorway, staring out into the night.

Lillian stepped past Eli and closed the door. Breathing heavily, as if she had run a long race, she leaned against the door and peered into her husband's pale face. He continued to stare straight ahead, a dazed look in his eyes. With his sagged features and slumped shoulders, it seemed that he had aged ten years in the past few minutes. Lillian swallowed a lump of worry and sorrow. "Eli?" She touched his arm. "Should you go check on the animals?"

"I will get dressed and go, too." Henrik whirled toward the hallway.

"And me!" Joseph trotted after Henrik.

"Nä!" Eli's stern tone brought both boys to a halt. They turned and looked at their stepfather. Eli waved his hands at them. "You stay with your mother. I will go."

The boys flanked Lillian while Eli pulled on his boots and put on his coat over his nightshirt. He strode out, the crunch of hailstones beneath his boots reaching their ears even with the door closed. It seemed hours passed while she and the boys waited, standing in a silent row, watching the door for Eli's return.

Finally, the string squeaked in the hole, and the crossbar rose. Lillian took one step forward away from her sons as the door opened and Eli entered the house. He closed the door behind him, and with slow, measured movements removed his coat and lay it across a trunk. Only then did he face his family.

Lillian wrung her hands together. "The animals?"

"The horses and oxen are nervous, but fine." He looked past Lillian to Joseph. "I am sorry, boy, but the chickens . . . they did not fare so well."

Joseph clamped his hand over his mouth, and Lillian quickly slipped her arm around his shoulders.

Henrik strode forward, his hands fisted. "What of the wheat?"

Eli closed his eyes and drew a long breath through his nose. When he opened his eyes, Lillian glimpsed pain coupled with peace—a combination she could not understand.

Eli placed his hand on Henrik's shoulder. "The wheat is gone."

30

Eli tightened his arm around Lillian. She lay with her cheek on his shoulder, her fingers toying with the buttons of his nightshirt. Despite the shattering loss of their crop, she didn't wail or complain. Yet he had seen fear in her eyes, and he sought words to appease her worry.

"It is only one crop." He forced a soft chuckle. "What is the loss of one crop in a man's lifetime? Nothing . . . an inconvenience." He flicked his fingers as if shooing away a pesky gnat and coiled a strand of her hair around his finger. The dark blond tresses resembled spun gold in the firelight.

Without shifting from her position, she asked, "Will you be able to salvage any seed to replant?"

"Nä." The thought brought a sharp stab of pain. The hours of careful choosing, of filling that sack with Jakob's help, flooded his memory. No bag of seed would ever be as special as that one he brought from Gnadenfeld. "But when the others come, they will bring more seed. We will buy some and plant again."

Lillian's thick lashes swept up and down, and her forehead

puckered. "Eli . . . will we have enough money to carry us until you harvest next year's crop?"

Despite himself, Eli smiled. That she was considering next year's crop told him she hadn't given up on the land. He kissed the top of her head before answering. "We will be all right. The Lord is good to put us in a place where we can hunt and fish, and glean nuts, berries, and roots from the land. We will not starve."

Suddenly, a remembrance twisted his heart. "I did want to build you a solid house before next winter." Even with the fireplace, the sod house remained damp and chilly. Lillian needed a warm, permanent home. "But lumber . . . that costs much money. It will have to wait." Her sigh stirred his beard. "But do not worry. The Lord has always provided. He will continue to do so."

She rose up, propping herself on one elbow to peer into his face. "Then you believe we will be all right?"

Eli cupped her cheek with his hand. Her skin, warm and silky, soothed him. "I believe God will not fail us. We will be all right."

For several seconds, she stared into his eyes, seeming to search for something. Then she gave him a gentle smile. "*Nä-jo,* I trust God . . . and you."

Mingled emotions—gratitude, love, protectiveness—fought for prominence, creating a huge knot in his throat. He drew her back to his shoulder. "Sleep now, Lillian."

She nestled, and he wrapped both arms around her. Contentedness enfolded him. Together, with God's help, he and his Lillian could weather anything.

Henrik startled awake, his body drenched in sweat. Images from a nightmare replayed in his mind: trying to plant wheat only to have the seeds stolen by birds or blown away by the wind. In his dream, he demanded nature leave the seeds alone—he had to grow wheat or he wouldn't be able to earn money for school—but the birds and wind laughed at him.

Now fully awake, he shivered beneath his quilts and stared at the sod ceiling of his little room. Anger—hot, fierce, all-consuming—made his heart pound just as the hailstones had pounded the wheat into the ground. Eli and his grand plans . . . what would happen now?

Joseph's soft snore rattled from the other side of the room. His brother would probably sleep until midmorning, given the late evening and nighttime excitement. That suited Henrik fine. He had some things to say to Eli, and it would be best if Joseph didn't hear.

He rolled from his bed, cringing as the dried grass crackled beneath him. Henrik shimmied into his clothes and then opened the trunk very slowly, holding his breath when the hinges complained. But Joseph slept on. Relieved, Henrik removed the two pairs of Father's trousers Ma had modified to fit him. He set them aside, then stacked a few shirts, a pair of long johns, and all of his socks on the bed. He closed the trunk lid with a soft thud, and Joseph snuffled, scrunching up his face.

Henrik stood perfectly still, holding his breath as he waited to see if Joseph would fully rouse. To his relief, his brother rolled to his side, pulling the quilt over his head. His snore resumed. Henrik tiptoed from the room, releasing his breath when he reached the hallway.

A faint glow cast by the dying coals guided him to the larger half of the sod house. He stepped into the main room, then immediately drew back. Ma and Eli, sound asleep, lay coiled together in the far corner on Ma's mattress. The sight brought a new rush of anger coupled with nausea. He clutched his stomach, breathing hard to gain control. Maybe he should just take his things and leave without a word.

But no! He needed money. Eli had promised him money for school, and he would have it. He didn't know where Eli kept the money pouch—he would have to ask for it. He puffed several breaths, gathering courage. Then he cleared his throat loudly.

A shuffling noise came from the main room.

Still in the hallway, Henrik called, "Eli?"

"Jo." Eli's voice sounded croaky. "Just a minute, boy."

Soft whispers and more shuffles sounded, and then Eli's voice again, stronger. "We are dressed. Come in, Henrik."

Henrik strode to the trunk where they ate their meals. The crumbled chunk of sod from the ceiling lay on the floor next to his stool. He toed the mess. The shattered lump reminded him of his crumbling dreams. Eli must make things right!

"You are up early," Ma said. "I thought you would sleep late on New Year's Day."

"I cannot sleep." Henrik avoided looking at Ma, focusing instead on Eli. The man ran a comb through his tousled hair, following the comb's path with his broad palm, unaware of Henrik's inner torment. "I need to speak to Eli."

"Nä-jo." Eli returned the comb to the little shelf pressed into the wall and crossed to the trunk. He sat on his stool and gestured to the spot across from him. "Sit down. Your mother will get some coffee brewing."

Ma began ladling water from the bucket into the coffeepot as if the man's every wish was her command—the same way she had always followed Father's instructions.

The lump of fury in Henrik's chest expanded. He remained standing. "I want the money you promised me."

Eli's complacent expression immediately tightened into a puzzled scowl. "What?"

"Mon-ey." Henrik drew out the word, his tone deliberately belligerent. "You promised me money for schooling. I want it now."

Eli flicked a quick glance at Ma, who stood beside the fireplace with a pile of grass logs in her arms. Then he faced Henrik again. "I promised you money from the harvest, *jo*. But, boy, you know . . . after last night . . . we will not have a harvest."

Henrik slammed his fist onto the trunk's top, and Ma jumped, dropping one log. He leaned toward Eli. "It is not my fault that there will be no harvest. I should not suffer because this land chose to destroy the crop rather than nurture it." He jerked upright, folding his arms over his chest. "You and I had an agreement. You said if I would put on a happy face and work hard, you would give me money to attend a university."

"*Jo*, I did, but—"

"I have fulfilled my part of the agreement. Now you fulfill yours. I want to go."

"And I want you to be able to go, too." Eli's unflappable attitude further stirred Henrik's ire. "But you must wait for a harvest."

"I will not wait another year to see a second crop fail!" Henrik hissed the words through clamped teeth, his temples throbbing with the intensity of his frustration. "I will not be stuck on this land, turning sod, cutting grass, and mucking out animal stalls for another season! You promised me money for school. Are you a man of your word or not?"

Everyone in the room froze with Henrik's challenge. For long seconds, Eli stared into Henrik's face, his expression stoic. Henrik waited, unblinking, his heart hammering. He heard Ma's rapid breathing, and a part of him wished to soften, to apologize, but fury held him in place.

Finally, Eli rose, pressing his hands against the trunk's top. "All right, Henrik. You want your money, I will get it."

"Eli?" Ma took one forward step. She shot a look of disapproval toward Henrik before turning back to her husband.

Eli shook his head, and Ma fell silent. He knelt and rolled the feather mattress aside. A flat circle of tin lay on the dirt floor. Eli lifted it, revealing the leather money pouch tucked into a hollow. He carried the pouch to the trunk and flopped it onto the top.

Straddling a stool, Eli untied the pouch's flap. "I said you would receive half of your father's portion." He removed a stack of bills and fanned them out. Propping his elbow on the trunk, he held the fan aloft. "Is that what you remember?"

Henrik nodded, staring at the paper money.

"All right, then." Eli began counting aloud, making four equal stacks on the trunk top. While he counted, Ma's face grew pale. Her gaze darted from Eli to Henrik and back again, but she didn't speak a word. Henrik, observing her from the corner of his eye, fought a rising tide of remorse. Should he leave Ma? Could he?

He steeled himself. Ma had Eli. She had no further need of his presence. Besides, he was grown, no longer a boy to be ordered about. He didn't want his livelihood forever tied to a successful wheat crop. It was time to pursue his own dreams.

Eli slapped the last bill onto the stack. "Your share comes to two hundred and eleven dollars." Leaning heavily on the trunk, he added, "Much less than what you would receive if you waited for a harvest."

Henrik clenched his jaw. "I will not wait for a harvest that may never come."

Eli clicked his tongue against his teeth. "Boy, where is your faith?"

Henrik snorted. "Faith . . . in what? This *land*? We know nothing of this country other than it grows tall grass and in one night hail can take everything away. You cannot promise there will be a harvest, but there will always be schools and a need for teachers. I want what is known rather than something hoped for." He held out his hand.

Without hesitation, Eli lifted one stack and placed it on Henrik's palm.

Henrik rolled the bills into a wad and pushed them into his pocket. A thank-you hovered on his lips, but rather than voicing it, he clamped his jaw shut. Without looking at Ma, he strode to the hallway and lifted a limp burlap bag. He shook it, and a dozen potatoes bounced on the floor, a reminder of last night's hailstones pounding the fledgling wheat. Leaving the potatoes scattered in the hallway, he headed to his room. It took only a few seconds to shove his clothing into the bag. As he tied the bag shut with a piece of leather string, his brother roused.

Rubbing his eyes, Joseph yawned. "What are you doing, Henrik?"

"Leaving." Henrik snatched up the bag and marched into the main room.

Joseph bounded past him, his nightshirt hiked up around his knees. "Ma! Henrik says he is leaving!"

Henrik removed his coat, hat, and scarf from the peg on the wall. As he did so, Ma stumbled forward and grasped Henrik's upper arm. "Son, please do not go!"

Henrik shrugged loose and shoved his arms into the sleeves of his coat, sidestepping away from her when she reached for him again. "I have to, Ma." She recoiled from his harsh tone as if he had slapped her. Guilt struck, but he resolutely refused to give it root. "How will I ever become a teacher if I stay here?"

"B-but where will you go?" He noticed her eyes shimmered with tears.

"To McPherson Town. I can buy a train ticket there." He jammed his hat on his head and wove the scarf around his neck. Bending over, he grabbed the tied end of the sack and flung it over his shoulder. "I will send—" But then he realized he couldn't send word. No mail service reached their land. How would he communicate with Ma and Joseph? For a moment, he wavered.

But then he glimpsed Eli standing tall and stern beside the trunk, and his resolve returned. Eli and his faith in God . . . the man was a fool. How could one trust in a God that pummeled their hard-won crop with hail rather than blanketing it in protective snow? God had not kept Henrik's people from hardship in Russia. God had not kept Father and Jakob safe. Why should they think God would grant them endless blessing in America? Henrik must take care of himself, and to do that he must be far away from this place.

He yanked open the door. "Good-bye, Ma."

"Henrik!" Lillian dashed toward the door. Strong hands gripped her upper arms, stopping her flight. She fought against Eli, grunting in frustration. "Let me go! I must go after my son!"

"Lillian, stop!"

Eli's stern command brought a momentary end to her struggle. But she held out her arms toward Henrik's departing form, anguish twisting her stomach and tightening her throat. "But I must bring him back!"

Eli spun her around, holding tight to her shoulders. "Let him go." He edged her back into the sod house and closed the door.

With a cry, she scrambled to open the door again, but his restraining arms prevented her from reaching it. She thrust her fists against his chest. "Let me go! He will get away! Let me go, Eli!"

"Lillian, Lillian . . ."

His soothing tone did nothing to calm her. Trapped within the circle of his arms—a place that had meant sanctuary and security in months past—she bucked to free herself. Eli lifted her and carried her to a trunk. He sat and held her in his lap. No matter how she tried, she couldn't escape his iron grasp.

After several minutes of frantic struggling, she collapsed against his chest. Only then did he relax his grasp. He lowered her to a stool and knelt beside her, his hands gently cupping the sides of her head. "Lillian, you cannot go after him. He—"

She clutched his shirt front. "Then *you* go. Take one of the horses. You can catch up to him. Bring him home to me, Eli. Please! Please bring him home to me."

"No."

"Why, Eli? Why?" Her throat was so knotted with emotion she could barely get the words out.

"He has made his choice. He wishes to be a man."

"But he is not a man! He is a boy—my son! And I want him here!" Pressing her fists to her quivering lips, she groaned. "Oh, how can you understand? You have never nurtured a child from infancy."

Eli jerked as abruptly as if she had stabbed him with a knife. But when he spoke, he retained his tender tone. "It would be pointless to drag him back. He would only resent the interference and leave again. We must let him go to make his way. To make his mistakes. In time, wisdom and maturity will bring him back again. But it must be his choice."

Lillian threw her arms outward, forcing his hands away from her head. Her hair caught on one of his fingers, but she welcomed the sharp pain. It took her attention away, be it ever briefly, from her aching heart. She stood, glaring down at his kneeling frame. "His choice! His choice?"

Clutching her hair, she paced the room. "What of my choices, Eli? I choose to have my remaining sons with me! I want them *here*, on this land, at my table, under my roof!" Hysteria raised her voice to a near screech. Joseph scuttled back into his half of the sod house as Lillian continued to rail. "Was it my choice to leave my beloved village of Gnadenfeld? Was it my choice to have my husband and my little boy tossed over the side of a ship like a bundle of garbage?"

Rushing forward, she grabbed Eli's shirt and yanked, drawing him to his feet. She shook his shirt and thumped her fists against his chest. "I cannot reclaim my home in Gnadenfeld. Reinhardt and Jakob cannot return from the dead. But you could bring Henrik back! Go get him, Eli!" She shoved him toward the door. "Bring me my son!"

But Eli remained in place, as if his boots had sent roots into the ground. His impassive expression, his hands hanging limply at his side, infuriated Lillian. How could he stand there like a lifeless scarecrow when her son wandered away into the cold?

"Eli!" She screeched his name. "Eli, please!"

And finally he moved. Very slowly, he shook his head from side to side. Sympathy glinted in his eyes, but his set jaw showed stubborn denial. "I will not go after Henrik, Lillian. He must find his own way. I will pray he returns to us, but he must *choose* to return."

She gaped at him in silent disbelief as he moved slowly to the hooks and took down his coat.

"I will see to the animals now." He nodded toward the fireplace. "Rebuild the fire. This room is cold." He stepped out the door.

Lillian stood for a moment, staring after him, her body so tense she couldn't move. Then her muscles dissolved. Incapable of holding her upright for another second, her legs buckled, and she crumpled onto the floor. With her face pressed into the cold dirt, she sobbed until she feared her lungs would collapse. But the tears—a means of release in the past—did nothing to remove the agony of betrayal.

31

Would Lillian mourn forever? Eli tossed a pitchforkful of hay to the horses as he pondered the thought. For three weeks he had been waiting for his sweet Lillian to return. He longed for the days when her face lit with pleasure and her arms opened with invitation each time he entered the room. Her persistent withdrawal cut worse than the bitter wind that coursed across the land, chilling Eli from the inside out.

He forked up a load for the oxen, and something in the hay caught his eye. He shook the hay loose and then reached into the dried strands to withdraw a faded, dry thistle bloom. He pinched the thistle head and the brown petals crumbled and fell away, leaving him holding an empty stem. He had carried thick clusters of these purple, cone-shaped flowers to Lillian. The thistle—once bursting with life but now dry and dead—painted an ugly picture of Lillian's heart.

The thistle would not blossom to life again. Would Lillian's love for Eli?

After hanging the pitchfork upside down on two nails pounded into the side of the barn, Eli pulled his collar around his chin and walked to the field. Now, well into January, snow had finally fallen. He looked across the endless, soft blanket of white that would have created a perfect protective cover for his wheat. He sighed, his breath hanging heavy in the frigid air.

So much work turning that sod, planting the seeds. So much anticipation, waiting for the seeds to sprout. So much celebration at the first growth. So much hope for a bountiful harvest. "Why, Lord, could You not have held back the hail? Our lives had melded together, Lillian's and mine. Those months as her husband . . . as her *true husband* . . . brought me more joy than anything. But the hail . . ." He swallowed the lump of bitterness that filled his throat. "It took everything from me. . . ."

As the words left his mouth, Eli experienced a twinge in his soul. He replayed his own statement until remorse sent him to his knees. "Oh, my Father *Gott*, please forgive me. The hail has not taken You from me. My joy . . . my greatest joy . . . is in my salvation. I can never lose Your love. Thank You for the reminder." The wind whisked by, carrying crystallized snowflakes that stung Eli's cheeks, but he remained in his bowed-low position, praying, until the wet soaked through his pants and his limbs turned stiff.

He rose, brushed the crust of packed snow from his knees, and turned toward the sod house. A tiny trail of white smoke rose from the chimney, spiraling against a pale blue sky. The dark sod stood out against the carpet of white like a welcoming beacon, and his heart twisted as he considered the lack of welcome waiting within the thick walls.

The joined houses once held peace and contentment, but now tension and anger encased the cramped space. Even Joseph suffered. How many times had Eli awakened, stretched out on Henrik's bed, and heard the boy crying softly into his pillow? As often as the sound of Lillian's nighttime weeping had carried to his ears. Too many times.

He set his feet in motion, plodding slowly across the soft snow. Somehow they must repair all that had been broken between them. But how? Lillian would hardly look at Eli, let alone speak to him. And without communication, there could be no reconciliation. His foot scuffed on something hard, nearly tripping him. He stopped and looked down. His boot had encountered a stone the size of a loaf of bread.

Blowing out a breath of annoyance, Eli crouched down and tried to pry the stone from the hard ground. In his plowing, he had discovered that the land was littered with large stones. The troublesome rocks worked their way to the surface, dulling or even chipping a plow's blade.

He almost fell on his backside when the stone came loose, but he caught his balance and rose, lifting the rock with him. He carried it to the nearest of the four piles of fieldstones that stood around the plowed field. The largest pile measured almost as high as Eli's head and was as big around as the small sod house. Underhanded, he heaved the rock toward the top of the pile, watching it hit and then tumble until it caught between several others halfway down the miniature mountain. Whisking his hands together, he started to turn away, but then he spun to face the rock pile.

An idea formed rapidly, his heart beating against his ribs. He had promised Lillian a house—a sturdy house with many rooms. Without a harvest, he couldn't buy wood for such an undertaking, but what if he built a house of rock? Hadn't he told Lillian that God provided all they needed on this land? Their need for food had been met. Now he saw how a shelter—a permanent shelter—could be constructed from resources available right here on this land.

It would take many rocks and much work to build a house, but what else did he have to do until the others came and he purchased seed for a crop? Yes, he would build a house for Lillian. He would keep his promise, even if he did not move into it with her.

Sorrow wrenched his heart as he considered remaining estranged for the rest of his life from the woman he loved. Could he stay on this land, living separately, now that he knew the ecstasy of being her beloved?

"I promised to care for Lillian." He spoke aloud, his voice echoing across the rolling prairie. "We are bound to one another, and I will see to her needs, even if . . ." Resolve lit a fire in his soul. Balling his hands into fists, he raised his face to the sky and vowed, "Even if she never accepts me again, I will fulfill my obligations to her, Father. I will love her unconditionally, just as You have always loved me."

His arms pumping, he headed for the house to fetch Joseph. He could use the boy's help.

Lillian sat in front of the fireplace, angling the fabric and needle toward the blaze to catch the light. Her stitches, usually straight and perfectly balanced, appeared jagged and uneven. With a huff of displeasure, she crumpled the patchwork quilt in her lap. How could she do anything correctly in this dark, shadowy hole?

She closed her eyes, battling an attack of tears. Oh, how she wished for sunshine pouring through windows, painting a yellow path across the floor! The sod house, with its solid walls and tightly closed door, felt like an animal burrow. How had she lived for so many months in this dirt hovel without losing her mind? Surely living in constant shadow contributed to the state of despondency she now experienced.

Setting the unfinished quilt aside, she crossed to the door and cracked it open. Cold air whisked inside, making the fire dance. She hugged herself and peered out through the narrow opening, basking in the thin band of sunlight, even though it carried little warmth.

Her gaze roved the snow-covered ground, noticing the trails of boot prints—the larger ones left by Eli's feet and the smaller ones, Joseph's. One set remained conspicuously missing: Henrik's.

A knot of anger clogged her throat, and she slammed the door. She stomped to the discarded quilt and snatched it up, crushing it to her aching chest. If only she could hold her absent sons the way she held this quilt, her heart would be soothed.

Sinking onto the stool beside the fire, she smoothed the quilt across her knees. She touched each patch in turn with her fingertips, her lips trembling as she battled another wave of tears. This quilt—her remembrance quilt—had been formed from Jakob's little shirts and those Henrik had left behind. As she'd cut into the clothing, turning finished items into squares, she had wept, feeling as though she cut into her own soul. But putting the squares together, arranging the plaids and solid colors into a pleasing design, had brought a small measure of comfort.

When she finished this quilt, she could wrap herself in memories of her sons. The thought sent her hands scurrying to retrieve the needle and resume stitching. She longed for the comfort the quilt would bring. Nothing else provided comfort. Not Eli. And not God.

Anger—a too-familiar companion—once more assailed her. Eli should have gone after Henrik. He should not have given Henrik money and sent him out into the cold. How could she trust a man who cared so little for her feelings? All of the intimate moments they had shared now tortured her. She wove the needle in and out, in and out, while her thoughts continued to tumble.

Where was Henrik now? The not knowing nearly drove her mad. Was he warm? Well fed? Ill or mistreated? Her hands trembled, skipping a stitch as the unknowns ate at her insides. Every day in his morning prayers, Eli asked God to keep Henrik safe and guide his footsteps. She would have no peace until Henrik's footsteps led him back to her—and she would hold herself aloof from Eli—and God—until Henrik was safe in her arms again.

Lillian sat bolt upright as crunching footsteps approached. Her hand pressed to her chest as the door swung open. But Joseph, not Henrik, entered the room.

Joseph stepped just inside the sod house. He rubbed his mittened hands together while globs of snow dropped from his boots. In the past, Lillian would have teasingly scolded him to remove his boots and come to the fire. But, too weary to speak, she simply sent him an unsmiling look.

"Pa says to tell you we will not be in for lunch. He is hitching up the oxen, and we are taking the wagon down-creek for more rocks."

The lack of enthusiasm in Joseph's voice sent a twinge through Lillian's middle. Her cheery, energetic son—the one who'd blossomed on American soil—had retreated into the quiet boy of Gnadenfeld again. And she had no more means of restoring him than she had of returning Jakob to life or bringing Henrik home.

"Do you want some bread and butter, then, to take with you?"

He gave her a hesitant nod. Slowly, feeling like a creaky old woman, Lillian set the quilt aside and retrieved a loaf from the crock in the corner. She broke it in half, slathered the exposed middle with butter, and wrapped the pieces in a length of toweling. With a sigh, she placed the bundle into Joseph's waiting hands. "*Nä-jo*, tell Eli I will keep a soup pot warm for when you are ready for something more."

The boy slipped back out without a word. She shook her head. So this is what she and Eli had resorted to: using Joseph as a go-between. Remembering the days when Eli would have found any excuse to return to the sod house, when he would kiss her lips or nuzzle her neck and whisper in her ear, a spiral of longing tried to overpower her. But she pushed it away.

That part of their kinship was dead. Thinking of what used to be only increased her dissatisfaction with the now. Determinedly, she returned to the quilt. She must stay busy with something concrete, useful, mindless. . . . When she finished this quilt, she intended to make a similar one for Joseph out of Reinhardt's shirts. The boy continued to call Eli "Pa," stinging Lillian's soul with every usage. Eli had made a mockery of the name. A true pa would have fathered Henrik, too. Reinhardt would not have given Henrik a fistful of cash and sent him alone into an unknown world. Reinhardt had always protected his sons, kept them close and safe. But Eli . . .

The needle jabbed her finger. She gasped, jerking her hand from beneath the folds of fabric. A bubble of blood rose from the tiny wound. She sucked on her throbbing finger, and the pain abated. If only the gaping hole in her heart could be so easily repaired.

With a huff of annoyance, she rolled the quilt into a ball and carried it to Reinhardt's trunk. When she lifted the lid, her gaze fell upon the black leather Bible. Another wave of longing nearly drove her to her knees. Her comfort in God's presence had slipped away the day Eli sent Henrik from their sod house.

Tears flooded her eyes. She closed the trunk and sank onto its lid, pressing both palms to the trunk's sturdy surface, envisioning the book trapped inside. Her heart begged her to pray—to call out for God's arms to draw her close and whisper peace into her soul. But her heart, withered and sore, couldn't find the means to open.

God had taken Reinhardt and Jakob home to Him long before she was ready to bid them farewell. He had given her a taste of security here on the prairie with Eli and her remaining sons but then callously snatched that away, too. Knowing all she had lost,

God should have prevented Henrik from leaving. He should have prompted Eli to keep Henrik close.

Shaking her head, she acknowledged the truth. She would be denied peace as long as she was denied the presence of her oldest son.

"Pa?" Joseph grunted the name as he heaved a rock into the back of the wagon.

Eli paused in prying loose a gray stone from the hard soil. "*Jo*, son?"

"Do you think Ma will like the new house?"

The hopeful note in Joseph's voice pierced Eli. Could Lillian not see the harm she inflicted on Joseph with her continued withdrawal? Was Henrik the only important one now?

He forced a smile to his face. "For sure your mother will appreciate having a big kitchen, and separate rooms for sleeping and sitting. This rock house will be fine house, and every time she looks at it, she will remember how hard you worked to build it for her."

"You work hard, too." The boy sounded defensive.

Eli's heart turned over. It would be easy for Joseph to pull away from Eli to show loyalty to his mother, but he had not forsaken the one he called Pa. Although Eli disliked that Joseph was forced to choose sides, he couldn't help but rejoice in the continued closeness he and his stepson shared. He considered it a precious gift, and he would not treat it lightly.

"*Jo*, we work together. You are a fine worker, and you make both your mother and me proud." A crooked grin tipped up Joseph's chapped lips. Eli jerked the shovel's blade, popping the stone loose. "Come now—get this one and put it in the wagon."

Joseph obediently lifted the stone, grunting with the effort. He walked straddle-legged and hefted the rock over the side of the wagon. Slapping his hands against his thighs, he said, "How many more stones do we need, Pa?"

Eli scratched his chin. They had used all of those from his four rock piles to lay the foundation and build the first layers of the walls. It pleased him to walk the circumference, to envision doorways and windows and rooms inside. Had he not chosen to make the house so large, the walls would already be higher. But he had promised Lillian a big house, and he would build her a big house.

"We will need many, many stones, Joseph," he answered, "but this land has plenty. We will keep collecting until the walls are as high as my arms held over my head. Then we will know we are done."

Joseph followed Eli, placing his feet into the larger tracks left in the thin coating of snow. "When you finish the outside, will you use stones to build Ma's *Spoaheat*?"

Eli scanned the ground, searching for stones as he considered Joseph's question. In Gnadenfeld, the cooking hearth had been constructed of Mennonite-fired mud bricks. Lillian missed her little thatched house in the village; a familiar kitchen would please her.

"We will fire bricks for the stove and oven." He flashed a smile over his shoulder. "And the *Meagrope.* Your mother wants to raise pigs, so she will need a lard cauldron, too."

Joseph nodded, his face brightening. Then he stopped suddenly. "Then . . ."

Eli came to a stop, too, and turned to face the boy. *"Jo?"*

"Then you will not . . ." Joseph's chin quivered; he blinked in quick succession.

Concerned, Eli placed his hand on the boy's shoulder. "What is bothering you, boy? Tell me. Do not be afraid."

Joseph swallowed, peering into Eli's face with a pained expression. "You will not give up? You will keep . . . loving Ma? Until she loves you back again?"

With a strangled gulp, Eli pulled Joseph into his arms. The boy clung, burrowing his face into Eli's jacket front. *Oh, Lord, please work Your miracle in Lillian's aching heart. Let what is broken be restored. . . .* Pressing his chin to Joseph's cap, Eli made a promise. "I will not give up, boy. I will love your mother forever." *Even if she never loves me back again.*

32

Through snow, rain, sunshine, and shadow, Eli worked on the house, with Joseph beside him. Winter faded into a spring so rife with scents that Eli sometimes felt almost drunk from breathing in the aromas. Musky soil, tangy grass, sweet moisture—a potpourri designed to thrill a farmer's soul. This was a good land—he refused to think otherwise.

The house, constructed with an assortment of brown, tan, and gray rocks, reminded Eli of the patchwork quilts Lillian worked to complete. But unlike a quilt, which eventually became tattered and worn, this house would endure for centuries. Just as his love for Lillian would endure.

He heaved a stone to chest level and rolled it into position, pressing it firmly into the thick slab of mud and clay mortar. Joseph stood to the side, his lips sucked in as he held his breath. Eli held the rock and counted silently to ten before stepping away from the wall. The rock held.

Joseph let out his air in a mighty whoosh, then grinned at Eli. "I always worry it will fall on your head, like that sod did on Henrik when we built the fireplace."

Eli smiled, remembering. That had been a good day. "One of these rocks would do more harm than a lump of dirt, I can tell you." He pointed to the waiting pile of rocks. "Hand me another stone—a *lenkjlijch* one."

Joseph sorted through the pile and selected an oblong stone. He thumped it into Eli's waiting hands with a light laugh. "It looks like a gray watermelon!"

Eli chuckled in response. "*Jo*, but I would not suggest trying to bite into it. You would break your teeth." He added the rock to the wall.

Joseph laughed appreciatively. The sound of the boy's laughter, accompanied by the whisper of wind and the song of birds, brought a lift to Eli's heart.

"We need to clear ground for a watermelon patch," Joseph commented. Eli hid a smile when the boy tucked his hands into his pockets and rocked on his heels—just the way Eli often did. "Soon it will be planting time. Can we ready the ground Saturday?"

"I thought you wanted to go fishing on Saturday."

Eli and Joseph had developed a routine of hunting or fishing on Saturdays. The time together had bonded them as securely as two rocks joined with mortar.

"The creek will still be there next week." Joseph begged with his eyes. "We need watermelons so when Henrik comes back, we can have one for his birthday."

Rarely did Joseph mention Henrik's name, but often Eli saw the boy staring into the distance. He knew Joseph missed both his brothers. Eli chose another stone while Joseph went on pensively. "Where do you think Henrik lives now?"

"I do not know, son." He pushed the words past gritted teeth, speaking while lifting the thirty-pound rock. A grinding *thunk* sounded as the rock found its position, and Eli stepped back, rubbing his shoulder. "He wants to attend a university, so maybe he went all the way back to New York."

How long would two hundred dollars last in a big city like New York? Had Henrik learned enough English to communicate? He didn't like to think of the boy being cheated. Many unscrupulous people lived in the world, and they wouldn't hesitate to take advantage of a young Mennonite boy from a faraway country. But Eli didn't mention those concerns to Joseph. "Wherever he is, you can be sure he is saving his money for school. Being a teacher, that is important to him."

Joseph pushed his foot against a rock, his head low. "Wish he would come back, though."

Eli didn't need to ask why Joseph wanted his brother to return. Lillian's continuing despondence created a bigger chasm between mother and son each day. He and Joseph had begun praying together for Lillian, and Joseph's heartfelt petitions for his ma's happiness brought tears to Eli's eyes. When would God answer the prayers of this young, faithful servant?

"He will return." Eli spoke with confidence, praying his statement would prove true. "He loves you and your mother, and he will want to show you the certificate he receives from the university so you can be proud of him."

Joseph nodded slowly, his expression apprehensive. "If he waits until he has a certificate, it might be years before he comes back." Suddenly, he squared his shoulders, his chest puffing. "I will be grown by then—as tall as him, probably, but stronger."

Eli laughed. "Stronger?"

"Jo." Joseph hefted a large rock. His face reddened and the tendons in his neck stood out like cords. Eli quickly took the stone, and Joseph flexed his arms. "I carry stones, and Henrik carries books. I will be stronger."

With another laugh, Eli turned toward the house. "You are

probably right. Now mix some more mortar. We are ready to put another row on the north wall."

They continued building, one stone at a time, all morning and into the afternoon. The early-March sun beat down, warming them, and they removed their jackets. Midway through the afternoon, a movement caught Eli's eye, and he looked to see Lillian walking toward them. A bucket hung from her hand.

His mind skipped backward to the days when he, Henrik, and Joseph had cleared the land to receive seeds. Lillian had walked across the grass to bring them a drink of water. But in all of their weeks of house building, she had never come near the growing stone structure. To see her coming now sent quivers of anticipation through Eli's body.

"Ma?" Surprise underscored Joseph's brief query. "Did you come to see the house?"

Lillian set the bucket on the ground and stood upright, pulling her shawl back into position. "I brought you a drink. And I need to speak with Eli."

Eli's heart leapt. Not since the day Henrik had left had she initiated a conversation. Surely, despite her sober face, this was a good sign. "For sure we can talk." He gestured toward the half-built stone house. "Come inside, and I will show you the house while we talk."

For a moment, he thought she would refuse. Her lips puckered, a sharp V forming between her eyes, but then she nodded and moved stiltedly through the opening that would eventually frame the front door.

Eli, hands trembling with excitement, followed. "See, Lillian? This will be the sitting room, and over here"—he trotted to the opposite side of the wide space—"the kitchen. Your *Spoaheat* will go right here in the corner so the flue can send smoke through the attic to smoke your hams."

He waited for an answering smile, but she remained somber. His spirits dampened somewhat, he continued, "Back here"—he walked to the far corner and held out his arms—"this will be the main sleeping room, with a stairway over there leading to the loft. Then this space will be a dining room." Envisioning it, Eli's enthusiasm soared again. "When the others arrive, and our furniture builders set up shop, we can buy a good Mennonite-made table and chairs, and there will be room to host gatherings for Sunday *faspa* or—"

"Eli." Her sharp tone brought an end to his explanations. She caught the tails of her shawl and folded them in an X across her body. "We must talk."

"All right." He crossed his arms over his chest, chilled now that he stood still in the shadow cast by the shoulder-high wall.

She took a few small steps closer and glanced over her shoulder. "Will Joseph hear?"

Eli leaned to glance out the door. "I will send him to the sod house, if you prefer."

"Please."

He stepped past her, giving a wide berth, and stuck his head out the door opening. "Son, will you take the bucket back for your mother? Refill it at the well, and then go into the sod house and eat a snack—some bread or dried venison. You have earned a rest."

"Sure, Pa."

Eli turned. "He is going."

She nodded. For a few moments she stood silently, worrying her lower lip between her teeth. He waited patiently, his palms sweating. Finally, she released a heavy sigh.

"Remember when you said you planned to have the minister dissolve our marriage?"

Eli jolted, the comment catching him off guard. The conversation had been so long ago, and so much had transpired in the intervening months, he had forgotten the intention. But he nodded. "*Jo* . . . I remember."

"I would like you to speak to the minister when the others arrive—make arrangements for the dissolution of our union."

Eli licked his lips, his temples throbbing. "Lillian . . ." He cleared his throat, staring at the spot of ground between his boot toes. "That . . . that is no longer possible."

"Why not?"

The confrontational words brought his head up. Heat built in his neck and ears. Could she be so naïve? "We have . . . have lain together."

Color rose in her cheeks, and she turned her face away. Her throat convulsed.

"Why do you want this now, Lillian?" Pain laced his voice, and he made no effort to hide it. She needed to understand how her behavior inflicted hurt.

"We cannot go on like this." The words, strained and hoarse, barely reached his ears. "I cannot live with you now that I know . . ."

Although part of him feared the answer, the greatest part needed the truth. He stepped forward, stretching one hand toward her. "Know . . . what?"

She swallowed and met his gaze. Her wide blue eyes expressed disappointment, disillusionment, despair. "Our love was a farce."

Memories tumbled through Eli's mind—moments of sweet intimacy, moments of awakening. A farce? A pretense? He hadn't pretended. Every word, every touch, every emotion had been genuine and cherished. Until now.

"How can you say such a thing?" Anger lowered his voice to a growl. "How can you sully the memory of our lovemaking?"

"Do not speak to me of lovemaking!" She matched him in tone and volume. "Our bodies were joined—yes. But our souls?

I thought they were . . ." For a moment her voice faltered, but then she set her jaw and continued in a steely tone. "But I was wrong. Very wrong. And I will not continue in this make-believe marriage!"

She spun to leave, but Eli tromped forward and grabbed her arm. "*Nä*, Lillian! You tell me why you call our marriage make-believe." When she clamped her lips together, he shook her slightly. "Tell me!"

"All right!" She wrenched free and faced him, her body tense and her chin high. "You professed to love me. You promised to meet my needs. But my greatest need—to have my remaining children close to me—you . . . you tossed aside as if it were nothing of importance. Although I begged you not to, you sent Henrik away.

"Now you build this big house." She threw her arms wide, her disparaging gaze bouncing off each wall in turn. "But for what purpose? The family that could have resided here is no more. The family crumbled, Eli, the day my son walked away in the snow. And if there is no family, then there is no marriage. I . . . want . . . out."

The spiteful words hung in the air. They stood, facing each other across an empty expanse. Tears glittered in her eyes, but they didn't fall. Eli's chest felt as though it would collapse, so great his hurt and frustration. *Lord, how could we have shared so much and now be so far apart?* If only he didn't love her . . . But he couldn't do what she asked. To request a dissolution, he would have to lie to the minister. And he would not lie.

He took several deep, slow breaths. His next words shouldn't be spewed in anger. "Lillian, if you want out of this union, then we will have to seek a divorce."

Her face went pale. The ugly word, rarely spoken by Mennonites, loomed like a black cloud.

He gave her no time to respond but continued in an even tone. "If that is what you want, when the others arrive, we will go into McPherson Town and inquire about ending our marriage. Are . . . are you sure?"

Tears trembled on her lower lashes, and she swished them away with her fingertips in quick, impatient movements. "I cannot continue as we are. It is too . . . hard."

Eli agreed. But the thought of divorce tore his heart in two. She started to leave, but once again he caught her arm. He held her gently, aware of her tense muscles. "Lillian, will you consider something?"

She stared into his face, her eyes large and distrustful. Her chin raised in a slight nod.

"Sometimes the things that wound us the most deeply are channels to great blessing." He spoke firmly, addressing himself as much as her. "God is not a wasteful God. He can use everything—even our heartaches—for good if we allow Him to work."

Lillian withdrew her arm from his grasp, stepping sideways. "I want to believe you, Eli. I want to think that maybe some great blessing will come from this time of pain and disappointment. But to believe you would be to trust you. And I can no longer trust you any more than I can trust God. You . . . and God . . . have betrayed my trust."

"Lillian—"

"*Nä*! No more talk." She took two backward steps and paused. Framed by the doorway with sunlight dancing on her hair, she gave the appearance of an angel standing at the gate of heaven. She glanced around the room, and a rueful chuckle left her lips. "Build your house, Eli. Keep that promise." A tear trailed down her cheek. "But do not expect it to be enough to make up for the promises that have been broken."

33

The first day of April, Eli and Joseph planted the seeds saved from Henrik's birthday watermelon. Eli listened to Joseph's cheerful humming while they worked, bending over to poke a seed into the ground, tamping the soil with their feet, then taking two large forward steps and repeating the process. But despite the sunny day and Joseph's obvious good mood, Eli battled melancholy.

When these seeds sprouted, Lillian and Joseph wouldn't be here to celebrate the first white flowers or anticipate picking the first ripe, juicy melon. Was it fair to let the boy go blithely on, unaware of the changes that would soon be thrust upon him?

Lillian's demand for a divorce haunted Eli. Despite his frequent attempts to change her mind, she remained firm. When the others came, she would take the boy and what was left of Reinhardt's money and move to the village, leaving Eli the homestead. So he would again be alone. He almost wished he'd never been given this brief time of family life. When Lillian and Joseph left, the loneliness might destroy him.

Joseph stood and peeked over his shoulder. He rolled his eyes and grinned. "Will I plant the whole patch myself? Hurry, Pa, so we can go fishing before suppertime."

Eli chuckled and waved his hand. He removed a seed from his pocket and knelt to push it into the cool, moist soil. But then he remained hunkered low, his thoughts once more holding him captive. After a moment or two, a shadow fell across his knees. He looked into Joseph's teasing face.

The boy propped his fists on his hips and shook his head. "You are no help at all. What is wrong?" The teasing look drifted away, and his face pinched with worry. "Are you sick?"

Sick at heart. But Eli kept the words to himself. It was spring already. The others would surely arrive soon. Joseph needed to know that more changes awaited him. As much as it pained Eli to share the news, he knew Lillian wouldn't do so. So he must.

Rising, he clamped his hand over Joseph's shoulder and led him to the edge of the cleared patch. "Come here, boy. Let us talk."

Joseph squinted upward. "About what?"

Eli sat and waited for Joseph to sink down beside him. He plucked a green blade of new grass and examined it rather than looking at Joseph. "About your mother and me . . ." He forced a soft chuckle. "We have not been getting along so well. Not since . . ."

"Since Henrik left?" Joseph provided the words Eli was reluctant to voice.

Eli tossed the blade of grass aside and faced the boy. "*Jo.* Your mother is no longer happy here . . . and so we have made a decision." Although the decision was Lillian's, Eli believed it was best not to throw all of the blame at her feet.

Joseph waited quietly, his dark eyes unblinking and his face innocent.

"When the others come, and our village is built, she wants to move to the village instead of living here on the homestead."

Joseph frowned. "We will leave the farm?"

"*Nä*, boy. Not all of us. Only you and your mother."

The boy drew back, his eyes round. "Without you? But—but you and Ma are married! Married people live together!"

Eli nodded, his heart pounding hard enough to bruise his insides. "*Jo*, married people most often stay together, but sometimes they divorce. This is what will happen with your mother and me."

"Nä!" The word exploded from the boy. Joseph jumped to his feet and glared at Eli. "Divorce is against the Bible! I heard the preacher say so!"

Eli rose and curled his hand around the back of Joseph's neck. "I know this is hard, boy, but your mother . . ." Could he form the words without breaking down himself? It would do Joseph no good to see his stepfather cry like a child. He sucked in a fortifying breath and finished. "Your mother deserves to be happy, Joseph. If she cannot find happiness here with me, then it is best to—"

"*Nä,* Pa." Tears rolled down Joseph's cheeks. "It is not best. Not for me." He swiped his face with his sleeve. "I want to stay here, on the farm. We built that house. I want to live in it. You said we would get more chickens and a piglet. I want to help raise the piglet." His tone grew in belligerence. "Ma can go if she wants to, but I will stay with you."

"Joseph . . ." Eli thought his chest might split in two, so great was his pain.

The boy jerked loose. "Ma is not happy with you—that is why you are going to let her leave you. Well, she is not happy with me, either. All she wants is Henrik and Jakob, not me. So she can move to the village by herself! I will not go with her!" He spun and took off running.

"Joseph!"

The boy didn't slow. Stumbling, his sobs carrying on the wind, Joseph disappeared over the gentle rise that led to the creek. Eli started after him, but a soft whimper from behind him held him in place. He turned toward the sound. Lillian stood in the doorway of the large half of the sod house. Her pale face told him she had heard Joseph's outburst.

He stared into her stricken eyes, searching his heart for words of comfort. But none came. She had created this heartache; she would have to bear the burden of it.

He cleared his throat. "Do not worry. I will bring him back."

She pressed her fingers to her trembling lips and offered a short nod.

Eli turned away from his wife and strode after his son.

"Dear Lord, what have I done? Oh, what have I done?" The moan crawled from her tortured soul. What kind of mother allowed her child to believe she had no use for him?

On legs so unsteady they might have been carved from wood, Lillian stumbled across the newly sprouting grass to the rock house. Not since the day she had told Eli she wanted a divorce had she come near the structure. Although no windows or doors filled the openings, a thatched roof, similar to the roofs of houses in Gnadenfeld, topped the tall, sturdy dwelling. A chimney of the same varied, colorful stones that formed the walls rose from the center of the house to point proudly skyward. It was a beautiful house—big, like Eli had promised.

Other Eli-promises rolled through her mind—vows to protect her, provide for her, cherish her. . . . She looked across the property at the cropped grass, the well, the barn and animal pens, the sod house, and the turned soil of the wheat field. Everything he did, he did to create a comfortable home for her. Evidence of his provision greeted her from every direction.

"But he did not cherish me. He did not cherish my son. He dishonored my wishes and sent Henrik away." She spoke the insolent words aloud, but as she heard her own voice she was stricken with guilt. In typical Eli fashion, he had gone beyond the vows made to her and loved her boys as if they were his own. Yes, he had let Henrik go, but he hadn't driven Henrik away. Not like she had driven Joseph away with her sullen withdrawal.

She stood in the middle of the area Eli had claimed would serve as the sitting room. Sunlight streamed through a window opening, bathing her in light and warmth. Standing in the splash of sunshine, she allowed tears to fall. Hot tears, choking tears. Outside the windows, spring had arrived, bringing with it shoots of green grass and tiny unfurling leaves on bushes and scrubby trees. New life blossomed around her . . . but she felt dead inside. As empty as this carefully built rock house.

She had blamed God for taking Jakob and Henrik from her. But she couldn't hold God accountable for the loss of Joseph. She alone bore the responsibility for his loss. Nearly blinded by tears, she stumbled from the house. Aimlessly she crossed the grass and found herself in the middle of the empty wheat field.

All around her, brown, withered scraps replaced what should have been waist-high wheat. In her heart, a hollow ache replaced the feeling of joy and completeness she'd once known. She sank to her knees and buried her hands in the dry wisps while tears flowed.

"Dear God," she sobbed, her shoulders heaving, "I need a *gnadenfeld*—a field of grace. Your Word proclaims that Your grace is sufficient, that Your strength is made perfect in weakness." Lifting her face to the sky, she admitted, "I am weak,

God. There is no strength left in me. No strength to give Joseph what he needs; no strength to forgive Eli for letting Henrik go; no strength to crawl into Your arms of comfort. Fill me with Your strength, God. Give me grace. Please, bloom in me a field of grace."

She remained with hands and knees pressed into the Kansas soil, her head hanging low and tears flowing until she felt completely drained. When her tears ran dry, she cleaned her face with her apron and staggered to her feet. As she turned toward the sod house, she spotted Eli and Joseph cresting the rise from the creek. They froze in place for a moment, both looking toward her. Stiffly held shoulders and solemn faces evidenced the torment she had inflicted. Why had it taken her so long to recognize she wasn't the only one hurting?

Oh, to return to the days when Joseph came running to her, bubbling about an animal he had startled, a fish he had caught, or some other boyish joy. Her heart pined for Eli's soft, adoring gaze that prefaced sweet, tender touches. For several seconds they stared across the ground at one another, and then Joseph shifted his head to look up at Eli. Eli's arm rose to curve over Joseph's shoulders, and the two of them headed toward the garden.

Lillian remained rooted in place, watching them bend to work in the section of ground cleared for a watermelon patch. A lump of desire so great it threatened to choke her rose from her chest. New tears stung her already sore eyes. She had told Eli that a family no longer existed on this land, but she was wrong. Eli and Joseph were most certainly a family. But after her self-inflicted seclusion, would they allow her to be a part of it again?

Saturday morning Lillian rose early and mixed a batch of *pankuake* batter. Joseph particularly enjoyed the pancakes sprinkled with sugar or smothered in peach jam. Without eggs, she used saleratus to keep the cakes from being flat. After so many other accommodations to recipes, she didn't even blink when stirring in the crumbly white powder instead of beaten eggs.

The aroma of frying pancakes brought both Joseph and Eli from the smaller half of the house. She offered a shy smile as they entered the room, her heart catching when neither returned it. But she reminded herself it had taken weeks to build this barrier between them; it might take weeks to break it down. Her prayers, which had lasted long into the night, had given her the strength to try. She trusted that God would continue to give her grace to repair the damage she had done so she wouldn't lose yet another son.

"Here you are." She forked a steaming cake onto each of their plates. "Say your prayers and eat them while they are hot. I will make more." She turned back to the skillet in the fireplace, leaving them to eat in peace.

The soft clink of forks against tin plates and the mumble of voices was like music to Lillian's ears as she fried the remaining batter and watched the cakes disappear. Joseph reached to slide the last pancake onto his plate, but he paused with his fork in the browned cake. "Oh. You have not eaten."

Lillian whisked her fingers through the hair behind his ear. After months of holding herself aloof, the simple touch sent tremors through her frame. Her arms ached to pull him into a hug, but she sensed he would resist her. "It is all right, son. Go ahead if you want it. I am not hungry."

But instead of taking the cake, Joseph shook it from his fork. *"Nä."* He dropped his fork onto his plate and sent her a wary look. "I know what you are doing. You are trying to trick me. It will not work." He rose from his stool and took a step away from her. "I am not leaving this land. I am staying here with Pa."

"Joseph." Reproof laced Eli's tone.

Lillian swallowed the hot tears that filled her throat. Her lips trembled, but she forced them into a smile. "That is fine, son. I will not make you leave if . . . if you want to stay." She glanced at Eli, noting his puzzled scowl. Turning back to Joseph, she added, "And I did not make *pankuake* to trick you, but to say I am sorry. I know I have been . . . difficult."

Joseph stared at her in sullen silence.

She rushed on. "Not knowing where Henrik is or how he fares is very . . ." Her throat tightened, and she swallowed again before continuing. "Very hard for me. But I should not have let my worry about Henrik push you away. I am sorry, Joseph. Will you forgive me?"

For long seconds Joseph stood, peering into her face as if trying to decide if she was sincere. She held her breath, awaiting condemnation or absolution. When she thought she might collapse from the tension, he finally gave a miniscule nod.

"I forgive you, Ma."

Her breath whooshed out. "*Dank*, Joseph."

"But I still want to stay here, with Pa."

Father, give me grace . . . Although her son's words pierced her, she drew her shoulders back and met his gaze. "*Nä-jo*, Joseph, I understand. Your . . . pa"—she flicked a look at Eli to find him eying her guardedly—"and I will discuss this." Unable to resist, she tweaked the curl behind his ear again. "All right?"

Joseph sighed, but he didn't step away from her touch. "All right." Then he whirled toward Eli. "Pa, are we going to McPherson Town today for the chickens and piglets?"

Eli rose slowly, as if unfolding his body. His gaze brushed across Lillian, his eyebrows low, but his expression cleared when he turned to Joseph. "That calf is big enough to be sold, so *jo*, we will go try to make our trade today."

"Is . . . is Ma coming, too?"

Lillian couldn't decide if Joseph was expectant or reluctant. Before Eli could answer, Lillian said, "I have my own work today, Joseph. You men go ahead." She began stacking the dirty dishes.

Joseph snatched his jacket from the peg by the door. "Hurry, Pa."

Eli stepped away from the table. "I am coming, son." He took down his hat and jacket and slipped them on with unusually slow movements. Just before heading out the door, he glanced at Lillian.

She held her breath, hoping for words of affirmation or even a tender look. Would he understand that her request for forgiveness from Joseph extended to him, too?

"Did you mean what you said . . . about Joseph remaining on the farmstead with me?"

"I meant it." Her words came out breathlessly, as if she'd just run a long distance. "He loves it here. He loves you. He should stay."

Eli nodded slowly. "*Jo*, it is good that you are thinking of what is best for the boy instead of selfishly." His tone let her know he'd found her previous behavior selfish.

Heat built in her cheeks, but she didn't turn away. "I know I hurt him." *And you.* "I want to make things right." *With both of you. Will you let me, Eli?* She waited for him to ask if she would be staying, too, but his gaze bounced past her to the corner, where the basket of dirty wash she had collected awaited her attention.

"You need not wash my clothes, Lillian. I will see to them

myself when the boy and I return from McPherson Town." He closed the door behind him.

His message was clear: He did not need her. Which meant he no longer wanted her. Lillian's shoulders sagged. "Oh, Father, please . . . give me grace to bear this pain I have created. . . ."

34

Eli stood inside the rock house and watched Lillian through a window opening. Her bonnet hung by its strings down her back, leaving her face exposed to the sun, but she didn't pause in her hoeing to tug it back in place. Instead she kept a steady rhythm of *chop, chop, chop* as she made her way across the watermelon patch.

April's scattered showers brought new growth, including weeds. She had proclaimed her intention to clear the weeds so the watermelons wouldn't be choked out. He chose not to explore her sudden interest in working the land when in the past her focus had been on keeping house. Speculation would only lead to heartache. Although over the past two weeks her attitude had softened, giving him a glimpse of the woman she had been before Henrik's departure, and although she had given Joseph permission to stay on the land with Eli, she hadn't indicated a desire to stay. And he wouldn't ask. Not again. A negative answer would certainly shatter what remained of his battered heart.

He turned from the window opening and tapped his boot toe against the pile of lumber stacked in the middle of the floor.

"*Dank*, Father, for Your provision," he said aloud. The calf had fetched a good price in McPherson Town—better than Eli had anticipated. He'd also sold several pounds of walnuts and a bushel of mushrooms. With the proceeds, he had purchased four red hens, a brazen rooster, two scrawny piglets, and a few supplies. The remaining funds paid for a stack of lumber—hopefully enough to build walls to divide the rock house into four rooms and put in the floor of the loft.

Glancing again at the window opening, he heaved a sigh. He wished he had been able to purchase glass to enclose the openings. But the general store owner in McPherson Town had quoted a price beyond what Eli could comfortably pay. The man had suggested buying glass panes in Newton. Since the panes came on the railroad from the East, and Newton was a closer stop, freight charges—and consequently the heavy goods—were less at the general store there. So now Eli needed to plan a trip to Newton.

Eli smoothed his hand over a planed board, biting down on his lower lip. The money from the sale of the calf was gone. To buy panes of glass, he would need to use some of the funds from the leather pouch. He hated to deplete that supply—especially with no crop to harvest—but there was no other choice.

Unless . . . There was one more thing he could sell. It pained him to consider it, but it would mean preserving their available cash, which he considered a wise choice. "Lord, guide my thoughts and let me find Your will concerning this matter." With the situation safely in God's hands, he set his mind to the task at hand.

Joseph was already anxious to move into the loft of this house—so Eli needed to build it. He withdrew several nails from the cloth pouch at his waist and stuck them between his lips. Hefting a board, he carried it to the east wall and stood it in position. His hammer connected rhythmically on the nail's square head, the force of each blow sending a vibration from his palm to his elbow and the resounding ring echoing through the house. Six nails, six good whacks on each nail, and the board was secure.

By noon the framework was in place, with rough openings for doors, and he was ready to start on the walls. He planned to fill the open space with mud for insulation and to create a sound barrier. The clang of Lillian's pots and pans in the morning was a discordant start to a day. Eli preferred to be awakened by the first fingers of sunlight creeping through windows. He'd missed the morning sunlight while living in the sod house. In the sleeping room of this house, he would be sure his pillow faced the east to glimpse the first morning rays.

Sadness rolled over him like a wave, buckling his knees. He leaned against the pile of lumber and put his head in his hands. When he planned this house for Lillian, he had envisioned the two of them closing the door to the sleeping room, shutting away the cares of the world together. But now he would be living in that room alone.

At least, he reminded himself, slapping his own knee to drive away the attack of despondence, he would have the boy's company. So he and Joseph would share this house. Eli raised his face and spoke to the echoey room. "Lord, You have given me a great gift in Joseph. I praise You for the boy's presence in my life." Speaking the words aloud cheered him, and he returned to work.

At supper Eli watched as Joseph spooned fried noodles onto his plate. "Those chickens we bought"—the boy shook his head ruefully—"they are not so smart as the ones we bought in Topeka."

Eli chuckled, taking the spoon to dish a hearty portion of noodles onto his own plate. His stomach growled as the good smell of noodles and fresh eggs fried together in rich lard reached his nose. "Clucks are clucks. All have small heads and small brains."

He handed the spoon and bowl to Lillian. Her fingers brushed his, and he nearly dropped the bowl. With difficulty, he kept his gaze on Joseph.

"Helena, Matilda, and Katrina all came when I called. These four clucks run from my voice. And that *rooster.*" Joseph's eyes sparked. "He thinks *he* is the boss, and he chases them all around." He shook his finger. "They better learn to mind me or I will take a switch to them!"

Eli laughed, but when Lillian's tinkling laughter joined his, he fell silent. Leaning over his plate, he focused on filling his belly and allowed Joseph and Lillian to chat. After their long weeks of little communication, they were rebuilding their relationship. He wouldn't intrude.

He'd finished his last noodle and reached for a piece of bread to mop up the grease when Lillian said, "Eli?"

His senses immediately went on alert with the sound of his name on her tongue. He gulped, holding the bread in front of him like a shield. *"Jo?"*

"Joseph tells me you have started building the inside walls on the fieldstone house."

The tranquil tone, reminiscent of days past, filled him with a desire to return to those wonderful days of kinship with Lillian. He bit into the bread in lieu of a verbal response.

"When do you think the house will be ready for occupancy?"

He swallowed the bread, forcing it past his uncooperative gullet. He considered an appropriate response. With the boy's help, he should have the walls up and insulated by early May. "In two weeks, probably." He glanced in her direction, curiosity overriding good sense. "Why do you ask?"

She offered a delicate shrug, lifting a bite of noodles. "I thought I would make curtains for the windows and some rag rugs for the floor. I wondered how much time I would have to work."

Eli's scalp prickled. "It is kind of you, but the boy and I do not need window dressings out here away from everyone. Who will look in on us? And rugs, they are much trouble to make. Are there not other things on which you would rather work?"

Hurt flickered in her eyes, but her smile remained. "I enjoy those kinds of tasks, Eli. Curtains will give a finished look to the house. And . . ." She looked at her plate, using her fork to move a noodle back and forth across her plate. "I would like a soft rug to step on when I get out of bed in the morning." Her face glowed bright red.

Fire shot through Eli's chest. "You—" His voice squeaked. He cleared his throat and tried again. "You intend to live in the rock house?"

The noodle sailed back and forth across her plate, propelled by the fork's tines. Her head low, she answered so softly he had to strain to hear her. "You built it for me. I . . . I would like to live in it." Her chin shot up, her gaze smacking into his as the fork clattered onto her plate. "And Joseph is young yet. He needs his mother near. If you have to do the cooking and cleaning, it will be hard for you to get all of the other work finished in building and running this farm. So . . ."

Her words trailed off, but she looked into his eyes, her lips slightly parted, though it seemed no breath escaped.

Eli cleared his throat once and then again, battling frustration. How could she play with him like a cat does a mouse? He swallowed a sharp retort and stroked his fingers through his beard. "*Nä-jo*. If . . . if you wish to be near Joseph, I understand." A lump filled his throat, and he was forced to clear it again. "You are probably right that the boy would benefit from having you here, so . . . *jo*, you and Joseph may move into the house."

He glanced around the sod house. The door stood open, allowing in the evening air and a band of dimming sunlight. He had anticipated windows and light, but it seemed he would continue living in shadows. Still, Joseph's needs overrode his own. As Lillian had said, a young boy needed his mother. Having grown up without one, he wouldn't deny Joseph the presence of a willing mother.

"I can continue to use the sod house until the others come. Then maybe I can rent a room from one of the villagers and ride out to work the fields during the day." He shot her a sharp look. "You will need me to work the fields? You do not plan to do the farming yourself?"

The oddest look crossed her face—a combination of confusion and disappointment. But she was getting what she requested, so why look at him as though she didn't understand?

"I am not able to do the farming. We . . . we will need you."

Her voice quavered, further baffling Eli. "*Nä-jo*, then it is set." He pushed off from the table, eager to escape her presence. Her wide eyes begged for something he didn't know how to give. Turning to Joseph, he said, "I am going to go load dirt into the wagon so tomorrow early I can begin to mix mud for the insulation. Do you want to help me?"

Joseph tossed his cloth napkin aside and jumped up. "For sure, Pa!"

Eli slung his arm across the boy's shoulders, and they headed for the door. Lillian's voice called, breaking his stride.

"I will fold the dry clothes after washing dishes. Shall I put yours on the trunk in Joseph's room?"

Pressure built in Eli's chest. She had washed his dirty clothes after all. He didn't want a housekeeper. He wanted a wife. If she couldn't be his wife, then she should leave his clothes alone.

Lillian waved as the wagon rolled from the yard, carrying Eli and Joseph away. A strange weight had settled on her shoulders when she saw Eli put the oxen in the yoke and tie the horses' reins to the back of the wagon. Why did he need to take all four animals to Newton to purchase window glass? Did he worry she would climb on the back of one of those horses and ride after Henrik?

Joseph turned backward in the seat, waving, his smile bright. She pushed aside the dark thought concerning Eli and focused on her son. How good to see his smile, to know it was meant for her. After a tentative beginning, they had managed to rebuild the close relationship that had developed between them following Jakob's death.

An unbidden thought crept into her mind: If Jakob had lived, she would probably still feel distanced from her middle son. Eli's comment about good coming from deep suffering had proved true in this situation. Joseph was funny and sensitive, with a bright mind. It gave her great joy to truly know this unique, pleasant young man she had borne.

Turning toward the house, she pondered whether Eli's proclamation might be evidenced in other ways given time. Her heart still ached for Henrik's return. Daily she prayed for him, but instead of begging God to bring her son back, she prayed for Henrik to seek God's will in his life. Placing him into God's hands, trusting God to guide and protect her son, brought a greater peace than anything she had experienced even when Henrik resided beneath her roof. She recognized that a part of her would always long for Henrik's return, but she had ceased to allow the longing to consume her. The freedom that came with the release of worry was exhilarating.

She lifted the basket of torn scraps that she planned to weave into rag rugs, and carried it to the yard. The spring sun was bright and cheerful, warming the top of her head. After the winter months of being trapped inside the sod house, she welcomed the opportunity to be outdoors again. And next winter would be better because she would have windows that would allow the sunshine in and give her a view of the snow-laden landscape.

"But no more *Hoagelsteens*, please, Lord!" She giggled after she voiced the impetuous prayer. How wonderful to speak with God as a friend again.

Her hands stilled in tying strips into one long string. Would this painful separation from Eli ever end? Despite her best efforts to reach him, Eli still held himself at a distance. She had always thought him a forgiving man, but apparently he was unable to forgive her for her coldness toward him.

She plunked the tumble of rag strips into the basket and stood. Staring into the distance where the wagon had disappeared, her heart sought a way to convince Eli she had been wrong. She had tried everything she knew—seeing to his needs, engaging him in idle talk concerning the house and the land, inviting him to read the Bible with her and Joseph as he had before Henrik left. She wanted to boldly tell him that she was ready to be his wife again, but each time the words formed on her tongue, his aloof treatment silenced her.

"What can I do, Father?" Lillian lifted her face to the sky, where wispy clouds drifted lazily on a backdrop of soft blue. No answer came from the clouds, but a sense of well-being enveloped her. Just as she would wait for Henrik and trust God to keep watch on her precious son, she would trust God to guide Eli back to her.

Slipping to her knees, she folded her hands and closed her eyes. "Dear God, You love Eli even more than I do. You know what is best for him . . . and for me. We have made vows to be faithful. I . . . failed him . . . but now I wish to make amends. I trust You to open our hearts to one another again, binding us together with cords that cannot be broken."

As she rose, a song winged through her heart. She began to sing, "*Erstaunliche Anmut*, how sweet the sound . . ."

She sang of God's grace while she braided the rag strips. Her voice caught on the words "The Lord has promised good to me . . ." As she sang, she considered the Lord's promise for good, and she made a promise to herself: By the time this rag rug was ready to be placed on the sleeping room floor, her relationship with Eli would be restored. Just as the tattered rags would become something of use and beauty, the torn edges of their relationship would be woven together.

35

Eli pulled the oxen to a halt outside the livery stable, then turned to Joseph. "You stay here, boy. I will be right back." He braced his hand on the wood side to hop down.

Joseph caught his arm. "Are you sure you have to sell the horses?"

Eli understood Joseph's disappointment. He might never own a finer pair than Socks and Stockings, as Joseph had named the matching bays. But the oxen could pull the plow and the wagon; horses were an extravagance. Finishing the house was more important than riding behind a beautiful team of horses.

"*Jo*, I am sure." Eli softened his statement with a wink. "Now stay here, as I said." He landed flat-footed, dust rising with the smack of his soles against the ground. He swished at his pant legs with his gloved hands, then adjusted his hat and headed for the livery owner's office at the front of the stable.

"Bornholdt! Eli Bornholdt! *Goodendach!*"

The *Plautdietsch* greeting brought Eli to a startled stop in the middle of the road. He spun toward the voice, squinting against the sun. "Gustaf Plett!" Eli trotted forward to welcome one of his former neighbors from Gnadenfeld. The men clasped hands, laughing and speaking at once, their words tripping over each other in a cacophony of gladness.

Joseph jumped down from the wagon and raced to the men's sides. "*Oomkje* Plett, is Wilhelm here, too?"

Plett rubbed Joseph's cap back and forth on his head, laughing. "*Jo*, boy, my son is here, and *mein Frü*." Suddenly, the man's bearded face clouded. "But our Trina . . . she did not last the journey." His hand shot out to grasp Eli's shoulder. "Just as we heard Reinhardt and little Jakob were lost. Sorry we were to hear of it." After shaking his head sadly, Plett brightened, pointing with his thumb over his shoulder. "But good it was to find a familiar face in Topeka."

Eli's pulse skipped a beat. "A familiar face? Henrik?"

"*Jo.* He works unloading goods at the railroad. He saw us get off the train, and he introduced us to the land sellers. He told us . . ." The man's ears turned bright red. "You and *Frü* Vogt married. *Ekj graute'leare du.*"

Several responses came to mind: *We married only for respectability . . . Lillian wants a divorce . . . It was a mistake . . .* But he couldn't express any of them with Joseph standing beside him. So he nodded and offered a quick thank-you before asking, "How is our Henrik?"

"*Goot, goot.* He looks healthy. He sent his ma a letter—my Martha has it. Henrik has many English words in him now—he says he learns the English from a girl named Nora. He is becoming a real American. He says when he has enough money set aside he will go to university to become a teacher." Plett poked Eli's chest with his finger. "I told him we could use him in New Gnadenfeld."

"New Gnadenfeld?"

"*Jo.* The villagers wish to form a town and name it after the village in Molotschna. So we call it New Gnadenfeld."

A new field of grace . . . Eli liked the sound of it. He peered past Plett's shoulder, seeking other arrivals. "Did many families come with you?"

"Nä." Plett folded his arms over his chest, puffing with importance. "The village leaders sent Titus Richert and me ahead with money to buy land on which to build our American village. The others will arrive mid-summer. Titus and I are to stake out the village and hold the land until the others come."

Joseph whooped with excitement, socking the air with his fist. "They are coming, Pa, just as you said! We will have our village again!"

Plett grinned at Joseph. "*Jo*, boy, it is exciting for sure. God is *goot* to bring us here." He looked at Eli. "Henrik showed us on the land developers' plat where the land you bought is located. Richert and I chose sections north and east of yours—enough for the village square and our own homes." He shook his head, releasing a happy sigh. "It is good to know you are there, are familiar with the land. You can be a big help to us."

"For sure I will help you. Joseph, too. He is a good sod house builder."

Joseph made a sour face, and Eli laughed.

"Sod house?" Plett's brow crinkled in puzzlement.

Eli briefly explained the process of building a house of sod blocks. "It makes a good, sturdy dwelling that stands up to the wind and rain." He gave Plett's shoulder a solid clap. "So we will get you a house built, but right now I need to take these horses inside and see what the livery owner will give me for them. Have you yet purchased your supplies?"

Plett nodded. "*Nä.* In Topeka we bought our wagon and horses, but only enough supplies to get us here. We will need more."

"Nä-jo." Eli ushered Joseph forward. "Joseph, go with *Oomkje*

Plett now and take him to the general store. I will meet you there after I sell the horses."

Joseph piped up. "Pa is buying windows for our house today."

Plett's eyebrows rose. "Windows in a house of dirt?"

Pride filled Eli as he corrected, "Windows in a house built of fieldstone. A sturdy, big house. You will see it soon."

After making his deal with the livery owner, Eli assisted Plett and Richert in selecting supplies. Joseph chattered with Wilhelm, sharing every trial and triumph from their months in Kansas while the men loaded the wagons. The adults, listening to Joseph's excited storytelling, alternately raised their brows in surprise, pursed their lips in dismay, and grinned in amusement. The work went quickly accompanied by the boy's cheerful babble.

The small caravan of wagons rolled onto Eli's property early in the evening, and the delight on Lillian's face as she greeted *Frü* Plett sent a shaft of jealousy through Eli's middle, followed immediately by self-recrimination. Why did he still want her to greet *him* like that? Wasn't their union going to be dissolved? He resolutely set the emotion aside to assist the new arrivals in pitching tents near the sod house.

Lillian had already prepared supper—a bubbling pot of potato and deer meat stew—but she added a few more potatoes, wild onions, and several ladles of water. Along with the last three loaves of bread, the stew stretched to feed everyone. Joseph begged to sleep in the tent with Wilhelm, and both mothers approved, so as night fell, Eli found himself alone in the sod house with Lillian. He considered taking the deer hide and sleeping in the rock house, but knowing his action would raise questions in the minds of their guests, he decided against it.

Lillian hummed as she cleaned up the supper mess. A pile of dishes awaited washing, but no word of complaint left her lips.

Should he offer to help her? That would put him elbow to elbow with her—closer than he had been in weeks. He headed for the door.

"Where are you going?"

The question, stated in a gently chiding, wifely tone, drew him up short. He grasped the door release and kept his face angled away from her. "I want to unload the wagon." Truthfully, the glass panes, sandwiched between layers of burlap, could spend the night in the wagon's bed. It was only an excuse to remove himself from her beguiling presence before temptation to sweep her into his arms and kiss her breathless overwhelmed him.

She scurried across the floor. Although she didn't touch him, his skin tingled. He stiffened.

"Eli, when you left this morning, the horses were with you. Now they are not." A teasing smile played at the corners of her mouth. "Surely you did not misplace something so large as a pair of horses between here and Newton?"

He so loved her playful side, too long absent. He rubbed the underside of his nose, bringing the urge to smile in response under control. "I sold Socks and Stockings."

Her eyes widened. "Eli! You loved those horses!" Awareness flooded her face. "Did you have to . . . because of the failed crop?"

That was part of it. A harvested crop would have provided the money for windows. But he shook his head. "*Nä*. With the village being built nearby, horses are a luxury. They eat hay and do little to earn their keep. Oxen provide milk, work the field, and pull the wagon. We are better off just having oxen."

Her brow furrowed, as if questioning his reasons. But then she nodded. "*Nä-jo*, I am sure you know best. But"—the teasing look returned—"horses are much nicer to look at than oxen."

Did she know what an enticing picture she painted with her

face flushed from the fire's warmth, her hair wind-tangled into little coils around her cheeks, and her lips curved into a sweet smile? He pressed his shoulder against the door. "But you will be able to watch the oxen through glass windows."

"Windows!"

The delight in her voice brought a grin to his lips despite his effort to remain reserved. "*Jo.* That is what I am going to unload. I bought glass for windows in Newton at the general store."

She wiped her hands on her white apron and then tugged it off. "May I see them, Eli? Will you show me the windows?"

Eli shook his head. "It is only a stack of glass squares, Lillian. They will not be windows until they are in sashing and placed in the house's walls."

"I know, but. . . ." She sighed, her eyes drifting closed for a moment as an expression of happiness lit her face. Popping her eyes open, she curled both hands over his forearm. "It has been so long, Eli, since I have enjoyed the pleasure of the sun streaming through a glass window. Please, may I hold one of the windows?"

Only a few days ago he had bemoaned the lack of sunshine spilling through glass to fill a room with light and warmth. He understood her desire, and his answer came without conscious thought. "For sure you may."

He accompanied her to the wagon, where he lifted out one small square and held it out to her. She took the glass by its edges and peered at him through it. A smile broke across her face, and she laughed out loud. Then, with the glass in front of her face, she turned a slow circle, seeming to examine every inch of the landscape in all directions. When she shifted to face west, she gasped, and she whisked the glass down to peer over its top.

"Eli! The sunset . . . it is magnificent tonight!"

How long had it been since they had stood together and admired

God's glorious close to a day? His arm itched to ease its way around her waist, to draw her close to his side and rest his jaw on her temple. But he stood, arms stiff at his sides, his face aimed toward the sinking sun but his focus within.

As soon as the windows were in and the house was finished, he must leave this homestead. Being near Lillian—loving her while knowing their union would end in divorce—was too difficult. For his own sanity he must separate himself from her.

Lillian turned slowly, holding the pane of glass toward him. He took the glass and stepped away from her.

"Th-thank you, Eli." There was a tremble in her voice. She twirled and, with light, eager steps, returned to the sod house.

Eli, watching her go, experienced a rise of panic. How would he get through this night? He would not be able to sleep, not alone under that roof with her.

As he wrapped the glass square in burlap, an idea formed. He crossed to the Pletts' tent and spoke briefly with Gustaf. Then he accompanied Martha to the sod house. Opening the door, he called, "*Frü* Plett will stay here in the sod house with you, Lillian, and I will sleep in the tent outside. This is a better situation for her." He ignored Lillian's look of hurt surprise and bustled toward the tent.

Lillian nearly burst with pride the following morning as Eli led everyone in Bible reading and prayer. In Gnadenfeld, Eli had not been a leader in the church, and she half expected him to ask *Oomkje* Plett, a deacon, to assume responsibility for their morning time of fellowship. Yet how her heart sang at the sight of Eli standing tall and confident, the Bible open on his hand as he shared from God's Word.

That first day with their guests they established a pattern that would carry them through the week. The men left early to carve blocks from the hard earth and build sod houses to shelter the new arrivals. Joseph and Wilhelm saw to the animals and then walked the mile to the new home sites to help the men. Lillian and Martha stayed behind to weed the watermelon patch, prepare hearty meals, and chat.

Lillian had never been particularly close to Martha Plett in Gnadenfeld. The woman was ten years younger than Lillian and, in Lillian's opinion, a bit snobbish given her husband's position of leadership in the village. But here on the prairie they developed a friendship based on commonality and need.

Listening to Martha mourn the loss of her three-year-old daughter to illness on the voyage reopened Lillian's wounds, but she was able to offer empathy to the grieving mother. She shared, "Each morning I must give my son into God's capable hands for the day. Sometimes I have to do it again before the sun sets, but trusting God to hold him frees me of worry and pain. The burden grows lighter every day."

Although she knew Martha surmised Lillian spoke of Jakob, in her heart she pictured Henrik, who was far away from her protective care. The letter the Pletts had delivered offered assurance of Henrik's well-being. Lillian carried the one-page letter in her apron pocket, and with each brush of her fingers against the folded paper she whispered a prayer for her son and then entrusted him once more into God's safekeeping.

With several mouths to feed, cooking filled a great portion of the day. Lillian showed Martha how to kill, clean, and cook rabbits caught in Joseph's snares. When Martha turned up her nose, Lillian laughed and reminded her that until a butcher shop was established in the new village, Martha would have need of such skills—"Unless you want your husband and son to go hungry."

On sunny afternoons, the women sat outside and worked together to finish Lillian's rag rugs. Lillian had enough rag strips for three rugs—one for the sleeping room, one for the front door, and one to place in front of the kitchen hearth. The rugs, with their varying hues, would provide pleasant splashes of color.

When Lillian mentioned her desire to sew curtains, Martha offered to trade a length of green calico for some of their dried deer meat. Lillian clapped her hands in delight and eagerly made the trade. No matter what Eli said, a house needed curtains on the windows.

With Eli helping *Oomkje* Plett and *Oomkje* Richert, the fieldstone house remained unfinished. After lunch each day, while Martha rested—the woman claimed her system would not digest food unless she reclined—Lillian visited the rock house, imagining the day when glass panes would fill the window openings. She stepped through doorways, picturing the wood doors that would seal one room from another. In her mind's eye, the cooking hearth already loomed in the corner of the kitchen, ready to receive her pots and pans. Sometimes she even imagined a whiff of baking bread or simmering soup.

Each time she left the house, she paused to offer a prayer of gratitude for Eli's willingness to work so hard to provide for her. A second prayer automatically followed: *Lord, please restore our unity.*

With the others here, she had no time alone with Eli. He appeared satisfied with the arrangement, but she grew more frustrated by the day. Watching Gustaf and Martha Plett whisper together after supper as he held his arm around her waist and she rested her cheek against his shoulder increased her longing for Eli's strong arms encircling her.

Finally, on the fifth morning, as they gathered for breakfast, Lillian received a glimmer of hope that a reconciliation might be near. Eli pushed his empty plate aside and announced, "Today we will put the thatch roofs on the sod houses. So by this evening, you will be moving into your own houses."

Lillian refrained from releasing a cheer. She mustn't lead the others to believe she resented their company. But she couldn't stop a smile from growing on her face. She followed the men into the bright morning sunshine and handed Eli the basket of dried meat, bread, and berries that would serve as their lunch. When he took the basket, she curled her hand over his. He froze, his surprised gaze colliding with hers.

Her heart pounding ferociously at her bold gesture, she offered a trembling smile. "After the others move into their own homes, you will be free to work here again, *jo*?" She kept her voice low so it wouldn't carry to Plett's or Richert's ears.

Eli's Adam's apple bobbed in a swallow, but he didn't respond.

"So you will finish the fieldstone house?"

Silently, he nodded, his expression steady but wary.

Lillian licked her lips, gathering courage. "Then be thinking . . . When the windows are in and it is finished, I will want to prepare something special for our first *Owentkost* in the house. There is still some sauerkraut in the crock that I have been saving for a special supper, and—"

"Lillian." His voice sounded hoarse.

She tipped her head. *"Jo?"*

"As soon as I have finished the rock house, I will move in with Titus. So I will be eating supper with him."

"But—"

"Now that others are arriving, we can get that divorce you wanted."

She jumped back, pain stabbing so sharply she wondered briefly if an Indian had fired an arrow and impaled her heart.

He plunked the basket into the back of the wagon and climbed onto the seat. After taking up the whip, he flicked a glance at her. His unsmiling face drove the arrow deeper. "We will be back midafternoon to load the wagons. You and Martha get everything packed so we can load and be gone before dusk."

36

Eli held his breath as he gently tapped the wood frame holding four squares of precious glass. The frame must fit tightly enough to remain in place against strong winds but not so tight that the glass cracked when the wood swelled from moisture. During his two days of constructing and fitting windows, he had questioned the wisdom of two windows for each room. So many windows was expensive. Time-consuming. Tedious. Yet how else would sunshine flood the house with light? Lillian craved light.

A final, cautious *tap, tap, tap,* and he lowered the hammer. He took a slow backward step and scrutinized the top, bottom, sides, and corners. His breath released in a mighty whoosh. Some clay to seal the cracks, and the house would be weathertight. Satisfaction washed over him as he admired his handiwork.

The rock house was a thing of beauty. Facing north, with windows looking out in all directions, it would provide a pleasant view no matter which room one entered. No deep shadows would shroud this house . . . except on cloudy days. The steeply pitched roof housed both an attic, which would serve as a smoking room for the porkers growing fat and lazy under the springtime sky, and a sizable loft. Eli chuckled, thinking of how many items Joseph had already moved into the loft. The boy would have the space filled in no time.

Eli's meager funds hadn't stretched to cover the materials needed to construct a decent staircase, but the lack didn't seem to bother Joseph. He clambered up the ladder rungs, nimble as a squirrel skittering over tree branches. Eli couldn't imagine Lillian using the ladder, but Joseph would willingly do any climbing and fetching she required.

Thoughts of Lillian immediately dampened his joy in completing the house. When he'd envisioned this big house, his daydreams had been filled with images of them residing together within its walls. That dream lay crumpled, just like the wisps of crushed wheat stalks that were swept away in the Kansas wind. When other villagers arrived, Eli could purchase seeds to plant a new crop. But he couldn't purchase a new relationship.

"I still love her. . . ." He whispered the words to the house, knowing stones would never repeat his secret. But loving her wouldn't remove the wedge between them. He saw how she carried the brief letter sent from Topeka, repeatedly fingering her apron pocket while a wistful look crossed her face. She pined for her oldest son.

Henrik's continued absence would always be a reminder of the day she had hurled accusations at him, throwing his love back in his face. Despite her softened attitude, despite the recent actions that hinted at remorse, despite her decision to remain here on the farmstead with Joseph, Lillian blamed him for Henrik's leaving. And so he must go, too.

He had three more things to do before permanently moving in with Titus Richert: He must seal the many windows in the house, build Lillian's *Spoaheat* in the kitchen so she could cook, and build a bed frame to hold her feather mattress. The final chore, although less physically taxing, would be the hardest. Memories of being joined with Lillian in body and soul tormented him. The sweetness of those moments conflicted with the deep pain of her withdrawal.

With a huff of irritation, he ordered himself to get busy. He set his feet in motion, striding briskly toward the creek and the bank of clay. The sooner he finished these remaining tasks, the sooner he could move on with his life.

God, remind me that I can find contentment in You alone. . . .

"'Be content with such things as ye have: for he hath said, I will never leave thee, nor forsake thee.'"

The words from Hebrews, recited in Eli's deep, respectful voice, sent a shiver of pleasure down Lillian's spine. They seemed a direct message on this bright morning, affirming her choice to be satisfied despite the losses of the past year. As promised in His Word, God had not forsaken her. He had given her the strength she needed to face the conflicts, the sorrow. And, she realized with a rush of joy, she had grown in her relationship with Him.

She took Joseph's hand for prayer, but Eli kept his hands curled around his Bible rather than offering them as had been their custom in the past. The change hurt, but Lillian replayed the verse that she had adopted as her own private tenet: *My grace is sufficient for thee.*

Later this morning she would move her belongings into the fieldstone house. Eli intended to load his things in the wagon and cart them to Titus Richert's place. Lillian harbored a different plan—a bold plan. If her actions communicated correctly, then maybe he wouldn't leave this land. But if she failed, she believed God's grace would give her the strength to go on without Eli's steadfast presence in her life. She wanted Eli to stay—she prayed he would stay—but if he chose to go, she would survive.

"Amen." Eli finished his prayer and rose. "*Nä-jo*, I will go out and see to the animals now. And when I have finished . . ."

Even though he didn't complete the statement, Lillian knew his intention. She stood quickly. "I have much to do, too. You see to your chores, and I will . . ." She waved her hands at him. With a sober nod, he strode out the door.

"Do you want my help, Ma?" Joseph picked his teeth with his fork.

Lillian plucked the fork from his hand. "You want to help me? Get out from under my feet." She smiled as she spoke, letting him know she wasn't upset with him. "I can move faster by myself."

The boy shrugged and ambled toward the door. "What should I do, then? Pa said he did not need my help, either." He sounded forlorn.

Briefly, Lillian wondered if Eli's reluctance to let Joseph assist him was a means of separating himself from the boy. *Father, let my plan work. Joseph cannot lose a second father.* With a clap of her palms together, she flashed Joseph a big smile. "I know! I would like fresh fish for tonight's supper. Would you take your pole and see if you can catch some of those whiskered fish?"

Joseph's face lit. "May I walk to the Pletts' and see if Wilhelm can come, too?"

"That is a fine idea. Now go."

Lillian flew into action, quickly washing the dishes and slapping the clean, damp plates and silverware into a crate. On top of the dishes she piled her dish towels and extra aprons; then she headed out the door. She crossed the ground that led to the fieldstone house, following the narrow pathway carved by Eli's feet on his many trips to the house. Walking the exact line he had walked so many times sent a sizzle of awareness from her soles to her scalp.

Oh, please, please, let him stay!

She dropped the crate in the kitchen next to her newly constructed *Spoaheat* and then raced back to the sod house for a second load. Sheets, pillows, and her remembrance quilt made a bulky armload, but she staggered outside and scanned the grounds for Eli. She spotted him stepping from the animals' enclosure with a bucket in his hand.

"Is that the milk?"

He nodded. "Shall I put it in the sod house or the rock house's kitchen?"

"The sod house is fine—I will see to the churning later." She waited until he neared before adding, "Would you please carry the feather bed to the fieldstone house for me? It is *schwoafallijch*." She spoke the truth—the plump mattress was too unwieldy for her to carry.

He offered another nod, and she scurried out to the house. She entered the sleeping room, and the crisp scent of newly peeled wood reached her nose. A bed made of stripped saplings and rope stood against the west wall, facing the eastern window.

The sound of a throat clearing caught her attention and she spun, the quilt flopping over her arm. Eli stood in the doorway with the rolled mattress covering everything but his feet. She burst out laughing and dropped her bundle to catch his wrist.

"Come with me." She drew him forward until his knees bumped the bed frame. "Now drop it."

He let go, and the mattress flumped across the ropes. He swished his hands together. "Is there something else I could carry over for you?"

His polite yet distant tone gave Lillian pause. She bit down on her lower lip, gathering her courage before nodding. Her heart pounded in nervous anticipation, and when she spoke she sounded out of breath. "*J-jo.* There is a box inside the sod house door. It needs to come to this room." Heat rose from her neck to her hairline, increasing the frantic beat of her heart. "W-would you b-bring it, please?"

Eli turned and clomped out the door. Lillian considered dashing to the kitchen window to watch for his return, to see his face when he realized what she had asked him to retrieve, but her trembling legs wouldn't let her move toward the window. Instead, she rolled the mattress across the ropes and covered it with the coarse cotton sheet. Just as she smoothed the quilt into place, footsteps signaled Eli's arrival.

She whirled to greet him, a smile on her face, but the smile quickly faded when she realized his arms were empty. "W-where is the box?"

"You must have made a mistake. That box contained my winter shirts and thick socks."

Her heart thudded so raucously it stole her breath. Lacing her fingers together, she pressed her palms to her dancing stomach and responded. "I made no mistake. I want your things to come here . . . to this room . . . *our* room." The final two words rasped out in a voice as soft as the down that filled the mattress.

Eli glared at her for several tense seconds while varying emotions played through his eyes. Lillian waited, her stomach churning and sweat beading on her upper lip. But then, without a word, he spun and stomped out the door.

"Eli!" She dashed after him, catching up halfway between the sod house and the rock house. "Please stop!"

He halted and whirled, pinning her with a fierce look, his hands balled into fists. "Do you think it fun to toy with my feelings? What kind of game are you playing, Lillian?"

"I am not playing a game!"

"Then what? Why do you ask me to bring my own belongings to . . . to that room? Do you know what that speaks to me?"

His emotion-filled words nearly tore Lillian's heart in two. "I know what it speaks, Eli. I prayed you would hear the message. I prayed you would respond to the message." *Please, Eli, please respond. Please return my love again.*

He closed his eyes and sucked in several deep breaths; slowly, his stiff shoulders relaxed and his clenched fists opened. When he opened his eyes, the sadness reflected there brought the sting of tears behind Lillian's nose.

"Lillian, I am just a man, not a seer. I cannot look beneath your skin to read the intentions of your heart. If you have something to say, speak it plainly."

The simplest, most direct words she'd ever spoken spilled from her lips. "I love you."

He jolted, stumbling backward.

"Is that plain enough? I love you, Eli. I love you. Please believe me."

Slowly, he shook his head, his eyes meeting hers. "How can you say that after . . . after . . ."

"After I said you betrayed me and I could not trust you?"

He didn't need to answer. In his hazel eyes she glimpsed the pain her words had inflicted. She wanted to turn away, to avoid the consequence of her previous actions, but she refused to surrender to the temptation. Eli needed to look into her eyes and see sincerity as she shared her heart.

"Eli, I was foolish to say you betrayed me. It has taken some time, but God has awakened my heart to realize that you did not betray me. Far from it. You have loved me as God loves me—over and above expectation." Tears filled her eyes, distorting his image. She whisked them away with her fingertips, then clasped his hand between both of hers. "I am sorry I allowed my hurt to turn to anger. I am sorry I pushed you away. Do you . . . do you think you can forgive me and we can return to what we shared before I . . . before I hurt you?"

Eli pulled his hand free of her grasp and ran his fingers through his hair. Shaking his head, he turned away from her. "I do not know, Lillian." He looked at her warily. "Even though we know where Henrik is, I will not fetch him back."

"I will not ask you to."

"But always it will be there, this place at the table where Henrik used to sit. When you see the empty chair, will you not resent me all over again?"

Lillian hung her head for a moment, remorse sagging her shoulders. Had she really wasted so much time dwelling on her anger? Such damage she had reaped with her behavior. She glimpsed her own hands—open, not fisted—and peace flooded her.

She straightened and pinned Eli with an unwavering gaze. "I will not resent you. I have learned, Eli, to trust." Holding her hand toward the empty wheat field, she said, "Out there, in the middle of that hail-damaged wheat, I discovered a field of grace."

She allowed tears to flood her eyes and spill down her cheeks in warm rivulets. But she smiled through them. "Henrik is not here with me. I cannot see to his needs . . . but God can. My son may return to me someday. And when he comes, I will welcome him with open arms. But until that day, I place him in God's hands and trust that my loving heavenly Father is taking care of him."

Eli grasped her upper arms and leaned close, peering directly into her eyes. "You are sure, Lillian? I love you—that has not changed—but I will not live under a cloud of recrimination."

"The cloud is gone, blown away by the wind of faith." Lillian curled her hands around his forearms, clinging hard. "Other clouds may come, Eli. We cannot live together without disagreeing now and then. I cannot promise I will never feel angry with you, and you could not honestly make that promise to me."

Seeing his raised eyebrows and thoughtful nod, she released a short, self-deprecating laugh. Then she quickly sobered. "But I make a pledge to you now: I will not let anger take control." She tightened her fingers, giving his arms a little tug. "When disagreements come, we will talk together, pray together, and find peace together. My time of separation from you has shown me how much you mean to me. I will not risk driving you away again."

"Lillian . . ." He crushed her to his chest. She threw her arms around his middle and clung, burying her face against his chest. His scent filled her nostrils, his pulse beat against her cheek, and his beard teased her forehead. Closing her eyes, she marveled at the sense of homecoming. She belonged in Eli's arms, in his heart, in his life. *Thank You, my loving God of grace . . .*

She heard him swallow, and then his chest rumbled with a low chuckle. He pulled back and searched the grounds.

"Where is Joseph?"

"He took his fishing pole and went to fetch Wilhelm."

Eli's eyes glittered. "How long will he be gone, do you think?" His hands spanned her waist, his thumbs slipping up and down her ribs.

A smile twitched the corners of her lips. She looped her hands behind his neck. "Long enough."

Grinning, Eli swooped her into his arms. She laughed aloud with joy, but the sound was stilled as he pressed his lips to hers and carried her over the threshold of their fieldstone house, over the threshold of their new start as man and wife.

A Note From the Author

Dear Reader,

Although Eli and Lillian come from my imagination, the Mennonites in this work of fiction are representative of my own family history.

The Mennonite Brethren first emigrated from Germany into Russia (present-day Ukraine) in 1790 at the invitation of Catherine the Great, who promised them religious freedom including exemption from military involvement. There, on the *steppes* (grassy plains) of Russia, they developed a hearty wheat they called Turkey Red, and they grew prosperous on the harsh landscape.

When government reforms threatened their religious freedoms in 1871, they sent explorers to seek out land in the United States. Groups of Mennonite Brethren began to arrive on American soil in 1873. Several groups established homes on railroad lands that encompassed McPherson, Harvey, Marion, and Reno counties in Kansas. Their hardy, red-gold wheat kernels came with them. The crops of Turkey Red wheat and its derivatives made Kansas the "Granary of the Nation."

Although much of this story is fictitious, including the community of New Gnadenfeld, there are several factual portions. My mother's grandparents were among those who came from the village of Gnadenfeld (meaning "Field of Grace") in the Molotschna Colony in the 1870s. Children like Jakob were given the responsibility for choosing the "perfect" kernels for planting in American soil. Eli's strong faith is very much a part of the Mennonite Brethren heritage, just as Lillian's hymn singing is an important part of the Mennonite worship service.

Lillian discovered that God grants grace and strength to help us face the challenges of life. I pray you, too, have found God faithful to sustain you. May God bless you muchly as you journey with Him.

In His love,
Kim Vogel Sawyer

Acknowledgments

My sincerest appreciation to the following:

Mom and Daddy, Don, my daughters and precious grandbabies—you fill my life with reasons to sing. Thank you.

Crit Group 14, Ramona, and Judy—your suggestions and encouragement are always so welcome and appreciated. I'm glad we're in this together!

Carla, Connie, Cynthia, Kathy, Miralee, Rose, 1st Southern Choir—your prayers keep me centered and plowing ever forward. Bless your hearts . . .

Ruth Heidebrecht at the Hutchinson Public Library—thank you for helping me find an appropriate ship to transport Lillian and her family to America.

Herman Rempel (author of *Kjenn Jie Noch Plautdietsch?*) and *Irv Schroeder*—thank you for the help in constructing the Low German speech.

"Mama" Ruth Seamands—thank you for sharing your seafaring adventures with me . . . but mostly thanks for your enduring friendship.

Charlene and the staff at Bethany House—my eternal gratitude for making me a part of your "family." Dreams do come true.

Finally, and most importantly, thank You, *God*, for being my Compass in this journey called life. I am never without hope when I am with You. May any praise or glory be reflected directly back to You.

About the Author

KIM VOGEL SAWYER is fond of C words like children, cats, and chocolate. She is the author of fourteen novels, many of which have appeared on bestseller lists. She is active in her church, where she helps lead the women's fellowship and is active in music ministry. In her spare time, she enjoys drama, quilting, and calligraphy. Kim and her husband, Don, reside in Kansas and have three daughters and six grandchildren.

More Heartwarming Historical Fiction From

Kim Vogel Sawyer

Reunited with her betrothed after five long years, Emmaline discovers they hardly know each other anymore. With the futures they dreamed of shattered, can their promise of love survive more than just years of separation?

A Promise for Spring

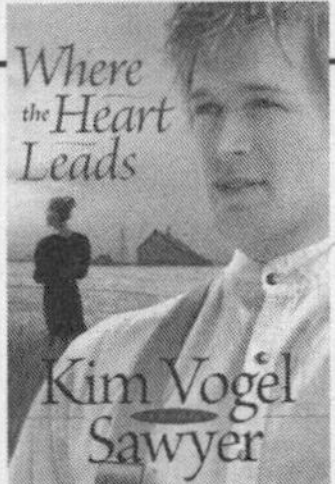

Torn between his Mennonite roots and his love for the city—and a girl in each place—Thomas' future seems uncertain. When his prayers are answered with silence, can he trust his heart to lead?

Where the Heart Leads

Orphaned and separated from her siblings, eight-year-old Maelle vows she will reunite with them one day. Seventeen years later, time has washed away her hope…and memories. Will she ever see her brother and sister again?

My Heart Remembers

When money gets tight, Harley takes a job with the Works Progress Administration away from home. But when the promised money never arrives, his wife fears Harley may be gone for good. Is the distance between them measured by more than miles?

Where Willows Grow

After losing her family to illness, Summer Steadman is hired by a Mennonite farmer to teach his young son. But widower Peter Ollenburger soon discovers that helping this outsider may have troublesome consequences.

Waiting for Summer's Return